3/3/23

BUS

Please renew/return items by last date
shown. Please call the number below:

Renewals and enquiries: 0300 1234049

Textphone for hearing or
speech impaired users: 01992 555506

www.hertfordshire.gov.uk/libraries
L32

Hertfordshire

B

531 865 87 2

First published in Great Britain in 2021 by Boldwood Books Ltd.

Copyright © Claire Calman, 2021

Cover Design by Alice Moore Design

Cover Illustration: Chuwy

A CIP catalogue record for this book is available from the British Library.

Paperback ISBN 978-1-83889-513-6

Large Print ISBN 978-1-83889-512-9

Hardback ISBN 978-1-80162-966-9

Ebook ISBN 978-1-83889-514-3

Kindle ISBN 978-1-83889-515-0

Audio CD ISBN 978-1-83889-507-5

MP3 CD ISBN 978-1-83889-508-2

Digital audio download ISBN 978-1-83889-509-9

Boldwood Books Ltd
23 Bowerdean Street
London SW6 3TN
www.boldwoodbooks.com

For Luce, my oldest friend – to me, you'll always look eleven

1

THE AUCTION

So... I'm lying in the bath, wondering exactly when my knees became so weird and knobbly, when my mobile rings. It's my husband, Carl. *Husband.* It still seems so unlikely. I never thought I'd meet anyone I could stand to spend more than a fortnight with on holiday, never mind a lifetime. We've been married for twenty-seven days.

'Hello, *darling.*' I never called anyone *darling* before. He's probably calling to remind me how much he loves me. I never had anyone call me every day just to do that, either. Sometimes I have this feeling lurking at the back of my mind that maybe I'm simply imagining the whole thing, that there is no Carl, that it's not possible to be this happy and it actually be *real*. It's as if I'm waiting for something awful to happen and unravel it all.

'Hey, *you.*' His voice sounds soft and sexy. Usually, Carl is almost allergic to lowering his voice. When we're out for dinner, I have to beg him to *sssh* because people keep turning round to stare. Maybe he's speaking quietly because he wants to say something seductive?

'I'm in the bath...' I make my voice low and breathy, to match his.

'Are you sick? You sound *awful*.'

'No, I'm fine. Must be a bad signal.' So much for sounding sexy.

'Listen, Nat. I've found the house! Exactly like we talked about. Our *dream* house.' Now he's speaking at a gallop. 'Loads of charm – beams, big fireplace. Huge garden, plus extra land. Hidden down a private lane. And there's a barn. God, you'll love me for this – it even has a whacking great duck pond.'

'A pond!' I sit up quickly, sloshing water over the side of the bath. Carl says I'm a dreamer, but even I never thought we'd find somewhere with a proper pond. He laughed when I put it in the 'MUST HAVE' column.

'That's incredible. When did you see it?'

We hadn't even started house-hunting officially yet, but Carl popped down to Kent for a day or two, to visit his children. We're supposed to start looking next weekend. Carl's just sold his amazing penthouse flat so that we'll be 'ready to pounce', as he puts it.

'Where is it? I can't wait to see it. Why don't you make an appointment for—'

'We can't, Natalie, it's up for auction. If we want it, we have to go for it.'

He sounds... not impatient exactly, but a bit frazzled, the way he does if I call him at the office and he's about to go into a meeting.

'Well, when's the auction?' I reach for my towel. 'I could—'

'*Now*. It's starting. I have to go.'

'But, Carl—'

'It's beautiful, darling. Will be beautiful. You'll love it, I absolutely promise you.'

'But surely I should—'

'Hang on a sec. I need to—' I strain to hear. He can't actually be bidding, can he, not when I haven't even seen it?

'Carl?'

'The setting is perfect. And the location. I have to go.'

'So it's good for your kids?'

'Yes, really handy. Natalie – *my love* – do you trust me?'

I feel myself melt. I love it when he calls me that. Of course, I trust him. I'd trust Carl with my life.

'You know I do.'

'Well then, my darling. Just say yes.'

I pause for a moment. Carl's always saying I need to trust my instincts more, like he does. I need to take more risks, be more decisive, throw myself into life boldly instead of being so cautious. I take a breath.

'Nat?'

'*Yes.*'

'Love you. Talk later.'

'Just tell me where it is!' I shout. But it's too late. He's gone.

* * *

Barely ten minutes later, my mobile beeps and it's a message from Carl:

It's ours! Just doing paperwork. Call u later. Love u. H x

H for Husband. I didn't dream it, then. We have a house. My husband has just bought a house. *Our* house. Without me. On the one hand, I'm excited, I really am. I feel like a kid the night before Christmas, wondering what will be in my stocking when I wake up. Our dream house! We'll be able to make it exactly how we want it. We've both looked forward to this so much. Sometimes we lie together in the dark, talking about it, how we'd have lazy days pottering about the garden, taking time to relax and be together. Carl works so hard, he never stops, but once we move, he's planning to work from home as much as he can. I'm sure he'll grow vegetables and take up fishing or rambling or wood-work; find something that will unglue him from his phone and his laptop, anything that will let him shrug off all that stress and simply *be* for a while.

Of course, he's much too young to retire – he's only forty-one – and we can't support both of us on what I make, but the idea is for him to cut back his hours; learn to live life at a slower pace, see more of his children. If he carries on at the rate he's working now, he'll burn himself out. Last year, one of his clients had a fatal heart attack and he was only a few years older than Carl. Maybe Carl will even change career completely – build tree-houses, or weave willow baskets or wattle fences – anything that's a world away from PR. We're going to be so happy. And it'll be much cheaper to live down in Kent anyway; you get way more for your money than in London. Carl got a really good price for his apartment so we don't even need to sell my tiny place too; Carl says we should rent it out for extra income, but I think he should use it when he needs to stay up in London for work.

On the other hand, I feel strangely flat. We have a house. We have a *house*! I splash the bathwater with the palms of my hands and say it out loud, but it just feels silly. I wonder why Carl didn't call me straight away afterwards, instead of sending a text. Of course, he'll be bound up in all the paperwork; there must be lots to sort out. Still, is it really so much faster to tap in a text than to phone for a minute, so we could, well, share the moment?

The bath is practically cold now. I get out and grab my towel and shove the thought away. I will focus on thinking about our new house. Our new *home*.

I try to gather up the few tiny fragments Carl threw my way when he called. Beams, he said. It's old then, ancient and lovely, with thick walls of weathered stone. Or more likely brick, as it's in Kent: mellow, warm brick that glows in the late spring sunshine. Down a narrow lane. I picture it in the perfect spot, a hidden dip, as if nestled in a gentle, giant hand. Maybe there are roses framing the front door. And honeysuckle, scrambling up to our bedroom window so we can breathe in its heady scent as we get ready for bed. I close my eyes, trying to picture it. I'm sure it's absolutely beautiful.

I open my eyes suddenly, remembering: 'Will be beautiful.' Carl said it was beautiful, then amended it to '*Will* be beautiful' – I remember now. Odd.

Carl's a wonderful man, but I wouldn't say he's an absolute stickler for the truth. He's not a liar or anything, but he's in PR and sometimes he has this slight tendency to... to... varnish the truth a tiny bit. To polish it up to make it more palatable. I can see how he needs to be able to do that for his work, it's just that sometimes it tips over into other areas of life. I suppose it's become a habit he finds hard to break. When we first got together, only six months ago, it was the thing I found hardest to adjust to. People say I'm very frank. They don't necessarily mean it as a compliment. My big sister, Celeste, is always telling me I need to learn when to be direct and honest and when to dial it down a tad, but I don't see why. Where's the benefit in lying? The truth always bubbles up to the surface in the end, doesn't it?

So... 'Will be beautiful'. Hmm. My guess is it's probably because it needs redecorating, which is fine. We never expected to find something ready to move into. Either the décor is old and tired, or it's not to our taste. Or... or it needs more than redecorating. A vision jumps into my mind of a picturesque ruin, a low assemblage of loose stones with a wooden door half off its hinges, swinging wildly in the wind. Keep calm, don't overreact. The house probably needs updating, maybe rewiring, a new kitchen and bathroom, that sort of thing. That's not so bad. In fact, it's good because we can make it the way we want it instead of having to live with someone else's fancy gold taps and hideous tiles simply because they're nearly new. Yes, once we put our own stamp on it, it'll be perfect. I can pick up bargains when I'm at antique auctions – gorgeous old rugs, a long oak table worn smooth by a thousand elbows over the generations... I picture a crackling fire in a huge inglenook fireplace flanked by squashy sofas. I add in a golden retriever sprawled in front of the hearth as a finishing touch.

I go through to my bedroom to get dressed, then plonk myself down on the bed, averting my gaze from the twelve test patches of different paint colours on the wall above the headboard. They've been there for nearly two years. Yes, yes, I will pick one. Eventually. Maybe Carl could choose the colour instead. I am terrible at making decisions. When we go out for supper, I sometimes secretly look the menu up online before we go, so that I can have extra time to think about what to order, otherwise Carl gets this sort of *look*. I can see him gripping his wine glass and know he's trying so hard to be patient; to not say, 'Please, please just order something! Anything!' Even I get annoyed with myself in restaurants.

Surely the house isn't actually *derelict*? The image of a ruin leaps back into my mind, this time with wild goats springing nimbly through the empty window holes. No, no – we said *no ruins*. We agreed. We've talked about it a thousand times, and we decided: no total renovation jobs. We're not exactly the king and queen of DIY. I can paint a room reasonably well, make curtains, put up bookshelves, and I've sanded a couple of floors, but Carl doesn't understand why you'd want do that sort of thing yourself, when you could pay someone else to do it while you're off doing something more interesting. I once took a photo of him, on my phone, as he was changing a light bulb, because it was such a freak occurrence. Before he met me, he used to ask his cleaner to do it.

I flip open my big road map, which I keep by the bed now. Carl laughs at me because no one uses paper maps any more, but I only like the maps app on my phone when I want directions from A to B. It's no good when you want an overview, is it? Even though we hadn't started house-hunting properly yet – well, not together anyway – we know the area we want. Carl has marked the *Strike Zone* on the map – a thirty-mile radius around Little Wyford, the village where his two children, Saskia and Max, live with their mum. There are plenty of villages to choose from; a couple of small towns that he says are lovely, too. Or the house might be completely rural, given that Carl mentioned it was down a lane. Wherever it is, I really hope it's near his kids. At the moment, the journey takes Carl over two hours from North London. He tries to go most weekends if the kids have space to see him in their scarily busy schedules – tennis lessons and riding and piano practice and so on. Usually, he takes them out for lunch or to the beach if it's nice weather, or to a film, then he drives all the way back to London the same day and spends the evening slumped on the sofa looking like a spaniel who's lost his bone.

It'll be so much easier now. He said it was, didn't he? 'Really handy.' Well, that's great. If it's only ten or fifteen miles away, he could pop over any time. It might even be a bit closer than that, I suppose. Five miles? Or less. Which would be fantastic. Obviously. He might have said how far away it was. I mean, 'really handy' could be twenty miles – compared with his journey now, that's relatively round the corner – or it could be ten miles or... or... it could be... it could be literally round the corner. Suddenly, my throat feels scratchy and parched, my skin clammy and cold, as if I'm about to address an audience of two hundred people on a subject about which I know absolutely nothing.

I look back down at the map, at the circle of possibilities pencilled on the page. Don't jump to conclusions. It'll be fine. There's a thirty-mile radius around the village. That's a circle with a sixty-mile diameter, so it's a huge area. I remember it's something to do with pi. Maybe pi times 2 to the power of $x = r$? No, that's not it. Pi x $r + 2 = ?$ There's definitely an r, r for radius. Hmm... r x pi to the power of 2? No, 2 pi r! Yes, it's $2\pi r$! I can't believe I remember that after all this time. Sitting in maths, secretly drawing silly pictures of the teachers under the desk with my best friend, Harriet, while Miss Hill stood at the front drawing a perfect circle on the blackboard, freehand.

Amazing what your brain can absorb when you're not even paying attention properly. So, multiply the radius by pi – call it 3.14 – times 2, and that gives you the... the... I think that was the point when I got sent out of the class for talking. It must be the area. So that's 3.14 times 30 for the radius, which is 90-something... Round it up to a hundred, then times 2. So it's 200. Two hundred miles. It could be anywhere within a 200-mile zone, say, which is obviously vast.

I try Carl on his mobile but it cuts straight to voicemail. I tell him I'm longing to know more about the house and to please call me back as soon as he can. Then I text him too:

Great news about house. Where is it? Love you. Wife x

Now I've remembered! It's not $2\pi r$ at all. That's the circumference, which is no use at all, is it? It's πr^2 for the area.

Why did Carl draw a stupid circle anyway? It would have been so much simpler if he'd drawn a square.

* * *

I'm dashing out the door, realising that I'm in danger of being late to open up my shop yet again, when my phone beeps. It's a message from Carl, responding to mine:

V nr vill. x

What? Which vill? Village. *A* village or *the* village?

And how near is 'V nr', for that matter? I have a bad feeling about this. Remain calm, it's probably an entirely different village. But then why not say which one? He was in a rush, pressed for time, that's all it is.

God, it's the same village, I know it is. OK, don't panic. I can live with that. He said 'V nr vill', so that means it's not *in* the village, right? At least there's a proper gap. It's not the same street or anything. We're not going to be popping in and out of each other's houses the whole time, are we? It'll be fine. Carl's always telling me I should try to be more positive, not always imagining every tiny little thing that could possibly go wrong. What he really means, I think, is that I should try to be more like him.

2

THE MARRIAGE EXPERT

It's nearly lunchtime. Well, actually, it's not even half past eleven yet, but I'm really hungry so, to me, it's nearly lunchtime. I'm teetering in the window of my shop, trying not to fall over while I lean right into the front to position a pretty rose ceramic jug on top of a Victorian washstand there. All morning, I've been trying not to keep checking my phone as if I'm fifteen again, waiting for some boy I fancy to call me. I have a small shop in Islington, specialising in antique clocks – rather ironic given my tendency to be late. The shop's called Second Hand, which now sounds corny and unsubtle, but seemed quite funny when I first thought of it. Anyway, obviously, I'm not hefting huge grandfather clocks about in the window. I once tried to shift one I'd bought at an auction into my van and pulled a muscle in my back. Yes, clearly a very short woman cannot lift a longcase clock single-handed into a van. I know that *now*. As well as the clocks, I sell small decorative objects: pairs of candlesticks, stylish 1930s teapots, vases, marquetry boxes, that sort of thing, the kind of thing that catches someone's eye when they're looking in the window.

My mobile rings and I practically fall over this annoying Edwardian footstool I've put in the window in the hope that someone will fall in love with it and buy it so that I don't keep tripping over it. I grab my phone and answer it before I've even seen who it is because I'm so desperate to speak to Carl.

But it isn't him. It's my older sister, Celeste.

I love my sister to bits, of course, I really do, but she can be quite... scary. I'm not entirely sure that she'll think letting Carl buy our house without me is a good idea. Luckily, after thirty-six years of being her sister, I know exactly how to handle her.

'Hi,' I say, my voice bright. 'How goes it?' I'm trying to sound light and breezy, la-la-la... 'How's work?'

'Work's a heap of steaming shit. Why are you sounding so creepy and cheerful?'

Celeste's been a bit prickly the last couple of months due to her impending fortieth birthday this summer. She's taking it personally as if God, Mother Nature and the Universe have somehow conspired to bring her to this unfortunate point.

'I'm not. I mean, I'm happy, of course I am. That's not creepy.'

'Yeah, yeah, whatever. Newly-wed bliss, I know, I know. You're supposed to be happy. It's... sweet.' Her tone suggests otherwise, as if there's something decidedly suspect about this type of behaviour.

There's a pause. Then I hear her inhale. Celeste has finally quit smoking after twenty years, but she's taken up vaping instead. Now when she inhales, she sounds like Darth Vader when an underling has failed to carry out an order to have someone killed.

'So, why's work so bad at the mo—' I start, but she cuts me off.

'Usual crap. Not worth your pretending to listen.'

'That's not fair! I *do* listen.'

'Sorry, Noodle, I know you do.' That's her pet family name for me when she's not being scary. 'Tell me something nice. Have you fixed up any viewings?'

'Actually, I've got some really good news.'

'Shit, you're pregnant. And I get to be the maiden aunt. Terrific.'

'I'm *not* pregnant. Honestly not. It's only – well, we've bought a house!'

'So fast! How come?'

'Isn't it great?' I prompt.

'But I thought you hadn't even started looking seriously yet? According to *Breakfast News*, the Great House Quest doesn't kick off until next weekend.'

I've been going on about the dream house for so long, she knows as much about it as I do.

'Mm, but this was really special so we had to grab it while we could. And it's saved us having to trudge round hundreds of hopeless places and—'

'But you've been looking forward to all that! I always thought you preferred the idea of *looking* for the perfect house more than the prospect of *finding* it. You know what you're like. You love nosing round other people's places and thinking how much better it would be if you'd designed the décor.'

She knows me too well. I've been trying not to think about that.

'You know, Nats, you haven't actually bought it yet. You've got the search, survey, all that to do, yeah? You should carry on looking, in case it falls through.'

'It won't fall through.'

'Seriously. Remember with my first flat when—'

'No, really. We've bought it. At auction. It's definitely ours.'

'At auction.' I can hear the note of disbelief creeping into her voice. 'When did you see this place?'

'Ah. I – Carl – we kind of bought it on impulse.'

The word hangs in the air for a few moments. I wish I could suck it back in, but it's too late. She's picked up the scent like a cheetah sniffing a sickly gazelle.

'On *impulse*? This from the woman who stands dithering in the supermarket for half an hour because she can't decide whether to buy medium eggs or large? Uh-uh, I don't think so.'

'That was only that one time!' I protest. 'It's our dream house,' I add defiantly, but it sounds a little feeble even to me.

Celeste sighs; she doesn't really go in for dreams.

'That's lovely,' she says in the tone she'd use to talk to a puppy or a toddler. 'But you have to be practical. I hope Carl didn't talk you into this?'

'No, no, he – we – it sounds so... I'm sure it'll be perfect.'

'*Natalie.*' Her voice has dropped about an octave. She *knows*.

'Oh, sorry. There's a customer. I'd better go!'

'You haven't seen the house yet, have you?'

'Hang on, I have to deal with a customer... *Yes, it is Edwardian. It's a really charming little piece, isn't it*?'

'You're fooling no one. You're the most useless liar on the planet. And since when have you talked to your customers as if you're auditioning for *The Antiques Roadshow*? Have you seen this house or not?'

'I don't need to see it! Carl and I always love the same—'

'Has your husband really bought a house – your first proper home together – without even letting you see it first?'

'It's different when you're married,' I blurt. 'You have to trust each other and—'

'And do things together, decide things together. You're in it *together*. I believe that's the whole point, isn't it?'

'What do you know? Who made you the marriage expert, all of a sudden?'

There is a silence. A deep, scary silence. Celeste is divorced; she describes herself as being 'amicably divorced' because she wants to make it clear to everyone that she's extremely grown-up and civilised about the whole thing, but actually she means 'amicably' as in: still sleeping together sometimes when they're both feeling lonely and/or drunk. I can't even begin to understand how she can stand to be in the same room as that man, never mind the same bed.

'Um, Celeste?'

'What?'

'I'm really sorry. That came out all wrong—'

'Whatever.'

'No, I didn't mean, you know—'

'Listen, Natalie,' (now I know she's really pissed off; usually, she calls me Nats) 'I wouldn't trust a man to choose a glass of wine for me, let alone a house, so maybe you're right. It's terrific that you can sit back and let someone else run your life for you. It's not what would work for me, but hey, as you say, I'm not exactly an expert on marriage, am I?'

The shop phone starts ringing. It's probably Carl, having failed to get me on my mobile, and I so want to talk to him, but I can't leave Celeste now.

'But you'll find someone perfect soon, the right man for you is out there, I know he is. They're not all like Jake—'

Jake, Celeste's ex-husband, had sex with the wife of Celeste's boss. For some reason, he decided a good time to do this would be during his own wedding reception. For some other reason, he decided a good time to confess to Celeste would be during their honeymoon. And then, when she returned home a week early, her boss fired her because he'd decided it was Celeste's fault for introducing them in the first place. Jake's a class act.

'Once upon a time, there was a stressed-out old bitch who lived in an enchanted apartment... Since when did you imagine I started believing in fairy tales?'

'But *I* found someone lovely! And you're a much, much better catch than I am! You're so gorgeous and glam and successful. And your hair's not mad and frizzy like mine. Any man should jump at the chance to have you!'

'The ones that jump at the chance nowadays are repellent, all droopy and drippy with soft, clammy hands and manicured nails. Hideous. The ones I like can't hack it with a woman who knows what she wants. They want some dim trophy wife with no hips and a permanent giggle.' Celeste sighs. The other call goes to voicemail. 'Don't feel sorry for me, Nats, or I'll shoot you. I am absolutely fine. In fact, I'm seeing someone at the moment.'

'But that's fantastic! Who is he? What's he like? Are you—'

'Keep your pants on. He's just a bloke. He's not exactly *Intellect of the Year* but he fucks like a god. It's what I need right now, OK?'

'OK. So, how long have—'

'There's no future in it, so please don't ask me any of that "Are you in luuuuurrrve? Are you moving in together?" crap. It is what it is. We're not sailing off into the sunset or any of that bollocks.'

'But still, if you're—'

'End of subject. And don't tell Mum. I don't want another lecture about being true to my inner self or my inner self will clonk her over the head with my briefcase.'

'No. Course not.'

She sighs again.

'So, what's this perfect house like then?' I hear her clickety-click-click her vape again and inhale deeply. 'Please don't tell me it has a thatched roof or I may have to vomit. More to the point, *where* is it?'

'Um, it's sort of quite near-ish to – to – Little Wyford. You know, the village where Carl's kids live. So that's really, really good – he'll get to see them much more.'

'How near?'

'Well, you know. Near-ish.'

'What – twenty miles, ten, what?'

'I'm not a hundred per cent sure of all the details right now,' I say as if she's asking me about the design of the wallpaper in the third bedroom. I clear my throat. 'Anyhow, it'll be so much more convenient for everyone.'

'You're such a hopeless liar, Nats. So, what you're saying – not saying – is that you will be living on the doorstep of your husband's ex-wife? That sounds like a top plan. I told you this move was a stupid idea. What on earth were you thinking of?'

'Why do you always have to exaggerate? It'll be so much better for Carl this way, being close to his children. I mean, naturally, his wife – ex-wife – lives there too, but she's remarried, remember? She's not still hankering after—'

'I'm not saying she is. It's only that your new life together with Carl, it sounds quite a lot to take on: a house you haven't even seen, round the corner from his ex-wife, who you've never seen either, and his sprogs. That's a big deal. It could be quite fraught.'

'They have a very civilised relationship! Carl gets on really well with her.'

'That's why they got divorced, is it?'

'Things are much better now.'

There's a pause.

'Good. I'm sure it'll be fine.' I have the feeling Celeste was going to say something else, something entirely different.

'It will be.' I say. 'Moving near his kids will make Carl so happy. He's not like Dad was, you know.'

'No one's saying he is, Noodle.'

'Well, you do see that I have to think of what's best for him?'

'Yeah. Of course. Trust you to do the right thing. He's bloody lucky to have you.' I hear her exhale sharply. 'I just hope *he's* thinking of what's best for *you*.'

3

CONVENIENTLY LOCATED

OK, confession time. It was *my* idea for us to move nearer to Carl's children in the first place. Since we've been together, I've always encouraged him to see them as much as possible, to have precious time alone, just the three of them, and I've never tried to muscle in on that. I would hate it if they ever resented me for taking their dad away from them. My own parents split up when I was seven and we never saw much of my dad. At first, he came every weekend to take me swimming then he'd come back to the flat for a meal. But, after a while, his visits became less frequent, and then in the end he just showed up at our flat sporadically, bearing piles of presents and gigantic bars of chocolate. The rest of the time, money was pretty tight at home, so being showered with gifts and treats felt like Father Christmas had suddenly blown in. Dad was loud and funny and laughed a lot, only he had very dark hair rather than a white beard, and a cool black leather jacket rather than a red, fur-trimmed costume.

I'm not sure our mum enjoyed his visits as much as we did. She'd smile and laugh, but looking back now, I think maybe it was hard for her to have him swan in, spoiling us with loads of gifts, then slope off into the night, not to be seen again for months. Once, he gave us a pair of old-fashioned toy telephones that actually worked (but only if you were in the next room). They were cream with gold dials, very fancy-looking, but they broke within a week and I remember crying when they wouldn't work any more. Mum gave me a cuddle and said we could still use them only it would be 'let's pretend' rather than like a real call. Then I overheard her talking to a friend about it and saying the toy phones summed up Martin to a T: 'all show and no substance'.

But it's fine. I'm completely calm. I know Celeste thinks moving down there is a crazy plan, but all I want is to make Carl happy. It was tearing him up every time he went down to Kent to see his children. He'd come back and throw himself on the sofa, then go into a sort of trance, gazing intensely at his mobile like a teenager, scrolling and swiping, or playing endless games, without looking up. And when I'd ask him how it was, he'd say, 'Yup, fine thanks, it was fine,' as if we'd only just met.

Then one time, he came back and he looked so... crumpled. You have to see Carl to realise how uncrumpled he usually is. He's tall and rather striking, with thick, dark hair and gorgeous, blue-grey eyes, and he always looks smart, even in jeans. I didn't say anything. I looped my arms around him and snuggled my face into his chest and he rested his chin on the top of my head (he really is a lot taller than me, but then most people are). Then I ran him a deep bath – getting into water is what I always do when I want to feel better about something – and I said, 'Look, as we're planning to live together anyway, why don't we move nearer your kids? I mean really *near*, so you can see them any time you want. I could have a shop anywhere; it doesn't have to be in London. And I'm sure you could work partly from home.'

He looked at me and, for a minute, he couldn't speak. He'd got undressed to get into the bath so he was naked and sexy but also suddenly looked so sweet and vulnerable at the same time.

He pulled me close and kissed me, and said, 'Really? Are you sure, my love?'

'Positive.' I nodded. 'I know how much this matters.'

'You're amazing. Absolutely amazing. We'll find our dream house and I'll have a blue plaque put up: "Residence of Natalie Glass, officially The Most Amazing Woman in the World." No arguments.'

'You're very silly. And I love you.'

'I love you more.'

Carl is quite competitive. Did I mention that?

And then we had sex on the bathroom floor, which was incredible until we rolled over and I banged my knee hard on the heated towel rail. Afterwards, he asked me to marry him. But I think he really wanted to propose; it wasn't just because he felt bad about my knee.

* * *

It's only in the evenings, after work, that I get to see Carl. We were both living in his enormous, swanky flat until it was sold, but now we're squashed into my tiny, unswanky flat until we move. I hear his key in the door and I run to him. He takes me in his arms.

'You...' He kisses me. 'Are...' Kiss. 'One.' Kiss. 'Incredible.' Kiss. 'Woman.'

'Oh, go on... I am *not*...' I squirm. Carl has the gift of making absolutely anybody feel as if they're really special.

'It's true.' He kisses me again, then picks me up easily and carries me through to the kitchen as if I weigh no more than a bag of shopping. 'How many other women would not only tolerate moving near their husband's ex-wife and children but would actually *come up with the idea* in the first place?'

Yes, but when I said 'near' what I now realise I actually meant was... not very near at all. I feel like a fraud. I don't want to be incredible. I want to be selfish. I want to drum my heels on the floor like a spoilt brat and say, 'I don't like this stupid game any more.' What was I thinking of?

'Well, the kids need their dad and you need them.' I do believe that, and in my head, I know it's right. It's just I didn't know that I was going to feel like this inside: all mean and pinched and horrible. I thought I was capable of being considerate and decent; I didn't realise I'd need a new personality as well as a new home.

He nods, his mouth tight, and the look in his eyes makes me want to cry. His silence says more than any words could. I know this means the world to him. I will make this work. I take his jacket and go to the kitchen to make him some coffee.

'So, tell me, where is the house exactly?' I say brightly. I'm fine with this. I practise telling people in my head as I fill the kettle: *Yes, we're moving to the same area as my husband's children and his first wife... yes, it's tremendously civilised... we all get along famously. Tra-la-la.*

'Your text said it's very near a village. You meant Little Wyford, did you?'

'Yes, of course. It's a fantastic position, down a private track. It's so secluded, yet it's less than a mile to the village.'

Less than a mile.

I clunk the mugs down on the worktop harder than I meant to. This was my idea, I remind myself, it was all my idea.

'It'll be so handy for seeing the children,' I say, struggling to keep my voice bright.

'Yes, as we're on the same side, they can cycle over in less than five minutes.'

'That's great.' I stretch up on tiptoes to try to grab the biscuits I marooned at the top of a cupboard so that I wouldn't be able to reach them. 'Sorry – the same side?'

'Yup. On the same side of the village.' Carl reaches up past me to get the biscuits. 'You know their house is a little way outside the village?'

'No, I didn't.'

'Well, it is.' His tone is slightly impatient as if he'd drawn me a detailed map indicating their exact location.

'So you could even walk to their place from the house? Our house.'

'God, yes. Easily. It's barely half a mile, I should think. It really couldn't be better.'

I know I should say something but at the moment the phrase on the tip of my tongue is: *Oh my God, what the hell have I done?* and I don't think that's what Carl needs to hear. I aim for a nondescript 'mm' noise, but it comes out as a panicked squeak.

Carl picks up his coffee and looks at me.

'You are still OK with this, darling?'

'Mm,' I say more enthusiastically, but into the depths of my coffee. 'Course I am.'

'You did say you thought it would be brilliant for us to be near Saskia and Max. But, well, if you've changed your mind, then of course we could...'

He sinks into a kitchen chair, suddenly deflated, without looking at me. He looks absolutely crushed. I have to learn to make a decision and stick to it. Even I feel frustrated with myself: the woman who takes half an hour to choose from a menu, the woman who can't even order a drink in a bar without dithering, the woman whose bedroom walls still haven't been repainted because I can't decide which colour I won't start to hate after two days.

* * *

I first met Carl a little over six months ago when he came into my shop. I rent a very small place in an arcade of antique shops in Islington. Of course, now that we're moving, I'll have to close it down and start all over again. It took me forever to find that place. I'm going to put a daily notification on my phone to remind me: IT WAS ALL YOUR IDEA.

Anyway, one morning I turned up – I was a few minutes late and I was standing outside, peering through the window, thinking about what to swap round to make the display more enticing – when a voice beside me says, 'It's never open, you know, so I hope you haven't set your heart on anything.'

I turn to see this tall, handsome man with thick, dark hair, eating a muffin out of a paper bag. He's wearing a beautifully cut suit and is carrying an expensive briefcase, though the immaculate effect is slightly spoiled – or, to my mind, improved – by the light dusting of icing sugar on his upper lip.

'It's open every day!' I reply, rather more forcefully than I mean to. 'Except Mondays,' I add, pointing to the sign.

'I wouldn't trust that if I were you.' He puts his briefcase down and leans against the window. For some reason, this makes me smile. It seems incongruous somehow; the kind of thing a teenager might do. He smiles back and it takes me unawares. I'm not prepared for a full-on smile at ten o'clock in the morning – OK, ten past ten – when I'm flustered and late and struggling with too many bags and a sticky Danish and a takeaway cappuccino the size of a small bucket. I fear I'm actually blushing. 'I've been here since five to, and yesterday I came at lunchtime,' he continues. 'There was a sign saying: "Back in 5 mins." I waited ten then gave up. This is my last shot at it.' He nods at my coffee and Danish. 'I see you've wisely brought some sustenance to prepare for the epic wait. You must be an old hand.'

'Maybe it's run at a loss as a tax dodge?' I say, addressing his reflection in the glass, which somehow seems easier than looking directly at him.

'That must be it.' He smiles. So...' He nods at the window. 'What's caught your eye? If it's that chrome clock there, you'll have to fight me for it.' He points to a small 1930s travel clock, which neatly folds up into its case. 'I think I've earned it by now.' He rests his forehead right against the glass for a moment and puts on a silly face of immense yearning, which makes me laugh. I find myself looking, *really* looking, at his face. He's not the kind of man I normally find attractive, to be honest. He's very clean-shaven, well-groomed and formally dressed, definitely not my type. I've never gone for men in suits. I've always thought there was something sad and repressed about them, as if there's a real person trapped in there who is never allowed out.

'Good choice,' I say. 'It's a really nice little piece.' I rummage in my bag for my keys and avoid looking at him. I swing open the door and flick on the lights.

'Ah.' He looks embarrassed even though, of course, I'm the one who's late.

'I'm really very sorry to have kept you waiting.' I pick up the clock and hand it to him. 'I'm not usually late.'

'Except for every time I've come here.'

'Mm. Except for those times.'

'Seems a little ironic, don't you think?' His gaze travels round the shop. I sell a range of small antiques now, but still there are over thirty clocks on display, including several handsome grand-father clocks, mantel clocks, plus a large case of restored watches.

Originally, I sold nothing but clocks, but then my whimsical desire to eat every week prompted me to diversify a bit.

'Astonishingly, you wouldn't be the first person to point that out.' He's looking at me directly now as I move away and start rearranging things; slightly altering the position of a green 1940s teapot and shifting a pair of candlesticks along a shelf. 'If you still want the clock, I'm happy to give you a discount,' I say over my shoulder. 'As compensation for keeping you waiting. Ten per cent.'

He glances at the price ticket.

'Twenty per cent?'

'All right.'

'Don't suppose you could wrap it for me as well, could you?'

I take it from him and explain how and when to wind it.

'Is it a birthday present?' I rummage under the tissue for the tape. 'Or, if it's for a wedding, you'll probably want fancier paper, won't you?' I wrap things in old-fashioned dark green paper and tie them with plain gold cord.

'Uh-huh.' He shakes his head, looks down at the floor for a moment. 'Actually, it's kind of a belated divorce present.'

'Wow – that's generous of you. Shouldn't they be giving you your original wedding gift back, not be receiving another present? I hope it's not for them to share or it'll lead to fights and another fifteen lawyers' letters. This one little clock could end up costing them another couple of grand.'

He laughs but it feels as if he's only doing it to be polite.

'True. Very true. No, it's just for the wife.'

I tug the cord tight and tie it in a double bow.

'My wife,' he adds, clearing his throat. 'Well. Ex-wife. Obviously.'

'Oh. I'm terribly sorry.' God, why don't I ever know when to shut up? I can feel a blush spreading over my entire body. I place the package between us on the desk. 'I didn't mean to be facetious about lawyers and... and fights and... and all that. Well. What I meant was, I... well. Anyway. Probably better if I stop babbling now. Yes. Good idea.' I attempt to laugh it off. 'Babble-babble, that's me. Shut up, Natalie.'

'It's fine.' He's looking at me with an expression of slight concern, as if he's worried that I might be unwell. Then he waves his hand airily and takes out his wallet. 'It's yesterday's news. She's actually already remarried. It's all very civilised now.'

'It must be if you're still buying her presents.'

'Ah.' He smiles again and hands over his credit card. 'The clock's actually a sort of joke.'

I raise my eyebrows. I wouldn't mind knowing someone who'd buy me an exquisite art deco clock for a joke. I put his card in the machine.

'Because she was late all the time,' he explains. 'I'm extremely punctual myself, but for some reason...' he pauses and takes the package from the desk, looking into my eyes, '... I always seem to go for women who are lousy timekeepers.'

Oh. OK, now I'm really blushing. I'm sure I must be practically crimson. And now the card machine isn't working. Again. I apologise, explaining that it has a mind of its own and days when it likes to be stroppy.

'Don't we all?' he says, opening his wallet again. 'I have cash.'

'Thank you. I'll just get your change!' I say, which comes out as more of a manic squeak than the calm statement I'd intended. I run into the back room and bring the cash box out, so I can set it down on the desk and unlock it. What I actually do is unlock it when it's still nowhere near the desk and, as I'm holding the handle on the lid, it opens and simply tips all the money straight on to the floor.

He calmly crouches down and starts marshalling it into a heap.

'I can do it! It's fine!' I can't deal with this, men flirting and smiling and looking at me like they can see right into my head. 'I'm sure you have to go! To a meeting or something! I can manage!' I'm picking up fistfuls of coins and notes and dropping them again all over the place. Notes are fluttering to the floor like feathers, coins are rolling under the big grandfather clocks.

'Hey, it's OK,' he says. 'I'm not trying to steal it.' He pushes the pile of money towards me. 'Here. I was only trying to help.'

I stuff the cash into the box and hand him his change without looking at him.

'I didn't think you were trying to steal it.' His shoes alone look like they cost more than I make in a week; I don't think he needs the paltry contents of my cash box.

'Well. You seemed a little –' he shrugs – 'hysterical.'

I pull myself up to my full height and attempt to look authoritative and regal. Not easy when you're five foot two.

'I was *not* hysterical. I was only very slightly flustered.' I attempt to look him straight in the eye, which seems like a good idea but is actually a lousy one because he simply looks straight back at me, and as he's tall and confident and clearly used to being in charge, and I'm short and hopeless and clearly used to being in a muddle, I get even more flustered and turn away briskly in an attempt to signal that that's now the end of the matter.

Which would probably work rather well if only I didn't fall straight over a footstool, banging my head on a dressing table. I grab at the nearest object to try to save myself but as it's only an old Bakelite telephone, it comes with me, so I crash to the floor clutching it.

I am lying on the floor of my shop with a sore head, a painful ankle and holding a heavy telephone.

'Oh my God!' says the man. 'Are you all right?'

'I think so.' I slowly sit up and rub my head, then my ankle. I try to stand up but my ankle protests and I promptly collapse back to the floor.

'Don't move. Stay there.' He looks round the shop and sees the chaise longue, then he bends down and starts to lift me.

'No, no! You can't possibly. I'm fine. I can walk. Please don't...' I'm flailing my legs and wishing I hadn't eaten two cream meringues yesterday. I was only going to have one, honestly, but they come in a box of two so what are you supposed to do with the second one? Crumble it up for the birds?

'Don't be silly.' He picks me up and carries me easily over to the chaise as if I'm no more than a bundle of twigs. 'Now,' he says, crouching down beside me, 'is there anyone I can call for you?'

We both look down at the Bakelite phone, still sitting on my lap. Its old, frayed, disconnected wire snakes over my knees. Then our eyes meet and, suddenly, we both start to laugh.

* * *

But there's a new me now; I can be as decisive as the next person. Well, not if the next person's Carl, obviously, but as decisive as the person next to him. Or maybe the one after that.

'Not at all,' I say firmly. 'Of course I haven't changed my mind.' I stand behind him and squeeze his shoulders and he rests his head back against me.

'Good.' He looks up at me and smiles. 'I'm sure you will adore the house, lovely Wife. All I want is to make you happy.'

I kiss the top of his head. 'I *am* happy! And I really can't wait to move!'

4

A VERY BAD DREAM

The village looks promising as I drive through, and I sink further back into my seat; I hadn't realised quite how tightly I'd been hunching my shoulders. It's bigger than I thought, a small town almost, rather than a village, with plenty of old-fashioned shops along the main street – I catch sight of a bakery, a butcher, a greengrocer, an ironmonger and a wool shop – exactly the kind of place I love. There's a pretty old stone and flint church at one end of the high street, and a picturesque green set back from the other end surrounded by tiny, beamed, white cottages like something on a postcard. The doorways look so low I imagine that even I would have to duck to enter.

Carl came down yesterday, straight after work, so that he could take Saskia and Max out for supper, then he stayed over at a local pub. I drove down earlier this morning to go to an auction in Sandwich, and picked up a couple of nice pieces: a rather well-made Victorian side-table and an inlaid tea caddy that I know will sell. There was also a really handsome long-case clock, but I was outbid. At auctions, you have to be very disciplined; decide on your limit, then stop. You must know

when to say *enough*. I was thinking the table might fit well into
the cottage, but I can always sell it in the shop if Carl doesn't
like it.

I left plenty of time to get here because, for once, I'm determined to be not just on time but slightly early. Carl is meeting me
at the cottage after he's picked up the keys, but I can peer through
the windows and look round the garden if I'm there first. When
he turns up, I will be wafting around looking quite at home.
Wouldn't it be lovely to have a simple picnic all ready for him,
maybe some crusty bread and cheese and apples? There's plenty
of time. I pull into a space near the greengrocer's and look around
for a pay and display machine. I can't see one so I ask a passer-by
how I pay to park.

'It's free parking, love.'

Free parking! Wow, I *love* it here. Never mind the dream
house, I may live here in my van, relishing the fact that I can park
for nothing. In London, when I have to unload something heavy
from my van to my shop, I have to pull in on a yellow line round
the back, put a begging note in the windscreen for the warden –
'Please, please, I need five mins to unload.'

I feel as if I've magically wandered into the pages of a child's
storybook. An elderly man actually tips his hat to me as he walks
by. A woman goes past with an old-fashioned basket over her
arm. A small girl is literally skipping along next to her mother.
Everyone looks so content. Where I grew up, walking down the
street required you to be constantly on high alert for weirdos,
junkies, dog turds, and sticking-up paving slabs. You'd have to
steer a course round the perpetually angry woman who would
shout at you if she caught you looking at her: 'I *know* you're wiv
the *pleece*!', and the old alcoholics mooching around the pub,
waiting for its doors to open. A lot of people there looked grey
and exhausted and only barely clinging on to life. But here,

people look like their biggest concern is whether to choose sultana scones or lemon cake for tea.

Inside the greengrocer, the air is cool and I breathe in the scent of fresh earth and sweet fruits, so different from a soulless supermarket. I can smell the apples. Some gorgeous-looking deep red tomatoes are marked by a handwritten sign: 'Grown locally'. I'll get some for a picnic with Carl and have a big bowl of fruit on the kitchen table. Or on the floor where we will one day have a table.

'Good afternoon, madam. What can I get for you today?'

She called me 'madam'! It's like being in an old black-and-white movie. I, too, should have a wicker basket over my arm. I smile and open my mouth to speak, but at that moment a tall, blonde woman dashes into the shop and starts talking straight away.

'Afternoon, Maisie. I'm in a mad rush. I'm absolutely frantic today, I can't tell you. Bung me a couple of lemons, would you?'

She doesn't look frantic. In fact, she looks cool and extremely well-groomed. Over her arm is a perfect rustic basket. She looks as if she's stepped straight out of the pages of *Country Life*.

The assistant hesitates awkwardly, looking at me.

'It's fine,' I say. 'Go ahead. I'm not in a rush.'

'Oh, were you ahead of me?' the customer says, though how she could have thought otherwise I don't know as I'm clearly the only other person in the shop aside from the assistant. 'How sweet of you. I'm running late.' She rolls her eyes. 'As usual.'

'That's OK.'

'Now,' she says. 'Let's see. I'd better have some grapes while I'm here. Yes, the red ones there. Hmm.' She pokes about in the box then extracts with finger and thumb a large, perfect bunch. 'These. And some mushrooms. Couple of peppers. And that's it. Literally nothing else. Ooh, asparagus! So early! OK, two bunches

of that. Is the watercress fresh?' She carries on and on, ordering a
bit of half the produce in the shop. There's way too much for the
basket so the rest is packed into a box.

'You wouldn't be a sweetie and pop it out to the car for me?'

For a moment, I think she means me and I take half a step
towards the box. The assistant doesn't notice and gets there first,
fortunately. The customer spots it, however, and can't resist a
smirk at my mistake.

As the woman turns to go, she says, 'Thank you so much.
That was really so darling of you. I'm in an awful hurry – another
mad day!' She bestows a huge smile on me and I feel somehow as
if I've been given a present, even though she pushed in front
of me.

I buy a few things and put them carefully into my canvas tote
bag, wishing I had a proper basket, and dreaming that I too have
a busy schedule and long, honey-blonde hair in luscious waves
rather than a mass of dark frizz that looks as if it's been statically
charged.

From the greengrocer's, I pop into the bakery for some crusty
rolls, then the deli for cheese. Next to the deli is a fabric shop and
upholsterer. Outside, I spot the woman from the greengrocer.
She's talking to another woman on the street, and gesturing at
something in the shop window. I must say, she doesn't really look
like a person in a mad hurry; she looks like a woman with no
worries and all the time in the world, chatting and laughing, and
oohing and ahhing over the swags of fabric on display.

On the way, I spot a shop with traditional, handmade baskets
hanging up outside. I go in and stand there for a minute. The
whole shop is packed floor to ceiling with baskets – huge ones for
logs and small ones for bread, and plenty with handles so I could
stroll along the high street, chatting to the villagers as I do a little
light shopping, carefully choosing the best grapes, musing over

the perfect curtain fabric for our dream house... I'll get a hand-made basket and put our little picnic in it so it will be absolutely perfect, and Carl will arrive and see me looking quite at home in the countryside, all wifely and wonderful.

As I get back into my van, I have a funny feeling in the pit of my stomach, the way I used to before taking an exam – a half-excited, half-terrified feeling. I try to ignore it and concentrate instead on not getting lost. Carl told me that the house actually used to be a small farmhouse, which is why it has a barn, but then most of the land was sold off, leaving only the track, the garden, and one field. I've set up my phone to issue audio direc-tions but Carl gave me a couple of extra pointers as he knows I have this slight tendency to lose my way and he said it's incred-ibly easy to miss the turn for the cottage, even with sat-nav, espe-cially as the track down to it is private so it's not on Google Maps.

Emerging from the village now, I see the houses are more widely spaced, and then suddenly I'm in proper countryside, with open fields on either side of the road, flanked by hedges and punctuated by large trees; I spot oak and ash and maybe hawthorn. This is amazing. I can't believe I finally get to live out in the country, like I've always wanted. I keep going straight along for a bit but then automatically slow down. Now, *that's* a serious house. It's gorgeous: a beautiful Georgian brick house, almost a small manor, with elegant sash windows, a wide gravel driveway and stylish clipped box bushes either side of a stone path to the front door. I try to avert my eyes, telling myself not to look at it. It'll only make me disappointed when I get to our house as it can't possibly be as spectacular as that.

I carry on, over a sweet little humpback bridge, round a very sharp bend, then suddenly spot the pointy tree that Carl told me to look out for. I turn left, then check Carl's directions again, though I have already read them at least twenty-five times.

Proceed until road forks, then take the right-hand fork downwards. Open gate – you'll need to untie it as well as unhook it – then close it behind you. Road becomes a track and looks as if it leads nowhere, but keep going. At the bottom, follow track round to your left to park, and – you're home!

In fact, the gate's already wide open, so maybe this isn't the right track after all? I reread the directions. No, it must be the one. Ah, Carl has got here first, that's it. Yes, I can make out faded painted lettering on the top bar of the gate: *Rose Cottage*. This is it!

I follow the unmade, bumpy track down and down, under a canopy of trees arching overhead. There's the barn, set back from the track. Gosh, it's beautiful, with rough-hewn stone at the base and dark wood planking above. I know I'm going to love this place.

Carl warned me that there are a couple of issues outside that need attending to so I'm not to panic: some missing roof tiles, an ugly separate garage that is almost falling down and the garden's a bit overgrown. Honestly, does he really think I can't see past a few weeds and minor problems? I'm good at visualising. I'm hardly going to be put off by a patch of nettles and a missing tile or two. You have to look at the proportions, that's the important thing. They're like the bones of a house and if they're good, then that's all that matters; you can always improve anything else, can't you? As long as the setting's nice. Well, it certainly is secluded. You could drive past the top of the lane a thousand times and never realise that there was anything down here. I swing the van round to park and come to a halt. You have to envisage the whole thing in all its glory once you've put your own stamp on it, not get bogged down in petty little details like a bit of peeling paintwork or dated wallpaper or – or – the fact that it has no roof.

Oh dear God.

I can't yet see the house properly because it's surrounded by towering thistles, triffids and other aggressive plant life taller than I am. But I can see the roof – or the non-roof, to be exact. I pick my way along what must once have been a path, clutching my new willow basket in front of me as a shield against various prickly, stinging, flailing weeds.

I can't believe it. I know Carl likes to put a positive spin on things – that's his job, after all – but how could he call this 'a few missing roof tiles'? From the front, well over half of the tiles are gone so that all you can see are the timbers and joists and I suppose the roofing felt. I go round the back. This side's not so bad, just a few slipped tiles halfway down, but otherwise intact.

My mobile rings. It's Carl.

'Hi, darling. Sorry, I'm running late. They'd mislaid the keys. Where are you? Are you in the village?'

'No. I'm at the house. At least, I think it's the house.'

'Did you turn left at the pointy tree?' he says in a teasing tone.

'Yes.'

'Did you manage the gate all right? It's very heavy.'

'It was open.'

'Really? That's odd. Still, isn't it amazing? What do you think? Don't you absolutely love it?'

'I haven't really had a chance to see it properly. I've just arrived this second.' I'm trying desperately hard not to sound so stricken. 'Um… I hadn't realised about the roof, darling.'

'It's fine. I spoke to a local builder yesterday. He says he's sure he can sort it out in no time.'

'Oh. OK. You might have told me, though, Carl. I did get a bit of a shock.'

'Oh, you funny little thing. Honestly, a few tiles… The place has been a bit neglected for some years; I did warn you.'

'Hardly a few.'

'Look, I'll be there in a couple of minutes. Have a stroll round, hmm? Go and chat to the ducks.'

I'm not really in the mood to chat to the ducks but still I take a wander down beyond the house around a stand of trees towards the pond. Now, this really *is* incredible. No wonder Carl thought I would love it here. It's so much bigger than an ordinary garden pond, and it looks natural. I crouch down at the edge. The water's surprisingly clear, and the edge is fringed here and there with rushes and yellow irises. There are coots and ducks dabbling in the water. Oh, that one has little ducklings, swimming after her. This is idyllic.

When I was a child, we lived in a rented flat in a grotty area. There was one sad, communal play area of very worn grass and a swing set, with only one swing seat remaining, the other three just empty pairs of chains hanging there. But at the weekends, sometimes our mum drove us out to the countryside, only for the day because we couldn't afford to stay anywhere overnight, but we'd pack up sandwiches and a flask of tea. One time, we found a pond and I remember lying on my tummy, gazing at the water, wishing I could stay like that for ever, watching all the insects zipping about, and the ducks and coots paddling to and fro. It felt like a magical, secret place where everything was beautiful, a completely different world from where we actually lived – a place where all I could hear was the drowsy buzzing of bees and the whispery rustlings of the reeds, rather than our neighbours slamming doors and shouting, or drivers leaning on their horns when they'd come to pick someone up as it was easier than having to climb the stairs because the lift was broken yet again.

* * *

After I've explored all around the garden, I head back to the house and am perching on the front step when I hear a large, angry creature crashing through the undergrowth, heading in my direction. It's Carl and he looks more furious than I've ever seen him.

'Where's the fucking roof?'

'What do you mean?'

'I mean – where's the fucking roof gone?' He looks round wildly as if it might be nestling beneath a patch of tall thistles. Somehow, I feel I'm the target of his accusation and that he's expecting me to suddenly produce it from behind my back.

'Then it wasn't like this before?'

'No, of course not. Why would I buy a house with no roof and not mention it?'

'You said it had a few missing tiles – I thought you were just, you know, being...'

'What?' He barks at me. 'Being *what*?'

Suddenly, I feel on the verge of tears. This was supposed to be our dream house but I've been here less than ten minutes and already we've got no roof and my husband is shouting at me.

'Being positive,' I say quietly. I stand up straight and look him in the eye. 'I thought you were doing a consummate PR job, putting a positive spin on it.'

'Why on earth would I do that?' he says, barely glancing at me and raising his eyes to the roof once more. 'Jesus. Look at it.'

'Because it's what you *do*.'

'For a *living*, yes.' He strides off round the side of the house. I start to follow him, then stop. I have a sudden vision of spending my whole life hanging on to my husband's coat-tails, whimpering in his wake like a puppy, scampering to keep up so he'll pat me on the head and take notice of me.

I stand well back from the house so I can see the roof more

clearly. It sweeps right down almost to my own height – I think it's called a catslide roof. The remaining tiles look original; hand-made, with subtle shifts in colour and tone. It must have looked amazing, er... *before*.

After a minute, Carl reappears. He seems surprised to see me still standing there.

'Where *were* you?' he says, as if I've been hiding in the undergrowth.

'Right here.'

'I thought you were going to follow me. What did you mean – it's what I *do*?' He addresses this to the house without looking at me, craning his head back to see the roof. 'You make it sound like an accusation.'

'Not really. But it *is* what you do – in life, not only at work. You put a positive spin on—'

'It's called being an optimist. I believe it's generally considered to be a good thing in life.'

'Yes, you are an optimist and that's great – it's wonderful – but it's not just that. You put a positive spin—'

'"Spin" again? Why do you keep saying "spin"? That's such a lazy argument. Whenever people want to have a crack at PR, they start using the word "spin" as if it's the ultimate evil. Instead of coming up with a coherent argument about why they object to something, they sidestep the issue by labelling the different view as "spin" so they don't have to have a proper reason. It's not—'

'I hadn't finished.' How come I've suddenly been lumped together in a mass as "people" and "they"?

'What?' Carl's not used to being interrupted.

'I was explaining what I meant, but you talked right over me.'

'Oh, please, carry on.' He waves one arm in an expansive gesture. 'Feel free to elaborate upon what's wrong with your husband at great length. Will it take long? Shall I make myself comfortable and order in a pizza?'

'There's no need to be melodramatic.' I take my hands out of my pockets and face him directly. 'All I'm saying is that – when it suits you – you put a p— you cast things in a positive light to make other people come around to your way of thinking.'

'So?' He shrugs. 'What's your point? Doesn't everyone want the rest of the world to see things from their point of view? Of course we all want other people to agree with us and to do what we want. And if we can make them think that's what they want too, so much the better. It's normal. Natural.'

'No, not necessarily. I don't think everyone has to see the world the way I do. I don't mind if no one agrees with me about all sorts of things any more than I demand that everyone should like ultra-strong tea or old clocks or singing songs from *West Side Story* in the bath. People should be free to make up their own minds without being told or persuaded – or... or, worse – *tricked* into what they should think. Why can't people be allowed to decide without being pushed? What's wrong with that?'

He snorts and takes out his mobile.

'I have to ring the builder and get this roof covered up before we end up with a second pond in place of a bedroom.' He turns to face me while he's waiting for the call to be answered. 'Not everyone is capable of making up their own minds. *Some* people,' he raises his brows, 'find it hard to make important decisions.'

He starts to turn away as the builder picks up, then says to me over his shoulder, '*Some* people need a little nudge. I'm sorry if you've been *tricked* into owning your dream house.'

5

A WILDLIFE SITUATION

I will not cry. I refuse to cry. Is that really how Carl sees me – as one of a throng of '*some* people' who can't make decisions? I know I'm indecisive, I know I'm hesitant and hopeless in hundreds of ways, but... but I do know what I do and don't want in life. I think.

What do I want? I *do* want to live in the countryside, yes. And I do want to choose a house with my husband rather than having it chosen for me. OK, it's too late for that, but I still want some say – in everything – in what sort of life we have. That's not unreasonable, is it? And, most of all, I want Carl to see me as a proper person, his partner in life as well as his wife, someone he respects rather than regards as an annoying adjunct. I know he loves me, I'm sure he does. But does he really care about what I think?

Carl puts away his mobile and tells me the builder is on his way. Anyone else would have to wait days, if not weeks, to get a builder to come round, but not Carl. I know how the builder feels: if Carl says *my* name quickly, I find myself jumping to attention.

'Well, we might as well go in as you're here.' He takes out the keys. 'If you can stand to be in the company of such a spin doctor?'

This should be such an exciting moment, stepping over the threshold of our dream home. Instead, I'm fighting back tears and wishing I were somewhere, anywhere, else.

We are in a cramped, dark hallway, with a dark brown swirly patterned carpet. Carl clicks on the light, but the bulb must be barely twenty watts because the effect is simply to illuminate a small patch of ceiling. There is a tiny, grubby window to one side of the door but dark strands of ivy have smothered it so it lets in no light at all.

'Try and see past the décor.'

'Of course.' I stand there with my arms crossed.

'I can't believe you thought I'd lie about the house having no roof. Is that how you see me?'

'No, I—'

'I thought you trusted me.'

'I *do*! I really do.'

We hear a vehicle pull up outside.

'That'll be the builder. Carry on. I'll join you once I've spoken to him.'

This is not the way things are supposed to be. I don't want to look around the house on my own. I thought Carl wanted us to do this together, relishing the good points, laughing at the bad, planning what we'd change, fantasising about what it could become. Maybe I should wait for Carl, then we can still look round together? I could go outside and explore the triffid collection a bit more. But no, there isn't time as Carl's arranged for us both to go over to see his children at their house. I've only met them a few times before, and they came to our wedding, of course, but I haven't asked to join them when he visits, mainly because I think it's important for them to get the benefit of their dad on his own.

Also, the times we have met haven't gone all that well, to be honest. Obviously, they're great kids – they're Carl's kids, so of course they are – but stepmothers have always had a bad press, haven't they? Think of an adjective to describe a stepmother and the first thing that will pop into your head is 'wicked'. There are no good stepmothers in fairy tales. So maybe it's just that.

I'm not saying they don't like me, as that might sound a little paranoid. Anyway, no doubt they will grow to like me eventually, won't they? Max seems a bit shy; he doesn't say much to me. He's eleven and in his last year of junior school, so will start secondary school this September. And Saskia, well, she doesn't come across as shy at all. In fact, she seems really confident. She's recently turned fourteen, is very pretty and is doing really well at school, and she plays the piano and goes riding. In other words, she's one of those annoying girls who seem to be good at everything. Not annoying. I didn't mean annoying – I meant accomplished. Plus, she seems to get whatever she wants. Carl says Antonia indulges her too much.

I'm going to meet Antonia for the first time, so I've got to buck up and stop feeling so pathetic and sorry for myself. I'm very, very lucky; I have a wonderful, loving husband and now a... a... potentially amazing house too.

Right, let's have a nose round. There are three doors leading off the hallway. I open the one on the right. Ah. Downstairs shower room. Never really liked the idea of stepping out and having to run up a cold staircase dripping and sneezing in a damp towel. There are grab rails everywhere and a pull-down seat in the shower cubicle, so the previous owner must have been quite elderly. Still, we can change that, I'm sure. To the left then. The kitchen. Ah, right. Well. This is certainly a project to get our teeth into. Still, everyone always wants to change the kitchen, don't they? And far better it's like this than all brand new with fancy, expensive fittings that aren't quite to our taste but which we'd feel guilty about ripping out. The cabinets are dark, wood-effect melamine possibly from the 1970s, and the worktops are marked with ancient coffee-rings, which is depressing. But the room is a good size, with windows on two sides. Amazing old sink – I love these, really big and deep, a butler sink, white ceramic with the – the – ay-ay-ayy, enormous spider lurking by the plug-hole. I back away quickly, feeling slightly sick. I try to slow my breathing right down and think of something nice.

There are very few things I'm really scared of, but spiders are near the top of the list, along with getting Alzheimer's or being forgotten about. What you mustn't do is try not to think about spiders. Once you try not to think of something, that's it, you can't think of anything else. Try *not* thinking of a brick wall – impossible, right? OK, so I'm mentally conjuring up these delicious baked peaches with Vin Santo we had in a restaurant on our honeymoon in Italy. They tasted of vanilla and almonds and lazy summer days. I'm picturing how idyllic it was, such a beautiful day, with a pretty vine-covered pergola over our heads and Carl looking into my eyes, saying, 'This is *perfect*. I'm the luckiest man alive.' I'm visualising the peaches now, the colour on the plate, the crisp white tablecloth – and now a spider comes suddenly scuttling across the tablecloth towards the peaches in my head.

That's not supposed to happen. The whole point is that you're directing your imagination in a positive way. Forget the peaches, focus on the house. I'll ask Carl to deal with the spider when he comes in.

I open the door to what I suppose must be a cupboard on one side. We could use it as a pantry or for storage. Where's the bloody light switch? I edge forward cautiously into the gloom and bump into a piece of furniture. Something touches my face. Aarrgh, a cobweb? I thrash out as if battling off an unseen assailant until I realise that it's a light cord. I give it a tug and the room changes from grey gloom to yellow gloom. It's not a cupboard at all, it's a dining room, but not large, and what space there is almost entirely taken up by a long, well-worn wooden table and some sad, mismatched chairs placed any old how around it. Now I see there are two windows but the ancient olive-green curtains are drawn shut.

Surely the previous owners didn't eat in here? It's so gloomy and poky and depressing. And why is their table still here? Another door leads off this room into what looks like a small sitting room, then another door from that to a much bigger living room with a beamed ceiling, an incredible inglenook fireplace and wonderful wide floorboards that look like oak. This is more like it. This definitely has possibilities. Polish up the boards, get a fire going. Change the lighting. Paint the walls. This room could be stunning. But, for now, there's a faded deep brown Dralon suite, and a tall standard lamp with a stained yellowish shade. I can picture it with a lovely old wooden carver chair set over there and perhaps a weathered leather sofa here or a long couch in grey linen or midnight-blue velvet, a beautiful rug in rich reds, little pools of light, a softly ticking clock... yes...

Odd that the owners left all their furniture behind, though.

Another door leads back from the living room to the hall, bringing me full circle. I'll nip upstairs and have a look at the bedrooms.

The main bedroom, directly above the living room, is large and light, let down by the fusty, old-fashioned, flowery wallpaper and yet more sad carpeting and an eclectic collection of furniture – over-sized chests of drawers and a dark wooden single bed so old that you can see how the mattress has sunk in the middle.

Still, this room could be gorgeous, although the ceiling is much lower than I'd expect, given the height of the roof. There are two other bedrooms, and a bathroom with a bath and basin and then a separate loo. Carl said that the barn is huge and, further down the line, maybe we could convert it into a guest annexe or something. I feel a bit better, though, because the house definitely has potential. It just needs a little bit of TLC, that's all. And a lot of work, obviously. And money. And serious planning. But it'll be fine. After selling Carl's flat, we have a decent budget to sort it out at least.

I'd better go downstairs and find Carl. He should be in a better mood by now. These stairs are REALLY steep – you can't skip merrily down; you have to take your time to look and – oh God.

There's a spider on the stairs. And when I say spider, I mean SPIDER. It must be the hefty sidekick of the one I saw in the kitchen sink. It makes that one look like a miniature scale model; this is the real thing.

I'm panting in small, shallow breaths now, the way women do on telly when they're having a baby.

I can't get past it. There's no way I can step over that. It will leap up at me. It'll pounce on my leg, then run up and scuttle over my face and in my hair. I think I've stopped breathing. Carl will come in. I'll be lying dead on the stairs and *IT* will have retreated to its lair. The post-mortem will say I died of fright and I'll never have had the chance to tell Carl how much I love him one last time. He'll never know that I didn't mean to be snotty earlier and accuse him of being a spinmeister. He was only trying to do what he thought was best. I love him so much and now he'll spend the rest of his life thinking I hated him.

'Carl...' I say, but it's barely a whisper. I try again. I slowly, slowly back up the stairs to the landing and remind myself to breathe, keeping one eye on the spider so that it doesn't trick me by sneaking on to a different step.

'I'm watching you,' I inform it. 'Don't think you can hide. My husband's going to come and get you any minute now. He knows I'm here, you know.' That's told it.

'Carl!' My throat feels dry and full of dust.

I go into one of the bedrooms. Ah, now if I can call out of the window, he can come and rescue me.

I open the window and shout for him as loudly as I can.

A moment later, Carl appears around the corner of the house, still with the builder.

'Hi,' Carl says. 'What's the matter?'

The builder looks up, interested. I thought he'd have gone by now.

'Um, well, it's a – a – thing I wanted you to see. Upstairs.'

'What sort of thing?' Carl is smiling and the builder has moved closer, clearly intrigued.

'Nothing really.'

'Well, hurry up and come down then. We should get going.' Carl turns back to the builder.

'Ah. You see there's a kind of a wildlife situation you might want to take a look at,' I call.

'Rats, is it?' says the builder. 'Or squirrels? In the loft, eh?'

'Not exactly. Carl, darling. If you could...?'

'You wanna get the pest man out if it's rats,' the builder shouts up, helpfully.

'I don't think that'll be necessary, thanks.' I cast a beseeching look at Carl.

A minute later I hear his footsteps on the stairs.

'So, what's up here then?' he calls. 'It has to be a lion at the very least.'

'There! There! On the step!'

'What? Where?'

'HUGE spider.' I cautiously edge on to the landing so I can point. 'That step.'

'Where? There's nothing there.'

I move round to see and, of course, it's gone. Coward. It's gone to skulk and lie in wait for me for another day.

'It *was* there.'

'Well, why didn't you just step over it?'

Carl thinks I have a silly little thing about spiders because he's never seen me in the same room as a big one. I always put the plugs back in after I've used the bath, basin or sink so that they can't climb up the drains to come and get me.

Only someone who doesn't understand about spiders could possibly say that.

'Well, because...'

'Because what?' He looks amused.

'Because, obviously, it might have jumped up and got me.'

Carl laughs.

'Oh, darling.' He kisses the top of my head. 'I do love you.'

'It's not funny!'

'It is a bit.'

'No, it isn't. And now it's hiding deliberately so you think I imagined it, don't you?'

'I don't. Really. I'm taking the hunt for the ferocious monster extremely seriously. Come out, come out, wherever you are! St George has come to slay you, ravening beast!' He shrugs. 'I think it's safe to venture downstairs now.'

'It's nearly as big as a hand,' I explain.

'Did it have fangs?' he asks, straight-faced.

'Yes, it did actually. Blood-stained ones.' I run down the stairs. 'I hate you, by the way. Just you wait till you have to face something you're frightened of.'

'Such as?'

That's the trouble with Carl, he's not afraid of anything. I know that's a good thing – of course it is – it's only that I sometimes think it would be nice if he weren't so perfect all the time and I could be the strong one for a change.

6

MAKING AN EFFORT

I had assumed that we'd drive in convoy to visit the children, but Carl says I should leave my van at the house and we can pick it up afterwards. He says it'll look funny if we arrive separately but I suspect that the main reason is that he's embarrassed about the fact that I drive a van. It would hardly be practical for me to be toting huge clocks back from auctions in the back of a sports car, would it? Mostly, Carl thinks my being White Van Gal is amusing, but apparently not today.

'See, it's only up here. No distance at all.' Carl stares straight ahead.

'Great.' My voice sounds flat, but not as flat as I feel.

I've been really nervous about meeting Antonia, and I was hoping Carl would say something encouraging, but he clearly has other things on his mind. He turns right, through wide open gates into a driveway that crunches expensively beneath the tyres, and I realise with a pang that it's the beautiful Georgian house I saw earlier. Of course. The path is lined with immaculately clipped box topiary, a miniature avenue of perfect cubes, smart and straight as soldiers on parade.

'Gosh, this is absolutely stunning, isn't it? I noticed it on my way to the cottage.'

'Ours will be stunning too,' Carl says, sounding cross. 'I'm sorry if the house isn't big enough or palatial enough for you.'

'I – I didn't mean that at all. Of course, we'll make ours into a wonder—'

'Well, we'd better go in. Aren't you going to put on some lipstick or something?'

I never wear lipstick unless we're going to a party or out somewhere special, and Carl knows I don't like the feel of it. I always end up scrubbing it off with a tissue so then it looks as if I've been scoffing strawberries. I rummage in my bag but there's only a stick of lip balm.

'This is all I have.' I put some on and turn to face him. 'OK?'

He nods.

'Mm. You look very nice...' he starts to open the car door, '... when you can be bothered to make the effort.'

I'm tempted to run back down the road to my lovely, grubby old van. I want to drive home to my funny little flat and curl up on the sofa under my mum's old paisley eiderdown, drink hot chocolate and watch a black-and-white movie and cry. I don't understand why Carl's being so horrible. Is he still cross about the roof? But then why be so snappy to me? It's hardly my fault, is it? I didn't sneak down in the middle of the night and nick half the roof tiles.

But I have to do this. I can't just storm off. This is part of my life now. It's in my job description. That's what marriage is. You can't say, well, I don't fancy doing this bit, it's too difficult or annoying or upsetting. You're in it for better, for worse, and you have to join in and try not to look as if you'd rather be at the dentist's.

Celeste told me this trick she used to use at job interviews or meetings if she was nervous, and she's very successful so it obviously works. In fact, I think she was so good at it that it sort of stuck and she ends up doing it even in situations where it might be better just to be Celeste, nervous or not. Anyway, you tell yourself that you're an actor, playing a part – you've already successfully auditioned so there's no need to be nervous – you have the role. So, let's see, I'm Caroline Cooke, with an 'e' – that sounds confident. I always think a Caroline sounds like someone who's very sorted. I'm a highly paid actor in this diverting new play, acting the role of the second wife, coming to meet the first wife. My nervousness only serves to make me more lovable to the audience. They can see it's an awkward situation and all their sympathies are with me. I walk briskly across the stage/driveway to catch up with my husband, the debonair and handsome A-list star Hugo Trill. No, that's not right – it sounds shrill. Hugo Till? Hugo Tull? Maybe Hugo's a bit wet. Carl's a better name for an actor, really. OK. Carl... Carl Cameron. But that is his *actual* name. And now all our names begin with C as if we're in a children's story about the alphabet. Oh, never mind. We're walking up to the front door. I tuck my hair back. Right. Lights, camera – action!

Carl's mobile rings and he checks the screen then answers it.

'Antonia?' he says, then, 'Really?' and, 'For God's sake, you're hopeless,' though this said with a warm laugh. How come she gets an indulgent laugh for being hopeless when I don't?

He looks at his watch. 'No, we can't.' He sighs. 'Honestly, Toni, we had an arrangement...'

Toni? Bleugh.

'Is he? That's nice for him... I'm not being funny...'

What's going on? I raise my eyebrows questioningly at Carl,

who shakes his head. Right, I shall stroll nonchalantly around the front garden. It really is amazing, straight out of the pages of a magazine. There isn't a leaf out of place. Every pebble looks as if it has been chosen and placed individually. I don't think a weed would dare poke its head up around here.

Carl lowers his voice a notch and I saunter a little nearer to stay within earshot while striving to seem completely uninterested.

'We will stay exactly half an hour. If you're not back by then, we won't be here. I have a work do back in London later.'

I must say, I'm really glad I don't work for Carl. He's very firm. Still, his tone has an undercurrent of indulgence in it, the way you might talk to a mischievous but lovable small child.

'They're held up.' He turns to me. 'We'll have a quick coffee with Dominic and if they're not here soon, then we'll go because I've got that work drinks thing and I'll need to change.'

Sometimes it would be nice to be asked what *I'd* like to do.

Before we can ring the bell, we hear the crunch of footsteps on stone chips and a man appears in the deep shadow at the side of the house. As he is dressed entirely in black, for a moment it seems as if a disembodied head is bobbing across the shadow to meet us. He is almost completely bald with very pale skin and rimless spectacles. He looks as if he's playing the part of a brilliant, yet slightly bonkers, scientist in one of those films about a mutant virus that turns everyone who gets infected into an amoeboid blob of jelly.

'Carl.' The man stretches out his hand. 'Good to see you.'

'Dominic.' Carl nods and shakes the proffered hand.

Why don't men say 'hello'? There's a guarded feeling in the air as if each suspects that the other might suddenly whip out a machete and start waving it about.

'And this is my *wife*.' Carl draws me forward proprietorially as if exhibiting a prize sheep at an agricultural show.

'Of course. Natalie, yes? What a pleasure to meet you at last.'

Carl puts his arm round me as Dominic leans over to shake my hand so I'm virtually affixed to his side and can't lean in too.

'Hello. I do love your house. It's beautiful.'

'And I love your name! Natalie... *Natalie*...' He rolls my name around his mouth as if it were a fine cognac. 'Like the delectable Natalie Wood. Though if I may say,' he pauses and looks right into my eyes, 'you have a particularly *natural* beauty all of your own.'

I feel myself blushing and I look down at my feet for a moment. I wish Carl had said that in the car rather than urging me to put on lipstick. Beside me, I sense rather than see Carl stiffen.

'Call me Dom.'

'Toni told you we were here, then?'

I've never heard Carl refer to his first wife as Toni before this afternoon.

A flicker crosses Dominic's face and I suddenly know Carl is only doing it to get up Dominic's nose. I can't believe he'd be so petty.

'No. Caught you on camera, in fact.' Dominic nods at a small wall-mounted camera aimed at the path and another by the front door. 'We have monitors in my studio at the back as well as all over the house. We can watch our visitors – welcome or otherwise – while we're in the bath if we so desire.'

'Um, is there a lot of crime round here then?' Have we bought a house in some hotspot for thieves and crack-dealers? What on earth will I do when Carl has to be up in London? Why did we have to buy a house here? Why? *Why*?

Dominic laughs. 'Hardly.' He opens the door and waves us in.

'We need some fairly serious security measures as I have a lot of expensive equipment – computers, et cetera – in the studio.' Dominic's an architect. 'Now, what can I offer you? Tea, coffee? Decaff? Wine? Gin and tonic?'

'Well, we don't want to disturb you if you're working,' I say. 'Do we, darling?'

'Gin and tonic's fine,' Carl says. 'Easy on the tonic.'

'Antonia is slightly held up. She's picking up Sasky from the stables and Maxie wanted to go along for the ride but they have to pick up or drop off some other extraneous child somewhere or other – you know how it is.'

Sasky? Maxie?

'I know. She called me.'

I wonder for a moment if Dominic is getting Carl back for the Toni thing earlier. *See how relaxed I am with your kids – I even call them by pet names.* If so, it's working. Well, this is fun. I thought Carl said they were all very civilised and grown-up? Honestly, they might as well be scraping their knuckles over the ground as they look for big rocks to chuck at each other.

Dominic leads us through a large hallway into a huge kitchen and flicks a switch. The worktops light up – they're made of some kind of milky glass suffused with a blue-green glow like a series of swimming pools. The floor is pale limestone, by the look of it, and there's an absolutely enormous long table made of smooth, pale, perfect wood. The overall effect is incredible.

'Wow! This is such an amazing house.' I have to at least try to ease the tension a bit. 'And the front garden is gorgeous, too – simple but stylish. I love the way you've clipped those topiary cubes. Sort of traditional but with a twist.'

Carl shoots me a look, which I ignore, and Dominic smiles.

'Thank you. That was our exact intention. When you own a house this stunning, you owe it to the building to bring out its best, don't you?' Dominic makes Carl's drink and hands it over. 'We've tried to preserve the integrity of the original structure while investing it with our own unique style. Would you like a tour?'

'I've seen it.' Carl pulls out a chrome and white leather barstool and lounges into it as if he's completely at home.

'Well, I'd love to – thank you. Might pick up some inspiration for our own house.' I take off my jacket and leave it on the barstool next to Carl's.

'Off we go then. Shan't be long.' We go back into the hall and into a sitting room.

'TV room, den, family room, et cetera.'

I make enthusiastic noises. It's not exactly my taste – high-shine chrome door handles everywhere and the walls are all shades of pale grey, taupe, and mushroom – tasteful but a bit samey. Opulent swagged curtains with outsize tie-backs, which are not really my thing, but it all looks *perfect*, with enormous vases of flowers like a posh hotel, and no clutter anywhere.

'I hope you will feel free to ask, if you want any ideas or help with the cottage?'

'That's very kind. We'll try not to. Doesn't it drive you mad, people picking your brains for free when it's what you do for a living? Like being a doctor at a party and having everyone you talk to asking you about their dodgy knees and flatulence problem.'

He laughs.

'Well, yes. But you'd genuinely be welcome. It's a very nice little cottage you've got yourselves there. And the setting is idyllic. But it needs a fair deal of work, of course.'

'Oh. Do you know it then?' Of course he knows it, you twit, it's only down the road.

Dominic is smiling in a slightly smug way.

'There was quite a bit of interest in it in the run-up to the auction. Looked like a very good potential investment. Though obviously quite a few people were put off by the...' he tilts his head to one side, '... circumstances.' He leads me into a much bigger room. 'This is our principal entertaining space.'

'Lovely.' I look round at the modern sofas and bold abstract artwork. Not really my taste, but certainly very stylish. 'Sorry... the circumstances?'

'Oh, didn't Carl tell you?' Dominic pauses, eyebrows raised.

'Oh, *that*. You meant the – yes, of course! I forgot. Mm.' I nod vigorously. Of course my husband's told me *that*. We have no secrets from each other. 'The *circumstances*. Yes. Absolutely. He did tell me, yes.'

'And it didn't bother you?' Dominic tilts his head again, takes off his glasses and rubs the bridge of his nose. 'Well, good for you. You're right to keep a cool head about these things. Antonia wasn't at all keen really. But then we were only looking at it as a little investment to sell on. We weren't planning to use it ourselves. And, as you know, I was outbid in any case.'

'What?'

'I was the underbidder. Didn't you know?'

'Um, no. I didn't.'

'Really?' Dominic replaces his glasses. 'Perhaps it slipped Carl's mind.' He leans forward conspiratorially. 'Or perhaps he realised he'd paid a touch more than he should have? I must confess I might have bumped him up a tad. But who could resist?' He laughs and winks at me. 'A spot of harmless fun.'

I'm not sure I would call making someone pay more than they need to at auction 'harmless fun'. I occasionally come across a dealer who does it at antique auctions, driving up the price when they don't even want it, but it's rare. I would never do that. Do he and Carl have some weird sort of rivalry going on?

'We should go, sweetie.' Carl is standing in the open doorway. He does not look happy.

'Such a shame. The children will be sorry to have missed you.'

'Well, I saw them this morning of course and we really can't hang around. Tell them I'll phone tonight.' Carl holds out my jacket to me. 'Come on, darling.'

'I was saying to Natalie what a charming little house it is you've got yourselves there.'

I'm probably imagining it, but is there the slightest emphasis on the word *little*? The house is certainly much bigger than anything I've ever lived in, so it didn't seem small to me. But, of course, next to this it probably seems like a garden shed.

'Yes, we *love* it, don't we?' Carl helps me on with my jacket and squeezes my arm for a moment. 'It's great to find something so authentic and unspoiled, something completely unpretentious. It just is what it is, with no silly affectations or—'

'It's wonderful,' I cut in, as Carl seems to be getting into his stride a shade too enthusiastically. 'And it's going to be even more beautiful once it's had a bit of love and attention.'

'Well, super to see you both. And, Carl, I must compliment you on having such a down-to-earth, clear-headed wife.'

Carl looks as baffled as I do. I don't think anyone's called me that before. I mean ever in my whole life. Carl can't stop himself.

'Oh?'

'Yes. Marvellous that Natalie here wasn't at all put off by its recent *history*.' Dominic savours the word 'history', letting it linger theatrically in the air. 'You know how sensitive some people are.'

Does he mean Antonia? Why didn't he say that then? So she's more sensitive than me, huh? More creative? More delicate? I imagine her as some beautiful pale flower, leaning gracefully towards the light, with petals so fine and translucent they seem spun from silk. And what does that make me? A potato?

Carl attempts a confident smile.

'Well, there you are. Natalie's a woman in a million. I'm a lucky man. A very lucky man,' he says, as he ushers me out of the front door. 'A woman like Natalie comes along *once* in a lifetime.'

7

ALPHA MALE

We don't have long because I've left my van at the cottage and we'll have to drive back to London separately, but there's so much I'm desperate to ask Carl. One thing at a time.

'Do you really think I'm a woman in a million or were you only saying that to get one up on Dominic?' I say, as we get into Carl's car.

'Oh, Natalie, darling.' Carl pats my leg. 'Of course I think you are. Why else would I have married you? I love you to bits. I don't give a toss about Dominic or what he thinks.' He pulls out of their driveway and heads for the cottage. 'He is a bit of a smug arse, isn't he? You have to admit.'

'Well, I suppose he is a little smug. I wonder if he's actually a bit nervous around you?'

'And he's so *old*. He must be sixty! Would you still love me if I was as bald as a coot, darling?' Carl runs a hand through his gorgeous thick hair, which is slightly greying at the temples in a highly attractive way. 'And those ridiculous black clothes all the time – trying to show how arty he is, like he's a drama student or something. He looks like a total twat.'

'I thought you all got on? You told me it was all extremely civilised.'

'It is. No one was shouting, were they? No swords were drawn.'

'Oh, come on, they might as well have been! The two of you were like gorillas beating your breasts and trying to prove you're the alpha male.'

Carl laughs. 'Well, maybe a bit. Only I really *am* the alpha male, of course. Dominic's well past his prime. If he ever had one. If we were gorillas, he'd be the old, grey one left in the corner, muttering to himself and chewing leaves.'

'Oh, Carl.' But I laugh anyway. 'Come on, you do seem a bit peculiar about him.' Now we're pulling off for the cottage. God, it really is close. 'As if he's a rival. You're not – well – jealous at all, are you?'

'Jealous! *Me*? You have to be kidding! Why would I be jealous? Of *him*?'

'Well, maybe just a bit, hmm? That house and everything! It must have cost a fortune. And I mean, you must have thought Antonia was a woman in a million when you married her. Didn't you?'

He doesn't reply, but stops the car.

'Could you open the gate, please?' He sounds like a stranger suddenly, polite and distant.

For now, the gate has been tied shut with baler twine, and the builder's made a good job of it. I struggle with it for a minute before Carl gets out with a sigh to help me.

He joins in but the knots are fiddly and it's hard to see here in the deep shade beneath the trees.

'Oh, this is fucking impossible! For God's sake!' His voice in the cool shade sounds suddenly crazily loud. 'That builder must be some kind of weird S&M freak.'

'Hey, hey, it's OK. We'll sort it out in a minute.'

'Why did you have to drive your van all the way down, anyway? You should have left it up at the top nearer the road.'

'But you *told* me to drive down.'

'Since when did you ever take any notice of what I say?'

'What?'

'Well, now you're trying to imply that it's my fault because I suggested you might want to park at the bottom. Why don't you make your own bloody decisions once in a blue moon? Why do I have to shoulder the responsibility the whole time? You *knew* we'd have to leave your stupid van here at some point. You should have realised it'd be better to park at the top. Think for yourself, why don't you?'

'That's not fair!' I grapple with the knots in the twine. 'I never said it was *your* fault. I didn't try to blame you. You're picking on me for no reason. You've done nothing but pick on me since I got here. I don't know why you married me. You clearly don't think I'm your one woman in a million – you act as if I'm nothing but a source of irritation. Well, I'm sorry, Dominic's got your precious, perfect Antonia and your kids and the alpha male house whether you like it or not. You've got me and my stupid van and my crummy little flat and a house with half a roof, no proper kitchen and a fuck of a lot of spiders and if you don't like it, you shouldn't have married me and you shouldn't have bought a house down the road from your ex with the perfect fucking life.'

I give up on the knots and quickly climb over the gate and stomp down the track towards my van. It's hard to storm off when you know you're going to have to come back up again. Still, I keep my head held high. It's not dark yet, but it's gloomy with so many trees branching over the track. Something touches my face – a low twig on a tree – and I jolt back. It's a bit creepy, to be honest. I wish Carl had come with me. Or at least I should have waited until I was safely in my van before shouting at him.

It's fine. I'm just not used to it. I'm far safer here than I would be near my flat in London. The biggest crime they have round here is probably someone nicking a cabbage from the allotments. Except there are burglaries or Dominic wouldn't have all that high-tech security stuff. And we had our roof tiles nicked. What if the thieves decide now is the ideal moment to come back and get the other half?

I reach the van and stop for a minute to look up as the sun is starting to set and the sky is streaked with pink and orange and purple beyond the furthest field. It's breathtaking. My row with Carl suddenly seems pathetically petty and irrelevant in the grand scheme of things. I do love him. I love him so much. And he loves me. At least I think he does. Maybe he still has a bit of a soft spot for Antonia, but that's all right. They have kids together – of course he still feels something for her. It's completely natural. I'll have to be sensible and grown-up about it. I can do that. I was sensible and grown-up only last Tuesday. For several minutes.

God, I wish we hadn't bought this house. Or I wish it were five miles away, at the very least.

I hear a footstep on the gravel and my heart skips a beat. I scrabble at the handle of my van and drop my key.

'Nat.'

It's Carl. He wraps his arms around me and I sink against him, my heart pounding.

'I'm sorry, I'm sorry! I didn't mean it,' I wail into him.

'Hush, hush. No, *I'm* sorry. It was all my fault. I'm a pig. You're right to hate me.'

'I don't hate you. I love you.' I bury my face in his chest and snuffle against his jacket. 'I don't know why you put up with me.'

'Ssh, ssh. You're my woman in a million, remember?' He pulls me close and kisses me tenderly. 'God, I wish we could drive back together. I hate being apart from you now.'

'Let's talk all the way back on speakerphone. It'll be like when we were first seeing each other and we used to talk on the phone late into the night.'

'Good idea.' He kisses me again. 'I'm sure we can transform this house into something wonderful. Whatever it takes.'

'I know we can, Carl. Hang on a sec.' I open the van and forage in the glovebox. Pull out a pair of scissors and a ball of string. 'For the gate.'

'I will never criticise your jam-packed glovebox ever, ever again. You are a star.'

'And, Carl, look.' I nod towards the setting sun.

It's so quiet I can hear him swallow. He takes my hand in his and squeezes it.

'My love,' he says. 'I have you, and a house in the country, and a perfect sunset. Who could ask for more?'

'This *will* be our dream house, darling.' I stretch up on tiptoe to kiss him. 'It will take time and work—'

'And money.'

'Ah, yes. And money. But it will be truly beautiful, I'm sure.'

'And Dominic and Antonia will be seething with envy. We'll have the best house for miles.'

Well, that wasn't exactly my top priority.

'And we'll have done it together – that's the point. It'll be *our* home we've created *together*. For *us*.'

'Yes,' Carl says. 'And it'll be better than theirs.'

8

_____

A QUESTION OF TRUST

After his work function in London, Carl comes back to my flat and we sit and have a late supper. He tells me that we will need a schedule of works for the cottage.

'Yes,' I say, full of enthusiasm. 'Let's do our bedroom first, then the kitchen.'

He laughs.

'That's not what I meant, sweetheart.' He stabs at his ravioli. 'I mean: anything structural, electrics, plumbing, sanding floors, then painting and decorating et cetera last. Don't worry about it. I'll get Steve the builder to sort it out, then we can hire a project manager to keep an eye on everything once the work gets under way.'

'Oh. Right. But couldn't we do that ourselves?'

'We can't keep running up and down to the country every two minutes when there's a problem with the bathroom tiles, can we?'

'But we want to choose the tiles and the paint colours and so on, don't we? I don't want to farm that bit out.'

'I'm way too busy with work, Nat. I can't take much time off to be down there to oversee the renovations.'

'But I could do it. It might take me a while to find the right premises for my shop, so I'll have time. Surely it makes sense for me to do it if you're too busy?'

'*Really?*' He says it with so much emphasis, I can tell he's not simply concerned that I won't have enough time.

'You don't think I can handle it, is that it? Carl, I do run a business. I did do everything in this flat. I know it's small but I did manage. I'm not an idiot.'

'I don't think you're an idiot – not for a second. But...' he sighs.

'*But?*'

'Look, you do need to be quite... *assertive* with builders and painters, otherwise they'll run rings round you and the next thing you know a six-week job is taking six months.'

'You think I'm a pushover?'

'No – no, not exactly.'

'By which you mean *yes*.'

'No, it's only that you're so nice and sweet to everyone that I worry they'd take advantage of you and have you running about making them tea while they put their feet up and ask if you could bring them more cake.'

'Carl, I think you need to learn to trust me – like I trusted you about buying the house.'

There's a pause, then he looks at me.

'OK, I'm sorry. Look, I can get the fast train down after work once or twice a week so we can do it together. The barn already has power and plumbing. Let's ask Steve to install a loo and shower in the little end room there, so we can stay over when we want to without being in the house, while the works are going on. It makes sense if we're going to convert the barn into a guest annexe or something later anyway.'

'That's a good idea. I'd love to stay there as much as possible. Now, what about the décor? And furniture? We could pick up some really good bargains at auction, I'm sure. When can you take some time off and I'll find—'

'Oh, we don't want to be faffing about with all that. If we want an antique, we can go to a proper shop.'

'But we'll pay more than double that way and it's so much more fun to unearth stuff at an auction house, to know you're going to give a good home to some lovely old wardrobe that no one wants any more.'

'A wardrobe's not a rescue dog, Nat. It doesn't need a good home.' He smiles and leans forward to kiss the very tip of my nose.

'You know what I mean.'

Carl draws me away from the table, over to the sofa.

'Yes, of course. You're such a softie, worrying about wardrobes and their poor little hurt feelings,' he teases me. 'Next thing we know, you'll be going round at night, kissing the chests of drawers and tables good night and reading them a bedtime story instead of devoting yourself entirely to me. Kiss me, Wife.' He holds me close, then draws back a little to look at my face. 'Now, darling, remember – we don't want to make it too cluttered, do we?'

I shake my head solemnly.

'It's perfectly acceptable to have some *empty* walls, you know.' He looks round at the small sitting room of my flat. The walls are generously occupied, it's true, but I love it. There are pictures and framed embroidery samplers, carved wooden masks and a couple of interesting hats I don't actually wear. Plus an amazing rug I lugged back from Morocco, even though when rolled up it was still bigger than I am. Wherever you look, your eye falls on something; a small pencil sketch, two tiny clay figures in a box frame, a white ostrich feather fan with mother-of-pearl inlay. There's a grandfather clock in the hall, which is too big for such a small space, so that when you enter through the front door, it seems to be confronting you, but I still love it. When Carl first came to my flat, he said it was like being in a miniature museum. At the time, I thought he meant it as a compliment.

'It will be a hymn to minimalism,' I assure him, trying to get comfortable; this sofa is way too small for both of us.

'Rugs only on the floors, not the walls?'

'Our walls will be a carpet-free zone.'

'No dusty hats that look like they've been chucked out of an am-dram props box?'

'My only hats will be a romantic straw one for swanning around in summer, a woolly one for winter walks, and a tweed deerstalker for embarrassing you in the village.'

'It's not that I don't like your taste.' Carl stretches and yawns. 'It's just that there always seems to be a lot of it.' His gaze roves round the room once more. 'Everywhere.'

I give him a gentle push. At least we'll be able to have a much longer sofa at the house. Two sofas, even.

'I suppose you think everywhere should be decorated like your flat was?' I suspect Carl is missing its spectacular views, huge bed, and luxurious bathroom.

'Well, you loved it, didn't you?'

'Ye-e-e-s. Who wouldn't? It was like staying at a deluxe hotel, where you could get great sex, cuddles and conversation from Room Service. But...'

'But it needed more clutter, right?' Carl laughs and pinches my waist.

'Tee hee. No, what I think it needed was a bit more... *you* in it. And maybe a bit more clutter.'

'More *me*?'

'Yes, more photographs, pictures, things you'd chosen, souvenirs from trips, special objects that meant something to you.'

'That's because you think a home is a nest and it has to have four million items from your life woven into it to be a real home.' He wriggles to get more comfortable.

'Well, a home is a sort of nest, isn't it?'

'Up to a point. But do we really want to fill the house up with junk the second we move in?'

'Thanks, Carl. Do you really see all my precious objects as junk?'

'No, no. Of course not. You know what I mean. But it'll look fantastic once we've done it up. It'd be good to enjoy it for a bit. *Then* we can slowly acquire a few things that really go with the house.' He turns to look into my eyes. '*Together*. Hmm?'

I like the idea of choosing furniture for the house together. We've never really bought things as a couple before.

'Carl?' I sit up because it's too squashed on this sofa with both of us, and perch on the armrest instead. 'Dominic mentioned that he was also at the auction. That he was bidding, too.'

'Hmm? What auction?'

'For Rose Cottage, darling. Our house.'

'Oh. Yes, yes, I suppose he was there.'

'He said he was the underbidder. Is that true? It was only down to you and him at the end?'

'Certainly is. I won, didn't I? We got the house.' He punches the air in triumph.

'Why didn't you tell me?'

'Didn't think it was relevant.' He shrugs. 'Or all that interesting.'

I look at him in disbelief.

'Oh, for God's sake. I thought you'd make a fuss and go all funny about it. And, see, what a surprise, I was right. You're going funny on me.'

'I'm not *going funny* on you, Carl. I just think it's a little strange that you bid against your ex-wife's second husband for a house and didn't even mention it.'

'So? What's worth mentioning? He wanted the house, but he didn't have the nerve or the vision to see it through. He wimped out, I won. End of story.'

'It's not a competition.'

'Of course an auction's a competition. God, you should know that – you go to auctions all the time. You really want something, you keep bidding till you get it. Or you want it but only at the right price to make a profit? Decide when to stop, then stick to it. That way you stay a winner every time.'

'I didn't mean that. I meant it's not a competition between you and Dominic. In life. There's no battle, is there?'

'Well, of course not. He's not in the same league. OK, so he's got a nice place down there, but he's not really a *player*, is he? In business, I mean. He's just pootling about, designing the odd extension.'

'Doesn't he own his company?'

'So what? He probably owns his own toothbrush, that doesn't make him a hotshot, does it?'

'But all his equipment, the studio, that amazing house. The *kitchen* alone must have cost an absolute fortune.'

'Family money.' Carl snorts, though his own family weren't exactly impoverished. 'His dad was loaded. Dominic's work is like a little hobby on the side. He's *playing* at it.'

'Really? But the house is incredible, and he did all that, didn't he?'

'Whose side are you on anyway?' Carl sits up suddenly. 'You're supposed to be *my* chief supporter, but you sound like you've taken on the job of being Dominic's PR manager.'

'Oh, for goodness' sake, Carl! I'm not on his side, I'm not on anyone's stupid side. That's not how I see the world. I don't understand why you seem so obsessed with being better than him. If you're going to be like this, what the hell's it going to be like living so near them all the time? I don't want to spend my life struggling to keep up with the Joneses and worrying about what car they've got or how big the swimming pool is or—'

'When did you see the pool? Did you see the crap statue? It's so naff.'

'Aaaarrrgggh! Just stop, will you? I didn't even know they had a pool. And I don't give a toss either way. I'm not playing your ridiculous, childish game. They can be richer than us, swankier than us and have the best of everything – I really, genuinely don't care, Carl. I've got you. I love you and we will be together in our own house, near your children, that's all that matters. Can't you forget about everything else?'

'You're right.' He pulls me close. 'I'm very sorry.' He kisses me. 'I can't help being competitive. Force of habit.'

Carl and his company have to pitch against rivals for new contracts. It's incredibly tough and he works fiendishly hard to be the best.

'I know. It's just the way you are. To me, you'll always be the best, you know that.'

'Yeah.' He smiles suddenly, that infectious, gorgeous smile that first made me feel all lit up inside. 'That's all that matters to me. Come with me. I have something vital to show you in the bedroom.' He takes my hand and leads me through.

I know, I still haven't asked him about the 'circumstances' that Dominic mentioned. I can't bear the thought of starting another row. And I can't ask Dominic when we're next in Kent because I said Carl had already told me. It's probably not as bad as I think, right? Chances are it's not that anyone died there or anything really dreadful.

9

IN TOO DEEP

String up the celebratory bunting – I am finally being granted an official audience with Antonia. I've had to be up in London solidly for a couple of weeks to sort things out, wind up my shop, put the remaining stock into storage and so on. Steve the builder has now put in a loo and shower in the small end room at the barn, so Carl and I can stay over in Kent when we want to. We can't sleep in the house until at least the electrics and plumbing are sorted out because he says the old wiring is 'a death trap'. Plus there will be so much dust when they rip off all the woodchip wallpaper then replaster the walls underneath that it would be horrible to sleep in the cottage.

I'm not exactly in a rush to meet Antonia, (when she couldn't get back to see us that first time, it was a bit of a relief to be honest, though at the same time, I felt like she was giving me a message: I can't be bothered to hurry back to meet you), but I know I can't avoid it indefinitely if we're going to be neighbours. And I am curious, of course. What on earth is my husband's first wife like? I remind myself that when they got married, presumably they thought they'd be together *for ever*. What if she's really beautiful? I don't think about my appearance much most of the time, but I hate the idea that Carl might look at me and think: hmm, I love Natalie, but it's a shame she doesn't look more like Antonia.

Anyway, she has invited me to a pool party at her house, which Carl says will be a lovely, informal introduction. Why can't I pop in for a cup of tea? Why does it have to be a *party*?

I've never been to a pool party before, so I'm not sure exactly what it entails. Swimming, presumably, but what makes it a party? I hate parties. Maybe I can swing by, say hello, immerse myself in their pool, do a few lengths, then scurry back to the cottage again?

I ask Carl what people do at a pool party but he waves his hand airily as if it doesn't matter, and says: 'You know, darling, swim, chat, have a drink. It's fun.'

I make a face. Enforced fun! My favourite.

'And what am I supposed to wear?' I ask him.

Annoyingly, he laughs.

'I don't know, darling. Who cares? Wear whatever you like.' He takes me in his arms and dips to kiss my neck softly. 'I know you'll wear jeans and a T-shirt whatever I say, so do that, but put your swimsuit on underneath. Then it's easy to change. OK?'

'So you think it'll be very casual, then?'

'How should I know? I'm not Antonia's party planner. But it can't be black tie and ballgowns if it's a pool party, can it? Anyway, she said it's literally just a handful of close friends. Hardly a party at all.'

'That's another thing. If it's her *close* friends, why on earth is she inviting me when we haven't even met yet? Isn't that odd?'

'Now, Nat, don't read so much into everything. That's partly my fault because I said I thought it would be nice if you could meet a few local people. And she's so keen to meet you, of course.'

'But you know how I hate parties.'

'I thought she'd ask you to join her little clique for coffee. I didn't know she'd make a whole big thing of it. Typical Antonia. Never have a quick sandwich if you can have a hundred people over and hire a caterer.'

'Clique?'

'I misspoke, OK? Group. I just meant group.'

'You said clique.'

'Guilty as charged. You should have been a lawyer or a judge.' He bends to kiss me again. 'OK, I might have mentioned that you're a really good swimmer so you'd love a chance to use the pool. I'm sure it's only Antonia and a couple of other women. Now go. Swim, make friends, relax and enjoy it, OK?'

* * *

I pull on to the gravel drive and park next to a red Alfa Romeo and a low silver Porsche. On the other side of the drive is a huge, spotless, white Range Rover and next to that a black Audi, all gleaming and gorgeous in the sunshine. I should at least have got my van washed. It can barely pass muster as the poor hick cousin of these glittering sophisticates; it looks like an entirely different species. I could have left the van down at the cottage and walked from there – why didn't I do that? Why do I always know what to do once it's already too late to do it?

As I get out of the van, a young man appears round the side of the house.

'Please no park here.' He's pointing at my van. 'Go other side, behind garage. Mrs says vans park round back.'

'Oh. OK.'

Is that a bit rude? I suppose Antonia must have spotted me on their CCTV. I now notice that there are three cameras at the front, not just the one I saw that first time.

I get back in the van and follow his direction to park at the back.

I can hear girlish giggling and chatter the other side of the high fence but I can't see how to get through from here and now the young man has disappeared so I go back round to the front and ring the bell.

I'm let in by a young woman, surely much too young to be Antonia? I think Carl said Antonia is two years older than him, which makes her forty-three, though he did say she has been 'thirty-eight' for quite a while now...

But the young woman says she is Katja, their au pair, and when I ask if there's somewhere I can change, she waves me towards the back door. Then she picks up a big stack of ironed clothes and scurries off upstairs.

I pause for a minute to look around the kitchen. It really is amazing, with those glass worktops and cool, metal, pendent lamps over the long table. On the worktop is a large chopping board with strawberries, cucumber, oranges and lemons, and there's a tumbler of water with a bunch of fresh mint in it and a bottle of Pimm's alongside. I glance towards the stairs, then dart over to the board and take a strawberry. I wish I could stay in here, in this gorgeous kitchen, eating strawberries and drinking Pimm's and not go *Out There* at all.

Or I could sneak back to the cottage and say I forgot to come. No. I can do this. I dump my bag down and take another strawberry just as the back door opens and a very made-up, blonde woman in a see-through turquoise kaftan, with a bikini on underneath it, comes in. Great. My first meeting with Antonia and here I am, sneakily nicking her fruit.

'Hi,' she says. 'Antonia says could you bring out another jug of Pimm's, please.' Ah, not Antonia then.

'Oh. Right. Yes. Sure.'

She says thanks and leaves by the back door. I start slicing fruit and slivers of cucumber for the Pimm's and look round for a jug. There's a tall white one on the top shelf of the dresser. Is that too big? Glass would be better really but I can't see a glass one. I open a cupboard at random to see two entire shelves of Champagne flutes. Who has that many Champagne glasses in their house? Don't people hire them for parties? I mean, for posh parties. Where I grew up, if anyone had a party, they used plastic cups. Though mostly they sat on the cold steps that smelled of wee and drank straight from the bottle. Not Champagne. Obviously.

I carry a chair over to the dresser to get the white jug down. God, being short is a pain at times – OK, most of the time. I can almost reach the bottom with my fingertips. I'll have to move up to the dresser itself. I carefully put one foot on to the dresser between a huge stoneware platter of fruit and a vase filled with tall grasses and seed heads. Reach up. Still not quite there so I bring up my second foot to perch on the dresser. Ah, better. Now I can reach the jug. I carefully take it and turn round to come down again. Now it seems a really long way down back to the chair, and the jug is incredibly heavy. At that moment, a beautiful tabby cat jumps up to the chair, then up on to the dresser and starts coiling round my ankles.

'Hello, Puss. Please don't make me drop this jug.'

I look round for a gap to put it down then I see that the au pair is standing at the bottom of the stairs apparently watching me.

'Ah, hello,' I say. 'I was just getting a jug down.'

'But you cannot take this,' she says.

'No, no. Not to take. It's for the Pimm's, you see.'

'No, not for Pimm's.'

'Yes, this woman came and asked me to make some Pimm's. So, I needed a jug...'

'No. Put back now.'

I feel ridiculous. I'm standing on a kitchen dresser, holding a huge jug and being told off by a stranger. The cat, disloyally, jumps down nimbly and darts off, clearly not wanting to be associated with a dishonourable person who purloins jugs. I carefully put the jug back and then climb back down. The au pair pointedly takes the chair and returns it to its original position.

'I was only trying to help,' I say.

'Is not for Pimm's,' she says, crossing to the far side of the room. She opens a cupboard and takes out a tall glass jug. '*This* for Pimm's.'

'Ah. I see. Should I... er, carry on... with the Pimm's?'

She looks at me as if I might be mad, then returns to the chopping board and picks up the knife.

'You are guest for the pool party?' She jerks the knife towards the back door.

'Er, yes... I'm a guest.'

'Go to party then. Can change next to pool.'

I really don't want to change in front of everyone. I know I have my swimsuit on beneath my clothes so I don't have to get naked, but I'd feel so conspicuous undressing in front of the other guests.

'Is there a bathroom?'

'Toilet there.' She jabs the knife towards another door.

I nip into the loo and remove my clothes down to my black swimsuit. It's a completely plain Speedo with a racer back as that's the best thing for swimming. I feel as if I'm practically naked when I emerge from the loo in my swimsuit and flip-flops.

I'm tempted to put my jacket back on top but think that'll look worse. I should have a floaty kaftan thing like that other guest had. That's what a proper woman would wear to a thing like this.

I brought my towelling bathrobe to put on after swimming, so I put that on top of my swimsuit. Now that I look at it, I can see that it's getting a bit worn and faded, but at least I won't be almost naked. 'Shall I leave my bag here?' I ask, but now the kitchen is empty. 'Hello?' There's no response, so I take my plastic bag and handbag and jacket, then open the back door. I stand in the doorway for a minute, wondering if I should put my swimming hat and goggles on, too. That way, there will be as little of me on display as possible. I try to think what Carl would do. Carl would avoid it altogether by having a meeting to go to, which is exactly what he's done. OK, Celeste then. Celeste would probably wear an amazing bikini with some sort of stunning cover-up on top. She'd have had a pedicure so her toes would be all pretty and perfect. Mine are clean, but that's about it. Why didn't I get a pedicure or at least paint my toenails? I look like an eleven-year-old.

Right, come on, stop being such a baby.

I step out into the sunshine and turn towards the sound of talking and laughing.

At the far end of the pool, a group of unbelievably glamorous women are draped over the sunloungers and outsize garden seats. There are seven or eight at a glance, surrounding one woman right in the centre, who is clearly the Queen Bee.

The chatter ceases suddenly and I hear a voice say, 'God, who on earth is *that*?'

I'm tempted to turn round and run for it, but then almost at once, another voice says, 'Ssh!'

The Queen Bee pauses a moment then raises one arm and waves.

'Is that Natalie?' she calls.

'Yes. Hi. Antonia?'

She stands up and slips her feet into gold criss-cross strappy high mules. She is wearing a translucent white filmy cover-up with gold embroidery across the bust, a white swimsuit underneath. Her hair tumbles around her shoulders in soft bouncy waves. She is tall and tanned and looks like she's just stepped down from Mount Olympus to say hi to the mortals.

Never have I felt so short, so earthly, so completely and utterly plain and ordinary. I can feel my hair sticking out from my head in an anxious frizz. My swimsuit must look as if I've turned up for a school swimming class. My plain flip-flops are the cheapest type you can get in a supermarket. My towelling robe is fifteen years old.

I take a step or two towards the group, wishing I could turn round and run, back to our little crumbly cottage with its half a roof, or back to my tiny flat where I could hide under the duvet and maybe forget about everything and go back to the way my life was before. That's a much better plan.

But then I'd have no Carl.

I take another step.

The golden goddess lopes towards me. I half-expect to hear background music accompanying her, maybe a little light angelic harp strumming. If I had music to mark my entrance, it would be clang-clang-clang, like a toddler bashing a triangle. Or hitting a block of wood – clonk-clonk-clonk.

She looks oddly familiar. Oh God, I've suddenly realised. She's the woman who queue-jumped in the greengrocer's when I first came down. I see a tiny flicker of recognition cross her face. Perhaps she's wondering whether or not to mention it? I'm certainly not going to.

'Hello and welcome. Dear Natalie, it's so nice to meet you at last.'

I put out my hand, but she bends down to kiss me on both cheeks.

'We're practically related really.'

Then she puts her arm round my shoulders and ushers me towards the group. They all look incredible, like a collection of Bond girls, albeit closer to age forty than twenty, but still stunning, with beautiful, brightly coloured sarongs or floaty kaftans over glamorous bikinis or swimsuits. They all have perfectly painted toenails and expensive-looking sandals. One woman is wearing flip-flops, I see, but even those have diamanté straps.

'This is Natalie,' says Antonia, 'Carl's Number Two. Be nice, girls.'

There's a chorus of 'Hi's. At least they're all smiling, though a couple of them definitely do that thing where they look you up and down. I want to stare at my feet but I force myself to meet their gaze and I am trying really, really hard to smile and not look grumpy or... terrified.

'Now let's get you a drink. What will you have? Katja should be coming out with more Pimm's in a tick.'

She turns to one of the women, the one who came into the kitchen earlier, and adds, 'Minty, did you ask Katja to hurry up with the Pimm's? She's taking *forever*. Really, how long does it take to slice a few strawberries and chuck them in a jug?'

The woman in turquoise looks embarrassed.

'Sorry, Toni, I thought this, er, I thought she was Katja...' She nods at me.

Antonia laughs. 'Oh, hilarious! You thought *Natalie* was Katja!'

'Well, I haven't met her. How should I know? You change au pairs practically every month.'

'I do not! That's such a lie.' But Antonia is smiling as she says this as if firing her staff regularly is simply a rather charming quirk.

'Now, what are you having? Pimm's? Or there's a half-decent rosé? White? Prosecco? Gin and tonic? We have literally *everything*. Whatever you like.'

'Actually, I'm driving so...'

'Just the one then? Go on.'

Katja appears with the tall jug of Pimm's then, giving me a look that says, 'I know you're a secret jug thief.'

'Let Natalie have some first. Drink up, Natty, or you'll never catch up with these drunken bitches.'

She pours me a glass and hands it over. It's absolutely delicious, though tastes quite a bit stronger than when I've had it before.

'I'd better go easy as I drove here.'

'Did you manage to fit your car on the front? These girls probably hogged all the space. They're so awful. Louisa can't park to save her life.' She smiles as if she's giving them a sweet compliment.

'Actually, a man told me to drive round the back – behind the garage.'

'What? Why on earth would Pavel do that? Oh, for goodness' sakes, can't anyone do anything properly! I'm so sorry, Natalie – having to park round the back as if you were a tradesman or the pool man!'

'Oh, well, perhaps he thought I was. I – I drive a van.'

'A *van*?' Antonia says this as if I've said I drive a motorised outsize carrot. Clearly, she's never actually met a person who drives a van. 'Shut up! You do *not*!'

'Er, yes, yes I do. I deal in antiques. A car would be useless to me.'

'How delightful! A *van*!' She tips her head back and laughs as if she's just heard the most hilarious joke.

God, does she talk like this all the time? She makes it sound as if the van is an amusing affectation I've developed to make myself seem charmingly eccentric, instead of a pragmatic solution for my business.

* * *

'So... er, how does this work?' I've already slurped my whole glass of Pimm's out of nervousness and I can't have any more. 'I mean, when do we swim? We do actually swim, right?'

One of the women, whose name sounds like Jinx (Jinks?) – but surely that's not a real name – laughs and says, 'God, no, we hardly ever actually get in the water!' She makes an outraged face as if she's never heard such a crazy idea. 'It's a pool party but the pool bit is...' she waggles her fingers dismissively, '... secondary. It does horrible things to my hair.'

'We only call it a pool party to give these fashionistas an excuse to wear bikinis and show off all those hours slogging away at the gym.' Antonia gestures at her friends.

'Oh, I see. I – I didn't realise.'

I feel like such an idiot. They don't even go in the water?

'But we must see you in action.' She turns towards the clique. Sorry, group. 'Girls, my spies report that Natalie is a serious swimmer. She can show us how it's done. We only get in when we want to cool off, Natty, and it's not exactly hot today. I can call you Natty?'

I'm trying to think of a nice way to say, 'No, please don't.'

Only one person ever called me Natty and it reminds me of him so I don't like it when someone else says it. Carl calls me Nat, usually. Or darling, which is sweet. Kind of old-fashioned.

'Um. I prefer Natalie really.'

I really don't want to swim for an audience. But the pool looks incredible.

'Aren't we all going in?'

'Come on, girls. Let's go in. Stop boozing for a few minutes and do some bloody exercise.'

There's a few 'Oh, no's, but three or four of them gracefully slip out of their cover-ups and sashay towards the pool. They all walk as if they think they're being secretly filmed or are practising for a catwalk.

'I hate this fucking expensive bikini – it's so uncomfortable,' one says, tugging at her strap.

It's really quite, um, tiny for a woman over forty, I'd have thought. The 'cups' are so small, they look like those mini cocktail napkins that have been folded into quarters. 'Christ,' the woman says, 'there's so little fabric in this thing, it probably works out at about £300 a metre.'

I laugh and she looks at me appreciatively. She might be rich and spoilt and vain, but at least she's funny.

'I'll come in with you, Natty. Sorry, sorry! *Natalie.* I'll never remember; you'll have to remind me.' Antonia shucks off her gorgeous cover-up to reveal what is possibly the most glamorous swimsuit I've ever seen outside the pages of a magazine. It's pure, bright white with a deeply plunging neckline and a large gold-coloured metal ring linking the suit at the cups and matching gold rings at the sides by her hips. I can't stop looking at her.

'Wow. That's an amazing swimsuit.'

'Thanks. It should be. Don't even ask how much it was.' She leans in as if we're conspirators in a secret plot. 'I told Dom I got it in a sale. As *if.*' She laughs.

I smile though I don't really understand why the idea of buying something in a sale is funny. When I was growing up, my mum had to get most of our clothes from charity shops or hand-me-downs from my cousin so, for me, buying something in a sale is a bit of an upgrade.

I cross to a chair and turn away to remove my bathrobe. I suddenly hate it that my swimsuit isn't nicer. I know it's petty and it doesn't matter, but I wish it were a bright colour at least, that it wasn't quite so determinedly plain and functional.

I grab my goggles and hat, and head for the pool, fiddling with the strap of my goggles as if I need to adjust them.

'Oh. My. God.' Antonia is standing in front of me, just staring. 'Is that really your swimsuit?'

Part of me is thinking: well, what a bloody stupid question. Why on earth would I be wearing it otherwise? No, my actual swimsuit is tucked away in a drawer at home. I put this one on as a joke to see what you'd say?

'Yes.' I stand up tall. Well, tall for me, which is still extremely short. I look her right in the eye, though as she *is* tall and still in her high-heeled mules, I am literally looking up to her as if I am offering a handful of manky grass to a beautiful giraffe. I refuse to be embarrassed. There's nothing wrong with my swimsuit. It's respectable and practical and really comfortable. Most important, it's great for actual swimming instead of lounging about next to a swimming pool looking at the water.

'But look at you – I can see you've got a gorgeous figure. Girls, will you look at Natalie's figure. Look at that waist. And fantastic tits, too. But you're hiding it in this *awful* swimsuit. I can't bear it. It's absolutely criminal. You must borrow one of mine.'

Did Carl's ex-wife really say I have 'fantastic tits'? I don't know where to look. This feels surreal. I can't even meet her gaze.

'Oh, no, I couldn't. I really couldn't.'

'They're perfectly clean, I promise.'

'No, no, of course. I didn't mean that. I'd really rather not. I'm fine in this one. It's good for swimming, honestly it is.'

'Well, all right, but you are mad, Natty. I'm going to tell our stupid husband to take you shopping and get you something lovely. I can't believe he's being so mean. He never used to be mean. Infuriating, God yes! But not *mean*. What on earth was he thinking of, sending you off to a pool party without treating you to something chic?'

'I don't need him to treat me. I don't expect him to pay for my clothes.'

'Oh, that's right. You *work*, don't you?'

She says it as if it's something extraordinary and slightly suspect. 'Girls, Natalie here is a proper career woman, unlike you lazy cows.'

They all laugh and a couple raise their glasses towards me. The one called Jinks comes up and says, 'So what do you do then?' She's wearing a leopard-print bikini with beaded side thongs (barely) holding it together.

'Jinks used to work until she had kids.'

'What did you do?'

'I was a lawyer, believe it or not.'

I try not to look astonished but I'm a hopeless liar even if I don't say a word. I immediately have a picture in my mind of her in a courtroom wearing her leopard-print bikini.

'Your face!' Antonia laughs. 'Hysterical.'

'Do you think you might go back to it?'

'I used to. I thought once the children had started school, I'd have so much free time I'd be desperate to go back to work, but the longer you leave it, the harder it is. You get out of the loop. Things change. If I went back, I'd have to start at a much more junior level. You lose your confidence. You know how it is.'

At least with clocks and antiques, the pace of change is very slow. Certain things go in and out of fashion: 1950s and 1960s furniture, for example, which you could have picked up for virtually nothing for years, is suddenly considered cool and it's now expensive. It's still horrible, but now it's expensive and horrible instead of cheap and horrible. I don't care because I rarely deal in furniture, aside from the odd item if I spot something promising at auction.

'So, what do you do?' One of the other women has come up alongside Jinks and Antonia. This one is wearing a fuchsia-pink bikini with no cover-up. Close up, I can see she's certainly older than me, maybe early forties. Like Antonia, her make-up is perfect. Her hair is perfect. They all look so... finished, like no detail has been overlooked.

'I have a shop, selling antique clocks and a few other bits and pieces.'

'Natalie has a shop, girls,' Antonia calls out to the others. 'Isn't that super?'

'Tell us it sells shoes or lingerie! Can we get a discount?' one calls back.

'But surely you're not going to drag up to London every day to open your shop? Or will your staff do it?'

I laugh at the idea of having staff. When I need a day off, Colin comes in. He lives in the flat below mine. Colin is seventy-four and likes minding the shop as it's warm and I get the teabags and biscuits he prefers, and he can sit there and read all day. He's less keen on customers, which isn't exactly ideal. He comes across as grouchy when you first meet him but he warms up after a year or two...

'No, I've closed it and put my stock into storage until I find premises, possibly in Canterbury, I'm not sure yet.'

'Oh, I know where it should be!' Antonia puts her hand proprietorially on my shoulder. 'The Hopwood Farm complex. It's such bliss!'

'Good idea, Toni. It's soooooo fabulous.'

'Well, of course, I will be looking at a few places because—'

'No, no. Now, Natty, take it from me. The farm complex is *the* place to be. They've only been there a year and already we all go there all the time, don't we?'

Antonia's sidekick chips in: 'There's the organic farm shop, the wine shop...' She starts counting off on her fingers. 'Then there's a yoga studio, physio, beauty salon. Plus, the café. Really good coffee. And a gorgeous little patisserie, if you're being naughty. The cakes look unbelievable.'

'Obviously, Miranda hasn't actually eaten a cake since she was about twelve, but she likes to look at them, don't you, darling? Cake porn.'

'I do!'

'She literally stands outside the patisserie window looking in and drooling. It's pathetic.'

Miranda smiles as if Antonia's given her a lovely compliment.

'But why don't you just have a cake if you want one?'

They're all slim. Surely, they can eat the odd cake now and then?

Miranda looks up at Antonia, possibly to see if she's allowed even to think about having a cake, then at me.

'Do you eat cake?' She says this as if she's asking me: 'Are you secretly a super-hero?

'Of course. Who doesn't eat cake?'

'But how come you're not fat?'

'Well, I do eat other food occasionally too, you know... not just cake.' That's supposed to be a joke but she looks at me as if I'm delivering a secret formula and she's trying to memorise it. 'And I suppose I exercise a fair bit. I swim a lot and I walk a lot, and I sometimes have to move big clocks and bits of furniture about.'

She's looking at me now as if I'm some sort of alien creature, intriguing but unintelligible.

Antonia takes my arm and announces to the others that we're going in for a swim.

'Now, Carl tells me you're a proper swimmer...'

Do they talk about me, then? Somehow the idea of Carl telling Antonia about me seems strange. What else does he say?

'Well, not really. I usually swim at my local pool, you know, most mornings. When I have time.'

'Super – well, let's get in then. You'll think my technique absolutely shameful, Natalie, if you swim properly. I know I'm simply awful.'

I can't imagine Antonia being awful at anything.

'And I don't want you to worry about your antiques shop. I know Mark, who runs the Hopwood complex. Actually, little

secret, I think he has a teeny bit of a crush on me. Not a word to
the chaps! Still, awfully handy really. I'll fix you up with a meeting. I know there are three units still vacant so you can probably
take your pick. Though I think you should have the one in the
corner. I know you'll absolutely love it.'

'Well, really I think—'

'Fizz, don't you think Natalie should rent the corner shop at
the Hopwood complex? For her antiques and whatnots.'

'Oh, yuh, perfect, Toni. Next to the salon, so literally everyone
will pop in.'

'Thank you, that's kind, but I—'

'No, don't worry. Leave it all to me. And I'll twist Mark's arm
and get you the best possible deal, I promise.'

* * *

Later, in the bath, I suddenly remember what it was that bothered me about my conversation with Antonia. I was distracted by
her talking about my figure at the time, but it was what she'd said
right after that:

'I'm going to tell our stupid husband to get you something
lovely...' Our stupid husband. Our husband. *Our.*

Is that how she still sees him? Why didn't she say 'your stupid
husband' or 'my stupid ex-husband'? Or why not just 'Carl'?

And it makes me wonder how Carl would talk about Antonia
to Dominic? Would he say, '*our* wife'?

11

PERFECT DAY

At last, Carl has taken a whole day off so we can do some things for the house. Top of the list: choosing a bed. I want to buy some plants too, so that we can have pots by the front door full of pretty flowers to greet us when we come home.

'But not too many, darling, yes? I don't want to come back in the dark and have to negotiate an obstacle course of mismatched containers cluttering up the front path just to gain access to my own house.'

'*Our* house.' I elbow him in the ribs. 'I suppose you'd have the front door flanked by two perfectly clipped bay trees in those poncy painted wooden planters?'

'Well, why not? Sounds good to me.'

'Why *not*? Well, one: because that's what Antonia has and I'm not copying her.'

'It's not *copying*. She doesn't have the copyright on having bay trees by the front door, does she? It's not exactly a startling bit of original thinking.'

'And, two: because this is a cottage, not a grand manor house.'

'Oh, come on, their house is hardly a manor house.'

'I didn't say it was.'

'No, but you implied that it's OK for them to do it because their house is practically a stately home while we're going to be living in a shack.'

'Carl, I completely don't see it like that. Antonia's house is quite grand and formal, so the planters fit in. It's a question of understanding the mood of the house.'

'It doesn't have a mood, my sweet. It's a *house*.'

'It *does*. OK, well, not a mood then, but a... sort of feeling to it. This is a rural cottage. It's charming but it's not grand. I don't want to tart up a country maiden in a rich lady's furs. It needs everything to be unfussy. Simple.'

Carl laughs and kisses me.

'Not too simple, please. Can we at least have hot water and not have to draw it up from the well, then wait for two hours while we boil it if we want a bath? And I'm not sleeping on a straw mattress either, even if it is simple and unpretentious. I'd like a very comfortable, very pretentious bed, with a top-of-the-range duvet and pillows and ultra-luxury, high-thread-count sheets because, gorgeous Wife, we will be spending a lot of time in it – and not all of it asleep...'

Carl is going to take his kids to the café at the farm complex for a quick breakfast of pancakes and waffles, but after that we have the day to ourselves. We're going into Canterbury to look at beds because, so far, we've only stayed over a couple of times in the barn; I was on a narrow camp bed we borrowed from Antonia, and Carl slept on a camping mat. And if you're wondering whether it's possible to have sex on a camp bed, the answer is: apparently not, or not without its tipping you both on to the floor, which was funny but not sexy. Later, we'll take a good look round the house and decide what we need to do in addition to all the plans we've already agreed, so we can tell Steve what the priorities are. He's finally managed to source some old roof tiles, so he wants to get going on that next week.

The first bed shop is huge and horrible, with an extraordinary range of beds, mostly extraordinary in that, despite there being hundreds of them, I don't actually like any of them.

'What about this one with the leather headboard?' Carl says.

'Too townie – won't look right.'

'Well, wooden then. That's rustic.'

'Wood is fine, but not that. It's too fancy, too dark, and too shiny.'

'Or no headboard? I don't care really, so long as it's comfortable.'

We lie down on the plastic-covered mattress side by side.

Carl reaches for my hand.

'This mattress isn't bad,' I say, wanting to sound more positive.

'Natalie?'

'Mm?'

He squeezes my hand. 'You're... well, you're not sorry you married me, are you?'

'What?' I turn on my side to face him and he turns towards me. 'Of course not. I love you. Don't you know that?'

'I suppose so. It's only... what with the roof tiles being stolen and – and the cottage needing kind of a lot more work than I'd realised, I worry it's not the dream house you'd hoped for. And, well, I chose it so it's down to *me*, isn't it? If it doesn't turn out right,' he scrunches his eyes shut briefly, 'then it's all my fault.'

'I don't see it like that. And it *will* be our dream house. I do believe that. I don't mind that it needs so much work. Better that than being bland and perfect already, with no opportunity to make it properly *ours*.'

He leans in close and kisses me.

There's a sudden cough as a sales assistant appears at the end of the bed, frowning at us.

'Were you *interested* in this one, sir? We are offering nought per cent finance at the moment.'

'Thank you, but we're still trying them out for now.'

'That is, we're still *looking*,' I emphasise as the man looks a bit startled, as if he thinks we are touring every bed shop in the country, having sex on all the beds to test them.

We quickly get up and pay a lot of attention to a nearby bedside cabinet, even though it's ugly, just to show that we're not bed-obsessed.

After the third shop, Carl says he must have coffee and please, please can we pick a bed, any bed, it doesn't matter – anything horizontal with a mattress will do, even a straw mattress at that. We go in search of a nice little independent café. I hate all the big chains because they're so soulless.

We turn into a side street and I see my favourite sort of sign in the world: 'AUCTION HOUSE'.

'Oh!'

'Oh-oh,' says Carl. 'I do really need a coffee.' He eyes up a café virtually opposite.

'Look, why don't you go and have a coffee and order me tea and cake if it looks good. You know what I like. I'll have a light-ning-quick look just in case there's anything perfect for the cottage.'

'You – lightning quick anywhere full of weird old objects? I don't think so. Please, please don't buy anything sad and creepy. I'm not sure I should let you loose in an auction house without a chaperone to protect you from yourself.'

'Funny. I will behave and I will be quick. I can recce in... let's say fifteen minutes – tops.'

'You promise? Otherwise, I will have to eat your slice of cake, you understand that?'

'I do.'

I dart into the auction rooms. The auction isn't until tomorrow, and much of it – like in many general auctions – isn't very enticing. Slightly sad, brown furniture. But over the years I've got better at digging out anything good. The only clocks are very ordinary, not worth bidding on, but there's a near-complete tea set from the 1930s, very pretty and with the original teapot. One of the side-plates is missing and one of the saucers is chipped, but it's otherwise undamaged. I take some pictures of it on my phone to show Carl.

I have a scoot round where the bigger furniture items are on show but there aren't any beds. I spot two guys, who presumably work for the auction house, hefting in a wardrobe.

'Hi. Any beds?' I ask.

'Don't think so. Oh, there was that brass one. Where's that, Gav? Is it still on the van?'

'Yeah, it's right at the back. Sorry, love. You're welcome to hop up into the van if you want to take a look?' He jerks his thumb towards the front entrance.

Outside, one of the men gives me a hand up into the back of the van and I wave across at Carl sitting outside the café. He immediately jumps to his feet, but I gesture I'm OK.

The man lifts a blanket and shows me.

'No frame?'

'Nah, probably rusted to bits. It's got the head and foot, though. See? You can get a frame made out of iron and bolt it on. Or wood. Easy. The frames weren't brass anyway. But the hassle puts most people off. Might go cheap, I reckon.'

It's mid-Victorian, by the look of it, wider than is usual for

these beds. The head piece, as always, is taller and more ornate –
brass, a couple of shallow dents but otherwise fine. It has ceramic
collars on the uprights. You don't see them often, and these
particular ones are really beautiful: sweet floral and leaf designs
in blue and white china. The whole thing is lovely, with the
matching foot section too.

I take some pictures of it on my phone and dig my extendable
tape out of my bag to check the dimensions. It's almost exactly
the width of a queen size; close enough anyway, that bedding
won't be a problem. Carl mocks me for having my handbag 'full
of weird crap', but you never know when a tape measure might
come in handy.

'Leave a bid at the desk if you can't make the auction tomorrow,' says one man. 'Or you can bid online if you want.'

I join Carl at the café and show him the tea set pictures.

'Are you going to be a very proper country wife then, having
ladies round for tea?'

'Absolutely. And we will share all the scandalous gossip as we
sip our Darjeeling. I do think it's really nice, Carl.'

'Then you should have it, my darling. Good. Anything else?'

'I also saw a bed.'

Carl makes a face. 'I'm not sure I like the idea of a second-
hand bed.'

I show him the bed pics.

'Actually, that is stunning. But where's the rest of it?'

I explain that we'd have to get a frame made.

'On the plus side, that means the bit we'd be sleeping on
would be brand new.'

'Sounds like a massive faff.'

'If I promise to sort it out, and not make any extra work for
you, then will you say yes?'

'All right then. I can see it fits with the house – sorry, the *mood* of the house. You look like a kid who's been given a packet of pear drops – your face is so sweet.' He dips to kiss me. 'Have I mentioned today how much I love you, by the way?'

'No. You've been very remiss. I've made a note in your "debit" column.'

After coffee, we go back into the auction rooms for Carl to see the bed for himself. It has been unloaded now, with the two parts left leaning against a wall next to a very ordinary 1930s wardrobe. I leave a bid at the desk.

Then I spot a really appealing chest of drawers. Mahogany. It looks late Georgian. There's a shallow scratch on one side, but I'm confident I can get that out. It's beautifully made. I give it a little pat.

'It's got a scratch,' Carl says, frowning. 'I know – here's an idea – why don't we look at some *new* furniture with no scratches for our house like normal people? Why does everything have to be second-hand? Or fifth-hand? Eighteenth-hand?'

'I *like* old things. They've lived a little. They have a *history*. Look at you – *you're* second-hand – not in pristine condition but adorable.'

Carl rolls his eyes. 'Hilarious. But I'm not having second-hand pillows...'

I leave bids on two more items: a fantastic old leather armchair and a pair of bedroom chairs with wicker seats.

'The house is going to look like this once you've had your way with it, isn't it?' Carl says, waving around at the cluttered show-room, but he's smiling.

'I promise not to get carried away.'

'I love watching you here, though. It's very lovable, the way you delve in and suddenly spot some gem with your sharp eyes.

The way you looked at that chest of drawers, as if it were a sweet little puppy. Do you know you even gave it an affectionate pat?'

'Is it silly?'

'No, it's lovely to watch you because I can see you enjoy it so much. So many women get excited about expensive new hand-bags or jewellery or designer clothes – Antonia is so extravagant about all that stuff – but you get your rocks off by looking at the back of a desk drawer to see if it's got dovetailed joints.' He takes my hand.

'Carl, I know we were planning to go back up to London this evening, but couldn't we stay here tonight?'

'You know I would love to, but I'm not sleeping on that bloody camping mat again. I'm too old.'

'Then let's buy a mattress, at least, to put on the floor. We can put it in the barn with a mat beneath it. If we buy a queen-size one, it'll fit the brass bed, and if we don't get that bed at auction, we can buy a plain wooden one in the same size.'

In a whirlwind, we buy a mattress and Carl talks them into delivering it this afternoon because he can talk anyone into anything. Then we go to choose pillows and some luxurious white bed linen with elegant blue piping.

As we're loading the pillows and shopping bags into the car, Carl suddenly grabs me and kisses me passionately right there in the car park.

'You know the mattress is being delivered this afternoon?' He looks at me in that way that makes me feel as if my insides are unravelling.

'Mm.'

'It would probably be wise for us to test it straight away.'

'Very wise. Mandatory, probably.'

We stop off at the farm shop on the way back and pick up some cheeses and salad as we haven't eaten since our coffee and cake. Then we walk around the house slowly, hand in hand. This is the way I wish it had been when we first looked around, the two of us happy and relaxed, taking time to talk about how we want the house to be.

We eat our very late picnic lunch out by the pond and I ask Carl if he wants to come in for a swim. He looks at me as if I'm crazy.

'I don't know, Nat – mud... bugs... do I have to?'

'Yes, you do. Don't be so feeble. The mattress guys aren't coming till after four, right?'

'Yes, why?'

I stand up then and take off my top. Undo my jeans. Strip off completely. Carl sits and watches me.

'You know what I love most of all about our dream house?' I say. 'It's not overlooked by anyone.'

Carl reaches for me but I twist out of his grasp and take two strides towards the pond and jump straight in.

'You're bonkers, but I love you.'

I swim slowly up and down the pond.

'It's honestly lovely once you're in.' I turn on to my back and float, looking up at the clouds. 'Are you coming?'

Carl stands up and starts to undress before clambering in awkwardly from the edge.

He swims up alongside me.

'Nat, I've realised we don't have any towels with us.'

'I have a big one in the van. With my swimming kit.'

We float on our backs, holding hands.

'This is *perfect*,' Carl says, squeezing my hand. 'Are you glad we bought this place now?'

'I really am. It's lovely. And once it's been rewired and deco-rated, it's going to be amazing. I can't wait to live here.'

'Me, too.'

There's a sudden toot from further up the lane and we scramble out quickly, naked, wet and a bit muddy from the bank. It must be the mattress being delivered early. Carl tugs his jeans on and says he'll run up and open the gate very, very slowly while I get dressed. Then he laughs and kisses me. I wish every day could be like today.

12

WHICH ONE?

Carl's mobile rings. It's on the kitchen worktop, charging. I bet it's Antonia. What on earth does she want *now*? I'm sure she never used to call this often. Or perhaps she did and I didn't know about it? I'm worried that she's still in love with him. But how does *he* feel about her? She's the mother of his children so he must still care about her – I accept that – but I wish she'd leave us alone. Then his phone beeps: a text. I'm not going to look at it. Well, I won't go *into* his phone, but I could glance at the notification on the home screen. That's not really prying, is it?

It's rare for Carl to be separated from his mobile unless he's asleep or in the shower. It's nearly always in his pocket or on the table in front of him, or clutched in his hand, like a magic talisman he's afraid to let go of even for a second.

This morning, he is over at Antonia's house, spending time with the kids while she and Dominic are out, but he left his phone here. It was my suggestion. The other day his hand actually seized up like a claw because he'd been on it so much.

I said, 'Look, why not leave it here for a couple of hours? The kids will be with you. It's good for them to have your undivided attention. I'm fine. What could possibly happen?'

It beeps again. Another message.

And, like every other brilliant idea I have, of course now there's a problem.

Then it rings again. I'm not sure Carl would like it if I answered his phone but maybe it's really important?

Two Missed Calls: Felix

Felix is Carl's younger brother.

There are texts visible on the notifications on the home screen. Also from Felix. The last one says:

CALL ME ASAP.

Then the phone rings once more and it's Felix again, so I pick up.

'Felix? It's Natalie. Carl's out with the kids but he left his phone here. Are you OK?'

'Yes, but our father is ill. Can you get Carl to call me, urgently?'

'Oh, I'm so sorry. I'll tell him. What should I say about your dad?'

'It's cancer, but it'll be easier if I talk to Carl. Please can you say Dad's OK for now but really not OK, if you know what I mean. I'll go down to Bristol when I can but Sima has a bad migraine so I can't leave yet as I've got to stay here with the girls.' Sima is Felix's wife and they have two young daughters, Ruby and Jasmine. 'Oh, yes – and tell Carl that Stefan will come from Amsterdam but can't leave till tomorrow and not to get stressed about it.'

Felix lives up north in Leeds, and their father lives in Bristol, in the West Country. From here in East Kent, it must be nearly two hundred miles. I have no idea who Stefan in Amsterdam is – possibly Carl's uncle? Did he once tell me that his dad's brother lives abroad? Carl's parents have been divorced for years, and his mother now lives in Paris.

I don't have the landline number of Antonia's house, but I do have her mobile number. She insisted on giving it to me even though I didn't ask for it. Is it weird to have your husband's ex-wife's mobile number? It feels ridiculous to call her to ask for the landline number so I can get hold of my own husband, as if she's the gatekeeper who controls access to him.

I could drive over there. It's less than five minutes in the van. But I don't want the children to feel I'm intruding. His kids need some time alone with him; they need to be able to see him without feeling I'm elbowing my way in the whole time. Also, I'm scared of Saskia. Not scared, no, that's ridiculous, obviously. I'm only a little nervous around her, that's all.

I call Antonia.

'Natalie! How super! We were just talking about you. How are you?'

'I'm fine, thanks, but I need to get hold of Carl urgently and he's left his phone here. Are you still out?'

'Yes, we are, but Carl's at the house with Saskia and Max. Only they're probably in the pool so won't hear the landline. I'll give you Saskia's number. She's never out of sight of her mobile.'

'Oh, no. I mean – I could... maybe I'll pop over there instead, if you don't mind?'

'Sure, as you like, but you'll have to shout over the side gate. It's Katja's day off so they won't hear the bell if they're in the pool.'

* * *

A few minutes later, I'm standing by the side gate, and I can hear splashing and shouting. It sounds like Carl and Max playing. I can't hear Saskia.

'*Hello*?' I call out by the gate, which they keep locked. 'Hello! Carl – it's *me*. Can you open the gate?'

Then I hear Saskia's voice, loud and clear.

'Daddy, it's *her*. Trying to get in.'

'Do you mean Natalie? Don't be a pain, Saskia. Go and open the gate then.'

'Do I have to? Why is it *my* job?'

'Because Max and I are in the pool and you're not. Just go and open it, please.'

'But you said I could go on my phone for a bit. You're so *mean*, Daddy.'

God, she's spoilt.

'Saskia, don't make me regret getting you a phone. Go and open the gate right now or I'll chuck your phone in the deep end and that'll be that.'

'You wouldn't!'

'Wanna risk it?'

There's a sigh and, taking her time, Saskia opens the gate.

'Oh, it's *you*,' she says, even though she must know that I'll have heard their entire conversation.

'Yes. Hi. I'm sorry to intrude but I do need to talk to your dad for a sec.'

'A sec? Is that like *one second*?'

'Well, not literally. I—' Why do I always end up feeling so hopeless around Saskia?

'You see him *all* the time. Why do you have to follow him here like you're a stupid lost puppy? It's like totally *pathetic*.'

This last bit she says with her voice lowered, so Carl won't hear. I can feel myself flush.

'I *didn't* follow him. I had to come to tell him something urgent. I know you and Max need time alone with him. I *do* understand it's important.'

She jabs two fingers towards her mouth and mimes vomiting over my feet.

I think of what Carl said about being the alpha male. Saskia is the dominant female when it's just her and me, no contest. Usually, I avoid ever being alone with her, and usually she likes to ignore me, so that's our shared strategy. Great.

'Well, I do really need to see him so...' I squeeze past her as she shows no sign of standing aside to let me through.

'Don't push.' She spins round. 'Daddy! She *pushed* me! She really hurt my arm.'

'Oh, I did not. Don't be such a bloody drama queen.'

'What did you call me? You can't say that. Dad! Daddy!'

Carl is fooling about in the pool with Max and ignores her.

'Hey, darling. Did you come to join us for a swim?'

Saskia stomps over to her sunlounger. She scowls at me, then puts her earphones back in, selects something on her phone then leans back with her eyes closed, oblivious to anything else.

I beckon Carl over to the side, away from the loungers.

'What's up, sweetie? Everything OK at the house?'

Max has stopped splashing about and is coming over to join us, so I pick up a couple of the coloured hoops from the side and chuck them to the far end of the pool. Max is brilliant at retrieving them from the bottom.

'Can you get the red one, then the blue one, Max?'

He dives underwater immediately and so I seize my moment.

'Felix rang – can you call him right now? I'm afraid your dad is ill.'

Carl clambers out of the pool and I pass him a towel, then hand over his mobile.

'Did Felix say what's wrong with my father? He's *never* ill. He can't be. The man is indestructible.' Carl looks down at his phone, at the string of missed calls and texts.

'I'm really sorry – I'm afraid it's cancer. Felix said to call him as soon as possible. He can't go today himself as he has to be with the girls. Oh, yes – and he said to tell you that Stefan is coming from Amsterdam.'

In a heartbeat, Carl's face goes from looking concerned to looking furious but he doesn't say anything, just jabs at his phone to call Felix.

'Felix said, um... try not to get... er... stressed about it.'

Carl gives me a look as though, somehow, it's all my fault, even though I have no idea why he looks so cross. Who *is* Stefan anyway?

'Can you keep an eye on Max while I call?'

'Of course.'

Carl heads for the house to make the call inside.

I stand by the edge of the pool.

'I'm right here if you want to carry on swimming, Max.'

'Come in, Natalie! Swim with me.'

'I'd love to, but I'm not wearing my swimsuit.'

'But you told me you keep your kit in your van so you can swim whenever you want to!'

Max swims over to the side towards me and asks me where his dad is.

'He's gone inside to call his brother. Oh, and I brought over some homemade cake in case you fancied it after your swim.'

Max shouts, 'Which one?' but then dives down to the bottom again.

I wait for him to surface then say, 'It's coconut and cherry – OK?'

'No, silly. Not which cake! Which *brother*?'

But then he ducks underwater again.

Which *brother*? But Carl only has one brother, Felix.

I turn round to see Saskia watching me. She looks back down at her phone.

'Max wants to know if Dad is talking to Uncle Felix or Uncle Stefan,' she says, not even looking at me. 'But it's *obviously* Felix because Dad doesn't talk to Uncle Stefan any more. Max is a moron.'

Stefan is Carl's *brother*?

'Uncle Stefan?'

'Yuh.' She glances at me with an assessing look, as if trying to work out exactly how dim I actually am. 'Dad's older brother.'

'The one in Amsterdam?'

'Yuh.'

'Maybe they don't see each other because it's tricky if he lives abroad?'

She swipes at something on her phone then, amazingly, puts the phone down.

'Huh. That's what Max thinks.' The implication is clear. I'm like a kid who doesn't know what's really going on.

'But...?'

'Uncle Stefan used to come over all the time. If he had a meeting in London, he'd always meet Dad for lunch or whatever, or come specially to see us. But now if you say like: "Dad, when is Uncle Stefan coming to visit?" his face goes all weird and he changes the subject, like we're too stupid to notice that's what he's doing. So obviously they had a huge fight. Uh-der.'

'He does do that a bit if he doesn't want to talk about something.' I perch on the sunlounger next to hers.

'He really does, right? But if I have a fight with a friend, Dad's like, "Oh, Saskia-sweetie-princess, you must learn to sort out your problems in a grown-up way by talking about them," la-la-la.'

Her impression is absolutely spot-on. And funny.

'But with Dad and Stefan, you can't even say the name *Stefan* without Dad looking like he wants to kill someone. Seriously.'

I nod.

Then I say, 'I wonder what they had a fight about.'

She shrugs. 'Probably something like totally stupid. Brothers are lame. Max shouted *I hate you – I hate you* at me just because I borrowed his pen and left the lid off.' She rolls her eyes.

'Natalie! You have to come *in*!' Max shouts from the pool. 'Hurry up!'

Carl has a whole extra brother he's literally never mentioned. We got married only a few months after we first met, but still, it's not as if there wasn't time for him to tell me. Why on earth would he keep him secret?

13

SHE'S NOT MY MUM

'Please, please, *please*, Natalie!' Max presses his hands together as if in prayer.

I see Saskia out of the corner of my eye, mimicking Max. Will my having a swim with Max make her dislike me even more? But nothing I do seems to make things any better, in which case I might as well have a swim. At least then I'll have one stepchild who doesn't hate me.

'I suppose I'd better get in the pool.' I say to Saskia.

'Whatever.' She shrugs.

'Wait a tick, Max. Let's see what your dad says, OK? When he comes back from his phone call.'

Carl emerges from the house then, and I get up to go over and speak to him away from the kids.

I look up at him. Carl always sees himself as the strong one, the person who can cope with anything, but now he looks visibly shaken, as if the ground has been suddenly tugged from under his feet.

I take his hand and ask about his dad and he tells me that his father has been diagnosed with prostate cancer and they want to start treatment almost straight away.

'So you need to go and be with him.'

'I suppose so. Well... I mean, yes, of course. But there's the house... and everything. We were going to... to make it nice... make it *better*.' He holds his hands palms up in a gesture of helplessness. 'I wanted it to be *perfect* for you. For us.'

'Don't worry about that. The house will keep.'

'But there's so much to *do*. I wanted to be around when I could, to keep an eye on the builders, not dump it all on you. It's not fair on you.'

'But *I* don't mind. Really. I don't have to look for new shop premises straight away. I have time.'

'Are you sure?' His face brightens for a moment, then darkens again. 'I don't want to ask too much of you.' He gently cups my cheek with his hand.

'I'm not a child, Carl. I can manage. You do believe I'm... capable, don't you?'

There's a slightly longer pause than I would like, to be honest, but then he says that of course he does.

He puts his arms round me and holds me close for a moment while Saskia sighs loudly.

'Any problems – promise you'll give me a shout, but I'll be back in a day or two, I'm sure.'

'Or shall I come with you?'

'Thank you, darling, but no. Felix will come when he can. I'll be OK.'

'Carl – about Stefan...? Do you want to—'

'I'm not getting into this now. I should go. I'll change and nip back to the cottage to get my bag, then drive to Bristol.'

'I wasn't asking you to "get into" anything. I wanted to – oh, never mind.'

'Can you stay here with the kids? Until Antonia gets back. I'll call her.'

'Yes, of course. If... if you don't think they'd mind?' I can't imagine Saskia would be too keen.

'*Mind*? Why should they *mind*? They don't care who it is – Katja or you or whoever.'

'Thanks.'

'Oh, Natalie, come on. I can't think straight.'

'I'm sorry. It'll be fine. You'd better get going.'

'Why did this have to happen *now*, for God's sake?' He sounds angry but I suppose he's really upset and doesn't know how to deal with it. 'When I already have all this other *crap* to deal with. It's too *much*.'

'Hey, hey, it's OK.' I stretch up to kiss him and wrap my arms round him. 'Carl, you *need* to do this. You've only got one dad. Don't worry about anything else. Go and be with him. I'll be fine here. I'll take care of everything.'

He nods but says nothing. I try to imagine what he must be feeling. Carl isn't exactly close to his father. They're a strange family – or strange to me, at least. They seem so unemotional, very controlled, so different from how Mum and Cely are with me. Carl is close to Felix, though, so I'm glad Felix will join him as soon as he can.

* * *

After Carl's got dressed, he explains to the kids that Grandpa isn't very well and he has to go to Bristol to see him.

'Now, Natalie's going to stay with you but Mum and Dom will be home soon anyway. Please listen to Natalie as she's in charge until they get back, OK?'

'OK,' Max says.

Saskia ignores him and carries on looking down at her phone.

'Saskia? Did you hear what I said?'

'Yuh. Grandpa is ill.'

'And so I have to go.'

'Yes. I heard you.'

'And you heard me say that Natalie is going to babysit until your mum gets back? So be nice.'

'I don't need a stupid babysitter – I'm not a baby.'

'I didn't mean it literally, Saskia. Just to keep you company. And Max needs a grown-up around, even if you don't.'

'She can't tell me what to do. She's not my mum.'

'No one's saying she is. But please do what she says. Don't be rude. You need an adult here by law. I'm not arguing about it. I don't have the time or the energy.'

Saskia sniffs but doesn't respond. Antonia and Dom won't be back for well over an hour. 'Maybe go in for a swim together or something, hmm?'

'I don't want to. Swimming's boring.' She returns to her one-to-one lovefest with her phone.

Carl sighs. 'Fine. But be nice, Squeaky, OK? Why don't you both make nice get-well cards for Grandpa?' He kisses her goodbye and Max quickly climbs out of the pool to give his dad a lovely wet hug. Carl laughs and squeezes him back.

I walk Carl out to the drive.

'Will you get in and have a splash with Max? I think he'd like that.'

'Yes, I've got my things in the van.'

'And have a chat with Saskia about ... I don't know... girlie stuff. Make-up? Hair?'

'Funny.'

'What? I wasn't joking.'

'Well, only if I'm asking her for tips. I don't know anything about make-up, and my hair is best hidden under a swimming cap.'

'Not true.' He leans towards me and rests his forehead against mine for a moment. 'I'm not looking forward to this,' he says.

* * *

Later, back at Rose Cottage, I suddenly remember something Carl said. I thought it was odd at the time but he was in such a rush that I shoved it to the back of my mind. He said, 'Why did this have to happen *now*... when I already have all this other *crap* to deal with?'

What other crap? Did he really mean that doing up our dream house is a horrible process to be endured instead of something to enjoy, something to bring us closer together? Or... or... maybe he wasn't talking about the house at all? Is it possible that he was talking about *us*?

14

USING UP OXYGEN

OK, I admit it. I don't really like Saskia. I know. It's an *awful* thing to say, or even to think, but it's true. We all know there are people we don't like much, and I've never expected everyone to like me; in fact, if anything I'm usually slightly surprised when I meet a new person and they seem to like me. But you're not supposed to dislike a *child*, are you? Obviously, I've never even hinted at it to Carl and, luckily, he's never asked me outright because he'd see through me in a moment. Part of it, I think, is because she reminds me of these incredibly bitchy girls at my secondary school. There were four of them, all very well off and kitted out in the most expensive designer clothes, led by this girl called Elisa. She had super-straight, very long, blond hair, and she was always flicking it or twiddling it or brushing it, drawing attention to it and herself. She was pretty, but only averagely so, I realise now that I look back, but she projected this glow of absolute self-confidence that made everyone think she was beautiful and amazing.

We didn't have a uniform at my school, so what you wore was up for scrutiny every single day. For some reason, Elisa would come and stand in front of me and look me up and down. Sometimes she'd say something mean, like 'Do you not know that your cords are too short?' and sometimes nothing, just give me a withering look that said, 'Oh dear, really no idea how to dress.' My clothes were clean but ordinary rather than fashionable. I wasn't that bothered about it most of the time, only when Saskia used to look at me with contempt. Elisa, I mean.

At school, my best friend, Harriet, told me to ignore Elisa.

'Don't stand there while she gives you the once-over. She's not a teacher. Walk away.'

'I always mean to but then I feel transfixed, like a rabbit in the headlights.'

'Or tell her to fuck off. She acts like she's in charge. She's not.'

Harriet wore cheapo jeans (not Levi's or any of the brands you were 'supposed' to have) and sneakers instead of flash trainers. Her family also weren't exactly flush. Her dad had become ill and lost his job but nobody ever looked down on Harriet. She was funny and fierce and absolutely fearless. Elisa kept well away from her.

Now I see Saskia does the same thing that Elisa used to do. If she wasn't good at something, she simply decided that it wasn't worth doing and acted as if anyone else doing it must be an idiot. Elisa worked really hard to do well at school but she was bad at maths. I mean so bad that she couldn't do it at all; she was always saying that maths was pointless and why did we have to learn it as we'd never need it when we were grown-up, and if you wanted to work something out, you could use a calculator.

Saskia does a similar thing. Carl's mentioned a couple of instances, like her giving up the violin when she'd only been learning it for six months (and after he'd bought her an instrument) and then doing exactly the same thing with the flute.

She's very pretty and slim and confident, and she gets excellent grades so she must be clever, but I suspect I know another thing she's not good at: swimming.

They have an incredible pool but I've literally never seen her in it, not once. Antonia doesn't love swimming the way I do, but she does use it often, and I know Dominic swims thirty lengths first thing every morning. I've seen Max swim lots of times. His technique isn't quite there but you can see he's relaxed in the water, which is the most important thing. He splashes about and has fun. But when I watch Saskia, she's always glued to her phone, on a sunlounger, and when she gets up to go and get a drink or whatever, she walks well away from the edge of the pool. I asked Carl if she can swim and he said, 'Yes, of course. She's not very keen, but of course she can.'

But then Carl would say that. Saskia is his little princess and he thinks she's perfect.

It's a shame Saskia doesn't like me, because swimming is the one thing I could almost certainly help her with. Of course, I would really like her to like me – not only for Carl's sake but because I hate the way I feel around her. She makes me feel as though I'm irrelevant and not worth her notice, as if I'm eleven all over again, that I don't fit in, I don't count, I'm just someone to be sneered at or, worse, ignored completely. When she gives me that look of utter contempt, I feel like I'm shrivelling away to nothing and it's all I can do to stand my ground and mentally remind myself that I'm supposed to be a grown-up. I mean, that I *am* a grown-up and so what if she doesn't like me?

What someone else thinks shouldn't diminish me. I know that's true. I read about it in a self-help book Celeste gave me, all about developing your sense of self-worth so you're not over-dependent on others to make you feel good about yourself. Practically, on every page there was something that struck a chord, but then the next time someone acted as if I didn't matter – oh, I remember what it was: a man pushed in front of me at a bar when I was trying to order a drink. He breezed ahead even though he could see I was standing there. And I felt like *nothing;* too small, too unimportant for anyone to notice.

But, for once, I summoned up the courage to be brave and I said, 'Actually, I believe I was here first. I've been waiting.'

It sounds like no big deal but I could feel myself flush and the blood racing round my body as if I were ready to seize my broadsword and do battle. I was so proud of myself that I'd stood up to him. I thought he'd say: 'Oh my gosh, I'm so sorry – I didn't realise – please go ahead.'

But he didn't. Instead, he shrugged, and said, 'It's just a drink. No biggie.' Then he turned away and carried on ordering.

Inside I was thinking, yes, it's just one drink to you, but this happens to me *all the time*. If you're a tall, confident man, it probably never happens to you. No one shoves in front of you or pushes past you or looks over your head as if you don't exist. But if you're a small woman who often wonders if she even has a right to *be* here on the planet, using up oxygen and taking up space, it happens all the bloody time. Mostly, I put up with it, but every now and then I want to scream and shout: I am *here*! I'm a person! I *matter*.

I thought all that but I didn't say it. When the barman finally turned to me, I ordered a double rum and coke instead of a small white wine and tried not to cry.

I grab my kit from my van and come back to the pool.

'Are you coming in now?' says Max.

'Sure thing. Just give me a min to change.'

'Give me a *min*!' says Saskia, not very quietly. 'Who even *says* that?'

I decide to pretend I didn't hear her, as what else could I do? Say: 'Don't be so rude, you spoilt brat'?

'Is Grandpa really properly ill then? If Dad had to go and see him?' Good grief – Saskia actually thinking about someone other than herself.

'Well, I'm sure he's in good hands. Your dad will call you later and let you know what's going on. Are you close to your grandpa?'

She shrugs. 'Uh-uh. I don't think he likes children much.'

'Oh, I'm sure he loves you and Max! You're his grandchildren. He's bound to.'

'It's OK. I'm not a kid any more. I don't think everyone has to love everyone else, you know.' She glances up from gazing at her phone to look me right in the eye. Well, that told me. Maybe she's right – why do I care so much if she likes me or not? So long as we're not actually chucking bricks at each other, maybe it doesn't matter?

'We love Uncle Felix, though!' Her face suddenly lights up and she looks completely different. In that moment, I can see the little girl in her and how maybe once upon a time she was really sweet, before she decided that being cool was the most important thing in life. 'He's really fun. When he comes, he flips me upside down and walks around with me like that for ages. It's *so* funny.'

I nip into the house to go to the loo and change, and am back out again in two mins – sorry, minutes! – I put my hat and goggles on and I hear Saskia snort with laughter as I walk past. The deep end is only six foot, but that's enough to do a shallow dive. Max is at the other end.

I pause for a moment, to be sure that Saskia is watching, then I do a very neat dive and swim the whole length underwater, coming up right next to Max.

'That was *awesome!*' he says. 'Can you teach me to dive? Please, please!'

'Sure. Have you got goggles?'

'They're up in my room, in my school swim bag.'

I jerk my head towards the house. 'Can you go and get them?'

Max scampers up the Roman steps and is running back towards the house in a moment.

I flip on to my back and float in a star shape. I sense rather than see that Saskia is watching. Then I take a breath and I slowly roll over on to my front and do an aeroplane float: face down, arms straight out to the sides, legs together, completely still. Yes, I am showing off, but for a good reason.

Then I bring my knees up slowly and stand up.

'Would you like to learn to dive, too?' I say, not quite looking at her.

Saskia sniffs. 'What's the point?' she says.

'It's really fun is the main point. Plus it's a good way of getting into the water quickly.'

'How do you do the – that floating thing?'

'On my back? Or the aeroplane float on my front?'

'Both.'

'I can show you. It's better if you have goggles on so you can see underwater. Do you have some?'

She shrugs.

'For school, maybe?'

'I don't do school swimming.' She looks away.

'Oh, right.' I sense that I shouldn't ask why. 'Well, you're welcome to use my goggles if you like.'

'The chlorine's bad for my sensitive skin. Our pool,' – she nods towards the water – 'doesn't use chlorine.'

'I know. You're right, it's much nicer without chlorine. When I swim in a public pool, I always shower straight away and then slather on loads of body oil. I look like a chicken ready for the oven.'

She laughs. She actually laughs. Admittedly only for about

two seconds, then she stops herself, biting her lip. For a moment, she looks more like Carl than Antonia. He does that exact same thing, biting his lip on one side when he's worried about something.

I'm pretty sure Saskia's persuaded her mum to get her out of school swimming because she's a lousy swimmer, nothing to do with the chlorine.

I give the smallest of nods towards the water, then take my goggles off and lay them on the side of the pool. I push off and swim backstroke, making it look as easy and relaxed as I can.

Saskia comes and stands by the pool edge. She's crouching down to pick up the goggles when Max comes running towards the pool and jumps straight in. I feel Saskia recoil from the splash and back away.

'Natalie! I couldn't find my goggles for ages and ages! Where do you think they were?'

'I don't know. Tell me.' I look across at Saskia, who's standing further away from the edge now, but with the goggles still in her hands.

'They were under my bed! Isn't that funny?'

'Do you often go for a swim under your bed then?'

Max laughs and puts them on and immediately plunges underwater to touch the bottom.

Saskia is still standing there.

Max comes up.

'Play an underwater game with me, Natalie!' he commands. 'Where are your goggles?'

'Probably under my bed!'

He laughs then spots them in Saskia's hands.

'Don't steal Natalie's goggles, Saskia!'

'I wasn't! I was only looking at them, that's all.'

'Well, they're not yours!' Max shouts.

'Hey, hey, it's fine. I said Saskia could—'

'I don't want *her* smelly goggles anyway. They're disgusting.' She throws them into the middle of the pool and goes back to the sunlounger, picks up her phone and stomps back towards the house.

15

INCONVENIENT DEMANDS

Carl sounded exhausted when he rang from Bristol last night. He's been there for two days. I don't think he actually likes his father very much; he's there out of duty, not love, and I can hear the strain in his voice. I must admit I didn't exactly warm to his dad when I met him. I don't think he smiled once. Even at our wedding, when you go through the photos, the man looks as if he chanced to wander in from elsewhere and has no connection with any of the other people there.

Once Carl comes back from Bristol, I'd like to move down to the cottage properly so I can keep an eye on things. Steve's lent me a camping stove and there's a sink in the barn so I can even cook myself something if I want to, rather than getting food from the deli.

I had hoped we'd both move into the house as soon as possible. When we first talked about relocating to the countryside, Carl said he'd *love* to work more from home. He looked genuinely pleased – relieved, even. But now that he could actually do it, and it would be the perfect time to start, he says he needs more 'transition' time.

So, I'll be moving to our dream house and starting our newly married life, on my own. I assumed that Carl would surely feel the same way I do. That he'd be desperate to move – to enjoy the house and the garden, being in the countryside and seeing more of his kids. And... spending time with me. I tell myself I'm being paranoid, that Carl has a lot on at work so can't take the time out to set up an office from home. Of course, now that his dad's ill and having chemotherapy, he'll have to go back and forth to Bristol a lot. I remind myself that it won't always be this way – of course it won't. But at the back of my mind, a stubborn, sneering voice keeps chipping away at me, whispering: does my new husband not want to live with me?

* * *

When we discussed our plans before we bought the cottage, we agreed that we'd have to sell Carl's flat but should hang on to my tiny flat because, although it's small, it's near the tube so it's very practical. Carl might need to stay in London once a week or so: if he has a work function that carries on late, or if he has a breakfast meeting one morning, he could come up the night before. And I will use it when I come up to see friends or Celeste, or if there's an auction I want to go to.

But this evening, once he's arrived back from Bristol and we start talking about it again, it's as if we'd never had the first conversation. We're at the kitchen table in my flat, eating supper.

'I think I should rent a studio flat near the office for when I need to be up here,' Carl says.

'But I thought we said you'd stay here? Use this when you need to.'

'It would be better to rent something closer to the office.'

'But it's three stops on the tube! It's hard to get much closer than this, surely.'

'Mm, but I'd prefer a studio right by work.'

'Carl?' I lean forward and top up his wineglass. 'What am I missing here?'

'*Missing*?' He does that look that drives me crazy, at once innocent but knowing, the look that makes me want to poke him in the eye. Not very wifely.

'Yes. You know we agreed we'd hang on to my flat because it's easier and cheaper, and less hassle than letting it out, then renting somewhere else. Why are you acting as if that conversation never happened?'

'I'm *not*. There's no need to be so melodramatic, darling. We were still considering all the options and, on further reflection, I don't think this is an ideal town pad for me. For us. I think somewhere a bit less... er... more... contemporary perhaps, would fit the bill better. I'm being practical.'

He flicks a glance round the kitchen and I get it. My kitchen is small and quite... full. I love it but no one could describe it as a shrine to minimalism. I've got this 1940s free-standing cupboard with little drawers, in pale mint green; it's full of interesting china, glasses, old enamel storage canisters and things from the thirties and forties. I think it looks really nice. The table and chairs, I bought from an old diner when they were closing down. There's a cute little café curtain at the window and a funny old gas stove.

As Carl is tall, I realise the flat must feel more cramped to him than it does to me, claustrophobic even. He doesn't look in scale with it. When I was a child, I remember Mum taking us to a museum where they had lots of old dolls' houses, which I adored, but in a couple of them you could see that the dolls were much too big, that they'd have to bend down to go through the doorways or, if you put one in a bed, its feet would hang off the end.

That's how Carl looks in my flat. He can't stretch out full-length on my sofa because it's a two-seater, so he hangs his legs over the side, but he can never get comfortable. My bed is a standard length but only an ordinary double, not a super-king size like Carl had at his flat, and it does feel squashed when we're both in it. I love sleeping with Carl, but sometimes sharing a bed with him can be quite challenging.

'You don't like my flat?'

He shrugs. 'I don't absolutely *love* it. But I love *you*, darling! Surely you don't really mind if I'm not besotted with your flat, too?' He makes a silly face, to try to tease me into laughing but I'm in no mood to be teased.

'But, Carl, we talked about this. If you're only staying up one night a week, it would be bonkers to shell out loads of rent money for a flat.'

'Well, it won't necessarily be only one night a week, will it? I mean, naturally it will vary a lot – I can't control my diary to that degree. If there's a vital work do, I can't skip it because I have to get back to Kent.' He leans back and takes a long swallow of his wine, as if the conversation is now over.

'And do you think it might have been a good idea to say all this before we bought a house seventy miles away?'

'We agreed there would have to be some flexibility.'

'Yes. And so far, all the flexibility has been on my side.'

'On your side? There shouldn't be any sides. We're married. I thought you said you were always on my side?'

'That's not what I meant and you know it. I mean – I actually did a decent thing here, Carl. I wanted you to have the chance to see Saskia and Max more because I know how important it is. I've packed up my shop and sold off stock and put the rest in storage and I'm looking into leasing premises in Kent. I want to make a new life with you – a new home, a new beginning. This should be the happiest time of our lives, but now it feels as if you don't want to spend time with me. It's as if you're clinging on to your old life so you can still be a bachelor about town and not be too troubled by the inconvenient demands of your wife, who you will keep tucked away in the country where I won't be too much of a nuisance.'

'That's completely crazy! Natalie, come on...' He reaches for my hand and gives it a patronising little pat as if I'm a misbehaving puppy.

'It's not crazy! Why should I have to let out this flat so you can rent another one? It creates a lot more work for no good reason. I need to focus on doing up the cottage and on setting up my new shop. I wanted to move a few things from here down there as we go along and work out what will fit in well.'

He laughs. 'Well, not much of it then.'

'That's just rude. None of the stuff from your flat would look other than bloody stupid at the cottage and you know it.'

'You said you *liked* that black leather chaise? *And* the mirrored chest of drawers? You're always making out you're so moral, that you never lie, but now it's all coming out.' He folds his arms and nods as if he's won this round.

'I *didn't* lie. I do love the chaise and the drawers. But I don't think they will look right in the house at all. They'll look like alien artefacts that have mysteriously been deposited from another universe with no explanation. They won't look *right*.'

'Well, why didn't you say that before?'

'Because, Carl, I didn't want to be rude or hurtful. I thought it would be better for me to live with them, rather than bossily telling you none of it would work down there. Why shouldn't you have things you love around you if they make you happy?'

Carl doesn't respond. He sits there, his face stony and unreadable. I clear the plates and put the kettle on and ask him if he wants coffee. Still no response.

'Carl? Do you want coffee? Please don't go into a sulk. You're not four.'

'I'm not sulking,' he says, sulkily.

I laugh and stand behind him and wrap my arms around him.

'I love you but you are funny when you go into a sulk!'

'I don't want to argue with you.' He pulls me round and on to his lap. 'Why do we keep arguing?'

'I think we're both stressed by the house – the roof and all the work that needs doing. It feels like a lot to deal with, that's all. It'll be OK.'

'Do you think it was a mistake, Nat?' He suddenly looks like a child, not his usual, confident self. 'Should we sell the cottage and start again?'

I lean my forehead against his and close my eyes for a moment. Is that what he really wants? Is that what I want? Maybe it would be better? Find somewhere, say, five miles away in a different village, somewhere where I don't have Antonia monitoring my every move, telling me which curtain fabric to choose, which bread to buy, which shirts Carl likes best.

There are so many things that haven't gone well. Not just the roof, but Carl buying the house at auction in the first place when I hadn't even seen it. And, yes, being too close to Antonia. Maybe I should take the easy way out that Carl is offering?

But. I close my eyes again and picture the cottage. That part of the lane once you go through the gate and proceed slowly down the potholed track. The way the trees arch overhead so you pass through a cool green tunnel and it feels as if you're entering another world. At the bottom you emerge into the light and the land dips down away to your right. There's the barn on your left, ancient and solid and reassuring. Then the house ahead of you, currently covered in bright blue tarpaulins, it's true, while Steve carries on with the roof work, but beneath those, you can see what a pretty house it is. A narrow stone path cuts through the grass to take you to the door. Then, a little way beyond, half-hidden by more trees, the pond, its surface glimmering in the sun, the ducks waddling and pecking around like the people on the village high street, stopping for a chat and a gossip. It could be the most amazing place to live, I'm sure it could. And it has to be good for Carl to be near the kids. I hated it after my dad left, not being able to see him whenever I wanted. This has to be the best thing for him, and for them.

I have never given up on anything in my life – except for crappy relationships, of course, and you can't count those. When I failed my physics GCSE, I resat it. I didn't need it, but I hated the fact that I'd failed it and wanted to do better. When I read a book I don't like much, I still keep going – because I've started it. Celeste thinks I'm crazy. If she doesn't like a book within the first few pages, she flings it across the room, then gives it to a charity shop. But I feel I somehow owe it to the book to carry on. Often, I'm right: sometimes it's only that the beginning didn't grip me but then I really start to love it.

Maybe this is like that? Maybe we will both grow to love the cottage? Being so near Antonia, Queen of all she surveys, even if I'm not madly keen on her, means Carl and his kids can see each other whenever they want. Saskia and Max can even walk or cycle over when they want to. If we buy somewhere a few miles away, they wouldn't be able to do that.

I have to believe we made the right decision. Not only about the house, but that I was right to marry Carl, too. Because if I was wrong... well, it doesn't bear thinking about.

I sit up straight and kiss him.

'Uh-uh. It's a beautiful house and it will be absolutely stunning. We are going to be very happy there. These are teething problems, darling, and we will sort them out.'

'I'm sorry I was rude about your flat. I was being stupid. I'm a bit strung out about work.' He looks strained and tired. 'And my father.'

'Of course you are. Look, what say I do my best before I move down to clear a bit of the clutter in the flat so it feels more... well, less... you know.'

'Less full?'

'Yes. I can box up some stuff and see if Celeste can store it.'

'Or we can take it down and put it in the barn?'

'Yes. I can do that. And maybe I could repaint the bedroom and bathroom here at least, to make it all feel fresher and nicer for you.'

'You're a star, Nat. But let me arrange a decorator to do it. We're both way too busy.'

'And you're not too stressed about work, Carl? You *do* look so tired.'

'Ach.' He shakes his head. 'A couple of things preying on my mind.'

'Want to talk about them? Maybe I can help?'

'Nope. I can handle it. No need for you to worry. You focus on the house.'

16

MR WHATSISFACE

It's a beautiful day today. I'm so glad I've moved down now. I make myself a big mug of tea and go and drink it by the pond in my dressing gown. This is where I'd like to have a small deck – not big or fancy, a simple wooden platform jutting out a little way over the water, with ladder-steps going down so that you can get in and out of the pond easily without having to slither on the muddy bank. It's not deep enough to dive in.

Carl is back in Bristol again for two or three days. Poor him – he's absolutely exhausted. I offered to go with him but he said he needs me here to make sure the works keep moving along. Also, there's no space at his dad's flat when Felix, or Stefan, is there at the same time.

Now I can see why Carl fell in love with this place. At first, I admit I was upset that he'd found it without me, and I felt a bit... well, manoeuvred into saying yes when he called from the auction. What else could I have said? It wasn't as if I didn't trust him or his judgement. I absolutely do. But the cottage – this was supposed to be our *forever* home, the place where we would make a life and, with any luck, a family. I know Carl thought he was doing the right thing, and there's nothing I can do about it now, but I did feel sad and angry that he didn't even seem bothered that I wasn't involved in choosing the house *with* him.

At last, the roof is completely retiled and the house is starting to feel more like a home and less like a building site, and I can see what Carl first saw. After all, he couldn't care less about having a pond, so he wasn't being selfish – he was only thinking of me and wanting to make me happy. But I do wish he were here more. There are times when I think: 'Am I really married?' Sometimes it feels like it did when I was single, like there's no one else thinking about me and no one else I need to consider.

Later, the water in the pond will have warmed up and I will go in for a swim. Late afternoon is the best time, if it's been sunny all day, so the water is at its warmest, but now is a good time for looking. If you get down on your knees or, even better, lie on your front, you can see right up close and watch the dragonflies darting this way and that, the whirligigs spinning in circles on the water, the water boatmen rowing with little jerky movements over the surface, and the pond skaters balancing so perfectly. It's like a whole beautiful world, with all the inhabitants intent on their individual business, only it feels calm and restful and it's fascinating to watch.

I hope Carl is all right. He mentioned he was stressed about some problem at work. I know – he's *always* stressed about work. I must admit I didn't pay much attention at the time because it seems to be his permanent state. When I say he should try to work less, ease up a little, Carl always says he *can't*, the clients expect his constant attention. And James and Jonathan, his business partners, are both so intense – there are no *off*-days. Even at the weekend he's always on his phone, glued to Twitter and Instagram, emailing clients and making voice memos to himself. I wish he would take a proper day off and put the phone away in a drawer, or bury it six feet under the ground so that when he's here, he's really and truly *here*.

How can I get him to relax more? And is that my job? I feel like I don't know how to be a proper wife yet. I can't ask Celeste as her marriage was such a disaster. Only two of my friends are married – Sarah, who now lives in a remote farmhouse in France, so I haven't seen her for ages, her main worry seems to be if the chickens aren't laying well, and Isabelle, who is so happy it's borderline annoying. When I saw her for supper recently, she was in a haze of happiness about how wonderful her husband is and their gorgeous flat – no spiders, no dust, no rewiring – perfect in every way. I am pleased for her but I felt it would be disloyal to Carl if I launched into everything that's gone wrong: half the roof stolen; house not yet ready to move into; husband's ex-wife popping up like an annoying jack-in-the-box every time I dare to venture beyond the gate; stepdaughter who hates me.

So, when Isabelle asked me how it's going, I said, 'Fine, thanks,' but she was so keen to tell me every single detail of her perfect life I don't think she even noticed I hadn't told her anything about my imperfect one, or that I rarely see my husband.

I do love him – I really do – I just thought we'd be seeing more of each other. Isn't that what newly-weds do? Isn't that why people make jokes about them – because they can't keep apart from each other? I can't even admit to Celeste that I've barely seen Carl. I edge around the issue or sidestep. When she asks how he is, I say, 'Fine, thanks,' as I did with Isabelle. Well, he *is* fine – although I only know he's fine because he's texted me or we've managed to chat for ten minutes on the phone when he's in Bristol or London, before he says he's exhausted and has to go to sleep.

* * *

Well, one little mystery's been cleared up at least, though I think I'd be happier if I'd never found out the truth.

I'm in the bakery on Saturday morning, queuing up for a sourdough loaf. They honestly only have about three so you have to either remember to order one in advance or be queuing outside the door by 8 a.m. when they open.

I'm almost at the front of the queue and toying with the idea of getting a bun or a Danish to have mid-morning on my regular stroll round the garden with a mug of tea, chatting to the ducks and looking at the pond and wondering what to plant where.

I reach the counter and am trying to decide whether to go for a Chelsea bun or a *pain au chocolat*. This place has a foot in two camps. It's basically an old-fashioned village bakery – cottage loaves, iced finger buns, cream cakes in a special display cabinet – but is also trying to be more trendy and artisan, thus the sourdough, *pains au chocolat*, etc.

As I reach the head of the queue, I hear a voice call out my name, or rather, not my name: 'Natty!'

It's Antonia. I've told her I don't like being called Natty multiple times yet she persists. Maybe if I ignore her, she'll stop saying it.

'*Natalie!*'

I turn round.

She pushes to the front, past the lengthy queue, saying, 'My friend here was saving my place.' I wonder what she'd do if I announced, 'I'm sorry, I've never seen this woman before.' Then she says, at top volume so I know it's really for the benefit of the other customers rather than me: 'Natty, you're such a sweetie for saving me a spot in the queue.' She twists to address the other people scrunched into the shop and lining back along the narrow part towards the door, who are now looking daggers at her and also at me. 'I couldn't park,' she says to them, shrugging. 'The high street's absolute mayhem.'

I look out the shop window at the village high street, which – though busy – seems a mayhem-free zone. Antonia really has zero idea how most people live if she thinks that's mayhem. Middle-aged ladies are pottering up and down with picturesque baskets over their arms while older women are wheeling their shopping trolleys. Kids are running in and out of the newsagent for their Saturday sweets. Elderly gentlemen are popping in for their *Daily Telegraph*s. It's all very calm and orderly. No drug dealers, no gangs, no breakdown of law and order. No mayhem.

'Hi,' I say, a touch coolly. 'How are you, Antonia?'

'I'm super, Natty.' Of course she is. Antonia is in a permanent state of superness. Or should that be superiority? 'Sorry, *Natalie.*' She puts a spin on the word, as if she's humouring me and my inexplicable demand that she call me by my actual name – 'And how are *you* today? Ooh, they've got still *sourdough*! Thank goodness for that! Morning, Sheila. I'll take a sourdough while you've got one, and four croissants, please.'

'Morning, Mrs Moore. A sourdough loaf – sliced as usual?' The woman behind the counter takes one of the three sourdoughs from the window over to the slicing machine. A number of people tut and sigh behind us but, as ever, Antonia is oblivious to other people's feelings.

'And, let's see, I'd better take a large granary as well.'

She turns to me. 'So how's the cottage coming along? Oh, I meant to say – Dom says there's an excellent deep-cleaning company based in Canterbury if you want...'

She turns back to Sheila. 'And two *pains au chocolat*...'

'Oh, thank you, but I can clean the house myself once the

builders have finished. There's not much point now. They're still working.'

Antonia makes a face as if I've said that I'm happy to put on a wetsuit and submerge myself in the septic tank to scrape it out.

'It's fine,' I say. 'I quite enjoy cleaning really.'

'But what about – you know...' She does a pantomime face of absolute horror, opening her mouth into a silent scream, then she turns back to the counter and says, 'Plus I'd better take two slices of pizza for the kids for lunch – the plain one – Margherita. You know what kids are like: "No bits on it, Mum! No bits!"' She laughs.

'Sorry – what?' What on earth is she getting at?

'And five white rolls. I freeze them for Saskia's packed lunches. She is *so* fussy – she refuses to eat school dinners. It's such a pain.'

I can't see how it's a pain when it's more than likely Katja makes the lunches rather than Antonia, but I don't care about that for now.

'Antonia? You were saying...?'

Back to me: '*You* know. *That* room.' She lowers her voice a fraction but, given that Antonia has clearly never whispered in her entire life, it's still distinctly audible to everyone in the entire shop. 'The room where he *died*. The *owner*.'

Back to Sheila.

'Actually, can you add another two croissants, Sheila. Oh, and you know what, I'll take another sourdough for the freezer. Sliced again.'

Antonia has broken bakery etiquette. There's an unstated rule that it's simply not done to ask for more than one sourdough when everyone knows they never have enough.

'Anything else?' asks Sheila.

'No, that's me done!' Antonia says, laughing, as if she's made a merry quip rather than pissing off half the village. 'No. What am I saying? Let's have a quiche as well. What have you got today?'

'Quiche Lorraine or mushroom.'

'Ooh – I don't know. Natalie, what do you think? Should we have the mushroom? We really all ought to be cutting back on meat, shouldn't we?'

What do I think? The previous owner died at the house, but do I have a view on whether Antonia should choose mushroom quiche or not?

'But he didn't die at the house... did he?' Oh God, the 'circumstances' Dominic referred to. I meant to ask Carl, then forgot about it with all the worry about his father.

'You know, I think I will take the quiche Lorraine. No, the mushroom. And that's it, I promise. That's definitely *it*!' She turns to the queue, as if to beg their indulgence for the adorable way she's just bought up half the shop.

'And you, love?' the woman says, passing Antonia's bags over the counter.

The queue is tutting and shifting behind me.

'Hi. I ordered a sourdough on Thursday for today.'

'Name?' She looks down at the order book.

'Oh, but, Natalie, I thought you *knew*!' Antonia is putting her many, many bread purchases into her preposterously huge willow basket.

'Um... Cameron.' I've actually kept my own name but I use Carl's name in the village. He says people will find it less confusing and they won't understand if we have separate names, which I think is slightly ridiculous nowadays.

'I've got nothing for Cameron.' She shakes her head.

'But I came in specially to order it.'

'Who d'you speak to?'

'Er, the girl with dark hair in a ponytail. The very young one.'

She looks about twelve.

Sheila shakes her head. 'Oh, Michelle. Yeah – no, she's not put it in the book. She's right dozy. You really need to watch her write it down. Well, you can have that last one in the window, OK?'

She takes it out of the basket in the window and puts it in a bag and I can feel little arrows of hatred pinging towards me from practically every person behind me.

'And a Chelsea bun, please.'

'Anything else?'

I'd really like to know what the other two types of pizza are but I think if I take any longer, I might get lynched. It's not my fault: I've been tainted by association with Antonia, buying up half the shop and sweeping ahead of the queue.

'No, that's it – thank you. Thank you very much.'

I smile and nod as I pay, then take my bread and start to follow Antonia out of the shop.

As we reach the door, she says, 'Are you saying you had absolutely no idea that old Mr Whatsisface died at the cottage? Oh, Natty! How *awful* that you should have to find out from *me*!'

But she's loving it – I can see she is – she's thrilled to bits to be the one who gets to tell me.

Everyone in the shop is staring at me. Why did she have to call him Mr Whatsisface? It sounds so disrespectful.

'Mr *Bailey*,' I say, hoping people will realise that at least *I* haven't forgotten his name.

'Oh, yes – that's him. Well, he died in his chair in the big reception room and you know he wasn't found for... guess how long it was till they found him?'

I'm not turning the death of a lonely old man into a game to amuse Antonia.

'I don't know, I really don't know.'

'Two weeks!' she says, practically grinning. 'Isn't that *awful*!' Her tone says not 'awful' but 'weirdly exciting'.

'Yes,' I say. 'It *is* awful. It's horrible. That poor, poor man.'

'Normally, Dave, our postman would look in on him every morning – he always used to go right down to take the post in, even though there's a mailbox at the top of the lane, but he happened to be on holiday for a fortnight and the replacement chap dumped the mail in the box. It was only when Dave came back that he found Mr Thing. It's so gruesome! And you, sleeping down there *all on your own* now Carl's away so much. I'd literally lie awake all night long, worrying his ghost might come back to torment me. I don't know how you can bear it, I really don't.'

Antonia has offered to let me use their pool whenever I like. She's obviously really trying to be kind and now I feel bad that I keep having mean thoughts about her. After all, she doesn't have to let me use the pool. Carl is in London, dealing with some problem involving a high-maintenance client, but then has to go back to Bristol to be with his dad for the next round of treatment. I miss him so much.

I'm still sleeping in the barn, but Steve has promised me I can move into the cottage very soon, which I really hope is true because my mum is coming to stay in a couple of weeks' time. Last night I lay awake for hours, listening to the wind rustling the trees and I confess I felt a bit spooked. It's not that I believe in ghosts or anything, but it feels so *sad*. I imagine Mr Bailey – Ted – dying and no one coming to see him or check on him, no one there to hold his hand. That's my worst nightmare, the thought of dying alone, being forgotten about; no one pausing to think, even for a moment: I wonder how Natalie is.

So today, to get away from the cottage for a little while and escape my thoughts, I'm off to Antonia's for a swim. She said I could come any time but suggested around 3 p.m. would be best as she should be back by then. Sneakily, I plan to get there at two thirty so I can have a proper swim while she's out, then a few minutes of polite chit-chat and, oh goodness, is that the time, I ought to get back to talk to Steve about the big bedroom...

It's not that I'm antisocial; it's only that I love swimming and I don't want to have to talk at the same time. It's one of the very few things I'm any good at and I like to swim fairly fast, but you can't really do that if someone else is swimming alongside, expecting you to talk about plans for the Christmas Fayre or the Wyford ball, or isn't it awful that they've put in plastic windows at Mulberry Cottage on the corner?

I drive because even though it's only a few minutes' walk, there is this really sharp bend about halfway, and if a car comes speeding round there you have to leap on to the grass verge to avoid being run down. I pull in to the gravel parking area, lock the van and go to the front door to ring the bell. There's no answer so I'm loitering for a minute, wondering if I should wave at one of the CCTV cameras to attract attention, when Dominic appears, having emerged from his studio.

'Ah, the fair Natalie.' He leans forward to kiss my cheek and takes my elbow. 'Have you come for a dip?'

'Yes. I hope that's OK? Antonia invited me. I can go away and come another time?'

'No, no, she's expecting you. She's popped to the station to pick up the girls, she said, and she'll be back in a mo.' He guides me towards the side gate, still holding my elbow as if I'm blind or infirm and I have to resist the urge to shake him off. 'Now.' He leads me behind a tall hedging screen and waves at a pretty little summerhouse with a pointy roof painted in that tasteful dull green colour that seems to prevail at National Trust proper-ties. 'There are changing cubicles and a shower in there, spare swimsuits, towels and whatnot, whatever you need – help yourself.'

Ah – that's what Katja meant when she said I could change next to the pool! I thought she was saying that I could get undressed by the side of the pool.

'Thank you, but I've brought my things.' I clutch my bag in front of me.

'Jolly good. Well, will you forgive me if I slope off for a bit? I'm right in the middle of something.'

'Of course. I'll be fine.'

Inside the summerhouse, there are two changing cubicles with wooden louvred doors, plus a shower and a loo. God, this place is amazing. Not that I'd want a pool like theirs really. It must cost a fortune to maintain and, next to our house, it wouldn't look right – too fancy and out of place. Still, it is pretty spectacular here.

If I hurry, I can probably get in a few lengths before Antonia comes back. By the sound of it, she's picking up Saskia and a couple of her friends too. I can imagine them sniggering at me in my utilitarian swimsuit so the sooner I get in, the sooner I can have my swim, then flee back to the cottage.

I nip into a cubicle and change, tuck my hair up into my cap and go out. Hurrah – still no one here. Nothing is nicer than having an entire pool to yourself and I almost never have the chance. The public pool I use in London is usually pretty busy, even if you go first thing when it opens. If you swim in the fast lane, it's often full of men swimming that very splashy front crawl and creating a huge wake as if they're a tanker steaming by.

I descend the Roman steps, rinse my goggles and put them on. I'd love to float on my back, drifting and dreaming, but I'm determined to get some proper exercise before Antonia gets back. The pool's not all that long so it's easy to do a whole length underwater. I put my face in and push off and glide. Heaven. I love that moment when you surrender to the water and it's so quiet and peaceful and you can forget about everything else. There is only you and the water, then afterwards the happy tiredness.

I reach the other end and switch to crawl, not rushing, focusing on my stroke and my breathing – one, two, breathe, one, two, breathe. I'm aware of some noise nearby, but it's muffled because of my swimming hat and with my head in the water. On my next breath, I spot a couple of pairs of feet by the side of the pool, but I swim on. At the end of my length, I pause to look up but there's no one there. They must be changing. After another few lengths, I switch to backstroke, which is better as now I can't hear anything at all, with my ears underwater. Through the tinted lenses of my goggles, the bright sky is muted, greyer than I know it is really.

They'll probably have changed by now and I suppose I ought to get out and say hello. I reach the Roman steps, climb out and turn around.

Antonia and three other women are clustered at one end by the table.

This time, Antonia is wearing an orange one-piece swimsuit with a deep plunge V-front and very high-cut legs. She's sporting huge sunglasses and is pouring Pimm's from a jug while laughing. One of the other women is wearing a silver swimsuit with a cut-out shape at the midriff as if she's wandered off the set of a 1960s sci-fi movie, and the other two are in bikinis. They are all tanned, devoid of freckles. They all have smooth, straight hair, similarly outsize sunglasses and are wearing teeter-tottery mules.

I wonder if I can somehow sneak back to the pavilion to change before anyone spots me, but Antonia waves and calls out:

'Natalie! How fabulous!' She beckons me over. 'You must have a drink! We're on the Pimm's again!'

'Toni, there's *air* in my glass!' one of the other women shrieks. 'Top up, top up!'

I walk along by the pool towards them, pulling up my goggles to rest on my head.

Antonia introduces them as her 'London girls', who've come down on the train for a day and a night.

Everyone says hello and they seem friendly enough, but I am acutely conscious of my style-free costume and that all of them are examining every inch of me as if I'm some curious species they've never come across before. I wish I had longer legs. I wish I had fewer freckles and skin that would tan rather than burn.

'You're a super swimmer,' says one of the women.

'Thank you.'

'Are you in training, then?' says another, slowly scanning me up and down.

I tug off my swimming hat and shake a bit to get the water out of my ears.

'Training? Sorry – for what?'

The woman shrugs. 'We presumed you must be entering a triathlon.' She takes a glug of her Pimm's. 'You look like you take it seriously.' She nods towards my swimsuit.

'Oh, well. I like to swim, that's all.'

'Now, Natty, you're putting us all to shame, you really are. Come and have a drink.' Antonia pushes a glass into my hand. 'Just because this lot would rather pose by the pool getting sozzled, they think anyone who actually goes for a swim must be some sort of dykey athlete. Pay no attention.'

The four sunloungers have been laid out in a straight row along one side of the pool and the women stretch out on them artfully, as if they are mannequins arranged in a shop window. Antonia sets her drink down and says she's going in for a dip.

'Will you come back in, Natalie?'

Given that the alternatives are: sitting on my own at the patio table away from the others as all the loungers except Antonia's are occupied, which might look a bit rude; sitting on the stone pool surround, which would be uncomfortable; or getting changed and dashing home, which is tempting but probably not the right move as I'm trying to get on better with her, I say 'Sure' and turn back towards the pool.

Antonia sets off at a stately pace, her head held high out of the water, still wearing her sunglasses and earrings. She swims a fairly smooth but achingly slow breaststroke. I'm not sure it's even possible for me to move that slowly. I take my time, fiddling with the strap of my goggles so that I won't have to swim alongside at her pace. I'm about to put them on when I see that the other women have all sat up on their loungers and are watching. Even though I know I'm a good swimmer, I suddenly feel overwhelmed by a wave of self-consciousness. I feel I should try to look more normal, more like them, so I leave my hat and goggles at the side of the pool and opt for backstroke as I hate swimming face down without goggles. At the end of the length, I find Antonia has paused, waiting for me.

'Thank you for letting me use your pool,' I say, remembering to be polite.

She waves a hand airily.

'Any time. Now, I hope this isn't an... er... inappropriate thing to ask, Natalie, so do forgive me, but... um... how are you managing *down there*?'

At that, she pushes off and begins to swim, so I have no option but to swim alongside her, with my head stuck up out of the water, feeling stiff and ridiculous. Oh God, I should never have come for a swim. It's been weeks since I had a bikini wax. It's usually all right in this swimsuit as the legs aren't high cut, but obviously a furry forest must have been curling its way round the sides and she's trying to tell me, in a tactful way, by asking how I'm managing *down there*. She probably wants to recommend a beauty salon for waxing. I'll have to stay in the pool for another six hours, then I can slip out into the dusk and slink away in shame. Oh, no – those women – that's why they were all staring! This is awful. How on earth am I supposed to answer her?

'Um. Well... er... I thought it was... um, OK... but...' This is *so* embarrassing. I don't want to talk to Antonia about bikini waxes but nor can I get out if they're all going to be covertly pointing and laughing. I honestly thought it was fine.

'Now, Natalie, be honest with me. Clearly, it's *not* OK. Of course you're worried about it. *I* certainly would be.'

'Er... well, this is quite awkward...'

'I *knew* it. Don't tell me that our awful husband is leaving you down there in a house that's not properly habitable yet?'

'Sorry – what?'

'He's letting you stay there when it's not remotely ready? All alone at the cottage?'

What? Oh. That *down there* – the *house*. Down the track! God, the relief that she's not going to advise me about my bikini line.

'It's fine.'

'Well, it obviously isn't – you sounded incredibly worried – I could hear the anxiety in your voice. Listen, you know what men are like. They don't understand that we can't be living out of a suitcase and managing without proper bathrooms and hairdryers and so on. Of course, you're welcome to pop over anytime you want a decent shower, but really, I don't see how you're managing.'

I explain that I'm only sleeping on a mattress in the barn

temporarily, and that as the builders have installed a shower and loo there, it's good enough. They've nearly done the kitchen, one bathroom and two of the bedrooms so I will be moving into the cottage properly any day now anyway, so I really am totally fine.

'But don't you find it *horribly* creepy down there on your own? Absolutely anyone could wander along that track in the middle of the night. If it were me, I'd be simply jangling with nerves. And it's *so* dark. You must get proper security lighting put in. Must, must, *must*.'

I do find it a little bit unsettling when I'm there on my own but there's no way I'm admitting it to Antonia.

'It's probably safer than my flat in London, I should think. And I don't mind the dark at all.'

'Well, possibly, but what if the ghost of Mr Whatsisface is roaming about, looking for revenge? If anything were to happen, no one would hear you screaming down there, you know.'

How on earth is this helping?

'We're having an alarm installed and it's the type where you can set only the ground floor at night if you want.'

'Oh, well, that's sensible at least. Tell Carl to hurry up and get it sorted, otherwise we shall all be off our heads with worry about you.'

'Thank you, that's kind of you to worry but I'm sure there's no need. Um... I think I'd better get out soon.'

'Thank goodness for that. I'm not keen on swimming really. I only do it because Dom insisted we have a pool and he likes to see it used. I'd much rather have had a tennis court.'

We swim to the steps and climb out.

'Didn't you get a say in it?'

Antonia waves an airy hand. 'Oh, you know what men are like. You have to know when to give way so they don't have their egos dented. Marriage is all about knowing how to manage them really, isn't it? It's rather like owning a rather large and annoying dog much of the time, I always think.'

I have no idea how to answer this, especially without pointing out the fact that she and Carl are divorced so clearly her man-management strategies must be a bit flawed. Did she really see Carl as a sort of misbehaving pet, who had to be kept on a lead and dragged outside for walkies? On the other hand, I don't seem to be doing such a good job myself, given that I barely see him and, when I do, we spend most of the time arguing. Could she possibly be right?

'Oh, and another thing. I have been giving a lot of thought to throwing a little gathering to welcome you both to the village.'

'That's so nice of you, but there's really no need.'

'Please let me. I honestly enjoy it. Just a handful of intimate friends so you get to meet some local people. A few drinks and nibbles. I'd love to do it, and you won't be ready to host parties down at the cottage for aeons until it's perfect – you know what builders are like.'

'Well, thank you, that's really very kind. But honestly, only something small and simple...'

18

LITTLE BLACK DRESS

Antonia is holding a party to introduce us properly to the village and it's going to be complete and utter bliss, apparently. She's thrilled that we're practically neighbours and is so, so glad that we're all grown-up enough to be civilised about the whole thing. It's a small party, she says, no more than fifty or so intimate friends, for Pimm's and bubbly and canapés. Everyone's dying to meet us, the new kids on the block. Especially me, she says. Why especially *me*? And how can anyone have fifty intimate friends? I don't think I even *know* fifty people, not even if I include the woman in the post office who's marginally less horrible than the other staff there, and Michael, the street-sweeper near my flat who's really good at whistling and always says hello to me.

I can't go. It'd be absolute bliss to go, of course, but I can't. Unfortunately, that's the day I'm washing my hair. I'm filing my toenails, I'm cleaning the oven, I'm polishing my Regency mahogany chiffonier/Louis Quatorze bureau/Ikea coffee table. I have to scrub behind my taps/ears/shed. I have some two-year-old popcorn that urgently needs popping. My books need to be rearranged chronologically by author's birth date. I'd go if I could but my mother's coming for tea/the weekend/all eternity. I have a prior arrangement with my old schoolfriend/dentist/gynaecologist. I have to pick the aphids off the roses. Individually.

Only I've already agreed, of course, because I'm a twit and I thought that when I asked Antonia to keep the occasion 'small and simple' that maybe she would actually listen. But of course, it's now clear to me that it's not going to be small and simple, it's going to be big and fancy, i.e. the kind of thing I absolutely hate.

Carl likes parties. Or at least he doesn't actively dislike them. Sometimes he thinks they're a waste of time, but mostly he thinks they're quite fun. *Fun.*

Carl and I don't have exactly the same working definition of 'fun'. For him, any kind of social occasion is almost guaranteed to be fun, and he can't understand how anyone could think otherwise. Lots of people! Food made by someone else! Free-flowing drinks! Talking to people you've never met before!

'But you're not especially shy, Nat. I don't get it. What's the problem?'

And he's right in a way. I'm not especially shy. I can talk to people without blushing or wanting to hide behind my mum. But there's a big difference between having a conversation that develops naturally and suddenly being plonked into a room full of people you don't know, then having to drum up an animated conversation with no warm-up. At a party, people expect you to be charming and sparkly and bubbly, and I'm none of those things.

Carl can go up to a total stranger at a party and start a conversation as easily as popping a slice of bread in the toaster. He simply cannot see why anyone could possibly find this hard. It's an entirely alien concept to him.

'They're not going to bite you, Nat. They're only people. Go up and say hello. What's the worst that can happen?'

Carl thinks the worst that can happen is that the other person will be boring. Being bored is Carl's number one nightmare and possibly the only thing he's afraid of. Once, we went to some very old friends of mine for supper and they'd invited some extra-especially dull people for us to meet. Carl fidgeted with his cutlery, the salt and pepper mills, the dripping wax on the candle nearest him, and jiggled in his chair like a two-year-old. When he started folding his napkin into a boat, I knew I'd better get him out of there. Now I know why people have children. It's so they have the perfect excuse to hurry home from hideous evenings 'because the babysitter can't stay late'.

Carl gives people about a two-minute trial to prove themselves. If they don't say anything remotely interesting in that time slot, that's it. At a party, he simply lifts a hand and waves at a complete stranger in a far corner of the room, says, 'God, that's Jeremy, haven't seen him for years! Do excuse me,' and shoots off.

From my point of view, what's the worst that can happen? The people in the group will look at me then at each other and share a knowing glance that says everything: Oh dear, she's not really one of us, is she? She looks common/dull/unsophisticated. Isn't she short/insignificant/freckly? Let's all hunch closer together so she gets the message.

Maybe they'll all simultaneously wave at far corners of the room and say, 'God, there's Jeremy!' and flee in several directions. Or they'll take one look at me and shake their heads sadly, then say, 'Oh, I don't think so. Run along now.'

Even when I was a student, I always used to take a book with me to a party. Then if I couldn't stand it, I could slink away to a quiet bedroom or a corner of the garden and read. Carl says I am absolutely not allowed to do this any more.

The other problem for me is that you're supposed to wear the *right* thing. If it's dressy, you can't turn up in jeans and trainers, even if that's your default setting and anything else feels like you're a kid playing dressing-up. And there are *so* many expectations. You don't want to stick to soft drinks or people think you're a killjoy, but nor do you want to knock back the booze and then have to prop yourself up against the wall so you don't fall over. You're supposed to do your hair so it looks 'done' as opposed to 'undone', which is the look mine favours. Then there's make-up, not just a smear of lip balm so your lips don't crack, but *proper* make-up – concealer, foundation, blusher, mascara and eye-liner, lip liner and lipstick – so that you don't look like *you* any more but instead, a weird mask-like version of yourself.

But the main problem, I think, is at grown-up parties, I always have this sneaking suspicion that I don't really belong and that it's only a matter of time before everyone else realises too. Sooner or later, a burly bouncer will appear and elbow his way through the throng towards me. He won't even need to explain; he'll just jerk his head towards the exit and I'll have to leave. He'll know, just as I know, that I'm still 'the girl from the flats' who has to wear second-hand clothes and can't afford to go on school trips. And no one's allowed to come back to our home after school because everyone knows those flats are where all the rough kids hang out. Anyway, you'd better keep away from me because I'm also 'Nitch the Witch' and I might put a spell on you if you cross me.

* * *

I hold up two outfits, so Carl can help me choose: a turquoise silk cheongsam or a bright floral off-the-shoulder top with my black jeans. Carl surveys them with that slow, assessing, frowny face he does sometimes.

'Hmm...' He looks away for a minute, fiddling with his cuff. 'Both of those are certainly very... ah... colourful, but I wonder whether something a tad more... er... sophisticated might be wise.' He glances at me, then back at his cuff, even though it's a button shirt, not links, so there's nothing to be fiddled with.

'I thought you loved the turquoise dress?'

'I do! I love it, and I love you in it.'

'But?'

'But you've seen Antonia and her friends. They're all very, well, they're very smart and glamorous and sophisticated and—'

'And I'm *not*. I get it.'

'No, you *are*. Natalie, darling, don't take this the wrong way. It's only that Toni and her acolytes – they're quite gossipy and judgemental and I think you'd make a better impression if you dressed in a more... elegant outfit. Just for the party. You know I don't care what you look like.'

'Thanks.'

'You know what I mean. I think you're gorgeous.'

'But I don't have anything like that.'

'Sure you do. What about that smart little black dress?'

'I don't own a little black dress.' Is he thinking of some other wife? I bet Antonia has ten little black dresses.

'You *do*. With the – I don't know – things around the neck. It was on top of the pile when we moved some clothes down the other day.'

The light dawns. He means my smart vintage 1960s dress with the restrained beading around the collar.

'My funeral dress, you mean?'

Carl sighs. 'It doesn't know it's a funeral dress, does it, Natalie? And nor will Antonia. It's a dress, it's smart and... and not, er, eccentric or ethnic or... or peculiar or anything like that.'

'You think my clothes are peculiar?'

'I'm not being drawn into this conversation because whatever I say will be wrong. You look lovely most of the time, but yes, some of your clothes are a little bit… eccentric – as if you're auditioning for the part of "crazy alternative therapist" in a bad sitcom.'

'Well, at least my clothes have some character and individuality! I don't look like Mr Perfect, who's just stepped out of a bloody Patek Philippe ad.'

His face flushes. 'That's not fair. Come on, Natalie. It's not like you to be mean.'

'I'm sorry, that *was* unkind – I'm really nervous.' I step closer and stretch up to kiss him. 'Fine. I'll wear the stupid funeral dress. I don't give a toss anyway. I'll come to the party but I'm not promising to have a good time!'

19

IT'S PARTY TIME

Antonia bends to kiss me on both cheeks. She's wearing vertiginous high heels so she really has to descend a long way to kiss me. I find myself stretching up on tiptoe as if I'm a tiny kid.

'What a simply gorgeous dress, Natalie. Is it vintage?'

'Thank you. Yes, it's from the sixties.'

'It's absolute bliss. Now, let's get you both drinks, then I can introduce you to some super guests I know you're going to love, love, *love*.'

'Can I help at all?'

'No, no.' Antonia waves the suggestion away as if it's absurd. 'I have people to help.' Across the other side of the pool, I spot Katja in a black skirt and top, offering a tray of canapés, and another woman in a short black dress coming out of the house with another tray. 'Pavel will bring you drinks.' She waves at a tall young man, also dressed in black, carrying a bottle of Champagne. Oh, yes, I recognise him – he's the one who told me to park round the back when I came for the pool party when I first met Antonia. Another of Queen Bee's worker colony. '*Pavel!*'

He scoots up and asks us what we would like.

'Now please tell me Carl's driving this evening so you can let loose, Natty?' God, I wish she wouldn't call me that.

'*Natalie*. We walked, actually, so we could both have a drink.'

'*Walked!* Gosh. How... er... how marvellous. Super. I'll be back in a tick but Pavel will bring you drinks.'

We both ask for Champagne and Pavel dashes off and returns with our drinks at once. Carl and I clink glasses and I take a sip but then he says, 'Darling, could you possibly hold my drink for a minute while I go and find the kids to say hi?' He passes me his glass of Champagne and scoots off.

A moment later, a woman gives me her empty glass and says 'Thank you' and then the man she's with gives me his too without comment as he's passing. I'm now struggling to hold our two nearly full glasses plus their two empty ones. Why would anyone give me an empty glass? How weird. Then I see Katja zipping past in her all-black outfit and I get it. Great – everyone thinks I'm one of the help. To be honest, I'd probably feel more relaxed if I *were* here to help. I go and find a side-table and put down the empty glasses but then Antonia swoops in on me like a hawk spotting a mouse that's foolishly broken cover.

'Now, let's see, who shall we introduce you to?' Antonia ushers me towards an elderly man. 'This is Alan, who does our accounts. Alan, I must introduce you to Natalie, Carl's Number Two.'

Why does she have to say that? It really makes me sound like second-best.

'Where's Carl gone?' Antonia looks round, but Carl seems to have melted away into thin air. 'Honestly, Natalie, you'll have to keep our husband on a much tighter leash to stop him from wandering off. Oh, never mind. Excuse me, I must gee up Katja to bring out more canapés. She's completely dopey if one doesn't keep on her case.'

I have a chat with Alan but I'm very distracted – is Antonia trying to tell me that Carl has a wandering eye? That he'll be unfaithful if I don't keep him on a tight leash? Is that true? I've never worried about it until now. And she called him '*our* husband' again.

The conversation soon turns to the issue of the VAT threshold for small businesses, and so I'm on the verge of excusing myself to say I need the loo when Alan suddenly waves at someone and says, 'Oh, I ought to go and say hello to Simon – excuse me.' Great. *I* am the bore that people can't wait to rush away from. Maybe I could take evening classes in how to be more sparkling?

Then I spot Carl, talking and laughing, with a semi-circle of women around him all looking up at him with rapt attention. He tips his head back and laughs, then runs his hand through his hair. It strikes me that my husband is actually incredibly good-looking. I mean, of course I've noticed this before, but I find him so attractive for all sorts of reasons: he makes me laugh, he's never boring, he's sharp but kind, dynamic and confident but then suddenly like a little kid. I love him. I honestly don't think about what he looks like very much.

As I'm watching, Antonia passes by the little group of Carl and his adoring acolytes and she briefly lays a hand on his arm proprietorially, leaning in for a moment to say something to him. The gesture is small, brief but intimate. Then she moves on, bestowing smiles and greetings; a one-woman charm offensive.

Max and Saskia have been allowed to stay up. I can't see Max at the moment but I spy Saskia standing by the back door.

'Hi,' I say, giving her a wave. I've decided not to try to kiss her in greeting unless she approaches me first. If she doesn't like me, it will only make things worse if I impose myself on her. 'That's a really pretty dress. Is it new?'

'Yes. I got it for the party.' She looks at mine. 'Is yours new?'

'No, actually it's vintage – from the 1960s.'

'That's so *old*!' Her face looks completely horrified, as if I have borrowed a frock from Miss Havisham and it's covered in cobwebs.

'Er... yes, yes it is.'

I'm spared any further mortification by Max, who comes charging up to me and throws his arms round me.

'Natalie!'

I bend down and he gives me a big wet kiss on my cheek.

'Hey, you. Don't you look smart?' Max is wearing a fancy silk waistcoat.

'Mum said we had to dress up for the party.' He frowns at me. 'Why are you wearing so much black stuff, Natalie? It's supposed to be a *party*. You're supposed to have fun!' He twirls round and round, then bumps into me. 'You look like you're going to a funeral.'

There is a reason I wear this dress for funerals. It's very simple, aside from the discreet beading at the neckline, very unshowy. Maybe a bit too unshowy for a party.

All the other women guests are wearing pretty, floaty dresses – the terrace is a sea of colour – pinks and blues, metallics, animal prints and floral patterns.

'Black is often thought to be elegant,' I say.

'But it's so *boring*!' Max says, laughing. I know he doesn't mean it rudely so it doesn't bother me, and he's right, it is a bit boring. 'You should have a rainbow dress in every colour there is. With a matching swimsuit underneath. Then when you get bored at the party, because it's only grown-ups being boring, you can take it off and go for a swim. That's what I want to do.'

That's what I'd rather do, too, but I'm fairly sure Carl would not be happy if I dived into the pool in the middle of the party.

Max runs off to go and play with his friend and I see Saskia talking to her friend, leaning in close and giggling. I wish I had a friend here to giggle with. I can't see Carl and, for a moment, I feel the need to be by myself. I draw back by the side of the house, into the shadows. I'm more comfortable, standing here and watching, sipping my Champagne on my own.

I notice a heavenly smell and wonder if it's from the flowerbed next to the house or one of the climbers that scramble up the walls. Jasmine, perhaps? Or honeysuckle. I move closer to the house when I hear voices coming from round the corner.

'... Carl's *Number Two*.' There is laughter.

'God, she is awful, isn't she? That's *so* bitchy. Classic Antonia, though.'

'True. I do feel a bit sorry for her, though, don't you? Number Two, I mean. Who'd want to be the next wife on the conveyor belt if Antonia had been first? Not me, thank you very much. Who could compete with that?'

'Yuh. She's such an amazing hostess. Did you see the crates of Champagne in the kitchen? Way more than we could possibly all get through, even if we were here glugging it back all night. And those canapés! I've been such a pig tonight.'

'And that lighting around the terrace. Gorgeous. She's so gifted at this stuff. She should be a party-planner really.'

'She looks killer tonight. That dress must have set Dom back a bit. And the shoes! They look like Louboutin's.'

'Fuck me. They're like £400, right?'

'At least 500, I think. Maybe more.'

'Jesus. I can't walk in those killer heels, though.'

'Wife Number Two should splash out on a pair. Apparently, she's a bit of a garden gnome, I hear.'

'Aw – poor little Wifey Number Two.'

'Yes, poor Number Two. Cheers to her, wherever she is.'

I hear their glasses clink, then one says, 'Bet you Carl moves on to Number Three in under two years. Fancy a bet?'

'No chance. Two years absolute tops – if she's lucky.'

I drop my glass and it shatters on the flagstones, my Champagne splashing back up on my legs.

I dart back into the house via the nearby side door and stand inside for a moment, trying to breathe.

I tell myself they're idiots. They don't know me – they don't know anything about our marriage. Who are they to say how long it's going to last? How can they make a judgement when they haven't even met me?

I go through to the kitchen to look for a dustpan and brush. I want to leave right now, this minute, but I can't leave broken glass out there. Tomorrow, Max will be running in and out with bare feet.

As I enter, I spot Katja going out of the back door with another tray of canapés. Pavel is in the kitchen, getting more ice, and I say 'Hi', then start to ask him where I might find a dustpan and brush, but he dashes out the back door too, rushing to attend to the Queen Bee's constant demands.

I walk into the utility room off the kitchen. There's a low stool, and I go and perch on it. I feel so much more at ease in here, sitting in the warmth behind the scenes, with the washing machine spinning away, than I do out there. It's as if I'm expected to perform on stage but no one's thought to give me a script or a costume or stage directions. Here, I don't need to pretend to be elegant and sophisticated.

At that moment, the washing machine beeps to show the cycle has finished. Without thinking, I stand up, turn it off and open the door. I might as well unload it while I'm here. I grab the laundry basket and start yanking out the clean washing into the basket. Should I put it in the dryer? I don't approve of them really. I hang our washing out on the line and let the sun and wind do the job for nothing. I can't imagine Antonia pegging out her pants for all to see, though.

What am I *doing*? I'm supposed to be out there, meeting people. I have to *try*. A couple of stupid women said some daft things. They've probably drunk way too much and get off on being bitchy. So what? I've got to stop letting everything get to me.

But first I must clear up that glass. I'd never forgive myself if someone got hurt. I find a dustpan and brush and head back out to the side patio.

Luckily, it's empty except for two other women, smoking and talking to each other.

One turns in my direction. 'Are there any more of those delicious prawn canapés?'

'I think so. Katja took some out but she'll probably go round the main terrace first.'

'Can't you ask her to come over to us?'

'OK, but I must clear up some broken glass over there.'

I knew this stupid black dress was a mistake. If I'd worn my turquoise dress, no one would mistake me for a waitress. I bet everyone thinks that's what I am.

I crouch down to sweep up the glass. There's not much light here so I hope I've got it all. I peer into the dark corner closest to the house.

The women are still chatting and laughing and I'm not really paying much attention until I hear one of them say, 'They still look so *right* together, don't they?'

I glance up to see who they're talking about, but already I know it must be Carl and Antonia on the terrace. Antonia is laughing and squeezing Carl's arm, drawing him closer to introduce him to someone.

'I know. Such a shame they broke up. Heartbreaking for those adorable children.'

'Awful. Though Antonia's done all right for herself with Dominic, hasn't she?'

'True – he's loaded. Still, don't tell me you'd drop your knickers for him if Carl was on offer?'

The other one shrieks hysterically.

'Where's his other one, anyway? Number Two? Isn't she supposed to be here tonight?'

Does literally everyone call me 'Number Two'? For God's sake. Bloody Antonia.

'Yes, somewhere around. No idea what she looks like. Do you know which one she is?

'No – I've got no idea either.'

'I wonder if she's that one in the red? Next to Carl? She's pretty.'

'I don't think so. Someone said she's tiny – like a little doll.'

'That must look hilarious with Carl being tall.'

I sweep up the glass as best I can and stand up straight.

'Excuse me, please,' I say confidently as I try to get past with the dustpan.

'Oh, do you think you could bring us two more glasses of Champagne?' One of them taps her empty glass with a long, manicured fingernail.

'Um. Actually, I really need to get rid of this broken glass.' I hold up the dustpan as proof. 'Perhaps you could ask Pavel, over there.' I point. 'The guy in black with the bottle.'

I move away and pause for a moment to look over at Carl and Antonia again. Yes, they do look right together. They *fit* perfectly, both tall, confident, entirely at ease with the world, never worrying that they're being judged or that they don't belong.

As I move on, I hear one of the women behind me say: 'Honestly, how rude. We were only asking for a couple of drinks. I know it's hard to get decent help in a village, but really – two glasses of fizz – how hard can it be?'

I'm tempted to swing round and tip the contents of the dustpan over them or sprinkle it over a tray of canapés as I swoosh past, but I don't. I go back in and put the dustpan of glass on the side in the utility room without even wrapping up the pieces in newspaper, the way I usually would. I run upstairs to the bathroom and lock myself in.

I am not going to cry. I refuse to cry. I bite the inside of my lip hard as a distraction. The window is open a little bit at the bottom and I kneel down on the floor to peer out and watch. From up here, it looks like such a lovely party. Everyone is so smart, and enjoying themselves, talking and laughing and drinking. They're all so glamorous, with their perfect tans and perfect teeth. They're not just a little bit different from me; it's like they're not even the same species. They're... cheetahs or lions, top of the food chain. And I'm... not even a gazelle. A rabbit, maybe, or... no, an amoeba in the pond.

I see Carl turn around, apparently looking for someone, Antonia presumably. Then he leans in closer to say something to the man he's talking to and moves away, raising his glass to people as he goes, shaking hands, kissing cheeks. He finds Antonia then and leans in really close. For a horrible moment, I think he's going to kiss her properly, right there in the middle of the party, but then he moves a fraction to one side and I see he's saying something. I don't know what. Perhaps he's telling her how stunning she looks? Or telling her he should never have let her go? She shakes her head then points towards the pool pavilion. Maybe she's suggesting he meets her there?

But now Antonia draws him to one side, away from the other guests. Their heads are only inches apart. She's speaking intently. Carl holds her upper arm, nodding. For a few moments, she lays her hand on his chest, her head tilting towards his. Such an intimate gesture. He says something else, then Saskia and Max suddenly appear and run up to them. The children look so happy. Saskia tugs at his lapel to get him to bend down so she can whisper something in his ear. Max curls himself under Carl's arm. Then Antonia squeezes Saskia close by her side and I see them the way everyone else must see them: as the perfect family.

Such a lovely picture. But where does that leave me?

20

THE PARTY'S OVER

I can't bear this. I don't belong here. I don't want to be here. Look at me, down on my knees, watching the grown-ups having fun. I remember my mum having very small parties at our flat occasionally, and Celeste and I were allowed to stay up a bit late and hand round the bowls of crisps and snacks to the guests. Then Mum would see us off to bed, but of course we got up again, peeping round our bedroom door, desperate for some of the grown-upness to rub off on us. How can I be thirty-six but still feel no more self-assured than I did when I was eight?

I'm going. I don't want to make a scene and, anyway, there's no need. Carl didn't mean for this to happen, I'm sure, but he must be kicking himself for having made such a horrible, horrible mistake. Antonia, too. I feel a bit sorry for Dominic but I suppose he'll be OK. And the children will be happy, that's the main thing. I shouldn't even be thinking about myself. This is what's best for them. I'm going to slip away and I'll send Carl a quick text to say I've gone home because I have a headache, so he doesn't worry. Then I can call him tomorrow.

I love Carl more than anything but we should never have got

married so quickly. If only we'd waited, I would have had time to see what I can see so clearly now: that he wasn't really over Antonia. God, I'm so stupid! That first time I met him, when he came into my shop, he was buying Antonia a present. Who buys their ex-wife a divorce present, for God's sake? I should have realised then that he was still crazy about her.

No wonder he was so desperate to buy the cottage, to buy it before I could even look at it and maybe interfere or stop him. It wasn't only about being close to his children; I see that now. Antonia's a glowing, radiant light and he's drawn to her like a moth. He can't help it. He can't keep away from her. And who could blame him? She looks stunning tonight. She's magnetic. Even though I find her annoying, in some strange way I've also fallen under her spell a bit, I admit. When I'm around her, I can't stop looking at her and noticing all the ways in which she's so perfect – her hair, her make-up, her nails, her clothes, her teeth, the way she's done the house, everything.

I slip silently out of the bathroom and pause on the stairs to check that there's no one there. Then I descend as quietly as I can. I don't want to bump into anyone. I didn't even bring a jacket as it is so warm. I check I have my house keys and phone in my bag, then I slip out of the front door.

At least I know I can walk in my shoes; they're my smart black suede ones, but they're not high. It's properly dark now, though. I get out my phone to switch on the torch app but I'm down to nine per cent and it drains the battery so fast. At that moment, the clouds clear and I can see pretty well by the light of the moon. I'm shivering a little in my short-sleeved dress but I'm fine. It's so quiet here and I was starting to love it: the peace and the fields, the village, those charming tiny cottages clustered around the village green, the beautiful old oaks at the top of our lane, and the pond. And the ducks. I even have a favourite, Humphrey. I'll miss him most of all. Well, aside from Carl, obviously. But I'm not going to think about that now.

The clouds cover up the moon again, and I can barely see the road ahead. I take out my phone. I'll have to use the torch or I could stumble in a pothole and twist my ankle. There's a sudden movement right in front of me and I'm being stared at by a pair of glassy eyes. For a moment, neither of us moves, then it darts away. Just a fox. But I can feel my heart racing as if I'm ready to run for it.

A little way off I hear the hum of a car engine, so I tuck further into the verge. You have to be so careful on the sharp bend up ahead. Carl says it's safer to be on the other side at that point because you can see better, but everyone knows in the countryside you're supposed to walk on the right side of the road, facing the oncoming traffic. Besides, it can't be safer to keep crossing backwards and forwards on every bend in the road, can it?

Suddenly my phone gives out and night cloaks the landscape. I can just about see the difference between the land and the sky, but if it's dark here, it'll be much worse down the lane. I'm sure I left our outside light on but you can't see it until you're right at the bottom where we park. I keep thinking about Carl, remembering that perfect day only a few weeks ago before we found out his dad was ill. I was so happy then, for once feeling safe and sure that everything would turn out all right, so certain I had found the love of my life, and that we'd share our life together in our dream house.

Suddenly, the roar of a car engine is incredibly close and I'm dazzled by its glaring white headlamps. I throw myself sideways on to the verge and there's a screech of tyres as the driver swerves to avoid me. It doesn't stop.

I'm lying face down, half in the muddy ditch, half on the grass verge. I reach out my hand to try to get up and press it down into what I assume is grass, but turns out to be a patch of stinging nettles.

Great – come to a party! It'll be such a super evening! Champagne! Canapés! Delightful company! Lose the love of your life and on the way home nearly get run over then end up wet and muddy and stung. This gets better and better!

What am I doing here? I'm a stupid fool. What did I expect – some romantic, ridiculous happy-ever-after ending? That's not real life. When I first started seeing Carl, I realise now I always had this thought lurking at the back of my mind that he was too good to be true. He was too tall, too handsome, too successful. He was bright and interesting and even made me laugh. He was sexy but not vain, fit but not boringly obsessed about getting a six-pack. Perhaps I *knew* in a way? Maybe that's why I felt I was inhabiting a wonderful dream and that any day I would simply wake up and there would be no Carl any more, no dream house in the country. It would just be me. It's only that I didn't realise it would happen so soon.

But then, once we got married and bought the house, at least it made it all feel more real. Because things *weren't* perfect. Far from it. The house had only half a roof, and Saskia was bitchy to me and Carl was never around. And Antonia made me feel... what? *Lesser*, I suppose. Not just less amazing than she is, because that must apply to almost everyone, but worse than that – *less than myself*.

When I'm around Antonia, I feel intensely aware of being so ungroomed: that my fingernails, although clean, are unpainted, that my hair is untamed, my clothes comfortable but under-whelming. But it's not only those things. I could handle all of that if that's all it was. Antonia is so confident. She seems to move through life completely undaunted and unabashed. She's like an elegant swan, gliding along without a care in the world, while I'm a stupid ugly duckling, frantically paddling but half the time getting caught up in the reeds or swimming in circles rather than achieving anything or going anywhere. When I saw her standing next to Carl, the way she gently laid her hand against his chest, I could see how they *fitted* – whereas Carl and I... Well, there is no Carl and me, is there? Not any more.

I need to be away from here, away from Carl, away from Antonia, away from the cottage. I need to be somewhere where I can feel like *me* again rather than Number Two – a second-hand, second-rate, second-choice wife that no one in their right mind would ever want if they could have the real thing.

I need to leave.

I let myself into the cottage. I want to say goodbye to it, but I know that's sentimental and stupid, that it will only make it harder. Still, I nip up to the bedroom, fetch the book I'm reading from my side of the bed, then go into the kitchen to drink some water. Thank goodness I only had half a glass of Champagne before I dropped my glass, so I can still drive. I grab the keys for the van. It's cold now so I put on a jumper over my black dress. I should change really but I can't wait to get out of here, so I tug on my jeans over my tights and put on my warm jacket. One quick glance into the sitting room. Oh, how I love this room. The fireplace. The red walls. The lights. The few evenings with Carl when we curled up by the fire. I was so happy.

It's just a building, I tell myself. Get over it. Don't be such a soppy fool.

I go out, lock up and climb into the van. Up the track, left on to the main road. Where should I go?

21

POTATO PRINTS

I think of going to my mum's, then to Celeste's. No, I'm not looking for someone else to rescue me. I'm not a child, I can do this myself. I'll go to my flat. My own space. A place where there's no Antonia in my face the whole time, reminding me how tall and glamorous and charismatic she is, how *right* she looks standing next to Carl, while I probably look like his pet labradoodle.

I've only brought my handbag because I still have some clothes here at the flat. I manage to find a parking space in the next road, and I let myself in at the street door, then slog up all the stairs to the top floor.

There's a funny smell – like new paint. Weird.

I click on the light in the tiny lobby and sniff the air. Definitely paint.

In the hall, some of my stuff is boxed up, ready to go down to the cottage, though now the boxes are covered with dustsheets.

I check the sitting room. The walls were a milky coffee colour in here but now they're magnolia. I look into the bedroom. The patches of test colours that used to be on the wall have been

painted over. Magnolia again. The bathroom used to be a bright
sky blue but that's gone too.

The whole flat is now the same colour – that same neutral
tone estate agents advise you to use 'to appeal to the wider
market'. I *hate* it. How is it possible to hate something so neutral?
I have no idea, but I do. I hate it with a deep loathing.

I know we spoke about getting the flat repainted, but we
hadn't even discussed colours. As usual, Carl assumes he knows
best and he's gone ahead and arranged it. Why didn't he even *ask*
me? It's still my flat, after all.

Most of my pictures have been taken down and boxed up. He
must have asked the decorators to rehang the few pictures he
considered appropriate. A glance at my bookshelves reveals that
my books have been reordered by colour instead of the way I had
them – fiction by author, non-fiction by subject. Most of my
personal bits and pieces are bubble-wrapped in crates in the hallway, waiting to be moved down to the cottage. Our dream house. I
feel sick.

I go into the bathroom and sit on the floor with my back
against the bath. My legs are shaking and I'm shivering all over. I
look around for a towel, but I can't see them. I used to have huge,
thick towels in mauve and peacock blue. You could wrap yourself
up in them and be cocooned in warmth. Now I spot a minimalist
metal shelf has appeared on one wall, with a perfect stack of
teeny-tiny aquamarine guest towels sitting on top, presumably for
teeny-tiny guests. The pile is aligned incredibly neatly, profes-
sionally even. I can't imagine Carl wasting his time and energy
fiddling about aligning towels.

I walk around the flat once more. The cushions are all placed
with contrived carelessness. There is a chi-chi chrome bowl filled
with lemons on the kitchen table. On the counter, two new
chunky white coffee cups and saucers send a tacit code: Rent this

Flat – Enjoy Lazy Sunday Mornings with Your Partner. The whole thing is a slavish copy of a lifestyle supplement.

What's with the lemons? Why would Carl need so many lemons when he stays in London? He likes a gin and tonic, but this is bonkers.

Suddenly I know he hired someone to make my flat lettable, without discussing it with me. Clearly, he didn't even feel able to trust me with something so idiot-proof as a little light towel-arranging and lemon-buying. God, what does he think I am? I know the flat was too cluttered – I'm not stupid. I was planning to clear it out and paint it in more neutral colours if we did decide to rent it out, of course I was. But the point is, I hadn't agreed to that yet. And now I'll be living in it again, I don't want aqua towels the size of hankies or chunky coffee cups too heavy to lift even when they're empty.

Maybe I'll have a red sitting room here? The thought of our beautiful red sitting room at home – I mean at Rose Cottage – hits me suddenly like a punch from nowhere. I think of the evenings, though there were precious few of them, when Carl and I sat talking or reading there, or curled up with a bottle of wine while we watched a film. I think of leaning back against him, his warm breath in my hair. His arms around me, casually, the two of us relaxed, content, feeling we had our whole lives together ahead of us.

I shake the thoughts away, impatient with myself. I'm a strong, independent woman. I can be by myself. I don't need Carl; I don't need anyone. Right. First, I want to do something – anything – to rescue this flat from Death by Neutral Tones. I have a look at my stacked clutter boxes by the front door, waiting to be transported out of sight somewhere. If only I had that red I chose for the sitting room at the cottage. Then I could paint one wall in it, at least. The one behind the bed would look great. All I've got are some old, tiddly, test pots I bought to try out for the bedroom here, all tones of red, plus a deep grey and one pot of gold, although each one is barely enough to paint a shelf.

I'm really hungry. I think of the fridge at the cottage – there's half a cold chicken, sweet cherry tomatoes, homemade pesto, fresh salad leaves from the local market, new potatoes. I open the cupboards: salt and pepper, sugar, a few dried herbs and spices, tea bags and the last of a jar of coffee. Some very stale crackers. Great. There must be something to eat, surely? I pull open the deep vegetable drawer. Three vintage potatoes. How appetising. I pick them out but they're soft and have white sprouts poking out of them. They look like something Damien Hirst would put in a Perspex box and recategorise as Art: *The Impossibility of Giving in to Death*. Or: *The Impossibility of Turning Three Extremely Sad, Sprouting Potatoes into Anything Resembling Supper*. When we were kids, we used to make potato prints sometimes, which is pretty much the only constructive thing you can do with potatoes when they're this far gone.

Two minutes later and I've phoned for a pizza to be delivered and the potatoes are scrubbed and halved, the test pots of paint are out and I'm dragging the bed away from the wall. I botch my first two attempts, but cut a reasonable star shape on my third go. Then I copy it as best I can, using the other potato halves. I get huge pleasure from taking the pristine white saucers from the kitchen and pouring paint into them. I decide against a regimentally ordered pattern and go instead for pleasingly random, using two shades of red, the grey and the gold.

I start to sing as I paint, belting out numbers from all my favourite musicals: *Guys and Dolls*, *Top Hat*, *West Side Story*, *Oklahoma*. I take a breath and stand back. This is really not bad at all. It could be the next big thing. Potato prints are the new wallpaper. Don't throw those old test pots away!

Then I begin singing more softly to myself, 'I Have a Love' from *West Side Story*.

But I barely get past the first two lines because, of course, it makes me cry. It makes me cry when I'm driving and that track comes up on my playlist. Sometimes, I even cry just thinking about that song.

I'm not a strong, independent woman who doesn't need anyone. I'm not reasserting my true self by being creative. I'm a self-deluding, lovesick fool, who's now spoiled a perfectly good plain wall by daubing blobby stars all over it like a nursery school kid on a sugar high from too many jelly babies.

I want Carl. So what if he was a bit economical with the truth a couple of times? Who could blame him? It would drive any sane man mad having to put up with me and my dithering. I love him and now he'll go off and be with Antonia. She's much more decisive than I am, more organised, more go-getting. He'll have the perfect wife again; the house will be all neat and tidy and she'll repaint the walls magnolia or this year's shade of grey, and there'll be huge bowls of lemons on the kitchen table and state-of-the-art gadgets and fancy taps. There'll be no clutter and no funny stones we found on the beach, by the bath, and no red sitting room and no badly sewn cushions with wonky seams, and there'll be no *me*.

Carl will be much, much happier than I've made him. So, I should be pleased. I should be really, really pleased because I love him so much that if I weren't such a selfish pig that's all I would care about: Carl being happy. I do want him to be happy. Of course I do. It's only that I wanted him to be happy with *me*, only now I've spoiled it. Tears roll down my cheeks and I start to sob. I sob so hard my ribs hurt. I hurl the suede and silk cushions off the bed and clamber in, tug the quilt over me, scrunch up into a ball, and pray for sleep to take me away.

22

Oh God, what's that noise! I'm suddenly wide awake and jerk upright. It sounded like the front door being opened. I reach for my phone, which is charging by the bed. My first instinct is to call Carl, but I shake the thought away. Why am I still expecting him to dash to my rescue? He's seventy miles away, asleep at the cottage. Or perhaps still up, talking to Antonia late into the night, leaning in towards her...

Should I call the police? Or Celeste? But she won't hear it because she keeps her phone on silent at night. I jab at my phone. What? It's dead. Oh, no – the power's off at the socket. It wasn't charging. I quietly get out of bed and look round for something heavy, but there's only a Victorian mantel clock, which is heavy but incredibly awkward. I can't possibly hold it in one hand. Maybe I could barricade the door, then open the window and shout for help?

I move across the room as quickly and silently as I can. There's a small Edwardian dressing table and I take the mirror off the top and carefully carry the table over to the door. The thought crosses my mind that, if it's light enough for me to lift it this easily, then the chances are it will be near-useless as any kind of barricade. Then one of the small drawers at the front slips out and crashes to the floor, spilling out a clatter of hairclips and earrings.

'Natalie? Are you here?' From the hallway.

It's Carl.

I set down the dressing table and yank open the bedroom door.

'You nearly scared me to death! What are you doing here?'

He strides forward and wraps his arms round me, then picks me up right off the floor and squeezes me.

'Jesus, thank God you're safe! I've been going mad. The whole way up here, I was going through all these possibilities in my head. I was shaking like a leaf as I drove. I called Celeste but it went to voicemail. And I called you and *called* you – about a hundred times. Did you lose your phone?'

'Could you put me down now, please?'

He deposits me back on the ground and takes my hands.

'My phone battery died.'

'Er... OK. And you haven't thought to recharge it? Or call me? You disappeared into thin air and no one knew where the hell you were!'

I did mean to text him saying I'd left but then my phone died and I jumped in the van and came up here. When I got here, I plugged it in to charge it – only, apparently, I couldn't even manage that.

'I knew where I was.'

'Natalie. Come on. That's ridiculous. You sound like a stroppy teenager.'

I shrug.

'You do know it's not normal to leave a party, especially one being held in your honour, without so much as a word to anyone, right?'

I cross my arms.

'I honestly didn't think anyone would notice if I went.'

'OK – that's clearly crazy. I was looking for you, for a start. When I couldn't find you anywhere at the party, I went back to the cottage and searched there. Then I saw the van was gone. I was completely freaked out. You scared the bloody hell out of me. Why did you leave?'

'I didn't feel I belonged there.'

'*What?* What does that even mean? Look, can we sit down properly? I need a coffee to stay awake.'

I tug on my jumper and we move through to the kitchen and I put the kettle on.

'I didn't fit in and I realised that it would be better for everyone if I left.'

'I *knew* it was something mad.' Carl puts his head in his hands and sighs. 'Even while I was totally terrified that something bad had happened, another bit of my mind was telling me: she's gone off for some crazy Natalie-type reason.' He looks at me then, exhausted. 'Nat, that makes no sense. Why would you feel you don't fit in?'

I shrug. 'I'm not part of that crowd, and I never will be. They're all rich and spoilt and awful.'

'Oh, come on, don't exaggerate.' He sighs. 'But, actually, so what if they are? OK, I accept that some of them are awful, but it doesn't *matter*. You'll find other women you have more in common with if you give it time. No one's saying they all have to be your best friends. Smile, be polite, chit-chat for a couple of hours and get tiddly. It's really not hard.'

'That wasn't the only thing.'

'OK. But why you didn't just come and find me and say, this is boring, can we go soon? You know – like a normal person.'

'Well, *because*.'

I take a deep breath. Then I turn away from him to make the coffee.

'Natalie.'

'Well, suddenly I could see the truth clearly. Things as they really are. So, I thought it would be better if I slipped away and let you all get on with it without me.'

'The truth?'

'Yes. Look, it's OK. I'm not exactly happy about it, of course, but I accept it. I'll get over it.' I shrug as if I'm talking about having missed out on a nice lot at auction rather than resigning myself to losing the man I love.

'Why would you put me through this? Natalie, I thought maybe you'd been abducted at the cottage and bundled into your van. I was bloody scared and panicking. Don't you get it? And what is this great truth that made you disappear without bothering to let your husband know that you're all right?'

He looks really angry, but I'm the one who has every right to be angry. *I'm* the one who's had my whole life snatched from under my bloody nose.

'That you're still in love with Antonia, of course.'

Why is he making me spell it out? So he can pretend it's not true? 'That you've decided to get back together and be a family again with Saskia and Max.' I shrug as if I'm not even that bothered. 'It's OK. I understand. I get it.'

'Is this some kind of really weird joke?' Carl says, looking at my face like he's trying to decipher some impenetrable code.

'Joke? How would it be a joke? It's not funny, or at least not to me. Maybe you and Antonia can have a good laugh about it at some point.'

'What? Who's laughing? Sorry to be a bit of a stickler for facts, but what exactly is the *evidence* that led you to arrive at this great truth?'

'Oh, Carl.' I pour us each a coffee and sit at the table. 'So many things. She's so glamorous and amazing, and everyone adores her and her incredible house. She's *perfect*. And, and... I saw you, the two of you at the party, standing apart from the guests, leaning in so close together, the way she touched you on your chest. It was so *intimate*. And then the four of you – you looked so *right* together, standing on the terrace with the kids snuggled up to you both. It was crystal clear to me.'

'*What?*' Carl frowns, as if trying to remember, then sinks his face into his hands. 'Oh, Natalie, didn't you think it might be a good idea to draw me to one side and say, hey, darling, are you trying to get back with your ex-wife?'

'It was *obvious*! That would have been crazy. Plus, I heard people talking about how good you looked together as a couple.'

'Which people?'

'I don't know who they were – just some guests.'

'And you think letting random people determine who I love and who I should be with is a good idea, do you?'

'Well... I can see it doesn't sound... quite right when you put it like that. But it really seemed one hundred per cent clear to me, so there you are.'

'And leaving without a word and driving seventy miles in the dark and not telling me you're alive and well – that's not crazy?'

'No, not at all. It made perfect sense to me.'

'I honestly don't know what to say.'

'So, you don't deny it? Look, the very first time I met you, you were buying an expensive present for Antonia. Who buys a present for their *ex*-wife? You're obviously still besotted with her! I *know* I'm right.'

'Well, think again, because you're not.' He looks at me directly. 'God, I *know* – that moment when she touched me, I know what it was.' he says. 'It was *Max*. He says he's not going to move up to secondary school. Antonia's really worried about it. She was asking me what I thought we should do. We're *parents*, Natalie. That doesn't go out the window just because we're divorced.'

'Oh. But still, answer me this: do you still have feelings for Antonia, yes or no?'

'Natalie – for God's sake.' He reaches across the table to take my hands but I withdraw mine. 'Of course I have feelings about Antonia. We were married, we have kids, that's natural. But my feelings are – they're complicated.'

He's not denying it, though.

'You still... love her, don't you?'

'No! Absolutely not. Christ, you can be a bloody idiot.'

'Thanks.'

'Why didn't you ask me, if you were worried? You're the one who's always going on about the importance of talking.'

'That's not fair. Any time I try to talk to you about anything important, you always deflect. You change the subject or say not now, you're too tired. It's impossible to get you to talk about anything when you don't want to.'

'I'm sorry. Look, you have to understand that I didn't grow up the way you did, with people talking about how they feel the whole time. In my family, if you were upset or angry, you went for a run or tried to think about something else. My father would say, "Best not to *dwell*, you know." That was his idea of paternal guidance.'

'OK, I get that, but this is *now*. Tell me – honestly – how you feel about Antonia. I can take it. I may be small but I'm honestly very tough.'

'I know you're tough, but you're also being bloody ridiculous and are going to feel like the biggest idiot on the planet.'

'Go on then.'

'When I first left Antonia—'

'I thought you had mutually decided to part?'

'No. That's what we told friends and the kids. We decided that would be a better story – that we were unhappy and thought it would be better for the kids to have an amicable separation. But when I first left, I hated her so much you wouldn't believe it. Never in my life had I *hated* anyone so much. My anger at her was like a physical presence surrounding me, inside me, absorbing every cell of my being. I couldn't think about anything else other than how much I hated her.'

'But *why*? What happened?'

He pauses. Gets up and goes to the cupboard, takes out a half-empty bottle of gin, finds some flat tonic from the fridge. Pours them into a glass and takes a swig. No ice. No lemon, even though God knows it's the one thing we have more than enough of.

'She slept with Stefan. That's why I don't see him any more.'

He turns round to face me. Takes another swallow of his drink.

Even now, over three years later, I can see the devastation on his face.

'Oh, Carl, that's awful. But do you still hate her *now*?'

'No, not really. Eventually, I ran out of steam. Now – I don't know – I tolerate Antonia because of the kids and it's much easier if we all get on, at least from the outside. And she doesn't get to me any more because, frankly, she's not my problem. If she wants to be late all the time, or ridiculously extravagant, it's her problem, and it's Dominic's problem. I don't have to deal with it or solve it or magically fix it. As long as what she does doesn't adversely affect the kids, it's better if I don't get stressed about it.'

'But you promise you really don't love her?'

He snorts. 'Really, really not.'

'And Stefan?'

'At the time, I couldn't even work out who I hated more – him or her. I was so angry with them both, but since then I've had time to think about it a lot. She did it to punish me. He didn't even have a reason.'

'Punish you? For what?'

He looks down into his drink then knocks back the entire thing. Shakes his head.

'Oh, nothing. Absolutely *nothing*. She was just being Antonia. It doesn't matter now. It's all water under the bridge.'

'But you're still upset about it.'

He sighs. 'I'm not really. It's only... it's soured my relationship with Stefan – for ever. I'll never forgive her for that.'

'That's so sad. Maybe things will change now you're seeing him more in Bristol?'

Carl makes a face.

'I don't think so. It doesn't matter. I don't care any more, and I really don't want to talk about it now. Christ, I'm tired. Can we go to bed?'

We go into the bedroom and he looks at the newly painted stars on the wall and opens his mouth as if he's about to speak. I give him a look. We can argue about the walls and the lemons and the hand towels in the morning. I haven't got the energy now. All I know is we are *not* renting my flat out. If I hadn't had it to escape to, where would I have gone?

'Er... nice stars,' he says. 'Have you thought of retraining as a nursery teacher?' He gives me that smile that normally makes me weak at the knees, but I still feel tight and pinched inside, like I can't breathe properly, even though I know he's explained everything.

'Not funny. Be kind or you're sleeping on the balcony.'

23

NOT-ANTONIA

In the morning, we can't have breakfast together because there isn't any food in the flat (aside from vintage potatoes, now covered in paint). There's no time to go out to a café because Carl has to drop into the office briefly, even though it's a Sunday. James, one of the partners, gave him a hard time about something to do with a client and Carl says he really needs to sort it out. We sit at the kitchen table, having a glass of water each because there isn't even any milk for tea, and we drank the remainder of the coffee last night.

'Carl, I have to say I'm not happy that you went ahead and got the flat painted without me.'

'But we'd talked about it! I thought it would be a nice surprise. I was sure you'd be delighted that it had all been done.'

'Well, I wasn't, because it looked very much as if you were tarting it up with a view to renting it out, even though that wasn't what we'd agreed.'

'What makes you think that?' But he looks guilty as hell.

'Er... let's see. Exhibit A, pointless huge bowl of lemons.

Exhibit B, strange heavy cups that have appeared from nowhere. Exhibit C, stack of tiny towels in the bathroom...'

'OK, OK, you've made your point. I'm sorry.'

'It's not listed with a lettings agent?'

'No. It isn't. I got a decorator-slash-stylist in to make it a bit more... photogenic so she could take pics, in case we then decided to let it, but I haven't done anything with the photographs, I promise.'

'Can we please agree that you're not going to decide on important things like this without me? I don't mean work issues, I mean about the house and this flat.'

'Yes. I'm sorry.' He looks at his watch. 'Nat, I really have to go. I want to talk to James face to face and he's in the office this morning. The man must sleep there.'

'All right. I suppose I'll go back down to Kent then – shall I? But will you come too? The new bed-frame isn't ready yet, but we can sleep in the second bedroom on that other bed I bought.'

'Yes, I'd love to be there with you. I'm sorry you've had to do so much without me. I'll come as soon as I'm done with James. Let's go to Kent. Home. We can have a long walk this afternoon, then a quiet evening in, yes? Some supper, a good bottle of wine, watch a film, maybe...'

'And we can *talk*.'

'Hmm,' he says, looking like I've said, 'We can take an ice-bath.'

'Sure.'

* * *

We have a wonderful long walk on the downs that stretch high above the village. There's a narrow path leading up from behind the church, marked by a wooden sign so discreet it is almost apologetic, saying simply: 'TO THE DOWNS'. I spotted the sign the other day and have been waiting for the chance to go and explore the footpath with Carl. We stride up there and it is absolutely stunning. At the top, the chalk downland dips down and away and we can see across the countryside for miles: mostly grazing for sheep, fields of grass bordered by hedges, but also pockets of farmland with crops – I think primarily wheat and vegetables round here – and, there, in the distance, shimmering waves of barley as it sways in the wind. Carl takes my hand.

'Now, here, with you, I do *get* it,' he says. 'Spending so much time at the office or on my laptop – well, it seems completely crazy, like – who gives a toss about that? But when I'm busy, it's as if I'm in this narrow tunnel, travelling very fast, too fast to stop and think for even a moment, and all I can focus on is making the deadline or landing the pitch or prepping for a client meeting. It's like some horrible never-ending marathon – only I have to compete at a constant sprint.'

'I know.' I stretch up to kiss him. 'You look worn out.'

There is something incredible about being in the countryside with someone you love and not being able to see a single other human being anywhere else. We face out towards the view again and stay like that for several minutes.

Above us, the sky is the clearest, fiercest blue you've ever seen, with only a few stray, filmy ribbons of cloud. The air is so fresh and clear I feel as if it's scrubbing me clean. With every breath, a little bit of the tension I've been storing up inside gradually dissolves. Then, far below us, I see a lone man out walking with a black and white dog, and that small sign of life brings us back to normality. We walk back to the cottage and potter around the garden, talking about how we'd like it to look, then go round the cottage, taking the time to savour how much progress has been made, though there's still quite a lot to do.

* * *

After supper, when we've both had some wine and are feeling even more relaxed, it's time to talk properly. I've bought some side lamps and they cast soft pools of light against the deep red walls. Although the sofa we've ordered, annoyingly, isn't being delivered until Wednesday, there's the big comfy leather armchair I picked up at auction. Carl sits on that and I perch on an antique wooden ship's chest near him.

'Now, please don't get upset Carl, but I do want to ask you about Stefan. When you come back from Bristol, you always look so stressed. Is that because of worrying about your dad, or because of St—'

'I'm OK, really I am. You don't need to fret about it. It's sweet of you, but it's not necessary.'

'But I think it *is* necessary.'

'You don't understand. You'll never understand.' He turns his face away from me then and I feel stung. I am *trying* to understand.

'Your family is different – you and Celeste and your mum. It's like the three of you belong to some special club, sharing family jokes and memories and teasing each other. Not all families are like that.' He sighs. 'I don't see why I have to go into this. I'll go and see a therapist if I need one, Nat. Look, you've seen what my parents are like. You can feel the blast from the Arctic when either one of them enters a room. They don't believe in talking and – I don't know – expressing your feelings or... or hugging... kissing, any of that. They don't deem it necessary. I was better off at boarding school. Honestly, Matron was way nicer to me than my mother ever was.'

It's so bleak, I don't know what to say.

'Well, you and Felix seem affectionate together, at least?'

He nods. 'With Felix, we've always had a goofing around kind of relationship. We used to play squash or go for a beer and we'd chat, sure, but mostly easy stuff – work, sport. But with Stefan it was different. You have to understand, my parents... they didn't talk to us, they didn't talk to each other. Once I was upset about something at school – I was about seven – and I was crying and my mother came in and she didn't even hug me.

'She said, "Oh dear, did you fall over?" I said "No," and tried to tell her about the boy who'd upset me, but she had this strange expression, half-frowning, half-smiling, and told me I shouldn't get upset about anything *silly*. I should forget it and come downstairs and ask Magda, our nanny, for a biscuit.

'And later when I saw my father he said, "Everything all right now, Carl? Your mother mentioned some sort of upset." And I said I was OK, but I clearly wasn't. Any half-decent human being would have sat me down and asked me what was the matter. But he didn't. He said, "Glad you've got past it. Doesn't do to *dwell*, you know."

'But Stefan wasn't like that. He would actually *listen* if I wanted to talk. And sometimes that's all you need – someone to take time to let you say what you're thinking. It wasn't that I was spilling my heart out to him every day, but I knew I could if I wanted to. In my teens, when I was going through a tricky time, he was the only person I could talk to.

'When Antonia slept with him, I was devastated, yes – but not really because of her – because of *him*. I felt bereft. Like he'd *died*. Like he'd been killed in a horrific accident. I cut him out of my life. I wouldn't answer his calls. But I had no one to talk to. Not Antonia, of course, not my parents, not even Felix.'

'But you must have still been upset? How did you deal with it?'

'Same way I deal with most things.' He leans forward

suddenly, with his head in his hands. 'Ignore it. Pretend there isn't a problem. Work so hard there's no time to think about it. That usually does the trick.'

'You do know that doesn't fix it, right?'

'Well, it's good enough in a way. It kind of works. It doesn't give you any headspace to think about anything else if you're really busy.'

'Or looking at your phone every second of the day.'

He has the grace to look embarrassed.

'After a while, it's not exactly that the pain goes away, but you have so many other things in your field of vision – urgent projects and people you have to call back and meetings you have to prepare for – that after a while you can't see the problem so clearly any more. It becomes more peripheral.

'Only every now and then the thoughts resurface and you catch yourself wondering about your brother. He hasn't tried to get in touch with you recently. Maybe he's happy never to see you again? Maybe he doesn't miss you at all?'

'I'm sure that's not true. And you spend time with him in Bristol?'

'Well – yes and no.'

'You must talk to him there, surely?'

'Of course. I don't ignore him, Natalie. But we don't *talk* talk. We speak as necessary about our dad's treatment and logistics, who's coming when. Mostly, only one of us is there at a time anyway, other than a brief overlap, or one of us plus Felix.

'But when we are there together, sometimes I look across at Stefan and I can sense that he's steeling himself to ask me, to see if we can move past it. Last time I was there, I could tell he was about to brave the subject, so I stood up and said, "Well, I'm knackered. I'm going to bed now."'

'Oh, Carl, don't you think you should have heard him out?'

'No, not really. Where's the benefit?'

'Well, you'd get to be close to him again for one thing.'

'I'm not sure I could ever trust him again. What if he tried to sleep with you, too?'

'Seriously?'

'Well, he might! He slept with Antonia. I told you – I don't trust him.'

'But don't you trust *me*? I'm not Antonia. You can't possibly think I'd sleep with your brother? Or with anyone other than you?'

He shrugs. 'I don't know anything any more. No, OK, I suppose not.'

'For God's sake, Carl. You *suppose* not? I know we got married quickly but you do *know* me by now. I have a million faults – I know that, I'm not blind – but I *don't* cheat and I *don't* lie. I wouldn't wander off and casually have sex with another man, and especially not your bloody brother, OK!'

'OK, OK, I'm sorry. I do know that you wouldn't. But I still can't get my head round Stefan doing something so appalling. What on earth was he thinking? Why did he do it?'

'Didn't you *ever* talk to him about it?'

'No, I was too angry. Once I knew, Antonia must have let him know that she'd told me. He called me – so many times – but I didn't answer. He even wrote to me, but as soon as I saw his hand-writing, I chucked the letter in the bin. I didn't read it.'

'But maybe he was trying to say how sorry he was? Or attempting to explain?'

'What explanation could there possibly be, Nat? Oh, yeah, I know I'm a strong, fit man of six foot two, but she overpowered me and forced me to have sex with her. Poor, poor Stefan, being taken advantage of by cruel, powerful Antonia. He's an innocent victim.'

'Of course I'm not saying that. I don't know why it happened. All I'm saying is that people make mistakes. We all do dumb things sometimes. And – and – even if there wasn't a reason... if you talk to him, maybe you'd get things back to how they used to be. You'd get your brother back.'

'Well maybe I don't want him back. I don't care any more. It doesn't matter.'

This is so obviously untrue that I can't even bring myself to challenge it. Carl's face looks like he's a little boy who's hurt himself but is desperate not to cry.

I stand up and go and put my arms around him and kiss him all over his face.

He kisses me back. 'How did I ever get through life before you were here to keep me sane?'

He pulls me close and draws me on to his lap.

'You've no idea what a difference you've made to my life, Nat. *My love.*' His voice softens and he kisses me again. 'You are *so* different from Antonia in every way, all good – not only physically, but in *everything* – like you're such an incredible cook but without making a massive palaver about it. Antonia doesn't cook but if she's assembling a meal, she makes such a song and dance. Everything has to be perfect and fussed over – finding the specific, best crackers to go with the artisan cheese that's she's driven twenty miles to buy. And there's the fact that you have your own business. Antonia couldn't possibly run a business; she's always in a flap about the tiniest thing. The way you've made a start on the garden, getting stuck in and dirt under your fingernails. I love it that you don't care about any of that – that you're so honest and real and true. Really, there can't be two women on earth who are more different from each other than you two are.'

Later, I lie in bed, looking up at the ceiling. Carl is asleep but I can't seem to fall to sleep myself. There can't be two women on earth more different? I know he was exaggerating, but now that I'm thinking about it, I can see it contains at least a grain of truth, and not only the obvious, physical stuff: Antonia is tall and blonde; I'm short and dark. She has a sort of languorous air while I'm always zipping about. She seems constantly bored. I'm never bored. She's perfectly groomed and I'm... not. She's always having her hair and nails done, or off for another facial, or booked in for a pedicure, or eyebrow threading or resurfacing (I don't even know what that is – it sounds like something to do with road-works rather than your face). So, I can see that it's true. But is that maybe rather odd? You'd think a man would go for quite a similar type. It's almost as if Carl chose me, not because he loves me, but because I'm as different as possible from Antonia; the 'Not-Anto-nia' aspects of me are more important than my being Natalie, my being *me*.

I try to shake the thought away and roll over closer to Carl. He's on his side, facing away from me towards the window. It's too hot for the duvet so we've shoved it off and have only a sheet over us. The sheet is right down at his waist. As it's so hot, we have the windows wide open and the curtains open too to let the air in. Outside, the moon is nearly full, its white light making it easy to see.

I know Carl needs his sleep but I wish he were awake so we could talk now in this half-light. I want to know how he really feels, why he's with me. I can't bear the idea that it's just because I'm like some sort of antidote to Antonia. I want him to love me for *me*.

I lightly touch his back and he stirs.

I say his name very softly.

He turns towards me and his eyes open a little.

'Mm,' he murmurs.

I stroke his arm. Lean forward to kiss his chest.

'Mm,' he says again, 'this is a good dream...'

'Is it?' I lean in to kiss him.

'Are you taking advantage of me while I'm asleep, Wife?'

'I'm considering it.'

'You might have to do all the work.' Then he suddenly pulls me on top of him and kisses me deeply. He tugs the sheet away from us and flicks it on to the floor so now there is nothing except us. His hands trace a shivery path down my spine.

He opens his eyes properly and looks at me.

'My beautiful wife.' He tucks my hair back on one side behind my ear.

Afterwards, we lie there, hot and breathless. I rest on his arm for a little while but then we're both so hot that I edge away, back to my own side.

'That was incredible.' He turns and kisses me lightly on the lips.

'It really was. I think I may have to hang on to you a bit longer.'

I get up to nip to the loo then and, in the bathroom, I can't stop the thought entering my head: was that different from how it was with Antonia, too?

I've noticed that when Carl doesn't want to have a potentially difficult conversation, one of his favourite ways to avoid it is by sending a text instead. It's almost impossible to have an argument by text. Yesterday was so lovely, but then he had to dash to London on the early train this morning for a whole string of meetings, and next weekend, when my mum's coming to visit, Carl will probably have to be in Bristol with his dad.

I have a long walk first thing after breakfast, and I've only this minute got back to the cottage when I see a text from Carl:

Hi. A is upset you left party without even saying goodbye. She did put a lot of time and money into it. Please extend an olive branch some-how… We do all need to get on! x

Oh. Did she really have to contact him about it? Looking back, I do see that leaving the way I did was really rude. At the time, it seemed obvious that they wanted to be together and so the only option was for me to leave. I've gone over it in my head a hundred times. Like Carl said, why didn't I take him quietly to one side and ask him if he wanted to be with Antonia? It didn't even occur to me. There's a name for it; I think it's 'confirmation bias'. You believe something to be true, so you only 'see' the evidence that supports that existing view and ignore anything that contradicts it.

Why didn't I ask him? I have an inkling. I think it was because I couldn't bear the thought of looking into his eyes and hearing him say the words: 'Natalie, I'm sorry – I don't love you. I still love Antonia.'

Better never to have to hear that, better by far to flee and run. So, I was the person who left, who took action, who didn't just sit there like a stupid fool, swaddled in self-deluding ignorance, waiting to be smashed to smithereens at the moment Carl came to his senses and the inevitable happened, and he left me.

Carl told Antonia I had to go because I developed a crushing migraine and needed to be somewhere dark and quiet.

I can't call Antonia out of the blue and say I thought she and Carl were getting back together, I just can't, and even Carl agreed I shouldn't say that because: 'She'll think you're barking mad. Let's stick with the migraine story, please.'

Last night, when we were talking as we got ready for bed at the cottage, Carl mentioned that Antonia has a book group and that maybe I should join it.

'*Really?*' I said.

'No need to sound so astonished. Don't assume that Antonia reads nothing but *Vogue*.'

'I didn't. I *wasn't*.' (I really was. I must stop being so judgemental).

'You really *were*,' he laughs. 'I'm not saying she has the same taste in books as you – but you might like the group – meet some other women a bit more like you, hmm?'

'Mm,' I say, trying to sound enthusiastic, but probably failing.

Late morning, in the village, I'm at the butcher's, trying to decide what to buy for supper and, as usual, unable to make up my mind. I'd love a roast chicken, but I'm not going to sit on my own, sadly staring at a whole chicken, reminding me that my husband isn't here to share it with me, and then have to work my way through the leftovers. In the end, I buy a single chicken breast because it's what I usually go for when I absolutely cannot choose, but I'm getting embarrassed that I'm taking so long. John, the lovely butcher, is getting used to me now, so eventually he prompts me with a gentle, 'Maybe a nice chicken supreme, hmm?'

My mind isn't really on tonight's supper, though. Yesterday, spending proper time with Carl was lovely but, if anything, it makes it even harder now he's had to dash off again. I am proud of him that he's doing the right thing, making the effort to go back and forth to be with his father even though they're not at all close. But I can see it's not helping that he also has so much on his plate at work. I have tried to ask him about it, if he wants to talk about it, but as ever, he says it's fine, it's in hand, no need to worry. If a tsunami were heading for our house, you can bet Carl would be the one saying, 'Don't worry about it – it's about to turn. It'll be fine.'

I'm toying with the idea of getting some sausages while I'm here, when the butcher looks up and says, 'Good morning, Mrs Moore.'

'Morning, John. Now what shall I have today? What would you recommend?'

Antonia has swept in. I turn to face her. Is she ignoring me? She must have realised it was me.

'Hello, Antonia. How are you?'

'*Me*? *I'm* extremely well, thank you.'

She turns back to John, but he looks at me.

'Is that everything for you now, young lady?' He winks. I think he says that to pretty much every woman under the age of eighty.

'Oh, could I have half a dozen sausages too, please – those ones there.'

Antonia is staring into the chiller cabinet as if transfixed by the display. Then she says, apparently addressing a steel tray of lamb kebabs, 'And are *you* feeling better?'

For a moment, I think she must be talking to the butcher, because clearly the kebabs have not been feeling good for some time. I look at John but he shrugs and nods back at me.

'Er – *me*? Yes, I'm fine thanks.' Better than what? Oh – *migraine*! I haven't seen her since I fled from the party. 'Antonia, I'm so sorry I had to dash away from the party. It was awfully rude of me, I know. I – I – really felt sick and horrible and had to – to be somewhere quiet.' That's true, so at least I don't have to look at my feet like a guilty child while I say it.

'Well, I'm sure you couldn't *help* having a headache, Natalie. I hardly think you conjured up a *fictional* migraine as a *flimsy* excuse to get away from my party... After all, what kind of person would do such a thing?'

'Uh – no, no, of course not. It was really incredibly kind of you to go to so much trouble with the party and everything. It must have seemed very rude and ungrateful of me. I do apologise.'

She shrugs and gives a slight sniff.

'I enjoy being a hostess. Still, it did seem a tiny bit...' She lets her voice peter out as if she can't even be bothered to engage in the conversation.

I put my purchases in my bag. I have to try a bit harder. Antonia is choosing lamb kebabs.

'Yes, and that one, John, please. No, not that one – the one underneath looks nicer. And the one at the back...'

'Antonia, Carl mentioned you have a book group?'

She nods, but doesn't turn to face me.

'And, John, could you set aside a large organic chicken for me on Saturday, please?'

'Certainly, Mrs Moore.'

'I'm not sure our little book club would be quite... highbrow enough for you.'

Antonia says this to a small jar of mustard she has taken off the display on top of the counter.

'Highbrow? Me?'

'Tell me, John, is this mustard very hot?'

'Not at all – and it's lovely-jubbly with sausages.'

She nods and puts the mustard with her other shopping.

'Well, I suppose you're quite the intellectual, aren't you?'

At this point, she's looking at John, who looks from one to the other of us, clearly confused, though he may well be an intellectual. I'm certainly not.

'I'm really not at all. I – I love to read, but my taste is very wide. I enjoy all sorts of—'

'Well, of course you're welcome to come along if you think it won't be too much of a let-down.'

'I'm sure it won't be. I'd love to – thank you.'

'But it's this Thursday evening at, um, eight. So, not an awful lot of time to read the book.'

It's Monday today so, actually, that's plenty of time.

I ask what it is and, luckily, it's a current bestseller which I already have a copy of, sitting in one of my to-read stacks. (That's hardly a coincidence: I have at least four teetering piles of books dotted around the house, so it would be a freak occurrence if I didn't have it.) If Carl sees me loitering by a bookshop, peering in the window, he drags me away – 'Please, please read the ones you have first before buying any more!'

'If you decide not to show up, or come down with some sort

of... condition, perhaps you would be kind enough to text me, Natalie. I do like to have an idea of numbers and so on.'

'Oh, yes, yes, of course – but I'll definitely be there.'

* * *

Thursday, 8 p.m. prompt. Antonia's drive is already full, so I park my van on the road. I recognise a couple of the swish, expensive cars of Antonia's friends, but I also notice a very old, dusty Citroën 2CV, a Land Rover with actual genuine mud on it, and a purple bicycle with a sweet, old-fashioned wicker basket on the front. Maybe there will be some *normal* women there?

I'm sure Antonia said eight o'clock, but it seems as if everyone else is already here.

I ring the bell and surprisingly the door is answered by Antonia rather than Katja.

As peace-offerings, I've brought an expensive bottle of red wine and a huge bunch of pure white lilies, which I've wrapped in gold tissue and tied with a raffia bow.

'Oh, Natalie, you did decide to come!'

'Of course – I said I would. Thank you very much for inviting me.' I proffer the wine and flowers.

'Oh, goodness. Well, there's really no need.'

'Well, I wanted to...'

'Oh, that's very sweet, but you shouldn't have.'

'I couldn't show up empty-handed.'

'But we have so much wine in the cellar already. Still, Dom always says there's no such thing as too much wine!'

They have a cellar? This house really is incredible.

'I hope you like lilies?'

'Oh. You really shouldn't have, Natalie...'

I think she's just being polite again but now I see she's frowning.

'...I'm afraid I can't accept these.'

'Please take them. I chose them specially for you.'

'No, no – oh, Natalie, I can't have lilies in the house because of Tabitha, you see?'

'Your cat?'

'Yes. Lilies are terribly poisonous to cats. Surely you knew?'

'Oh. No, I didn't, honestly. I'm so sorry.'

Does she really think I knew and am trying to kill her cat? So much for my olive branch.

'So...' She pushes them firmly back into my arms.

'I'll take them back to my van.'

'If you would.'

When I enter the hall a minute later, Antonia is standing, waiting there. She points towards the ground floor cloakroom.

'If you could wash your hands super-thoroughly, Natalie, that would be appreciated. For any traces of pollen, you know.'

'Oh, right, of course.'

I feel like a child who's been told off for leaving smeary fingerprints on the upholstery.

I enter their main reception room where there are eight or nine women. Some of them are Antonia's friends I met at the pool party, but I don't recognise the others. I think I can identify the owner of the bike, and of the 2CV, because of their clothes – faded jeans and one's wearing a tie-dye T-shirt and the other a loose linen blouse, but they are sitting together on the outer fringes of the group and there is no space next to them.

'Hello. I hope I'm not late?'

'Don't give it another thought,' Antonia says, though I'm sure she told me 8 p.m. 'Drink?'

Jinks, and a woman I don't know, shift along on one of the sofas to make room for me.

'You haven't missed anything,' Jinks says. 'We've only been bitching about our husbands up to now.'

Antonia passes me a glass of wine and says, 'Say hi to Natty, everyone! Sorry – oops – *Natalie*. Definitely Natalie. Don't want to get it wrong! Natalie is Carl's *second* wife and they've recently moved here to that neglected little cottage down the track. You know – the one where the owner died and wasn't found for a fortnight. The one where all the roof tiles were stolen. Such a shame.'

Is she saying it's such a shame that the tiles were stolen? Or that Mr Bailey died and wasn't discovered for so long? Or such a shame that we've moved here? Already, I feel wrong-footed. And 'second wife' makes it sound as if he'll be lining up a third one any day now. I smile tentatively and rummage in my bag for my copy of the book.

'Right. Who wants to kick us off then? Natalie, as you look ready there with an actual copy of the book?' She taps a long fingernail on her Kindle. 'Why don't you start?'

'Oh, OK. Do you have a format for the discussion? Do you talk about themes first or story or—'

'Goodness, no!' Antonia laughs. 'It's not a boring discussion programme on Radio 4, Natalie. Just plunge in wherever. There's no need to dazzle us with your intellect.'

'No, course not. I'm not... I wasn't.' I open the book and touch the pages, as if they might offer some comfort. I wasn't trying to show off. I'm doing my best to get it right. Now I'm worried that whatever I say it will sound pretentious, as if I'm trying to be clever-clever, and I'm not like that at all.

'Er... I really liked the story...' I say tentatively, trying not to dazzle anyone with my intellect even accidentally. I catch two of the women I don't know giving each other a look, a look that says: *Really? Is that it?*

One of the others interjects as I grind to an embarrassed halt.

'I thought the way the author used the imagery of the forest to echo the way the protagonist is struggling with her past was so effective – the metaphors about her being caught in a kind of thicket of memories, catching at her, entwining her in their branches, was incredible...'

'Yes! That's exactly what I thought.' I say.

The woman looks at me, clearly disbelieving because I'm the dimwit who said, 'I liked the story.'

'I'm afraid I'm still only halfway through,' says Jinks. 'I never manage to read more than a page or two in bed before I conk out.'

The discussion continues and I actually start to enjoy myself after a while. It's so nice to be around women all talking animatedly about something so interesting. Antonia, to my surprise, doesn't say very much, but when she's in the middle of making a rather good point about the ambiguous ending, I catch her glancing nervously at me, as if worried that I'm going to judge her.

As the conversation starts to wind down and shoot off at tangents on to other books and other writers, Antonia interrupts, saying, 'Now, forgive me everyone, but while I've got you all here, I'm going to be completely shameless and seize the opportunity to bend your ears about the village Christmas Fayre.'

'But it's only June,' I say, then wish I hadn't.

'Natalie, as you're a newcomer to the village, of course you can't possibly realise how much work is entailed in these key events.'

'No. Right. Sorry.'

'Now, one thing we absolutely must, must, must get sorted is...' she literally pauses at this point for dramatic effect as if she's hosting a game show, '... *Santa!*' She claps her hands together in excitement.

I nod sagely, as if I'm totally on board with helping to sort out Santa six months in advance.

Antonia is looking at me expectantly as if I'm going to leap into my van and drive to Lapland to issue a personal invitation. I smile cautiously. Why is she looking at *me*? I'm not doing it.

'So, Natalie, you'll speak to Carl?'

'Sorry – what?'

'To check he's up for doing the honours this year? Dom did it last year, and Carl did provisionally agree to step up this year.'

I'm speechless. *Carl?*

'Or I can speak to him if you don't feel you're up to asking him, Natalie? There are definite advantages to having the same husband at times!'

OK, now I do feel she's just trying to wind me up.

'I can ask him. I'm not promising he'll do it, but I will ask.'

'Excellent. And if he isn't keen, give me the word, Natalie, and I'll work my magic charm on him. I'm sure I still know exactly how to get round him.' She laughs. 'What next? Ah – music. A live band would be nice. Jinks, do you want to get on to that?'

I clutch my wineglass in one hand, my book in the other. Is this how my life is going to be – always at the mercy of Antonia and whether she's in the mood to torment me, like a cat toying with a terrified mouse?

25

FAMILY MATTERS

Hurrah! Mum is coming to see the cottage at last. I've driven over to see her a few times but this will be the first time she's seen the house, because only now is it fit to have anyone else stay over. It's not that it's all finished, but at least the roof, rewiring and plumbing are all sorted, the upstairs bathroom is done, and the kitchen and dining room are very nearly there, with only a few snagging tasks to do. The sitting room looks stunning, with its wide oak floorboards sanded and sealed, the red walls, and at last our extra-long velvet sofa has been delivered. The two smaller bedrooms are decorated, though not the big main bedroom that Carl and I will have when it's ready. Steve, the builder, is still trying to talk us into letting him knock out the later false ceiling – he thinks it would look amazing because the room would stretch all the way up to the roof ridge and we'd be able to see the original beams. His team don't work at weekends and they've cleared up, so I can enjoy a couple of days with no dust and no banging. Mum's only coming for one night. Carl is back in Bristol.

I'm in the kitchen, peeling potatoes to go with a roast chicken for supper when my mobile rings. It's Celeste.

'Mum says she's coming to see the cottage and stay over. Why haven't you asked me?'

This is typical of Celeste. No 'Hello', no 'How are you?' She bulldozes ahead.

'I was going to ask you, of course, but I thought you'd rather come a bit later, once it's completely finished. There's still quite a bit to do. It's not ready.'

'Why? Because I'm so mean and judgemental, you think I can't see past the fact that it's not perfect?'

Er, well, yes, obviously, but I'm not saying that.

'And there's no bedroom for you. Only two of the bedrooms are decorated and have beds in – a double and a single. Carl and I were sleeping on a mattress in the barn until recently. I've only – we've only just moved into the house.'

'I can bunk in with you if Carl's not going to be there. Or with Mum, if I have to. Though she's even more annoying than you are.'

'Oh, right...' Who could resist?

'Nats, don't you want me to come? Tell me if you don't – it's fine. But Mum called me and she seems to want me to be there.'

Why on earth did Mum do that without asking me first? And when Celeste says: 'It's fine,' I know that means: 'It's not at all fine.'

'No, of course I'd love you to come too. Mum's coming around four or five, but any time is OK. There are two fast trains an hour from—'

'Yes, I know. I looked it up already. Have you got any decent wine or only cheap crap?'

'Erm, I don't know... There's probably a bottle somewhere. Or I can go into the village.'

'Forget it – I'll bring some. See you later.'

* * *

Mum arrives first.

'Oh, but this is absolutely beautiful, Natalie! No wonder you fell in love with it. As I drove down the lane, I felt like I was entering a sacred enchanted dell.'

This is the way my mum talks: very sweet, slightly mad.

'I do think the setting is lovely.' I take her bag and put it inside, then we stroll round the area by the side of the house that I want to turn into more of a garden than it is now. For now, there are only a few rather boring shrubs and some bright bedding plants I put in to cheer it up, but I think it could look a lot nicer if I knew what I was doing.

'It's completely magical – and the house looks adorable. It's absolutely charming. That roof! The windows. The beams. The way it almost seems to have grown out of the land around it. You must love it.'

'I do, and I'm so pleased you like it.'

'And – listen!'

I listen but can't hear anything other than the odd chirruping bird.

'What?'

'*Nothing.* Glorious, precious *nothing* – apart from beautiful birdsong. Lord, do you remember in our old flat how much noise there was constantly? Buses thundering past on that awful main road, sirens at all hours...'

'The neighbours shouting at each other on the concrete steps... kids chucking glass bottles into the courtyard from the balcony to smash them... that old wino telling everyone to fuck off every time you passed him... Ah, who could forget?'

'Well, it wasn't ideal, no, but I bet it makes you appreciate this all the more?'

And she's right, of course, it does.

'Mum, Celeste's coming too.' We go inside and into the kitchen.

'Oh, that's lovely: both my little chickadees in one nest.'

'She said you called her and suggested she come? Tea?' I put the kettle on.

'Well, yes, that's right. I did.' She looks down. 'Natalie, I'm very sorry, I shouldn't have called her without checking with you first. That was quite wrong of me. It's only I do need to talk to you both and it seemed a good time.'

'Why? What's the matter?' I think of Carl's dad. 'You're not ill?'

'No, no. Tough as old boots, me. Nothing bad, I promise. It's rather awkward and... um... well, unusual.'

'Well, you can't leave me hanging now. You have to tell me.'

'I'm really sorry but we *have* to wait for your sister. Let's talk about something else. Show me the promised pond. Let's take our tea outside.'

Mum enthuses about the pond and we sit at the edge in the sunshine, watching the ducks dabbling to and fro. I try not to think about what important thing she could possibly have to tell us. She promised it's nothing bad and Mum never lies. She's been left a legacy by a distant relative? But would that be such a big deal? Oh God, I bet she's met someone: some awful ageing hippie, and they do tai chi and drink matcha tea and have tantric sex. Yeuch. I love Mum to bits, but she does have this unfortunate tendency to give you more details than you really want.

'Now, tell me about Carl's first wife – what's she like? Do you get on? I must say I do think it's awfully brave of you to move so close. I'm not sure everyone would be mature enough to handle it.' Mum leans forward and kisses the top of my head. 'It was a very *noble* thing to do. I know you wanted Carl to be able to see his children more easily. You're a kind girl. Now, tell me, tell me about the wife.'

'She's very... glamorous.'

'Hmm. Meaning?'

'Meaning, she's very glamorous.'

'Natalie, come on now. That's not a word you use much. What do you mean by that really? Do you find her intimidating?'

'Well, a little, yes I do. Oh, Mum, she's so *perfect* in every way. She's really tall and well groomed, with hair in perfect soft waves, like she's permanently about to walk up the red carpet at the Oscars. And their house is perfect, too. I love this cottage but their house looks like it's been styled for a magazine – outsize vases of flowers and gigantic bowls of fruit and no mess or clutter anywhere, and they've even got a swimming pool.'

'But what on earth would you want with a swimming pool when you have this idyllic natural pond right here?' She waves an arm towards the water. 'Look at that. It's glorious, the way those rushes dance in the wind. Have you been in for a dip yet?'

'Yes.' I smile. 'And it's lovely. You're right – it's pretty cold, but it's nicer than a posh pool really. You can chat to the ducks while you swim. That one over there with the funny crest sticking up is Humphrey. He's my favourite. Sometimes he even follows me around the pond. When I swim here, the dragonflies dance over my head. But the best thing of all is to float on my back and let myself just *be*.'

'Well, there you are then. And you have Carl and this magical house. Presumably, if she really were perfect, she and Carl would still be married, so I think you can safely cease to worry about it. Carl is very lucky to have you; I'm sure he knows it and thanks his lucky stars every single day. And if he doesn't know it, then the man's a fool. Now, I think I might be in need of a biscuit to keep me going until supper. What time is your sister turning up? And do you know if she's involved in a romantic *liaison* at the moment, or do I not want to know what she's up to? I know she'll only bite my head off if I ask her.'

26

THE NEWS

Celeste arrives in a taxi from the station.

One thing I will say about my sister is that she's incredibly generous. She keeps a small wheelie suitcase packed at her office in case she has an overnight work trip and out of it she now brings Champagne, a bottle of posh-looking red wine and a box of chocolates. And she's carrying a big bunch of flowers.

'You weren't kidding when you said it was tucked away. When the taxi driver turned off at the top, I thought he was bringing me down the lane to murder me. It's so creepy.'

'Thanks. I've been staying here on my own and I wasn't worrying about it until now.'

'Oh, you know what I mean. I only feel at home if I have traffic roaring past my door. Let's open some wine and you can give me the tour. Has Mum already had a look?'

'Yes, I have.' Mum emerges from the downstairs bathroom and kisses Celeste. 'It's beautiful. Natalie and Carl are doing a wonderful job.'

'Well, actually, Steve the builder and his team are doing a wonderful job. I mostly point to a paint chart and say, "That one, please," though I did sand the upstairs bedroom floor and paint the little room I was – we were – sleeping in over in the barn.'

We decide to open the bubbly as Celeste and I are ready for a glass, even if Mum isn't. I get out some olives and salted almonds, and give the chicken a baste and turn the roast potatoes.

'Right – the tour, the tour.'

'Shall we look at the garden first, though we haven't really done very much outside yet, other than the pots by the door, and I've put in a few plants by the side.'

We stand by the pond, watching the dragonflies dashing to and fro over the water.

'OK, I get it. I can see why you love it here.' Celeste raises her glass to me.

'It's really breathtaking, Natalie.' Mum puts her arm round me and kisses my cheek. 'Well found. And I can see you're breathing new life into it.'

'Well, it was rather sad when I first saw it. The setting was lovely, of course, but the house itself was depressing, with lots of dark carpet and low-watt naked lightbulbs.'

'But you managed to see past all that. You saw what it could be. Were the previous owners very ancient? Older even than I am?'

I nod, then say, 'Oh, Mum, it's so awful. The previous owner was an old man who died right here in the cottage. And no one found him for two weeks. That poor, poor man – all alone.'

'Oh, little peach.' Mum gives me a hug. 'These things do happen, you know. We live, we die. It's natural.'

'He wasn't murdered or anything truly awful?' Celeste asks.

I shake my head. 'No. It was heart failure. And he was eighty-seven.'

'Maybe you could plant something nice in the garden – you

know, in his memory?' Mum says. 'A rosemary bush? That symbolises remembrance.'

'You're right. I need to do something – to – to...'

'Ease his wandering spirit and grant him peace?' Mum closes her eyes as she speaks.

Celeste rolls her eyes at me.

'That's not exactly how I would put it, but, well – yes. I want to do a nice thing for him.'

We leave Mum to relax with her tea by the pond while I show Celeste the house. We start in the big sitting room.

'Hey, Nats, I'm sorry for what I said about Carl buying the house without you. He obviously does know you so well. This house is so *you*.'

'Really, do you think so?'

'Yeah, this room is beautiful. I'd never have thought of using such a strong colour but this red is really gorgeous, not overpowering at all. It feels really warm and welcoming. And I love this sofa.' She strokes the velvet with one hand as if it's an adorable pet.

'Thank you.'

'It's so great you're now doing it all together – even if Carl did find it without you in the first place. Now you're doing all that couply stuff, right? Picking out your china pattern or, knowing you, dragging him round weird dusty junk shops to find mismatched plates. Poor man. I should have warned him what you're like.'

'Mm. I know it's not cold but shall I light the fire later?' I look towards the fireplace rather than at Celeste.

'Nats? I was just kidding.'

'Yup, I know. It's OK. Actually, I need to go and baste the chicken again. Then I'll show you upstairs. There's a second little sitting room through there and a downstairs bathroom off the hall, but they're not finished.'

I dash out, into the kitchen and start humming as I take out the chicken to check if it's done.

I put the kettle on for hot water for the veg when I hear Celeste come into the kitchen.

'Chicken's ready,' I say. 'I'm going to let it rest while I do the gravy and the veg. You can have a nose upstairs without me, if you like.'

'Natalie.'

'What?' I turn away from her. The trouble with Celeste is she knows me too well. She knows I'm a hopeless liar so I tend to sidestep awkward things rather than telling lies. I sweep the carrots into a saucepan and put my hand on the handle of the kettle as if I'm about to use it, even though I've only just put it on so it clearly won't have boiled yet.

'What are you not telling me?'

'Nothing!' I turn to speak over my shoulder. 'Could you get some plates down from the dresser, please – over there!' I wave at the dresser even though of course she can see it.

'Look, Nats, I don't want to make you talk about – about stuff if you don't want to, but obviously you're upset about something – to do with the house or with Carl. Maybe I can help? OK, I'm crap at relationships, but I can listen, at least.'

I let go of the kettle but stay facing it. Maybe it'll be easier if I don't have to look at her.

'We're not doing lots of – lots of – couply stuff together.' My voice cracks then and I can't hold it any more. Before I know it, Celeste is holding me, holding me tight.

'You know you'll always be my favourite sister,' she says as I cry into her shoulder (even Celeste is taller than I am).

Then Mum comes in from the garden, calling out in the hallway, 'Do you know, I think I could manage a glass of wine now, if the claret elf has made a delivery...'

There's a pause as she clocks her daughters hugging in the kitchen, and then, being Mum, she doesn't say, 'Now then, why are you upset?' or, 'Goodness, what on earth's the matter?' She comes up close and I feel her arms go around both of us.

'My little chickadees,' she says, squeezing us. 'You're both so precious.'

We stand like that for a minute, then I rally myself and declare that I must get the veg on; Mum sets the table, Celeste opens the red wine, and I make the gravy.

And then we are sitting at the table. We have candles and a chicken and crunchy roast potatoes, and a mountain of vegetables, so for a while at least, there is happy chewing.

Then Mum picks up her glass and says, 'Well, here's to you, girlie! You've made a great start and it's going to be even more beautiful once you've done some more planting, I know. Well done.'

I smile and raise my glass.

'And...?' says Mum, which really is all that's needed.

'Look, you know Carl bought this house without me?'

'Did he, dear? That's a funny thing to do. Still, it is very *you* so I suppose it only goes to show he knows you very well.'

'It's very *me*, because I've chosen almost everything in the house. Carl and I had precisely one outing where we chose the bed and the bed linen for the big bedroom, and that's it. We haven't even used it yet because I've had to have a frame made for the base, which is taking forever. You know I mentioned his dad is ill? Well, Carl's had to be with him in Bristol – and I know this makes me sound horrible because, of course, he has to be with his dad and he's doing the right thing – but I've hardly seen him at all so I've had to make all the decisions on my own. And when he's not in Bristol, he's always dashing back up to London for work. He's almost *never* here.'

'But, Nats, it shows he trusts you, so that's not bad.'

'But it doesn't feel like that at all. Like that dresser with the plates on: I sent him a picture of it when I viewed it before an auction in Canterbury and he texted back, "Sure, fine". It doesn't feel like he trusts my taste or... or judgement, just that he doesn't care – about any of it.'

'Well, of course he must be preoccupied with his father, dear. You know that.'

'Ye-e-e-s, that's what I keep telling myself, but I don't know... It feels as if something else is going on. There's so much I don't know. We got married so quickly – which was wonderful and I do love him, I really do – but then all these things keep bubbling up and then I feel I don't know him at all.'

'What sort of things?' Celeste tops up my wine as I seem to have almost finished my glass.

'Well, OK, like his secret brother.'

'Secret brother? What – locked in the attic, you mean?'

'No, stupid. You met Felix, his younger brother, at our wedding.'

'Oh, yes, what a sweet boy,' says Mum, though Felix is thirty-eight.

'Well, it turns out Carl also has an older brother, called Stefan, who he literally never even mentioned to me until their dad got ill. Before that, Carl hadn't seen him for nearly three years.'

'Did I meet him at the wedding?' Mum sometimes comes out with things that make you think she's missing a chip.

'No, Mum – obviously not – as I haven't met him. How could he be a secret if he was at our wedding?'

'Well, I did wonder, dear... I thought perhaps he was in a different part of the reception or something...'

We had a small wedding of about forty people so how there could have been a different part, I really don't know.

'So, why did Carl keep him a secret all that time, you mean?'

'Exactly. It's quite a big thing not to mention, right? Did he really think I'd never find out?'

Mum suddenly knocks over her glass of wine and I leap to my feet to fetch a cloth.

'I'm awfully sorry, dear. That was clumsy.'

'It doesn't matter. At least we weren't using a tablecloth.'

Celeste gives Mum a look, then looks at me meaningfully. I wonder if she's worried that Mum is drinking too much. But she's only had about a third of the glass as she drinks a lot more slowly than Celeste or I do.

'Maybe he did have a good reason and will talk to you about it when the time is right,' Mum says.

'But we're married, Mum. There shouldn't be any secrets sitting between us.'

Mum tuts and shakes her head. 'That is one of the most unhelpful clichés bandied around about marriage: that there should be no secrets between you. In my view, every marriage is different. It's no use having flat rules that are supposed to magically work for everyone. They won't. Marriage is a journey. You find your path together, if you're lucky and if you work at it...'

We leave the rest of it unsaid. It seems rude to point out that I might not want to take advice on marriage from Mum, given that she and my dad split up when I was seven. I replenish her glass and sit down again.

'Talking of which...' she says, reaching for her wine and taking an unusually large gulp. 'Ah, now... this is a little bit tricky.'

Celeste and I set down our glasses as one and say, 'What is it?'

'I have something rather... er... difficult I need to tell you about your father and I'm not quite sure where to start.'

'Please say they've finally found his will and he's left us a ton of money,' Celeste says, rolling her eyes.

'Well, no, that's not quite it.'

'I was joking, Mum. More likely, you're summoning up the courage to tell us he was a bit of a crook. If that's it, it's not a huge surprise.'

'Ah,' says Mum. 'Right.'

'What? What do you mean?' I turn from Mum to Celeste and back to Mum. 'Why would you say that?'

'Well, it's only partly that.'

'Come on, Nats, didn't you wonder why he'd suddenly show up with loads of presents then disappear for ages?'

'Well... no. I mean, that's just what happened, so I never questioned it. I looked forward to seeing him so much. When I was little, he took me swimming every weekend. I *adored* him – you know I did.'

'Oh, Nats. He was a bit of a disaster, though, yeah?'

'But there is some good news,' says Mum, though she looks to be on the verge of tears. 'Some very good news.'

'He's left us a million quid and a football club in Spain?'

'No, Celeste, that's not it. Now I want you both to be very calm, can you do that for me?'

'Sure,' says Celeste.

'Carl always tells me to be calm when he's spotted a spider. Nothing makes me less calm than being told to be calm.'

Mum sighs and reaches out to take both our hands.

'Well,' she says, 'it's this. The thing is that your father is... in fact... um... *alive*.'

27

THE LIE

'*What*?!' Celeste and I say, as one.

'That's not possible, Mum.' Celeste and I exchange worried looks. Is Mum starting to get a bit... confused about things?

'Mum, don't you remember that you told us he had died? I was eighteen, in my first term at university, and I happened to be staying with Celeste for the weekend.'

'Of course I remember!' Mum looks irritated. 'I'm not losing my marbles, if that's what you think.'

'So, are you saying his family lied and, for some strange reason, they told you that he'd died?' Celeste squeezes Mum's hand.

'Ah. No, no, I'm not saying that.' Mum looks down into her wine, then takes a sip. 'I'm afraid I told you that he'd died, knowing that he was still very much alive. I can only say that I am really and truly very sorry.'

'But why on earth would you do that?' I can't believe it.

'It doesn't make sense.' Celeste is looking intently at Mum. 'You're a terrible liar, just like Nats. Why would you lie about something so big? Whatever for? What – because he didn't want to see us any more and you were trying to protect our feelings?'

Mum shakes her head. 'No, not at all. As you say, I don't usually lie. In my view, it tends to create more problems than it can ever solve, and I hope you both see it the same way. The fact is that Martin asked me to lie on his behalf and tell you that he'd died. He begged me to do it. I didn't want to, and I was never convinced that it was the right thing to do but – but I did understand his reasons, and so I agreed.'

'So *that's* why you called us on the phone,' Celeste says.

'Yes. I knew you'd have rumbled me immediately if I'd tried to lie to you face to face. I'm *so* sorry. I still feel thoroughly ashamed of myself.'

'It's not your fault, Mum. Nats, is there any bubbly left? I could do with another glass.'

'I think so. Hang on a tick.'

I go to the fridge and stand there with the door open, looking in as if I'm having trouble finding the bottle, even though of course it's right there in the door. I feel as if I've been hit with a sledgehammer. I can't seem to take in what Mum's told us. Dad is alive? Dad is alive. Dad is *alive*! It's incredible. The words are cycling round and round my brain, but beneath them, lurking in the shadows, darker thoughts come slithering towards me: he didn't want to see you... he didn't love you... he ran away... you don't matter... you don't count...

I will never, ever forget that night. Nearly eighteen years ago.

* * *

I am reading History of Art at university in Manchester, but this weekend I am staying at Celeste's rented flat in London because she has a fantastic, swish party to go to, where some man she has her eye on is going to be, and no way is she walking in the door on her own. Besides, she says, it's about time I had a proper taste of what a party should be like, not those sad cheap-plonk-and-twiglets parties that students seem to go in for.

Anyway, being at Celeste's is definitely a welcome break from our grotty, shared, student flat, with its odd combination of slobbiness – stacks of washing-up, sticky worktops, dingy bathroom – and obsessiveness: two of the four of us (not me) label every item of their food so that when you open the fridge you are confronted by pots of yoghurt and tubs of Marmite-smeared margarine, and even half-apples in cling film covered in fluorescent pink or green stickers with 'Property of Michaela – keep off!' or 'THIS IS ALEX'S'.

Celeste and I are getting dressed. She has flung aside the plain black skirt and top I have brought with me and is thrusting a choice of gorgeous dresses at me. They all seem fantastically glamorous and I feel like an imposter even considering them.

'They're not really me,' I say.

'Well, they bloody well should be!' Celeste barks back. 'Try on the gold.'

Gold! I've never worn gold in my life. Still, it's actually rather lovely – a soft, slightly shimmering fabric, not at all brassy or glittery, and the cut is very simple. I'm carefully pulling it over my head so as not to muss my hair when the phone rings.

'I'll come and do your make-up in a tick,' says Celeste, going to answer it.

'Oh, hi.' She mouths 'Mum' at me. Then she says, 'What is it?' Then 'Oh' and 'I see' and 'Oh' again. I draw closer until I am right next to her, trying to listen.

'Shall I tell Nats or do you want to? OK.' She passes me the phone and stays close. Celeste mouths something else at me. It looks like 'Dad' but that can't be it. We haven't seen him for well over a year – nearly two, in fact.

'I'm sorry, Natalie, but I'm afraid I have some bad news about—'

'You're dying! You've got cancer! No, no—'

Celeste grabs me by both arms so suddenly that I drop the phone. 'No, Nats, *no*. *Mum's* fine. It's Dad. He's dead.'

'Natalie? Are you there? Are you OK?' I hear Mum's voice coming out of the dropped handset as if she's far, far away, in a different country, a different time zone, instead of in her little cottage in Kent. Celeste picks up the phone and gives it back to me.

'What happened?'

'He's been quite ill for a while, I'm afraid... and then, you know...' her voice tails off.

'Was it cancer then?' I ask. One of our tutors at college is off having radiotherapy and I am somewhat obsessed.

'Oh, Natalie, darling, I don't want you to be too cut up about this. Your father had a good life in many ways and he—'

'But now we'll never see him again!'

Celeste puts her hand on my arm and takes the phone and asks Mum to hang on a tick.

'We haven't seen him for ages anyway, Nats.'

'That's not the point!' I pull away from her. 'We probably could have seen him if we'd wanted to.'

She lets the implicit thought hang in the air without voicing it aloud: we didn't really want to. We could have called him and asked him to visit, but we didn't.

'I just mean now it's not possible, now we can't—'

Celeste knows exactly what I mean. Now it's never going to get better, he's never going to turn up and suddenly be the dad we always wanted. There'll never be the possibility, however tiny, that he'll tell us he loves us again. There'll never be a grand reunion with hugs and tears and 'God, how I've missed you's.

The clock has stopped and things are as they are.

I take the phone back from Celeste.

'Well. Can I go to the funeral, at least?'

'Oh, no, dear. Do you really want to?'

'Yes. I really do.'

'Well – I suppose – ah. You see, it's a bit...'

'A bit what?'

'I'm afraid it's already taken place.'

'When?'

'Um – I'm not quite sure... Yesterday, I think. His sister called me and, you know, the family wanted a very small, quiet cremation with no fuss.'

'But *we're* his family!'

'Yes, yes, of course you are. I'm sorry.'

'How could they have done that without telling us? It's so mean.'

There is a pause.

'Oh, well, it's probably my fault. I imagine they thought it wouldn't matter very much to me as your father and I were divorced. I'm really sorry. I'm sure they didn't mean to – to...' Her voice fades away. 'It's my fault,' she says again. 'I wasn't thinking.'

'That doesn't make sense, Mum.'

'Hmm?'

I don't understand why I feel like this – angry and strange. But it's not Mum's fault. I mustn't take it out on her.

'I'm sorry, Mum. This must be hard for you, too.'

'Oh, peachy, you are sweet. I'm honestly fine. Don't worry about me.'

I wear the gold. Celeste does my make-up and I ask her to give me the full works. I want to be a vamp. I want to be gorgeous. I want to be someone else. She does my eyes with shimmering bronze shadow and smoky eyeliner and expertly paints my lips in confident red. My hair is pinned up, with curling tendrils framing my face. I look in the mirror as Celeste watches me, smiling to herself. It's the most extraordinary feeling: I'm looking at me, but it's not me. I look grown-up, sophisticated, assured and, well, sexy.

'Now do you believe me when I tell you you're beautiful?' she says.

'But it's the make-up. I don't look like this normally.'

'Oh, for Christ's sake, Nats, it's *not* the bloody make-up. Can't you see? What's wrong with you? You look amazing.'

I peer at my reflection, as if examining an interesting sculpture. It is sort of amazing. Still, who'd want to faff about doing all this every day?

'Come on,' says Celeste. 'Let's knock 'em dead.'

For a moment, the word reminds us about Dad and we face each other in silence. Then she picks up her bag and heads for the door.

'I think we should get very, very drunk,' she says.

28

THE TRUTH, THE WHOLE TRUTH AND NOTHING BUT THE TRUTH...

I take the bubbly out of the fridge and bring it to the table. I pass it to Celeste and slump back down in my seat.

There's so much I want to ask, but I don't know where to start. I look at Mum, trying to shape my maelstrom of thoughts into a meaningful question, but I cannot even say the word: *Why*?

Mum looks at me, then at Celeste, and takes our hands.

'There's no way to sugar-coat this, I'm afraid. Your father was sent to prison. When he received his sentence, he was devastated, of course, but the thing that worried him most – more than managing life in prison, more than anything – was the effect it would have on you girls. Now, as you know, by then we'd been divorced for several years anyway and his visits had become somewhat... sporadic.'

I nod dumbly, remembering how pathetically excited I used to get when he showed up, even though as time went on it was only a couple of times a year.

'Martin couldn't bear the thought that you'd be ashamed of him or that you'd feel you ought to visit him in prison, or that you'd have to lie about where he was to your friends. He believed that this was the only way.'

'What did he *do*?' I hear my voice ask the question but for a moment, I think it must be Celeste who has spoken. My voice feels detached from me. I have to know the answer, but I don't want to know.

The words hang in the air for a few moments before Mum takes a deep breath and gives us the story: our father had carried out a burglary on a mansion in Surrey. The planning had been thorough. The owners would be away over Christmas and New Year on a skiing trip. There were two members of live-in staff, a housekeeper and an elderly gardener/chauffeur, but both would be out at a New Year's Eve party. They were a small, experienced team: our dad, Martin, plus three others. Martin was the clever one, the strategist. He had thought of everything.

Except that he hadn't, because you can't. Life is unpredictable. The gardener felt ill while out at the party and came back early. And, instead of running away and calling the police, he confronted the intruders. They were masked in case of hidden CCTV and Martin wanted to tie the guy up and get out of there pronto, but one of the other men refused and started waving a gun around even though it had been agreed in advance – no weapons. Martin told him to put it away but instead he bludgeoned the gardener over the head. And the man *died*.

When they were caught, they were all sent down for aggravated burglary because of the weapon. Apparently, our dad already had a criminal record for breaking and entering and also for handling stolen goods. He swore he didn't know about the gun, but he was unquestionably the leader of the gang and the architect of the whole plan and was not believed. He was sentenced to eighteen years.

'I don't want to see him,' I say.

'Nor me,' says Celeste.

Mum argues on his behalf. She says that if Dad swore he had no part in killing the gardener, then she believes him.

'It's still his responsibility,' I say. 'He went there to burgle the house. It was his idea. No one made him do that.'

'And, Mum, how can you believe anything he says?' Celeste asks.

'Because I *know* when he's lying. I know him so well.'

'Oh, Mum, aren't you being naïve?' Celeste shakes her head.

'Why does he suddenly want to see us now?' I ask. 'What does he want?'

'Don't tell me – he's got kidney failure and wants one of us to stump up a kidney? Well, it's not happening. You can tell him to sod off and die, for all I care.' Celeste knocks back her wine but I can see her eyes are brimming with tears.

'*Is* he ill, Mum?'

'No, sweet pea. He's OK. I promise you he doesn't want anything. He actually called to say he wants to offer you both some money.'

'We can't take stolen money, Mum.'

'He must be crazy if he thinks we'd accept it.'

Mum explains that it's *not* stolen. He never got a penny from the burglary because they ran before they'd opened the safe. He's running an upscale ranch with riding holidays out in Portugal. The money is legit.

'Oh, no, Mum, you're not getting back together with him, are you?' Celeste asks.

At this, Mum throws her head back and laughs.

'Good Lord, no! Perish the thought!'

She carries on laughing for a bit then gradually calms down and wipes her eyes.

'Look, girls, I remain fond of your father, mostly because he helped produce you two – my finest achievements. So, really, how could he ever be unimportant to me? But when I first found out that he was... not earning his living honestly, that was the end for me. We argued about it, but after that I told him I couldn't be with him and that I wouldn't take any money from him either, unless he'd earned it. And I was clear I meant *earned* it.'

'Oh, Mum, poor you.'

She shakes her head. 'I'm not asking for sympathy. You girls bore the brunt of that decision because I didn't earn much myself. I'm afraid we were often short when you were growing up. You often had to go without things that other children had, and there were many times when I thought maybe I was wrong and I should take the money, but I didn't.'

'I'm glad you didn't.' I pat Mum's hand. 'You were right.'

'We managed OK,' says Celeste. 'And it taught us both to be super-careful with money.'

'Listen, your dad has married again. He's happy. He's very well off. He wants to do something nice for you two.'

'It wouldn't undo the past though.'

'I know that. And he knows that. He's done some bad things in his life, but he's not stupid.'

'Well, he is if he thinks we want to see him.'

'I did warn him that you might not want to, but...' Mum shrugs, '... he asked me to ask you.'

'Well, you have, and we don't.' I stand up abruptly and start clearing the table.

'So where is he now?' Celeste says, standing up too, to help.

'Actually, he's staying not that far away.'

I dump the dishes by the sink and spin round.

'*What*? Why is he here?'

'He wanted to be nearby in case you girls agreed to see him. He's staying at a pub in the village. The Cross Keys.'

'Well, you can tell him to go away. I don't want him anywhere near here.' God, can you imagine introducing my ex-con dad to Antonia? She'd have a field day: 'Dad, this is my husband's perfect first wife, and Antonia, this is my father, Martin, who's been in prison...'

'You have to make him promise not to try to get in touch with me.'

'I will tell him, but—'

'There is no *but*, Mum. I'm trying to build a new life here with Carl, and it's hard enough as it is with his bloody perfect ex-wife and spoilt brat daughter, and Carl never, ever being here. It's really *hard*, OK, and I can't deal with having Dad swaggering about the village with his gold chains and his spivvy leather jacket embarrassing me, OK?'

I sit back down at the table with a thud and glare at Mum, even though it's not her fault.

'Oh, he's not like that any more, Natalie, he really isn't. He looks rather respectable and distinguished now. His hair's grey. It suits him. I think he's what they call a silver fox.'

'I don't care what he *looks* like. I don't want anything to do with him. You tell him. Promise.'

Mum promises and she goes into the sitting room to phone him.

She leaves the door open, but whether by chance or on purpose, I don't know.

'I'm sorry, Martin, they don't feel ready to see you at the moment... Yes, yes, I did... as well as I could... You do have to try to see it from their point of view... Mm... Yes... I will do that if you think so.'

She comes back in while I'm putting on the kettle.

'Your father would like to reiterate his offer to give you both some money. He swears it's entirely legitimate, from the ranch venture and holiday flats he lets out. Purely as a gift – no strings attached, no obligation to see him.'

'No, I don't want it,' I say at the same moment as Celeste says: 'How much is it?'

I give her a look.

'What? I'm only asking.'

Mum tells us. It's a lot. Not enough to buy a house, but more than enough to finish doing up this one, enough to convert the barn into a guest annexe or even a holiday let. Maybe Carl would take me more seriously if I were bringing a bit more to the party, and the cottage restoration wasn't solely from the proceeds of his flat. Maybe he'd start to see me more as his equal. Or I could use part of it for a lease on a shop premises in Canterbury...

Celeste and I look at each other.

'We should take it,' she says, then turns to Mum. 'You absolutely swear the money is *clean*?'

'Are you auditioning for a part in a gangster movie? Who talks like that?'

'It's what people *say*.'

'Which people?'

'Crims' daughters – like us.' She makes a face at me and we both laugh.

'You take your share. I don't want it.' I pass Celeste a cup and push the cafetière towards her.

'You know I can't take it if you don't.'

'Why not? It's up to you. I'm not judging you.'

'God, I hate it when you're being perfect.'

'*Me!* I'm not remotely perfect. What's that supposed to mean?'

'Yes, you *are*. Nats, you don't know what you're like. You *always* do the right thing, you're always so honest, kind and caring, you're never mean or bitchy. You never lie. You set such high standards all the time. It's impossible for anyone else to live up to!'

'But I'm *not* like that. I often have mean thoughts. I'm always thinking bitchy things about Antonia, for a start.'

'Yes, but you don't act on them. You don't gossip about people, you're not rude to her, are you?'

'Now, now, girls, let's calm down, shall we?' Mum smiles at us both. 'Do you want to know what I think?'

'Actually, yes, I really do.' I sit at the table.

'Shoot,' says Celeste.

'I think you should take the money. Call it compensation for having to go without so many things when you were kids. Or call it a gift from the gods. Take it, enjoy it, put it towards the house or do whatever you want with it. Life is short and you probably won't get money handed to you on a plate ever again. There – I've said my piece.'

29

THE CRIM'S DAUGHTER

I was hopelessly disorganised yesterday and only prepared for supper so I've had to pop into the village again this morning for supplies for breakfast, for Mum and Celeste. I've picked up a fresh cottage loaf from the bakery (no sourdough left obviously – presumably Antonia has already swooped in like a vulture), and some sausages, bacon and eggs from the butcher, then I nip into the newsagent to buy a weekend paper. As ever, it has multiple sections – review, property, motoring et cetera – falling out of it and, as I come out of the shop, I can feel them slipping from under my arm. I rest my shopping bag on the pavement for a minute, so I can marshal the newspaper back together, and crouch down to fold it into the bag. As I stand up, I happen to glance across the street. There's a man standing outside the door to the pub opposite, staring straight at me.

He has grey hair now and he's wearing a cream linen suit. No gold chains. No leather jacket. But it's *him*. It's my dad. I know it's real but I feel suddenly detached, as if I'm watching him and myself from above, playing out a scene in a film and now I'm waiting to see what happens next.

He lifts his hand.

I don't know what to do.

I want to turn away and run to the van and drive off without a backward glance.

And I want to shout at him right here in the middle of the street. How dare he abandon me – us – then try to saunter back into our lives as if nothing happened?

And I want him to cross the road and hold me and tell me he's sorry, so, so, sorry, and that he missed me. Like I missed him.

I'm so confused. I feel absolutely paralysed. I can't deal with this now. I'm too stressed about Carl never being here. And I need to get back and make breakfast. Celeste gets incredibly grouchy if she doesn't eat. I can't think clearly. No. I'm not doing this. I *can't*.

I start to turn away then, but he shouts, '*Natty!*'

He is the one person who calls me that, the only person I've ever loved calling me that.

I start to turn back and, as I do, Dad steps straight into the road towards me. A huge black four-wheel-drive swerves madly with a screech of tyres and a blast of the horn. It drives off but Dad – my dad – is lying in the road.

'*Daddy!*' I drop the shopping and run to him, crumpling to my knees on the tarmac. 'Daddy, Daddy! Are you OK? Please be OK. Oh, please. *Please.*' I clutch his arm and lean in close and touch his cheek gently with my hand. I can't lose him now. Not again.

He takes my hand then and squeezes it, and I help him to sit up.

'I'm all right, Natty.' But he reaches behind him to rub his back and gives a sharp intake of breath.

'You're *hurt*! Are you hurt? Don't try to move.'

'I'm not hurt. It's OK.'

'Did the car hit you? He drove off! What a tosser!'

'No, no. I was startled, that's all. I jerked back out of the way and I stumbled.'

I carefully help him to his feet.

Now we are standing on the pavement, face to face. I reach towards him and try to brush the dirt off his smart jacket. People have stopped to stare, I realise, but now they see he's OK, they trundle on about their business.

'Don't worry, love. It's just a jacket.'

'Why did you step into the road? You always told us to be careful! *Stop, look, listen* – remember? What were you *thinking*?'

'I dunno. I'm an idiot. It threw me – seeing you. I was so desperate to see you, Natty, honest I was. Then it looked like you were turning away, like you didn't want to see me.' He looks down. 'I don't blame you, but I... didn't want to lose my chance.'

'I – I didn't know what to do.'

'Yeah, course. I'm sorry.' He lifts his arm up, offering me his sleeve to dry my tears, the way he used to sometimes when I was little, but I shake my head. 'Look at you now – all grown-up and beautiful. How are you doing?'

'I'm OK, thanks. I'd better get my shopping. I dropped it.'

We cross the road together and I gather up my bag and newspaper, looking down as if I need to concentrate because I can't look at him.

'Natty...'

'I don't get called that any more.'

'Oh. Right. Sorry. Listen, I know what I done – what I *did*—'

'*Natalie!*' It's Antonia. Of course it is. She's everywhere. I've moved to her hive, so why am I surprised to discover that the Queen Bee is at the centre of everything?

She dips to kiss me on both cheeks.

'How *lovely* to see you!' She always says that, as though I'm her long-lost sister she hasn't seen for five years, even though it was only on Thursday after the book group that she was trying to boss me into using her upholsterer to do our curtains – everybody round here is described as Antonia's possessions – *my* builder, *my* decorator, *my* interior designer, *my* plumber, *my* upholsterer. She probably refers to me as *my* husband's Wife Number Two. I tried to explain that I was intending to make the curtains myself, but Antonia looked completely baffled and asked if Carl's work was drying up. She doesn't understand why you might want to do something yourself, that it's not necessarily about the money.

'Oh, hi. I'm afraid I have to dash, Antonia. I've got guests at the cottage.'

'Ooh, guests! Are these your first? How exciting! I didn't think it was finished yet.'

'No, it isn't. It's getting there, though.'

'Well, you're so brave – that's marvellous. I wouldn't even think of letting anyone across the threshold until it was all absolutely one hundred per cent perfect, but that's silly old me for you!' She shrugs and gives a little laugh as if she's describing an utterly lovable peccadillo. 'So, who are your guests then?' She looks sideways at my dad, then back at me. 'Do tell.'

'Just family. I really have to go.' I gesture to my shopping. 'Can't keep them waiting for breakfast.' I smile and heft the bag on to my shoulder.

'And are you staying with Natalie, too?' Antonia has turned to Dad and is addressing him directly. Why can't she keep her nose out of it? It's none of her business who he is or where he's staying.

Dad looks at me, then at Antonia, then back to me.

'Ah... er... no... I...' He meets my eyes. 'I happened to be in the area.'

'Really? In our little out-of-the-way corner of Kent? How intriguing! Whatever for?'

Dad looks her right in the eye. He's not keen on people being nosy either.

'Business,' he says, without elaborating. 'I bumped into Natty just now.'

'*Natty*! You mustn't call her that, you know, or she'll bite you!' Antonia laughs uproariously, as if she's made the cleverest joke. 'It is absolutely forbidden. Our Natalie doesn't let *anyone* call her that.' She leans in towards my dad conspiratorially. 'I suspect it was what her first great love called her. It was obviously someone very *special*.'

Dad and I exchange a look. It was his name for me and it reminds me of him. He knows that.

'No, it wasn't. I just don't like it.'

I can just see Antonia winkling the whole horrible story out of Dad and then I'll be the crim's daughter for ever. I jerk my head a fraction to one side to indicate he should go.

'So...' Antonia puts her hand on my arm to waylay me. 'Aren't you going to introduce me to this distinguished gentleman?'

Dad looks at me, waiting to follow my lead.

'Should Carl be jealous about this mystery man? I know he's away. Have I tumbled into a naughty liaison? Ooh, I know, shall I send him a little text to tease him?' She laughs and reaches into her poncy designer handbag for her mobile.

What is wrong with her? Why can't she sense that I don't want to talk to her now and graciously back off like a normal person?

'Actually, no, Antonia. There's zero mystery but as I've already told you I have to get back to my guests. I really don't have time to chat. Sorry, but there it is. Have a good day.'

Antonia's face falls. She looks like a pantomime character acting outrage. No one ever says no to Antonia.

I'm not leaving my dad, alone and defenceless, on the street with Antonia ready to dissect him, no matter what he's done, so I link my arm through his and march him off along the pavement towards my van.

I hear a funny snorting sound, so I look and see that Dad's laughing. His whole face is creased up and he's leaning over like he can't walk. I'd forgotten how he looks when he laughs: he gets the giggles and he can't stop, and then everyone around him ends up laughing too.

'Jesus – well, you told her! She's a piece of work, that one, isn't she? How nosy can you get? But you were brilliant! I love it: *There it is. Have a good day*. Priceless!'

I smile. I am quite proud of myself, though no doubt Antonia will complain to Carl and he'll tell me off later. But, for now at least, I don't care.

'You know, she really *is* a piece of work. She's my husband's ex-wife.'

'Fuckin' hell. What's she doing in your village?'

I unlink arms and stand facing him.

'It's not *my* village. It's *hers*.'

'Well, she ain't the Queen though, Noodle, is she?'

'No, but she was here first. We bought a house here so Carl could be nearer his kids as they live with her.'

'Oh, right. That was nice of you, Natty – agreeing to that. Not easy.'

'I bet you're thinking: well, that was a bloody stupid idea, so I should tell you it was *my* idea. And it *was* stupid. Unbelievably stupid. And I only have myself to blame because I suggested it.'

'I'm sure you meant well, love.'

'You know I did. I really did. And I – I—' The words won't come. They feel like sharp stones, stuck in my throat.

He puts a hand on my arm but I shake it off at once.

'I just thought it would be good if they could see their dad more often. You know. Whenever they wanted to. If they wanted to. Because it's good for kids. To see their dad. If they have one. So, there you are.'

He looks down at his feet then.

'Right,' he says. 'I guess so.'

He takes out his handkerchief and wipes his nose briskly.

'Well,' he says, 'that was kind of you, Natty. You done well. You got a good heart.'

No, I haven't, I want to say – I *haven't*. Half the time I hate myself for making us live here, and Antonia's always trying to tell me what to do, and Saskia looks down on me, and Carl is never here, and sometimes I'm so lonely without him I feel as if I might shatter into a thousand pieces. It was a stupid, stupid idea, trying to make up for the past, to try to give Carl's kids what I didn't get to have myself. You can't change the past. It is what it is. I don't need my dad now. I needed him when I was growing up. It's too late, it's all too late. I can't fix it. I can't fix any of it.

'They do love their dad,' I say.

He looks at me and says, 'And I bet he loves them like you wouldn't believe. I bet even if there were times when he didn't tell them or didn't know how to tell them, or whatever, because – because some men are just bloody useless at that sort of thing, still, you know, I bet he loves those little kiddies to bits.' He nods emphatically. 'I bet he does. I know he does.

'Listen, Natty, I know what I did was wrong – really wrong – and I'm not asking you for anything. But could I maybe come with you now – and see Cely too?'

I pause, unsure what to do. But no, I'm not going to spring him on Celeste. That's not fair and she wouldn't thank me for it.

'No. I need to tell Celeste I've seen you first, OK?'

'I'll go and have a coffee and you can call me later. Is there anywhere that does a decent coffee round here?'

I laugh.

'Look at you – all sophisticated! There's a massive choice of two cafés. One has better coffee, but the other one is run by a really nice woman so I usually go there. It's called The Copper Kettle – along there on the right. The other one's further down on the opposite side.'

I turn towards the van, then back again.

'And – Dad – Martin,'

His shoulders slump.

'Yeah?'

'If you get chatting to anyone, the waitress or whoever, well, could you not... you know...'

I can't look at him.

Don't tell them you're my dad. Don't tell them your life story. Don't tell them you were in prison.

He nods. 'Right. If anyone asks, I'm your mysterious uncle, back from overseas...'

'No, you don't need to make things up. Just ...' I shrug.

'Just don't offer information.'

'Right.'

'I get it. One thing you learn in— inside: know when to keep your mouth shut.'

Back at the cottage, I unpack the shopping and pass the news-paper to Celeste, who fishes out the gardening section to give to Mum.

'Proper cooked breakfast, yes?'

'Lovely!' says Mum. 'So nice to be cooked for.'

'No mushrooms for me, please,' says Celeste.

'I know. Mushrooms are the devil's work.' I get out the big frying pan and another one for the eggs and ask Celeste to make tea or coffee.

'Mum, there's time for a little wander in the garden before breakfast, if you want? We'll give you a shout when it's ready.'

Mum goes outside. In bare feet.

'So, guess who I saw in the village.' I know I should simply tell Celeste but I'm worried and somehow it seems right to try to make light of it if I can.

'Was it Number One, the one true wife, who reigns supreme, you lowly interloper?' Celeste says as she fills the kettle. 'How very marvellous for you to be able to share the pavement with her. Did you pay homage?'

'Well, actually, you're right. I did see her. But I also saw... um...
Dad.'

She thunks the kettle down on the worktop.

'What?'

'He stayed at the pub in the village last night – remember,
Mum told us he was staying nearby?'

'Is that why you insisted on going into the village – to see
him?'

'No, of course not. I went in to get the food for breakfast. I saw
him by chance.'

'Did he try to talk to you?'

'Yes, I – well, I did talk to him for a minute or two.'

'*Why*? You were the one being all high and mighty and not
wanting to see him!'

'I know. I *know*, but it was different, suddenly seeing him. And
then – look – he stepped into the road and nearly got run over
and so I ran across to check he was OK. It wasn't his fault.'

'Well, it sounds as if it was his fault. Why did he step into the
road? What a moron.'

'When I suddenly spotted him, I was completely fazed. All
these things were whirling through my head – how angry I was
with him – I wanted to scream at him. And I wanted to ignore
him completely, spin on my heel and walk away as if I didn't give
a toss. Oh, Celeste, you know, I did turn away. It was my fault he
nearly got run over. I feel awful.'

'It's *not* your fault. None of this is.'

'Hmm. Also, I really wanted to see him. I couldn't help it.'

Celeste puts her arms around me.

'It's OK, Noodle, I know it's complicated. I don't really know
how I feel about him either. I mean – I do – I'm fucking pissed off,
for a start. But I can see that I'm angry because I'm also really sad.
I'm not saying I would have wanted to visit him in prison because

maybe that would have been much worse, but I would have liked to *know*, so we at least had the choice.'

'Exactly. But do you want to see him now?'

'I honestly don't know. Can we have breakfast first? I can't think till I've eaten something, at least.'

Mum comes in from the garden then.

'How is my little head chef getting on? I seem to be ravenous this morning. Normally, I have porridge with a sliced apple but must admit I'm looking forward to a proper cooked breakfast. Though only one egg for me, Natalie, please.'

'Nats saw Dad in the village, Mum.'

'Goodness. Did you? And how was that?'

'Completely strange and oddly familiar at the same time. Though surreal to see him in the village.'

'And, Celeste, would you like to see him too, do you think?'

'I don't know, Mum. If Natalie hadn't bumped into him, I think I'd have been perfectly prepared not to see him at all. I mean, what kind of person pretends to his own kids that he's died?'

'I think he was so deeply, deeply ashamed of what he'd done and of being sent to prison.'

'So he bloody well should be! Why couldn't he get a normal job and earn money like a normal person? We wouldn't have cared what it was. He could have cooked in a café or whatever...'

Celeste waves towards me at this point and I know we're all remembering Dad did the best breakfasts. Before he left, when I was little, he'd pretend he was a chef and put on a hat and a stripy apron. We'd have to call out our order and he'd relay it back as if he were shouting to a waiter across a busy café kitchen instead of only three feet away with me and Celeste perched on high stools at the counter, swinging our legs.

'He could have been a bin man, a street sweeper – anything – so long as he *earned* his money.'

Mum comes up and gives Celeste a squeeze.

'I know, my peach, I know. I felt the same way. But...'

'But *what*? Don't make excuses for him.'

'I'm not. It's not my job to do so. If you do agree to see him, I'm sure Martin will do his best to explain.'

Celeste snorts.

'Cely, I do think, if you can stand it, then we should see him.'

'What made you change your mind? *You're* usually the one taking the moral high ground. *You're* the one who never does anything bad.'

I shrug. 'It's just...' I focus on doling out the food on to the plates and pass them over. 'He's all there is. It's not as if there's a choice of dads and we can pick a better one, can we? And maybe if we at least talk to him – for half an hour – maybe we'd start to understand a bit more. What do we have to lose? If he starts trying to justify himself or what he did, we can say, OK, well, sod off then.'

Celeste stabs her sausage as if trying to kill it.

'OK then – but remember it was *your* idea.'

* * *

I say to Mum she can call Dad to tell him he can come over. Then she passes the phone over to me to explain where the cottage is.

Less than half an hour later, we hear a car coming down the lane (I keep popping outside because I'm so nervous). Dad pulls up next to my van and Mum's old Renault. He's driving a BMW sports car – gun-metal grey – with the hood down.

'Flash car.' I say, lifting my hand in a half-hearted way.

'Just a rental.' He gets out and comes towards me as if to hug me but I hold up my hand.

'Let's take this slowly and see how we go, OK?'

'Fair enough.' He looks down, abashed. 'Cely still here?'

I nod.

'This your spread then, Natty?'

'Yup.'

'You done well, love. Nice place. Beautiful setting. Bit of land, too?'

'Yes, all this area around the house and up to that fence, and also that field there.' I wave towards the field beyond. 'More than enough for us.'

'And you got married? I'm sorry I wasn't... that I didn't...that I wasn't there, you know.' He pauses.

Of course, I didn't invite him because I didn't know he wasn't dead at that point, but the thought crosses my mind that perhaps I wouldn't have asked him anyway. '*Yes, this is my ex-con father...*' introducing him to Carl's posh parents.

'I would at least have sent a present. Cash or something.'

'I know. It's OK. It was only a small wedding anyway. Whirl-wind romance.'

He smiles. 'And is the lucky man here, too?'

'No. His father is ill so he's away seeing him.'

Celeste comes out then and stands at a distance.

'Hello, you,' Dad says.

She nods and gives a small wave, as I had, but doesn't speak.

Then Mum comes out too and Dad goes towards her and they kiss on the cheek like affectionate old friends. Celeste gives me a look and rolls her eyes.

I make a pot of tea and bring it out to the garden.

Dad asks how long we've lived here and I explain, and tell him about the roof and how much work it's needed. He tells us he's bought a ranch, with horses, up in the hills in Portugal, to offer riding holidays, plus he's got some holiday flats on the coast, and he also has a few commercial properties in the UK he lets out.

'So is that how you've made your money? You swear it's completely kosher?' Celeste asks, frowning.

'Hundred per cent – I swear.' He makes a quick crisscross sign over his heart and raises one hand as if swearing in court. Huh.

'You could maybe do with a bit extra, Natty-love, if you're doing up this place?'

I look across at Celeste. I could certainly use some money to get a lease on a shop in Canterbury. I can't wait to start earning my own money again, to feel like I'm contributing something. And some to do up the barn. A stray thought is niggling at the back of my mind though, and I can't quite pin it down. Something doesn't fit properly.

'Well, maybe...'

'Girls, you should take the gift your dad is offering,' Mum chips in. 'Whatever your father may have done – and I know he's deeply ashamed of his past – he has promised me that this money comes from his property rentals. And the ranch holidays.'

'You're saying he's ashamed.' Celeste looks at Mum. 'But he's not, is he?'

Dad looks down into his tea cup. It feels so odd to be seeing him here, as if two separate parts of my life have suddenly collided and I can't quite make sense of what I'm seeing.

'I *am*,' he says simply.

'Is that *it*?' Celeste asks.

'I can't make excuses for what I done. What I did,' he corrects himself. 'I was greedy and I was an idiot – and that's a recipe for disaster.'

'You mean an idiot for committing crimes?' I ask. 'Or for

taking someone with you who turned out to be violent and impulsive?'

'Both. But I mean for getting mixed up with dodgy types in the first place, and for thinking there's a short cut to making money. Stupid!' He suddenly punches his fist into the palm of his other hand.

'You have to understand, girls, that your father had a very difficult upbringing.' Mum and Dad look at each other. 'No help, no encouragement, no support of any kind. And no money. That's not easy.'

'But that's true for lots of people and they don't all break the law!' I hear my own voice and think I sound like a kid. Naïve. Rosy-spectacled. Wanting everyone just to work hard and do their best the whole time, then everything will work out fine, even though I know that's not true.

'It's OK, Judy. I won't make excuses for myself.'

He puts his cup down.

'Anyway – can I get a tour of the place, Natty? Show me round.'

'OK.'

Mum and Celeste come too. Dad says all the right things about the downstairs, even though it's still not finished. We head upstairs and into the largest bedroom.

'This is all right, isn't it? Really good size. What's happening in here then?' He turns around. It's still completely empty.

'It will be the main bedroom. For Carl and me.' What's the point? I think. Carl's never here. Will we ever get to sleep in this room together? 'The builder thinks we should knock out the ceiling. It's got amazing beams hidden above it. You can take a look, there's a hatch inside that cupboard there.'

I asked Steve to put off decorating it until we decide about the ceiling. I have tried to get Carl to discuss it, but I can never pin him down. It's as if he doesn't care about making our bedroom special. Now I've stopped asking him because it makes me feel so sad.

'Sounds like a plan,' Dad says. 'Can I have a recce of your barn?'

We go outside and head towards the barn.

'This is massive. You could use this for all sorts.'

'You could use it to host painting workshops,' Mum says. 'Or meditation – something like that. Zen retreats. Tai chi classes. Something peaceful.' She closes her eyes and starts breathing deeply.

'I can't actually teach painting or meditation, though, Mum. I don't know about anything much, other than clocks.'

'Well, someone else could do that bit. You could provide the venue and the idyllic setting.' She waves a hand around airily as if it will all magically fall into place with barely a thought.

'And lunch,' Celeste adds. 'You're a really good cook.'

'You could rent it out for small conferences,' says my dad. 'There's good money in that. Or for parties, events. Or – simplest thing – convert it into a holiday let.' He marches off into the end area. 'Loads of space, two bedrooms, big reception room. You've already got a shower in there. Kitchenette the other end. I've done a few conversions myself, could give you a hand. Advice and that.'

'I'm not sure Carl would like guests staying so close to the house.'

'Oh. Fair enough. Or he could run his business from home? What does he do? Good job, is it?'

'He's in PR.'

Dad makes a face. 'At least he's not a banker.'

'Dad! You're hardly in a position to be making sniffy comments about other people's jobs!' Celeste says.

'Yeah. Fair point.'

It suddenly clicks what's been bugging me at the back of my mind.

'Anyway, Dad, I meant to ask you, how come your ranch holidays have been so successful so quickly? I mean I don't understand how you can offer to give away this money so soon.'

'Judy?' He turns sharply towards Mum. 'I thought you would tell them the whole story?'

Mum looks at us, then back at him.

'Martin, I think you should do it. It's not my responsibility to try to explain it all to them, is it?'

'No, no, you're right, course you are.' He puts his hands in his pockets then and his demeanour shifts from well-off, confident businessman to apologetic and hunched small boy who's broken the best vase.

'*What*?' Celeste and I both say at the same time.

'It's... sorry... I thought you knew. I been out a while, girls. I made my money doing up and developing property in the UK once I was out on licence. Then I moved to Portugal and got the ranch, and a couple of flats. But I didn't just get out last week.'

Celeste comes over to stand next to me and I say what we're both thinking.

'When? When did you get out?'

'Well, it's been a while, you know. I wanted to – you know – make something of myself before I got back in touch so you wouldn't be ashamed of me. Make you proud, like.'

'*When*?' I repeat.

'Eight years.'

Eight years? He's been out of prison for eight years. That's a hell of a lot of days in which not to call someone, not to write, not to send a fucking postcard, even. I am so angry I can't even speak. I take Celeste's hand and squeeze it. Dad looks at us and I look him back, straight in the eye. I wish my vision were a flame-thrower and could raze him to the ground.

'I'm sorry, girls, truly sorry.'

I turn away.

'You have to go now,' I say.

'Natty.'

'No!' I raise my hand like a shield. 'Please go.'

He looks at our mum and she lays her hand briefly on his arm and says something to him quietly. I leave the barn with Celeste and we walk down to the pond and sit on the grass looking across the water at the reeds moving in the breeze and the dragonflies weaving back and forth. I try to imagine what it would be like to be a dragonfly in this moment, to have no worries, no past, no fears, no anger, nothing to think about other than moving from this reed to that one.

I am sitting with my back to the barn but Celeste reports that Dad has now left the barn and that Mum's walking him round to his car.

I hear the engine start up and the sound of him driving up the track. And then he is gone.

'I'm sorry,' I say to Celeste. 'I'm sorry I made you see him. You didn't want to and I talked you into it.'

'Not your fault, Noodle. You were trying to give him a chance, that's all. You always do what's fair.'

I shake my head, too upset to speak any more. I don't want to be fair. I'm all done with being fair.

31

Carl isn't due to come home until tomorrow. I don't know why I even mention it – Carl's being away – because that's his default setting now. I should get a loudhailer so I can run through the village shouting about it on the very rare occasions when he's actually here. I must sound mean and bitter. I know he can't help it, but I feel like I've had enough. Dad, Carl, Antonia, Saskia. I'm sick of being treated by everyone as if I don't matter, like I don't count.

My dad's been out all this time and didn't even bother to get in touch, and now he wants to give us money as if that will make up for all those lost years. It *doesn't*.

I call Carl but it goes straight to voicemail. Perhaps he's at the hospital again. I realise that I've lost track of where he is; I don't even know if he's still in Bristol or gone back to London to be at the office. I only know that he's not here with me. Maybe I shouldn't bother him with stuff like this, but I have to know what he thinks about the ceiling. I had a text from Steve saying:

Time to decide! Let's go ahead with the ceiling! Bet you'll love it.
Swinging my sledgehammer in readiness!

I text Carl:

If we take out bed ceiling, it will give you more headroom, Tall Husb.
Need to decide. What do you think? Nx

I walk into the village as I really need the exercise and to clear
my head. I'd love a proper, long swim in Antonia's pool but I'm
not in the mood to deal with her today. I can go in the pond later.
It's really hot today so it should be lovely and refreshing.

At the greengrocer's, I'm looking around for a minute,
deciding what will go with supper tomorrow and realising I
should have chosen the meat or fish first, when Antonia swoops
in. Of course. Why did I think I could dare venture into the
village for half an hour without tripping her secret radar that
makes her spring up wherever I go?

'Oh, Maisie, be a love and give me some of those apples,
would you?'

'Morning, Mrs Moore. Actually, this lady was here first. Mrs
Cameron, isn't it?'

Antonia turns towards me.

'Hi, Antonia.'

'Oh, I didn't see you! It's only Natalie. Natalie, you don't mind,
do you? Please, please! I've got to hurry home because my hairdresser is coming at eleven and I look like a complete scarecrow!
My hair is an absolute disgrace.'

Sometimes I wonder if Antonia is inhabiting a parallel
universe, in which hair that is ninety-five per cent amazing is an
absolute disgrace.

'Sure, go ahead.' I wave my hand towards the produce. Why

did I say that? Why do I always let everyone go first? I mean, it's true that I don't really mind if I'm not in a hurry, but I have things to do, too. I have a load of compost being delivered for the garden at eleven, so I'm not in any less of a rush than Antonia is and in fact the cottage is further away and I'm on foot.

As ever, Antonia makes it sound as if she's buying only one thing then proceeds to order nine or ten bits of this and a little of that.

'You're an absolute darling, Natalie, thank you! I'm in a tearing hurry, as usual!' She rolls her eyes. 'I honestly don't know what on earth I'd have done if you hadn't let me queue-jump!'

I shrug. 'Well, you'd probably have done what everyone else has to do...'

'Oh?' Antonia half turns towards me as Maisie picks up the box of fruit and veg and takes it out to Antonia's car.

'You'd either have had to call your hairdresser to say you'd be a bit late, or you'd have had to buy up the greengrocer's later on in the day when you have more time. Like a normal person.'

'Oh. Well. Yes. I suppose you're right.'

I cross my arms and wait for Maisie to come back in.

'But, as you say, I'm *only* Natalie, so I can wait.'

'Oh gosh, Natalie – did I really say that? I honestly didn't mean it like that. You know what an awful fool I am. Speak first, think later, that's me.'

Maisie comes back in and turns to me, smiling.

'Now, Mrs Cameron? What can I get you?'

'Call me Natalie. Please.'

I turn away from Antonia and I hear her quiet, 'Bye then' as she leaves.

I suddenly feel as if I'm about to cry. What on earth is the matter with me? I lean in close over the grapes to shield my face for a moment, and select a bunch. I realise Antonia's done exactly what she did the very first time I ever saw her, before I even knew who she was – she's pushed in front of me because she thinks I don't matter. And now, months later, absolutely nothing has changed. I still don't count.

'We've got some lovely local tomatoes fresh in, too. Really good flavour.'

'Great, yes, some tomatoes then. And one of those lettuces, please.'

I pack the items carefully into my backpack. So much for my poncy willow basket – I never use it. I was going to be a country lady-who-lunches, swanning up and down the high street with my purchases but, actually, a basket is completely impractical for when I walk into the village – far too wide to be easy to hold if you're striding down a country lane, leaping into the ditch every two minutes to avoid being flattened by a nutter in a Range Rover.

I go to the butcher, pretending to check out the display in the window while actually peering in to check that Antonia isn't in there. If she were, would I dare to push in ahead of her? Would I say: Ah, I see it's only you, Toni, you won't mind if I rudely elbow you aside as I am busier and more important and have a jam-packed, fascinating life to attend to?

I buy some lamb chops, then head to the newsagents for a paper. Antonia is standing on the pavement outside, chatting away animatedly to another of her never-ending supply of cronies. She smiles and waves her hand. So there you are, chatting – clearly not in a hurry at all then. In a hurry when it comes to pushing in front of me, but not in a hurry when it comes to talking to your adoring acolytes. Right, I get it.

Normally, I'd wave back and smile. Normally, I'd go out of my way to be super-friendly, to show how delighted I am to be living so close to my husband's ex-wife. How civilised it all is! How amicable! Isn't it all marvellous! But now I don't even lift my hand in a gesture of acknowledgement. I simply blank her. It's so completely unlike me but it feels wonderful. I walk past as if she doesn't exist or is no more than a speck of dust on the pavement, invisible to the naked eye.

As I pass, I hear her crony – it's Louisa, the slightly mousy one – say, 'Oh, isn't that Carl's wife?'

I don't hear Antonia's response because I've swished straight past them by then and am marching off back to the cottage.

When I get back, I put the food in the fridge, deal with the compost delivery, then dash upstairs to the main bedroom to take a look.

I go into the barn to see if Steve's left his tools in there – he locks them up there sometimes – but I can't find what I'm looking for, just the floor-sander and the tiles for the splashback in the downstairs bathroom. Maybe the garage?

I get the key for the padlock and go in. It's a bit cobwebby, but for once I'm not scared. I know exactly what I want. Yes, there it is, in the corner.

I grab what I need and go back into the house. I take a clean tea towel from the kitchen and run it under the tap, then wring it out. Tie it around my face. I am the Lone Ranger. Do not fuck with me. The thought is oddly comforting.

I enter the big bedroom, shut the door and open the windows wide. The dust is going to be phenomenal. I set up Steve's stepladder right in the middle of the room and climb up. Then I swing the sledgehammer up as high and hard as I can and smash it into the ceiling.

32

DUST IS A FOUR-LETTER WORD

I am sitting on the floor of the bedroom, surrounded by rubble and plaster. Most of the ceiling is now on the floor, except for the edges. The air is swimming with dust. I crawl to the door and stretch up to open it, then sit out on the landing with my back to the door. I tug off my tea towel mask. What have I done? What am I *doing*? I've been playing at making a home with Carl, making a marriage with him, but nothing ever goes right. And now all I've done with my customary skill is make it worse. The room was fine as it was. Now it looks like a bomb site. This is my life. Before I met Carl, it was fine. OK, so I wasn't happy all the time, but who is? Then I met him – and I was happy! *So* happy. I loved him so much I thought that love alone would magically make everything else fine – that whatever happened, we would face it together, that being a couple and so in love would make us invincible.

But of course, that was ridiculously naïve – as if I believed that love makes the world a place of prancing unicorns and endless rainbows. What a fool. Instead, I have a husband who is never here and I have to face everything on my own, only it's even worse because everyone assumes that Carl is shouldering the burden with me. Celeste assumes he's shielding me from the worst of Antonia. Antonia assumes Carl is dealing with the builder. My mum assumes the pixies in the garden are lending a hand…

Only no one is helping. All right, that's not true: Steve and his guys are doing most of the work. But all the other stuff – making decisions and working out what to do – it's just me, muddling through and getting it all wrong. Like the ceiling. I've asked Carl multiple times, 'Shall we get Steve to remove the false ceiling in the bedroom? What do you think, Carl? What do you think?' And each time, he's said, 'Do we need to decide this minute?' Or 'I'm too tired to talk about it now.' This time, he didn't even respond to my text, so there we are. *I* made the decision.

When I first stepped inside the hallway of this house, my first thought was not: 'Wow! How beautiful this is! We'll be so happy here.' My very first thought was: '*Yeuch, how grim, how gloomy, how depressing. I hate it.*'

But I believed we could fix that. Together. I thought Carl would… I don't know… actually take some proper time off and come with me to choose furniture. We'd have fun looking at paint charts and going to antiques auctions and deciding which tiles to have in the bathroom and which taps in the kitchen. I thought we would get closer and closer and grow to love each other even more. But that's not what's happened, is it?

I know he can't help it. Of course Carl has to be with his dad. I'm not inhuman. It's only that when he's not in Bristol, he's at work or on his laptop or his phone, working. Even when he *is* here, too often it feels as if he isn't quite here. He's so distracted, so absent, he might as well not be. We won't get a second chance further down the line to do all this. If we want the house to be habitable, we have to make decisions now, get furniture now. I hate having to decide on so many things myself – paint colours, tiles, taps, light fittings, rugs –

without any input from him. At long last, the ironworks guy called to say the bed-frame will be ready any day now, and then Steve will bolt it to the antique brass head and foot I got at the auction house in Canterbury. It's a beautiful bed, but it doesn't *mean* anything to me if I have to be in it all on my own.

I am slumped on the floor of the landing, my hair thick and matted with dust, my clothes caked, crying. Crying because I have no idea how to make my life work, make *this* life work. I want to be with Carl so much but I don't know how to be a good wife or even a good person. I feel like I'm absolutely *nothing* – that now and forever I will be 'only Natalie', the person who doesn't matter, the person of no account that anyone can push past or shove to the sidelines. I'll always be Number Two, the second thought, the back-up.

Suddenly, I hear the front door open. I didn't even lock it. You don't really need to around here.

'Hello?'

A voice from below. Is it Steve, come back for his ladder, maybe? But he definitely said he wouldn't be back until tomorrow – Tuesday. No, it sounds like... like Carl.

'Nat?'

My voice comes out in a croak. 'Carl?'

He takes the stairs two at a time, then comes to a sudden halt when he sees me.

'Oh my God! What's happened? Are you OK? Did you have an accident?' He crouches down and looks into my eyes, strokes my face.

I shake my head, then burst into tears again.

'My love, my love – my extremely dusty love – what is it?' He holds me tight, then kisses my dusty face and hair. 'Tell me. What can I do?'

For answer, I reach up and open the bedroom door behind us and let it swing open.

'My God, the ceiling collapsed on you! Are you hurt? Can you move?' He gets out his phone. 'I'm calling an ambulance.'

'No, no! No need – I'm fine. It didn't collapse. It was *me*. I... I knocked the ceiling down. Myself.'

'What? *Why*? Why didn't you get Steve to do it?'

I sink my head forwards to rest on my knees.

'I... I really wanted to do it myself.'

'Er... OK...'

Carl doesn't say 'What were you thinking?' or 'Are you crazy?' or 'What the hell!' He holds me tight while I cry, then he gently helps me to my feet.

'Now, should I run the vacuum over you or take you to the car wash?' he says, carefully picking chunks of plaster out of my hair.

'Pond, please.'

'OK – pond it is.' He leads me by the hand, grabs a couple of towels, and then, by the pond, he slowly undresses me, handling me very gently, as if I were a wounded animal. 'My beautiful wife. Bonkers but beautiful.'

I sniff and he kisses me again.

'You come too.' I can't even speak properly.

He hesitates for a moment, then strips off and takes a running jump right into the middle of the pond, making a huge splash.

'Hurry up, Dusty!'

I do a running jump too, but slip on the bank with my last step so I careen into the water sideways.

But the water works its magic, not only removing the dust but restoring me, making me feel human again, nice again, not like some horrible scrunched-up ball of anger and pain.

Carl and I linger in the pond for a while, swimming on our backs and floating, and *being*.

'I thought you weren't coming back until tomorrow. Shouldn't you be at work?'

'I cancelled my meetings. Why do you think I came back early?'

'I don't know. Did your dad's treatment go well?'

'It was all right, but that wasn't it.' He reaches across for my hand, then we turn on to our fronts to swim for a bit.

'I *missed* you, Natalie. I've never been able to talk to my dad. Felix isn't there that much because of the girls, and it's too hard to – it's not – I can't talk to Stefan right now, that's all I'm saying. I *need* you, darling. A hundred times a day, I think: oh, I must ask Natalie that, or I must tell Nat about this. She'll know what to say or she'll find that interesting. But nothing means anything when you're not there. Don't you get it?'

'I...I didn't realise. Sometimes it feels as if I don't matter to anyone else. Not even to you.'

'Well then, you're a bloody idiot!' He laughs and splashes me. 'How could you think for a second you don't matter? Good God, woman, what do I have to do to get you to believe me?'

'I don't know.' I can feel my eyes welling up again.

'Come out, Nat.' We scramble up on to the bank and I stand there while Carl dries me, taking his time, tenderly rubbing me all over, crouching down on the grass to dry between my toes.

'You're not expecting anyone, are you?'

'No. No one. Steve won't come until tomorrow.'

'Well then?' Carl spreads the towels out on the grass by the pond and draws me down to lie beside him, then he turns on his side towards me.

'Do you accept that I love you?'

'I suppose so.'

'Not good enough. You should *believe* it. I've never felt like this before about anyone.'

'But you did get married before. I mean you must have—'

'Shush! I'm going to stop you there because I don't want to talk about bloody Antonia right now, OK? All I will say is yes, of course I thought I loved her at the beginning but only because I was a fool and didn't have a clue what real love is. This... you ... how I feel about you ... is fundamentally different. When things are grim in Bristol, I close my eyes and think of you here at the cottage, like you're some magic medicine to soothe me. You know how much I adore the kids, but I've never felt so happy and alive like I do now, not only as a dad but as a man– as *me* – like I'm one lucky bastard for having you in my life.'

I feel completely overwhelmed.

'Do you... do you really think that?'

'I do.' He leans in and kisses me, pulls me closer. His hand strokes down the line of my back to my bottom.

'But what if someone shows up? Remember, last time we attempted this...the mattress guy—'

'Well, let's hope, if any delivery drivers appear, they have the good sense to tiptoe away again, and if not, they get to enjoy a free show.'

It's the following week and I'm driving to the station to collect Carl. He's had to be away this whole week. I park the van and go to meet him on the platform, thinking that will be more welcoming than waiting in the van for him to come out. He must be exhausted. His dad suddenly got worse again, so Carl had to rush to Bristol then spent the rest of the week in London, embroiled in some sort of work crisis. He promised he'd try to come down midweek but then said he couldn't, there were problems he needed to fix. Probably nothing all that important, in reality, but Carl does get so stressed about work. I wish he would chuck it all in and find something else to do.

As usual, only a handful of people get off at our tiny station. There's a cluster at the far end and I shield my eyes against the strong August sunshine to scan their silhouettes; a woman with a small child, a couple, a tall but stooped, elderly man, two older women, one helping the other down the step to the platform.

Where's Carl? If he'd missed the train, surely he'd have called me? Maybe he's fallen asleep so failed to get off? The train only stops at Little Wyford for about thirty seconds so you have to be primed and ready with your bag as it pulls into the station, other-wise you get carted off another five miles further along the line to the next stop. It happened to me once and I had to wait nearly an hour for the next train going the other way.

I run along the platform, peering through the train windows in case Carl is there, asleep, but then I hear my name called and Carl is right there, back near the exit. How on earth did I miss him?

I run to him and we hold each other on the platform.

'I *missed* you.' He dips to kiss me. 'So much. You have no idea.'

'Me, too. I didn't see you get off the train.'

He looks slumped, defeated, not like himself. Suddenly, I realise that I *did* see him – only I didn't recognise it was Carl. In a bunch of people at the far end. I'd assumed it was a much older man, a droopy-looking silhouette I'd barely given a second glance; not like Carl at all, who is always so confident, always striding, upright, ready to take on the world.

I ask how his dad is doing now.

'The treatment is really taking a toll on him. Psychologically as well as physically.'

'It must be very tough.'

'Mm, my father's always been so in charge, you know. Born to command – the boss, the leader, the one other people turn to for decisions. Now, he seems so diminished.' Carl shrugs and he looks strained. 'He actually looks smaller. Fragile. Scared.'

I reach up and cup Carl's cheek with my hand.

'That must be really hard for you, too.'

He nods.

I take his hand and we head towards the van.

'And how is it with Stefan now? Are things OK?'

Carl sighs. 'He sometimes stays at a hotel but the last couple of occasions, when Felix hasn't been there, Stefan and I have both been at Dad's flat, which I could really do without, on top of everything else. He has, at least, taken the sofa and given me the spare room. Not exactly compensation, but better than nothing.' He gives a snort of annoyance.

'Carl? Don't you think—'

'Darling, look ... Stefan and me... I'm not really in the mood to go into it all right now, if you don't mind.'

'Sure.' I nod and unlock the van. Inside, I'm thinking: *But when will you ever be in 'the mood' to talk to me about it? To talk about anything that really matters? You're always too tired or too stressed or too busy. It's never the right time. This matters – I know it does. 'It affects us and our lives,' I want to say, 'you can't pretend it isn't important.'* But, for now, I leave it, while telling myself that perhaps I should be braver and persist.

On the drive back, Carl tells me more about his dad's treatment and prognosis. He'll have to go back to Bristol again next week, the day before his dad's next bout of chemo.

'You must be exhausted. It's hard caring for someone else so intensely.'

'Mm. I am. And my dad's not exactly the easiest patient.'

We reach the lane. Usually, whoever is the passenger hops out to do the gate, but Carl looks shattered, so I do it.

He dumps his bag in the hall with a massive sigh.

'Tea? Or wine?'

'Wine,' he says. 'Definitely.'

I take his jacket, open the wine and pour him a large glass and he goes into the sitting room and slumps on to the sofa. He leans back and shuts his eyes. I bet he's strung up about Stefan, too – that's why he looks so strained, I'm sure – I know he hates talking about anything difficult, but I have to *try*.

'Carl, I understand that you're reluctant to talk about Stefan, and I realise you must be tired, but surely talking about it will help you feel less stressed? If there's stuff in the past bothering you, you should air it.' I perch on the edge of the armchair and lean towards him. 'It's not good to bottle it all up. You have to try to commu—'

'Seriously?'

'Hmm? What?'

'I can't believe this. I am absolutely *shattered*. The last thing I need is a lecture from you about how I should learn to communicate with my tosser of a brother, OK?'

'But I'm only trying to—'

'Well, *don't*! Don't try to interfere. Stop.' He covers his face with his hands. He won't even look at me. Then he suddenly leans forwards and stares right at me, and it's as if I'm looking into the eyes of a total stranger, a man who not only doesn't love me, a man who at this moment looks as if he'd rather be anywhere else in the world than here in his dream house with his new wife.

I jolt back as if I've been burned.

'Natalie, let's get this straight. This is *none* of your business. I'm perfectly capable of communicating with my brother if I choose to do so. But I choose *not* to. Please stay out of it.'

He gets up then and leaves the room. Then I hear him say, 'I'm exhausted. I'm going up to bed. Please – for pity's sake – just let me sleep.'

* * *

It's only a little after nine now. I was sure Carl would be hungry. I turn off the oven and take out the potatoes and the ratatouille and leave them to cool down. I thought... what did I think? I thought Carl would be exhausted, yes, but that he'd want to eat something and slowly unwind and talk to me – not only about his dad's treatment, but all of it – how he feels and what's the deal with Stefan and have a vent about this week's work crisis. Isn't it partly my business, now we're married? I'm not asking just because I'm nosy. I want to know because I want to help make things *better*. I'd do anything to bring Carl happiness, but in the sitting room he looked as if the only thing that could possibly make him happy would be for me to be somewhere else.

I clear up in the kitchen, then stretch out on the sofa and try to read my book, but I can't concentrate at all. I keep thinking of the way Carl sounded, the way he looked at me.

I climb the stairs to bed and look into the big bedroom. Steve and his guys have cleared up the aftermath of my ceiling work. Steve thought it was a hoot that I'd knocked it out myself. He said, 'Good for you – it's a blast, isn't it?' as if I were in need of a fun diversion to amuse myself. They have to wait for the new plaster to dry out; then they will decorate it.

In the guest room, where we've been sleeping, Carl is absolutely out for the count, spread-eagled right across the plain wooden double. we've been using for now. I'd been so looking forward to when our brass one will finally be ready – our first proper marital bed – but it looks as though he's happier sleeping by himself.

Quietly, I grab my nightie, creep out and go through to the little, third bedroom. At least the single bed is made up, in case my mum or Celeste suddenly wants to come to stay.

I brush my teeth and get ready for bed, trying not to think that my husband is sleeping in another room. We've been married for five months. Is this how things are going to be?

* * *

Morning. It took me an age to get to sleep. I kept turning things over and over in my head, veering from one extreme to the other.

Was I being insensitive and pushy, trying to force Carl to talk to me when he wasn't ready, so I made things even worse? Or was I right to press him, and it isn't my fault if he can't ever talk about anything difficult?

There's a gentle tap on the door and Carl pokes his head round.

'Why are you in the tiddly single room, Wife? Do you hate me?'

'Course not. You looked exhausted and I thought you might sleep better on your own.' But I can't quite look at him. 'Plus, you were hogging the whole bed.'

He comes towards me and sits right on the edge of the bed as if he's a hospital visitor.

'Natalie, I'm truly sorry. I know I was vile to you last night.'

'Yes, you were.'

'But you have to let me take things at my own pace. I can't be... press-ganged into talking about stuff if I'm not ready to.'

'I wasn't press-ganging you. I could see you were stressed and I thought if you could only talk about it, it would be better.'

'I do need to talk to you about something, in fact,' he says. 'Something important.'

I start to sit up.

'Actually, can we go down and have some coffee and breakfast? I'm starving.'

We go down in our dressing gowns and Carl makes a pot of coffee for him, and tea for me, and I start making scrambled eggs with tomatoes and cut some bread for toast.

Once we've had some breakfast, I say, 'So, it *is* about Stefan, right?'

'*No.*' I see how quickly he's ready to flare up. He takes a swig of his coffee as if it's a slug of gin and sets his cup down with a bang.

'I do not want the S-word mentioned for the foreseeable future, OK?'

'OK, OK. Remain calm. What is it, then?'

'It's bad. Really bad.'

'Well, don't keep me in suspense. How bad?'

'It's my work. It's...' he shakes his head, '... gone.'

'*Gone*?'

He nods.

'How can it be gone?'

I wait. What on earth does he mean? Is he saying that the firm's gone bust? But for once I manage to shut up and let him tell me when he's ready.

He drinks some more coffee, then tells me he's been ousted. The other guys in the small PR firm, James and Jonathan, have taken the decision to cut him out.

'But how is that even possible? You're a partner, aren't you?'

He explains that, contrary to what I'd thought, actually no, he wasn't. Technically, he was an employee. The other two initially started the firm then brought him in a bit later on. They treated him like a partner, so he still had a share of the profits, but from a legal standpoint, he's been an employee all this time. Only I didn't know any of that because, Carl, a PR man even when there's no need to be, always referred to it as 'my company'.

'You should see an employment lawyer. They can't fire you, surely? You must have a contract? Something?'

He nods.

'They've offered me three months' basic pay, which is what it states in my contract. It's nothing.'

'But you've always earned really well, I thought.'

'Yes, because I brought in a lot of the business so we shared the profits. The basic pay is not good. I've got some savings at least and you know we made money on my flat so we're OK, we won't starve. It's just I feel such a fool!'

'Oh, Carl, that doesn't matter. You're not a fool. But how could they do this to you? You said you've attracted lots of clients. You're so brilliant at what you do. *Why* would they do this?'

He pushes his plate away from him.

'James and Jonathan took it in turns to take pot-shots at me: "Carl, you're *never* here", "You're very high-handed", "You always act like you know best", "We've both had enough", "You're an arrogant son-of-a-bitch, frankly". On and on. It was horrible.

'Apparently, I went ahead and made high-level decisions about spending levels on a couple of campaigns without consulting them – but so bloody what? I had to, Nats: they were faffing about and I needed to crack on. But they're saying it put me in breach of contract. And, OK, they had warned me about it a while back.

'James said they could let me go without a penny, if they had a mind to, because of the breach of contract, but were being decent, offering me three months' basic to walk away. It was take it or leave it.'

'But... but... you've only not been there because of having to be with your dad so much! That's not fair.'

'I know, but they don't care. James referred to me as "constantly swanning off to Kent to play happy families in the country".'

'Well, that's not true! You've hardly been here at all!'

He gives me a sharp look.

'Natalie, I'm doing my best. Don't give me a hard time.'

I stand up and start to clear the table. Whatever I say is wrong.

'Look, at least we have the rest of the money from the sale of your flat and, if you don't need to go up to London, we could rent out my flat, or even sell it to give us a safety net. And I'll start looking for shop premises later this week, so...'

'We can't possibly live on what you'll make from your little shop!'

'Well, it's unlikely to be much, no, but we could rein in a bit and—'

'I was thinking of starting up my own company.'

'As a PR?'

He shrugs. 'What else can I do?'

'I'm sure you could do anything in the world if you set your mind to it.'

'I'm not ten, Nat. You don't need to give me a pep talk.'

'I wasn't. It's only that, well, you do seem to find it stressful. Perhaps you could think about other options?'

He snorts with laughter.

'Other options? Right. I'd like to be an astronaut, please, because that's what I really, really wanted to be when I was six.' He clasps his hands together. 'Please can you make that happen?'

'All right, there's no need to be facetious. I'm trying to help. Be a bloody PR then. I don't care.'

I start plonking things in the dishwasher and I dunk the eggs' pan in the sink and start scrubbing at it as if I'm trying to erase it from the planet.

'Oh, Nat.' He comes up behind me and puts his arms around me but I hold myself stiffly. He nuzzles into my neck in the way he knows usually makes me go all wobbly but I bite my lip. That's the trouble with Carl – he thinks he can circumvent any argument by luring me to bed.

'But is it true, do you think? That I'm high-handed? Or arrogant? That I think I always know best?' He laughs, maybe trying to lighten the mood.

I don't know the right way to phrase this because the truth

is, of course, that Carl is a little bit arrogant. And he does act as
if he knows best. Look at the way he bought this house –
without me – even though it's our first proper home together. I
would never have done such a thing. There must be a tactful
way of indicating that without being hurtful. I need a minute to
think.

'Nat?' He pulls my arm to turn me round, but I can't look at
him. 'Oh my God, I was *joking*! You think I'm arrogant! You *do*! I
can't believe it.'

'It's not that, exactly. It's only that... well, you can be a little...'
How on earth can I put this diplomatically? 'You know... um... a
bit high-handed... at times,' I add pointlessly, trying to soften it.

'I see. Example, please?'

All I can think of is this house. There has to be a smaller
example, there has to be. But if it's too trivial, he'll say, well, that's
nothing, so bloody what?

'Right, well, when you found this house, you rang me from
the auction, Carl. You'd clearly already made the decision to buy
it, but then you called—'

'But you love this house!'

'That's not the point.'

'*Of course* it's the point! What else matters, for God's sake? OK,
so it's needed a fair bit of work, but it's a lovely house in a great
setting with a barn and a *pond* and down the road from my kids.
What more could we possibly want?'

I resist the urge to say, 'Well, if we moved it about five miles
away from your ex-wife, that would be a lot, lot better,' as I'm
guessing that's not going to help this little talk.

'Carl, it really isn't the point. All I'm trying to say is that you
effectively made the decision without me and—'

'I'm not talking about this. This is absurd. We've got a
fantastic house and you should be grateful that I'm the one who

got it for us. Instead, you're having a go at me when I already feel like shit. Thanks.'

He stomps off upstairs to shower and dress, and when he comes down, he says he's texted the kids and he's going over to Toni's to pick them up and take them to the beach.

'See you later!' And he slams the door.

After Carl returns from taking the kids out, I hear him come in the front door and he calls out 'Hi'. At least he's talking to me, though it's a very flat sort of 'hi'. I call back.

I'm sitting on the floor of the big living room, making the curtains for our bedroom as Steve's painter will decorate it this week. We'd left the old curtains in place up until now, but they were very worn and sad-looking. I have the new material spread out on the rug and I'm pinning the heading tape in position before I stitch it on my machine.

He appears in the doorway.

'What are you doing there?'

'Making curtains for our bedroom.' I take a deep breath. Yes, the room we still haven't got to sleep in. 'The big room, I mean. I did send a picture of the fabric to your phone, remember?'

'Oh. Can't you get them made? Antonia said there's a wonderful place on the high street where they can do it properly.'

'They *will* be done *properly*. I want to do it myself.'

He snorts. 'What, like the ceiling? Taking DIY to new levels...' He sighs. 'I'm making myself a drink – you want one?'

I fix my gaze down at what I'm doing so that I don't have to look at him. I know bashing the ceiling down was incredibly stupid, but Steve told me that's how they do it anyway; I didn't damage the house. I made a lot of mess, which of course the builders had to clear up, but I didn't murder anyone or anything. Carl's being nasty because he's still cross about this morning.

'Yes, please. I'd love a tea. Thanks.'

'I meant like a gin and tonic or a glass of wine.'

I glance at the wall clock.

'It's only five o'clock. Bit early?' Carl does seem to be drinking a fair bit these days.

'Since when were you appointed Drinks Monitor?'

'I'm not. I'm not saying that... I just... Oh, never mind. Forget it.' I stand up. 'I'll make my own tea. Careful in here. There are pins there.'

There's a strange awkwardness as we move around each other in the kitchen, as if we don't know each other all that well. Carl gets out ice for his drink and I put the kettle on for my tea. We're like two mates in a flat-share who've had a row about who finished off the last of the milk.

'It's pasta with some sauce and a salad for supper later.' I say as if I'm speaking to a guest I'd rather not be entertaining. 'Nothing special.'

'Great,' he says, his voice conveying not 'great' at all but 'I don't give a toss.'

I stand by the kettle, looking out towards the garden at the front, or what in theory will be the garden once I've put more plants in.

'Oh, I know what I meant to ask you.' Carl leans back against the counter a little way away. 'Who's the mystery man?'

'Mystery man? What are you talking about?'

'My network of spies report that you were spotted with a mystery man in the village last weekend.' He takes out his phone and pretends to be reading a report on it. 'Yes, here we go – older, quite distinguished, smart linen suit, flash sports car. Anything you want to confess to? Or do I not want to know? Strange that you didn't mention it.' He looks at me, raising his eyebrows, unsmiling.

'Was it Antonia? What is *wrong* with that woman? Bloody hell, I can't so much as sneeze in the village without her announcing to the world at large which bin I dropped my tissue in!'

'Hey, hey, steady on, Nat. I'm only teasing you. Actually, it wasn't Antonia. It was Dominic. I saw him earlier when I took the kids back. He was obviously trying to wind me up. I didn't take it seriously. I thought that, knowing you, you'd probably stopped to help some elderly chap with his shopping and were being kind, and Dominic was trying to make out you had some secret thing going with a Sugar Daddy.'

'It's none of their business what I do or who I talk to!' I take a mug from the dresser, then bang it down on the counter. 'He's *not* a Sugar Daddy! That's a horrible thing to say.'

I don't really want to have to explain about my dad to Carl. I don't want to lie to him but I don't feel ready to tell him. Especially not when we've been arguing so much.

Since I met Carl, I've always had the sneaking feeling that I'm not in his league. I never expected even to meet someone like him, never mind marry someone like that – I don't just mean good-looking and well-off and successful, but all of it – someone who had so many advantages. Carl grew up in a huge house with a live-in housekeeper, a nanny and a gardener. I mean, all the time – not having a cleaner come in once a week for a couple of hours, but living there – to plump your cushions and make you a

cup of tea, dust your chiffonier and snip your lawn with a pair of
nail scissors, should you so desire.

Secretly, I've felt as if I'm inhabiting one of those old-fashioned sagas where our heroine, a lowly servant, falls in love with
the young master of the household, a debonair and dashing
ne'er-do-well who, in the end, sees that she is his true love. He
forsakes the wealth and title, and his previous life of drinking and
gambling, to keep chickens and grow vegetables with her deep in
the countryside.

Yes, I know it's not at all like that. I didn't grow up with money
but I've never been out of work. I did start my own business and
I'm not having to get up at 5 a.m. to black-lead the kitchen range.
And Carl is successful... er, *was* successful, not because he had it
handed to him on a plate, but because he's brilliant and works so
hard.

I do see it's not logical, it's only that it sometimes *feels* that
way. Even more so with Antonia. Sometimes, she'll say something
that seems so astonishingly out of touch with how the average
person lives. I don't even mean people who are really poor, or in
the developing world, but someone on an average income, where
a holiday is something you save up for once a year, not: 'I'm in
such a dreadful dilemma about where to go after Christmas.
Saskia does so want to go skiing again, but Dom really wants to
go to Guadeloupe.'

Is that really a 'dreadful dilemma'? Having to decide between
ridiculous, expensive Option A or crazy, expensive Option B?
Surely a 'dreadful dilemma' is having to decide whether to pay
the electricity bill, so you don't get cut off, or buy food for supper?

When I was a kid, we never went on flash holidays abroad. At
junior school, that was OK, because a lot of the kids came from
families who were short of money, so they'd have a week on a
caravan site in Dymchurch or at a holiday camp in Wales, nice

but cheap. Occasionally, someone went to Spain, but that was about it. For our summer holiday, Mum usually took us camping in Scotland, and we loved it, but she was exhausted. As she was the only grown-up, she had to do all the driving.

But at my secondary school– it was a grammar – the girls came from a range of backgrounds. Some were like us, not well off, but many of them lived in large houses in North London: Hampstead, Primrose Hill, Chalk Farm. Their fathers had well-paid jobs in offices and were described as 'businessmen'. So, when other girls asked, 'What does your dad do?' I'd say, 'Oh, he's a businessman', then change the subject because I didn't understand what he did for a living. Mum had at some point told us that he was 'in business'. When they first got married, I suppose that's what she believed: that he was involved in wholesale trade in some way.

But at the end of the summer term, the girls would start saying, 'So where are you going this year? We're going to Tuscany.' And I didn't want to say 'Nowhere' or 'Just camping', so I'd say 'Oh, we still haven't decided' or 'We might stay with our grandparents,' even though I knew Mum couldn't stand to stay there for more than two nights. Once, we went to France, camping again, but Mum nearly had a nervous breakdown trying to deal with driving on the wrong side of the road, and the next year, Celeste and I said, 'Why don't we camp somewhere nearer, Mum? What about Sussex?' and she looked so grateful that we knew we'd said the right thing.

Carl comes close and tries to put his arms round me but I wriggle out of his grasp.

'What is it, Nat? I was only teasing you to try to make things better between us. I don't really think you have a Sugar Daddy on the side. You seem awfully tense.'

'I'm fine.'

'Come on now. You're a lousy liar. You're *not* fine.' He tries to turn me around, away from the sink, but I stay rooted to the spot. So, he picks me up as if I'm a toy and simply plonks me down the other way round so that I'm now facing him. 'What's going on?'

I don't know how to say this: Sorry – you shouldn't have married me. My dad's an ex-con. A criminal. You should never have let me think I could live in your world. I don't belong here.

'I...'

He can see I'm struggling so he puts his arms round me again and holds me close. I sink into him. There is nowhere else I'd rather be. This is where I feel safe and happy and loved. 'Oh, Carl.'

He takes one of my hands and kisses it.

'My love, you're starting to scare me. How bad can it be? Or not bad? Oh God, are you pregnant?'

I sniff and shake my head. 'Uh-uh – not pregnant.'

'Well, that's a relief at least. What with the minor problem of my not having a job any more.'

I nod, though – ridiculously – a part of me is disappointed that he's relieved. We did talk about having children before we got married, of course. Carl said he'd like only one because he already has Saskia and Max, but I'd love to have two because I'm worried it might be lonely if we had only one. Also, I really want two so that they would be absolutely equal in Carl's eyes with Saskia and Max, not like an afterthought who doesn't count as much.

He leads me to the dining table and sits me down.

'Now, what's going on, Nat? You're always telling me I should talk more but now you're the one who's clamming up. Spill it. What is it? You've written off your van? All your stock's been stolen? You drowned a kitten? How bad are we talking?'

'How could you think I would drown a kitten?'

'Oh my God – sense of humour failure. I only said it at random as something crazy and madly unlikely.'

'OK.' I take a deep breath. 'Right, you know I told you that my dad died when I was eighteen, during my first term at university?'

'Yes – have they suddenly found his will and you're rich? Well, I suppose I can live with that. Especially now.' He laughs.

'Well, he didn't die then.'

'All right. So, when was it?'

'No, I mean, he's still alive.'

'But why on earth would you lie about that? I don't get it.'

'I didn't lie! Obviously. I didn't *know*. My dad begged Mum to tell us he'd died and that the funeral had already taken place. Celeste and I believed he was dead.'

Carl raises his eyebrows and for once says nothing.

'My dad felt that was the preferable alternative to the truth.'

He reaches for my hand, waiting.

'He was sent to prison. For eighteen years. He claims that he hated the idea of our having to visit him in prison, or having our friends know that our father was a criminal. By then, we only saw him perhaps once a year anyway, so I guess he thought it wouldn't be that big a deal if he slipped out of our lives.'

'But it *was* a big deal.'

I nod.

'Ah, I see. The mystery man? He's back?'

I nod again.

'So, do I get to meet him or what? Though it's a bit late for me to ask him for his daughter's hand in marriage!' He laughs.

'How can you laugh? You're married to a crim's daughter! And you haven't even asked what he did!'

'I'm assuming you will tell me when you feel ready.'

I let out a sigh and rest my head on the table on my hands. Carl gently strokes my hair.

'I'm not sure I'll ever be ready.'

'Well, OK then, but I'm assuming he didn't just nick a packet of sweets from the corner shop. Eighteen years is a seriously big deal.'

'Mm.'

'But Dominic said Toni saw you with him well over a week ago?'

'So?'

'Why didn't you tell me? You're the one always lecturing me – telling me I've got to learn to talk about problems, express myself. It's a bit rich, Nat.'

'This is completely different.'

'Why is it?'

'Because... because my dad was in *prison*. I am mortified. It's completely shameful. You have no idea. With your posh background and your expensive school, you haven't got a clue what it's like to always feel as if you've been – I don't know – allowed in for a little bit, to watch the rich folks in their fine clothes dancing in the ballroom, but any minute now you'll be sent back to the servants' quarters and told to get scrubbing the pots!'

Carl laughs.

'It's not funny.'

'But you've never been a servant. That's just *silly*.' He squeezes my arm but I shake him off.

'It's silly to you, but not to me. I'm trying to tell you what it *feels* like.'

'But I don't care if your dad's been in prison. Not really. If he's paid his debt to society...' Carl shrugs as if it's nothing, an oversight, a couple of unpaid parking tickets. 'Anyway, why does he want to see you now?'

'It doesn't matter why. It's irrelevant because I sent him away and I don't want to see him again.'

'So says the woman preaching tolerance and forgiveness, and badgering me to talk to my brother.'

'This is *totally* different.'

'Course it is.' He knocks back the rest of his drink and stands up again. 'You're the renowned expert on communicating with estranged family members so I am sure you are one hundred per cent correct.'

I want to create a veg patch near the garage, where Mr Bailey had his before he couldn't manage it any more; the open area that gets the sun most of the day. I need to have something positive to focus on to stop me thinking about my dad or worrying about the fact that Carl doesn't have a job any more. It probably sounds ridiculous but I also want to do it partly for Mr Bailey. I've been wondering about what he was like and thinking about how he died. I can't do anything about that, I can't undo it, of course, but somehow this feels like the right thing to do. Dave, the postman, told me that Ted was very proud of his veg. It's one of the reasons Dave always used to drive down the lane instead of leaving the post in the mailbox at the top – partly so he could see Ted was all right, but also the pair of them used to swap bits of produce. Dave would bring Ted some courgettes and Ted would give him some rhubarb and they'd chat a bit about the garden. Dave feels awful about what happened.

When Dave came with the post this morning, I told him my plan and he thought it was a great idea. The rhubarb is the one plant that's still there; you don't need to plant it each year like you have to do with potatoes and carrots and so on. He suggested I try a few crops to start with, as it's quite a lot of work, and I still have the rest of the curtains to make for the house, and I need to get my shop up and running, especially with Carl now out of a job.

'What kind of shop is it?' he asks.

'Antique clocks. Well, I specialise in clocks but I sell other antiques too.'

'Have you got premises already or are you still looking?'

'Actually, I'm still looking. Someone – er... Mrs Moore, up the road, recommended I rent a place at the Hopwood Farm complex.'

Dave laughs and shakes his head.

'*Don't*. Take it from me. Those units are overpriced and you've got a tiny number of potential customers and not enough passing trade for something like antiques.'

'That's what I thought, but... um... Mrs Moore says—'

'She's your husband's ex, right?'

God, does everyone know everything round here? Er, well yes, I suppose they do. Don't move to a village if you want your private life to be remotely private.

'Um – yes, yes, she is.'

'Well, 'scuse me for saying, but what's it got to do with *her*? There's loads of them rich wives round here and they know diddly-squat about anything so normal as running a business. They've got money but they're bored as hell and all they do is have parties, drink too much, and stick their noses into everyone else's business. If you've been running a shop successfully in London, then you know what you're doing, right?'

'Well, yes, I suppose I do.'

'For my money, I'd look at Faversham or, better yet, Canterbury. Way more punters – tourists, some rich residents. It's a beautiful city and there's plenty of shops in the backstreets;

tourists wander all over. You don't need to be on the High Street where the rates are high.'

'Thank you. I've been a few times but I'll go and recce the backstreets.'

'You do that. And if you want help, I know a man who handles commercial lets there.' He gives me a wink.

'Don't tell me, he's your brother?'

'Brother-in-law, actually, but don't hold that against him. Let me know if you go and I'll text him and tell him to look after you.'

* * *

I bump into Antonia in the village. Inevitably. It seems almost impossible to enter the village without seeing her. Whether I walk in or drive, as I enter the high street, I can't help myself – I can feel all my senses prickling, like a rabbit cautiously emerging from its burrow and sniffing the air in case there's a fox nearby. I start scanning the road ahead for her white four-wheel drive so that I can at least have some warning before she spots me. It's not exactly that I feel like an intruder, daring to venture on to her turf – but I bet *she* sees it that way.

'Natty!' I swear I'm going to kill her if she calls me that one more time.

'It's Natalie. *Please*.'

'Oh, Natalie! Of course. What am I like!' She laughs as if it's endearing, the way she insists on getting my name wrong. 'You did tell me a thousand times and I forgot. Hopeless!' Whenever she talks, it's far louder than necessary, given that we're standing together on the narrow pavement. It's as if she's announcing every single thing she says to a wider public. Her audience is the entire village.

'Now, what was it I meant to tell you?'

Obviously, I have no idea, but I bet it's yet another thing that involves her telling me how to run my life: which fabric I should choose for the guest bedroom curtains ('Don't pick anything with green in it – Carl really isn't a fan of green'); which breed of dog I should have ('You absolutely must, must, must get a cockapoo! They're soooooo gorgeous.' Though we haven't even said if we're thinking of getting a dog); and what colour I should wear ('I do think we ought to get you a red swimsuit, Natalie. With your dark hair, it would look absolutely super.' And who's 'we' in this scenario? Is she my mum, going to take me shopping? Will she buy me a milkshake afterwards?). As ever, I fight the urge to be rude. I try to think how Carl says he handles clients he doesn't like. Be polite, be professional; you don't need to be over-friendly, but be beyond criticism.

I make a conscious effort to smile.

'Well, I should be running along...' I say, turning towards the newsagent.

'Oh, I'll come in with you. I need to pick up my copy of *Vogue*.'

'Right.'

I was only going in there to get away from her.

'So, what are you getting, then?' She turns to me expectantly.

I reach down and grab a local paper from the stack.

'Just the paper!'

I really want some chocolate but I don't want Antonia to get all judgemental and make some irritating comment about diets. Oh, bollocks to her! I'm not letting her control what I do and what I eat.

I choose a bar of hazelnut chocolate plus a box of peppermint creams to have when Carl returns from Bristol and we can curl up and watch a movie together. Maybe things will be better next time.

'Ooh, *naughty*! What goes in the lips stays on the hips!'

'Carl loves peppermint creams. They remind him of being a kid. His aunty used to give them to him.'

'Really? I never used to get peppermint creams for him. Perhaps that's where the marriage went wrong!'

The thing with Antonia is, I can never tell when she's trying to be funny. She's not really funny, but sometimes she laughs as if she thinks what she's saying is hilarious.

'Probably!' I laugh, trying to join in and make some headway with her.

'Oh, no, not really, Natty – *Natalie*.' She puts her hand on my arm in a concerned way, as if I'm so dim I really thought she got divorced over peppermint creams. 'Actually, it was all really quite awful, you know. I don't know how much Carl has told you...'

'Um...'

'I'm happy to fill you in at some point. You know, when it's just us girls together! If you think that might be helpful... give you some... some context for everything?'

'Er, thanks, but it's OK. There's really no need.'

'Also, you know you'll only have heard Carl's side of it, obviously.'

'Mm.'

I don't really want to have this conversation in the middle of the newsagents. I get out my purse to pay and the woman behind the counter meets my eyes. I can't quite gauge her expression – is she looking at me with sympathy? Or something else?

'Good morning to you, Mrs Moore.' She turns towards Antonia. 'What can I do for you today?'

'I'm only picking up my *Vogue*, Marjorie, if you could pop it on our bill.'

And there it is. I clock the newsagent's expression and I see exactly what Carl was trying to tell me: be professional, be polite, be beyond reproach. But I can see that she doesn't like Antonia.

'Marjorie, you must know Mrs Cameron? She's my ex-husband's Number Two.'

Really? Can't I just be me for once?

'Hello. I'm Natalie. Nice to meet you properly.'

I've been in there loads of times of course, but I never thought to introduce myself. If you did that in a London shop, they'd think you were crazy.

I hate this weird lopsided thing, the way Antonia – and others – often call the shopkeepers by their first names, while they in return say, 'Mrs Moore', etc., like there's some horrible hierarchy. Either you're both on formal terms or you both use first names. Anything else is strange.

'You're in Ted Bailey's cottage, aren't you?' Marjorie asks me.

'Yes, that's right.'

'That's such a lovely place, but I know it must have needed a lot of TLC. Ted let things go a bit at the end. It was hard for him to manage with his arthritis.'

'I'm sure it was.'

'Have you kept up with Ted's veg patch? Sorry – *your* veg patch. He was so proud of his veg. We can give you some plants in spring. My Robert grows a lot from seed so we've always some spare.'

'Thank you, that's really kind. I do want to get going on the veg patch as soon as I have time.'

'Well, the seasons won't wait, you know. Autumn's round the corner. You could get some spinach and radishes in, at least. They're dead easy.'

'I didn't know that. There's so much to learn.'

'I hope you won't mind me saying – but I hope you'll keep the spirit of the cottage in mind as you're doing it up...?'

She looks at me, then back to the till to get my change.

'Oh, yes, definitely, we've really tried to. I know what you mean. Believe me, I'm the last person in the world to want to spoil it with fancy-schmancy taps and chrome door handles!'

I'm taking my change when the thought pops into my head about Antonia's house. That freakishly tall mixer tap in the kitchen with its weird hose attachment. And the one in the downstairs loo that looks like a modern sculpture, and the water comes out like a waterfall. Oh God, and the chrome door handles! I wasn't thinking. Why didn't I say 'granite worktops' or 'marble statues'? Actually, she does have that horrible statue by the pool. Why didn't I say 'Mm', then shut up like a normal person?

Beside me, I can feel Antonia flinch. Do I apologise or try to distract her? We start to leave the shop.

'Er... do you grow any fruit and veg, Antonia? I imagine you're too busy. I suppose it is a lot of work. I grew up in a flat so we didn't have a garden. Then when I met Carl I was also in a flat' – I'm babbling madly, I know, but I can't help it, I'm so embarrassed – 'a different flat, of course – well, not of course but definitely a different flat. There's a teeny-tiny balcony but really, it's barely big enough even to stand on it with your coffee – I couldn't fit more than a couple of pots out there – so, yes, I do want to grow some veg. But I suppose Carl will be too busy with ev—'

'Well, Natalie. Super to see you, but I must get on. So much to do.'

'Oh, yes, yes, of course.'

'Taps to shine! Door handles to polish!'

'Antonia, I'm really so—'

'Oh, there's Jinks!' Antonia waves frantically at Jinks on the other side of the road and calls out. 'I need to speak to her. Bye!'

Why is it that every time I see Antonia, even though I try so hard to get it right, all I do is make things worse?

36

THE BALANCE OF POWER

I hear a car pull up and I run to the side window to see who it is. Uh-oh: a gleaming white Range Rover. Antonia. Not content with lording it over me if I'm at her house, or popping up in every shop if I dare to tiptoe covertly into the village to get food, now she's stalking me in my own home, and I can't escape. Has she come to tell me off for sneering about her taps? I wouldn't blame her, actually. I can't believe I said something so rude.

I toy with the idea of not answering the door. My van is parked by the house, but I could easily have gone to the Hopwood Farm complex or to the village, or be out for a walk. I need to hold my nerve and crouch down and she won't see me and I can—

She's waving. She's seen me. Why did I stay right by the window like a sitting duck? But I ought to be able to be in my own house near my own window without having to hide behind the sofa surely?

I lift my hand in a not very enthusiastic wave, and head for the front door to open it.

'Antonia! What a surprise! Um, a nice surprise.' I look away. I can't lie. At all. That so obviously wasn't true that she gives me a sharp look.

'Hi. I was passing so thought I'd pop in, see how the work's going. No workmen today?'

'Steve had to go and get some stuff. He'll be back shortly.'

'You do have to crack the whip a bit, you know. I know what you're like.'

'Oh?'

'Carl says you're far too sweet, and then people take advantage. A friend of mine – her kitchen took over a year! I'm not kidding.'

'I don't think he's taking advantage. He went to collect the new taps for the downstairs shower-room.'

The word 'taps' hangs in the air between us. She looks at me, then quickly looks away.

'Well, he says that but he's probably off on another job, you know.' She sniffs.

'Antonia. I do want to apologise. What I said yesterday ... I ... I can see it must have come across as awfully rude and I honestly didn't mean to offend you. I was babbling on and it... it—'

'There's no obligation for you to like our house. Of course, we all have different tastes. It's absolutely fine.'

'But I *love* your house. I think it's absolutely *stunning*, I really do. You've done an amazing job. And I understand now how much work it must have been. This cottage is much smaller but still, it's taken way longer than we thought and there are always so many decisions to make. And your house always looks so calm and beautiful – with the flowers and everything – and there's never any clutter anywhere.'

'Oh, that's because I shove it all in the clutter cupboard.'

'The what?'

'I have this big cupboard in the utility room. If people are coming over, I simply swoop on all the crap everywhere – unopened post, flyers and magazines lying about, bumf from school, et cetera – and I dump the whole lot in the cupboard. Sometimes I forget about it completely until the next time I do a clutter swoop. That's when I find urgent post I haven't dealt with. Oops!'

Antonia comes into the hallway then. Short of literally barring the way, I can't really see how to stop her. Maybe I should buy an electric cattle prod and jab it at her if she tries to cross the threshold? She moves on into the kitchen.

'Now *this* is a lovely colour. What is it?'

I can't help it – I love talking about this stuff. I've thought so hard about what would work in each room. I'd like to say *we've* thought so hard about it, but that wouldn't be true. Every time I tried to raise it with Carl, he'd say he was too tired or too stressed to think about it or couldn't we paint everything white and have done with it? But I wouldn't want it all white. I don't think it's right for the house. In the end, I emailed him a list of the rooms and my suggested colours, like this:

Kitchen – Buttercup yellow – not actually buttercup at all, like a very pale, soft primrose yellow. Cheerful but not in your face.

I did that for every room.

This is how I have to communicate with my husband, half the time: by email if it's anything long; otherwise, by text. Even though he's no longer at the PR firm, he's still up in London a lot when he doesn't have to be in Bristol. He says he needs to 'network' and see people, consolidate his contacts in case he does start his own firm. Occasionally, we're actually in the same building at the same time and can pretend to be a proper married couple for a brief period.

Anyway, after I sent him a long, descriptive email, his response was:

Yes, OK. Thanks. x

After my three pages of descriptions and details and notes about what sort of mood each colour would create. Did he even read it?

Antonia moves on through to the big sitting room.

'Now, this is really a delightful room, Natalie. I honestly think it's almost as nice as our main reception at Greystokes. I see you did go for the red in the end. It certainly makes quite an impact. I thought you might think better of it?'

'Well, I love it. *We* love it.'

'I probably would have chosen something more neutral in here. Do you know the Farrow & Ball shades? They have one called Manor House Gray that really is marvellous. That's what I would have chosen for in here.'

'Right.'

'Does Carl honestly like the red? I can't believe you've managed to rope him into looking at paint samples. Well done, you! When we did our house in London, I had to use an interior designer; I couldn't get Carl to sit down for five minutes to look at so much as a bathroom tile or a fabric swatch. He was *awful*. I'm so glad you've successfully house-trained him, Natalie, it's fabulous. You're doing such a good job with him.'

Why is it that, even when Antonia is supposedly complimenting me, I feel as if I've been put down? She's making it sound as if I've done a super job training a misbehaving rescue dog.

'Would you like some tea? Coffee?'

'Super. Absolutely love some. Only if it's no trouble?'

'No, it's fine.'

'Coffee then, please.'

I'm presuming Antonia never drinks instant coffee, so I go to the fridge for the real coffee and make her a cafetière for one, and I top up my lukewarm tea with a dash of hot water to jolly it up a bit.

'Biscuit?'

'Oh, I shouldn't!'

Well, don't then, I think. This thing so many women do: ooh, I'm being so naughty, I'm having a biscuit! For fuck's sake, have a biscuit or don't have a biscuit. The world is full of actual real problems. No one gives a toss either way if you have a biscuit or not. If you want one, then eat it and stop wittering on about how awful it is. Or don't have it and shut up.

I shove the open packet towards her ungraciously, instead of transferring the biscuits properly to a pretty plate like my mum would do. I think of what Mum would say: always be gracious. No matter how rude or ill-mannered the other person is, always keep to your own standards of behaviour. She's right. So I go to the dresser and choose a pretty small plate and arrange several biscuits on it, then offer Antonia a napkin and go through to the little sitting room, which leads off the dining room then connects back through to the red room.

'Thank you,' she says emphatically. 'How nice. What a lovely plate. Family heirloom?'

Hardly. There aren't any family heirlooms because our family never owned anything significant to hand down to the next generation, other than a predisposition to bowel cancer and bad colds.

I shake my head.

'Well, now this is such a nice colour in here! I'm amazed. Carl doesn't usually like green, but this is charming as it's so pale. Very soothing.'

'Thank you. Please – sit down.'

She perches on the very edge of a seat as if she's waiting to go into the dentist's, then glances at the bare windows.

'And – oh, yes – curtains. Now, you must, must come with me to see Angela on the high street. I'm sure I've mentioned her to you a couple of times before, but really, it'll be so much better if I come with you so she understands you're an important customer. She does absolutely all our curtains and blinds. The finish is absolutely marvellous. She's rather expensive, of course, but really you don't want to be a cheapskate about these things. I bought some ready-made curtains once, and I can tell you I was kicking myself for months until I gave in and had proper ones made to replace them.'

Doesn't she have any idea at all how most people live? When I was growing up, Mum made all the curtains for our flat. We couldn't afford ready-made ones, never mind custom-made ones.

'Thanks, that's kind of you, but I'm planning to make them myself. I did the curtains in the red room, next door, and the guest room, and I've just finished the ones for the main bedroom upstairs.'

'Make them *yourself*?' She comes closer. 'Oh, Natalie. How awful! Is Carl in... financial difficulties? You should have said. Perhaps Dom could lend him some—'

'No, no. We're fine.' I am not going to tell her that he's lost his job. Carl would be furious with me. 'It's only... I'm used to doing things myself when I can. It's normal for me.'

I realise that phrasing it that way makes it sound as if I know it's a freakishly abnormal thing to do, that I'm somehow buying in to Antonia's world view, where everyone has to have the best, most expensive option available all the time rather than making do, or getting it second-hand or in a sale.

'Right. Well, that's... um... lovely. It's good to have some interests, I always think.'

I feel my shoulders slump. She doesn't get it.

'True. And what are *your* interests? What do you like to do with your free time?'

She gives me a nervous glance as if I've asked something totally inappropriate.

'Free time! Well, you know... I can't say I have two spare minutes to rub together, what with the house and the children and... and Dominic... you know, planning meals... and of course we do entertain a fair bit... and the garden, and I usually have one or two... special projects on the go.'

'Special projects?'

'Yes, like say, helping out with Saskia's school summer fair, organising the rota for the face-painting stall. That sort of thing.'

'Right.'

I know she hasn't worked for years, but I wonder if she doesn't get bored. That doesn't sound like a full calendar to me. Maybe she is bored and that's why she feels the need to interfere with my paint colours. Or maybe I'm a Special Project? Turning Number Two into a Proper Wife? God help me.

'Oh, I remember the other thing I meant to tell you! About the Hopwood Farm complex. I know you'll be thrilled. I've fixed for you to see Mark. Remember, I told you about him, and I've been meaning to get on to it but it's always so busy during the school holidays, as you can imagine. I've been up to my eyes with sorting out the kids' activities. I've arranged for us to see him on Thursday at twelve. Does that work for you?'

'Sorry – to see him about what?'

'About taking on a unit at the complex, of course. For your antiques shop. We talked about it.'

Ah. What she means is that she went on about it more than once while I listened patiently and failed to tell her a flat no when I should have done, so now she's convinced herself that's what I want to do. And what's with the 'us'? Why would she be coming along to a business meeting with me? She really does need to take up crochet or something. I think her chief hobby at present is: interfering in Natalie's life for no good reason.

'Actually, that's nice of you, but it's not necessary, thank you.'

'Oh?'

'Yes. I've been thinking about it and I've decided that I need a shop with more passers-by. I'm going to look at some premises in Canterbury.'

She sighs. 'I do think you might have let me know. It's going to be terribly awkward to let Mark down. I'm not sure what on earth I'm going to tell him.' She's literally pouting as if I've broken a sacred promise.

'If he's in business, I'm sure he's used to the fact that things change. And in fact, I didn't say I wanted to have a shop at the complex.'

'But you were so keen! I told you how super it was there and you seemed completely on board.'

'I'm sorry if that was the impression you got, and I do appreciate you were trying to help, but I have to trust my own judgement on business decisions and really, it wouldn't be the right position for my shop. I need a spot with more passing trade.'

She sniffs and turns away.

'I see.'

Now I've offended her again. I do need to try to get on with her.

'It's such a lovely day – shall we go outside and see the pond?' I say, trying to lift the mood.

The water is looking beautifully clear and the ducks and coots are paddling about serenely.

'This is actually awfully nice,' she says, and for once she sounds sincere. 'It really looks *so* natural. Clever. But I'm sure there was already some sort of pond when Mr Whatsisface lived here.'

'Yes, it's the same one. It's a natural pond.' Does she think I'm trying to claim credit for it?

'Oh, I see.' She looks disappointed as if somehow that's inferior to an artificial pond that has been designed to appear natural. I really don't understand her at all.

'Maybe the kids would like to come for a swim in it?'

She laughs.

'Max might, but not Saskia. Too muddy. Too many insects – *oh Mummy, can't you get rid of all the horrid bugs? They're annoying me!*'

'It's really not bad. I never put my feet down though. You're right, the bottom isn't very nice – sort of slimy mud, and if you're not careful I think you might get stuck in it.'

'You're honestly welcome to use our pool whenever you like rather than...' She waves a hand at the pond. 'I mean, I wouldn't want you to think I have any... ill-feeling towards you. As Carl's wife, I mean. I'm not jealous of you.'

'I'm sure you're not.' Why would she be jealous of me? It never crossed my mind even for a second. 'But thank you.'

She lays her hand on my arm for a moment.

'Now, I suppose Carl's told you about why we – why our marriage ended?'

'Um, he's told me a little, yes. But not much, I promise. He doesn't like to talk much about the past.'

She rolls her eyes. 'Ha! Well, that's true. Trying to get Carl to talk about anything important was always absolutely impossible! Fine if it's to do with the kids, but anything else – forget it!'

She looks away across the pond, remembering, perhaps. 'I hope you'll do a better job with that than I ever managed to. It's only that...'

'Yes?'

'I wanted to – to tell you my side of it.'

'Oh. Well, that's not necessary. I honestly don't see it as being about sides. I do have friends who are divorced. I understand that it's complicated, that there are rarely any villains. It's life, that's all. I don't see you as the baddy, if that's what you're worried about.'

'Ye-e-e-e-s, I suppose so. It's only that sometimes I do get the teensiest impression that you don't like me. That you're *judging* me, you know. And I wondered if that was because of... well...'

Maybe if I let her say her piece, then she'll leave and I can get on with the hundred and one things I need to do. Making some inferior curtains for the small single bedroom, for a start.

'I really try not to judge anyone.' But of course, she's right in a way. Since Carl told me about her and Stefan, a part of me can't help thinking of that every time I see her.

She sighs and glances at me, then looks back out over the water.

'I presume Carl told you that I went to bed with his brother Stefan?'

'Actually, yes, he did.'

'And did he tell you that he slept with someone else first?'

'Um, no. No, he didn't mention that.'

She snorts. 'Well, no surprises there. Typical Carl. Keep the brand clean – Perfect Carl.'

'I'm not sure I feel very comf—'

'So you see, what happened is that Carl had sex with someone else while away on a business trip. Completely unprovoked.'

'Unprovoked?'

'Yes. I hadn't done anything wrong at that point. I mean, he wasn't punishing me for something I'd done.'

God, I can't get a handle on Antonia at all. I don't understand how her mind works. Does she see relationships as being all about a balance of power?

'Er... OK.'

'So, he slept with this woman and then he confessed to me and I was absolutely furious, as you can imagine. I really had no option but to pay him back for it. So, I slept with Stefan.' She shrugs as if the matter was entirely out of her hands. 'But to be fair to me, I was rather drunk and I'm sure Stefan had been lusting after me for years, only we'd never acted on it. I thought, well, why am I being such an angel and not succumbing to temptation when it's right there being offered to me on a plate, and if Carl doesn't give two hoots about our marriage, then why should I? And Stefan was so persuasive.'

'But then Carl and Stefan became completely estranged!'

'Well, that's up to them. It's nothing to do with me. That's Carl being Carl. Anyone else would have forgiven us both and moved on by now.'

God, she's infuriating.

'Well, I should be getting on, Antonia.'

'I've upset you, haven't I?'

'No, it's fine. I have a lot to do, that's all. With the house. Curtains to make and so on.'

'Oh, of course. Well, I'll speak to Mark and square it with him about cancelling the meeting, so you've no need to worry.'

I really wasn't – as I hadn't asked her to get involved, didn't want a meeting, and don't want to rent one of his outlets – but still I find myself saying thank you so much for sorting it out.

And I really didn't want to know the details about her and Stefan, though I'm starting to see that maybe the whole episode was more complicated than I realised. I suppose it's not surprising that Carl edited out his part in it all rather than giving me the whole story, but why did Antonia feel the need to tell me? Surely, she doesn't care what I think?

37

NUMBER ONE

Celeste is here for another visit. It was her fortieth birthday on Thursday, and to say that Celeste is not at peace with ageing would be the understatement of the century. Usually, for her birthdays, she has a party in a wine bar with an incredible, but unheard-of, band she's discovered, amazing food, with loads of cool people there. It's all very glam. Only this year, Celeste said she couldn't face it. On the day itself, she went out for dinner and then drinks with a couple of friends, and at the end of the evening they put her in a cab (she was quite drunk). When she got home, she'd keeled over on her bed fully dressed and cried and cried because she was forty and single, and she'd never get married again or have kids, and it was completely horrible. But then she heard my message on her voicemail, singing 'Happy Birthday' and saying 'I love you', so she called me – at 2 a.m. – and asked if she could come down to the cottage on Saturday. So now it's the weekend and here she is.

Carl has taken the kids out for the day, to the beach, then they're going for pizza and a film in Canterbury in the evening.

Anyway, Celeste and I have had a good day so far. We had a

wander round the village, bumped into Antonia. It was actually pretty funny because I'd been explaining how it's impossible to enter the village without seeing Antonia. One of the things I love about Celeste is she'll take something like that and exaggerate it so that, instead of being annoying, it starts to become funny. We were walking along the high street and I was showing her the shops, and she was pretending to spot Antonia in unlikely places (she hadn't met her at this point).

'And this is the chi-chi fabric shop where Antonia instructed me to have my curtains made,' I say, 'because, you see, it's a false economy to have nasty, ready-made curtains like ordinary people have, when you could let yourself be ripped off and shell out the equivalent of the output of a small country just so no one can see in while you're getting undressed, even though you live down a track where there are literally no neighbours.'

'Yup,' says Celeste, peering in. 'There she is, see, ducked down behind that display of fabric samples, waiting to pounce on unsuspecting second wives.'

'Here's the bakery.'

'Is this the place where Antonia nearly caused a riot by buying up Kent's entire supply of sourdough loaves?'

'Yes, pretty much.'

'I think she's in there. Look, that's her, disguised as a shop assistant in a pink overall!'

So we'd been talking like this when I hear, 'Natalie!'

Well, at least she's finally got my name right. Hurrah! Shall I give her a medal?

I make a face at Celeste and hiss '*Behave!*' at her as I turn around.

'Antonia. Hi. How are you?'

As ever, Antonia kisses me on both cheeks, *mwah-mwah*, as if I've arrived for a super-marvellous dinner party instead of simply sauntering along the high street, wondering what to get for supper.

Celeste, mouth twitching in the effort not to laugh, turns to face her. I'm about to introduce them properly but of course Celeste gets in first.

'I'm Celeste, Natalie's sister,' she says. 'Now, let me guess, you must be one of Natalie's *marvellous* friends in the village?'

Celeste is so unsubtle. I'm afraid I was doing impressions of Antonia when we were at the cottage, saying everything is marvellous all the time: the sourdough is marvellous and Saskia is so marvellous at riding and she had a simply marvellous rosé at that gorgeous new wine bar and the weather has been so marvellous...

I can see a tiny flicker of doubt cross Antonia's face as she tries to suss out if Celeste is taking the piss or not, but then she smiles.

'Well, I do hope Natalie would count me as a friend, but actually I'm Carl's Number One.'

Who on earth would insist on phrasing it like that? Only Antonia– instead of saying she's Carl's ex-wife or first wife or the mother of his kids– would say she's his Number One, making it sound as if she's the most important person in his life and I'm just Number Two; second best. Does she have to keep doing that? I tell myself it's not actually deliberately bitchy. It couldn't be, could it? I'm probably being paranoid, but sometimes it feels as if it might be.

'Oh, really?' Celeste laughs, completely unfazed. 'His Number One what?'

'Oh. Wife, I mean – his Number One wife.'

'Gosh.' Celeste turns to me. 'Nats, honestly, you never said that Carl was a polygamist and you have to share him with multiple wives. How many are there? Are you Number Two? Or Number Five? Number Twenty-Seven?'

I bite my lip to stop myself laughing.

'No, no.' Does Antonia actually think Celeste believes that? 'Sorry, perhaps I wasn't clear. I meant that I'm his *first* wife. Carl's ex-wife, you see?'

'Oh, I *see*!' Celeste hams it up unashamedly. '*Ex*-wife!' With a massive exaggeration of the word '*ex*'. 'Ah, of course. Natalie had mentioned that Carl had been married at one point to someone...' Celeste does an understated but dismissive shake of her hand at this point as if flicking away an irritating little piece of fluff. '*Ex*-wife,' she says again. 'Right. I'm divorced myself but must admit it's never entered my head to refer to myself as his *Number One* wife. Not under any circumstances. Is it some sort of local custom? How interesting.'

Celeste is really pushing it now. I sidle closer so I can nudge her discreetly to get her to stop.

'Er... well... I don't think so, no, I... I suppose...' It's rare to witness Antonia looking so ill at ease. 'I wasn't thinking,' Antonia looks down for a moment. 'Sorry,' she says. 'Well,' she adds, 'I hope you have a nice visit. Bye.'

'Bye, Antonia. See you soon.'

She nods and scurries off into the butcher's.

'That was a bit mean,' I tell Celeste.

'It was *not*. She was doing a number on you. You shouldn't let her get away with it.'

'Was she, though? Surely it wasn't deliberate?'

'Oh, Noodle, you're the nicest person I know, but sometimes you are so naïve it's like dealing with a tiny child. She was putting you down. Now, being you, you're going to make excuses and say she can't help it or she's insecure or some other bollocks, but, trust me, she was trying to make you feel you don't matter. But you're my little sister and you're amazing and I'm not having anyone speak to you like that or make you feel you're not important. I don't accept it and neither should you.'

We get some food to cook for supper later, then pop into The Copper Kettle for tea and toasted teacakes. It's a sweet little tearoom, with blue gingham tablecloths and mismatched china, and proper leaf tea and decent cakes, too. We sit down at a table and I say hello to a couple of people I recognise, and I introduce Celeste to Hazel, the friendly woman who runs the café. Hazel asks how the house is coming along and do I want any onion sets to plant as she hears I'm reviving Ted's veg patch.

After we leave, Celeste says, 'You're so settled – you seem to know half the village. People offering you stuff for your veg patch, you horny-handed daughter of the soil.'

'I wish I were. I'm having to learn about gardening as I go along, but people have been really so kind. Dave, our postman, has even rotavated the veg plot for me. And, to be fair, Antonia did introduce me to her clique – I mean friends – so she's not all bad.'

Celeste rolls her eyes, then says, 'That's super-marvellous, absolutely marvellous, sweetie.'

Back at the cottage, it's too cold to swim in the pond and the sky is getting darker and darker as if there's a storm brewing. It's been so humid today.

We're standing in the big bedroom, freshly painted in the softest, palest blue, which is pretty and calm and I absolutely love it. The new bed-frame has finally arrived, and Celeste admires the beautiful Victorian brass head and foot. Steve's been up to his eyes on a new job, so fixing it all together has been delayed a bit, but he's promised to do it after the weekend. For now, Carl and I are still in the guest double, and Celeste will sleep in the little single room.

I tell her about my assault on the ceiling. She understands. I knew she would. I think Carl thought I was doing it for no reason, as a fun bit of DIY that went awry, not because I was so crazily angry and upset that all I wanted to do was smash something to smithereens.

'Nats – has Dad been in touch with you?'

I shake my head and shrug.

'I need to tell you, I contacted him via Mum. You should know: I'm taking the money.'

'OK.'

'Is that it? I need to know you're really OK with it?'

I nod. 'I promise you I am. Carl's lost his job.'

'Oh Lordy, he hasn't! Nats, that's awful. How?'

I fill her in on what happened and she says I must definitely take the money from our dad.

'I think we can manage without it.'

'But what did Carl say when you told him about the money? Doesn't he want you to take it? Even if he starts up his own company, like you said, it would give you a bit of a cushion.'

'I didn't tell him about the money.'

She gives me a look, then raises her eyebrows.

'I didn't tell him because I thought he'd insist I accept it and it's not up to him.'

'Nats, come on, you're married now – you should at least *tell* him. He can't make you take it, but it's not fair to keep him in the dark, is it? You said you want to do more things together, but you have to do your part. You were annoyed he didn't tell you about his other brother. You can't have it both ways.'

I shrug. 'I like to be self-reliant. I don't want a hand-out.'

'Cheers! How's that supposed to make me feel? It's not a hand-out, it's a gift. And being too self-reliant isn't always a good thing. Take it from one who knows.'

True, Celeste is the most self-reliant person I know.

'But it is a good thing, surely? It has to be.'

'Is it? Sometimes I wonder if that's partly why I'm single. I know I'm not unattractive, and I'm not crazy or alcoholic. There's nothing *obvious* wrong with me. Men want to sleep with me, but they don't want to settle down with me. Maybe they're subconsciously put off because I seem like I don't need anyone else?'

I pause to think and we go back down to stroll round outside before the rain comes. It's so humid; the air feels like a claggy wet blanket all around us. Overhead, the clouds are thickening and the sky is getting darker.

'Where did you suddenly gain all this self-insight?'

'Therapy,' she says. 'Should have done it years ago.'

'Think I'm beyond help. All I do is say the wrong thing. Every time Carl is here, we end up arguing. And you've seen I'm not exactly hitting it off with Antonia. My only therapy really is swimming in the pond, preferably naked. At least it doesn't cost anything, and it's so private down here. We're not overlooked at all.'

'You don't!'

'Yes, you prude. No need to sound so shocked. Only on my own or with Carl. Though we did nearly get caught when they came to deliver our mattress. Which was actually pretty funny.' It seems aeons ago. We were so happy that day.

'God, you weird hippie. You really do take after Mum.'

'It's honestly so nice. It's lovely to swim there. I'm only not dragging you in because it looks as if it's about to start tipping down.'

'Yeuch. No, thanks. If it's not the Caribbean or a really warm, really clean swimming pool, I'd rather not bother.'

'Now you'll be regretting you didn't turn on the charm for Antonia. Their pool is perfect. No chlorine and really warm.'

'Why don't you swim there then? It's so near.'

It starts to rain and we scurry back into the kitchen.

'Well.' I get out the food and start preparing things for supper later. 'You've seen what she's like. I see her practically every day when I dare to go into the village so I don't exactly feel I'm suffering from a shortage of Antonia in my life. I have swum there a number of times, but it's not that relaxing. I can't go and just have a swim. I have to make polite chit-chat.'

'I bet it's because you're afraid of her and the spoilt-brat daughter!'

'I'm not! Well, not really afraid exactly...' My voice peters out. 'It's not always easy, that's all.'

'Look, Nats, no one on the planet aside from you would ever have agreed to moving so close to "Wife Number One". I'm surprised she doesn't get herself a diamond brooch emblazoned with it so she can wear it in the village. But you've made a great go of it and this house is really beautiful. Don't let her intimidate you, that's all. It's *your* village too now – don't let her lord it over you. She's not your boss, your parent, or your spouse. She has no sway over you whatsoever.'

* * *

Later, the rain has intensified and blown up into a proper storm. The sky is leaden and, in the distance, we hear the low growl of thunder. It's raining so hard now that it's bouncing off the path, and the wind is roaring through the trees.

Celeste and I are in the middle of supper, talking and laughing, when there's a sudden knock on the door. Because the parking is round at the side, you don't always hear or see visitors, especially now with the wind and rain drowning out everything else, but I'm not expecting anyone. Surely even Antonia wouldn't 'pop in' during a storm? It's only about half-eight, way too early to be Carl, and anyway he texted from the cinema to say he wouldn't be back until ten.

Celeste is standing behind me, holding my heavy cast-iron frying pan behind her back in case it's a would-be burglar or mad axeman. I tell her she's being crazy but she says I should be more careful. It might be some nutjob who's seen me swimming naked in the pond and wants a closer look.

'Don't say that. You'll get me worried now.

'Who is it?' I call out.

'Please let me in. It's Stefan,' the voice says. 'Carl's brother.'

I open the door at once.

'Come in, come in! It's horrible out there. You must be soaked.' I stand back to welcome him in. 'Celeste, could you run up to the airing cupboard and bring a towel please?'

Here I am, alone in the hallway with Carl's secret brother. I look up at him because of course, he's tall, like Carl, maybe even an inch taller. He looks like Carl and also not like him, with brown eyes and shorter hair, so that it's incredibly disconcerting to be with a complete stranger who at the same time feels so familiar.

'Um, I'm Natalie,' I say, though as soon as I say it, I realise it sounds dumb. Who else could I possibly be?

He does that funny half-smile exactly the same way Carl does, a sort of wry, lopsided grin.

'Obviously,' I add. 'Well, it's very nice to meet you at last.'

I know I'm sounding stiff and formal. Really, I want to hug him, but I don't know what to do. Does Carl know Stefan is here? If so, why on earth didn't he tell me he was coming?

'If I weren't soaking wet, I would like to hug you,' Stefan says.

Well, that's enough for me.

I reach up and give him a hug.

'It's only water.'

He squeezes me back.

'It's so good to meet you...' He sounds choked up. 'I need to see Carl. In Bristol... he doesn't... it's horrible. He won't talk... I have to...' His voice peters out.

'I'm very sorry you weren't at the wedding.' I take his hand. 'I didn't know about you then or I would have insisted you come.'

'Ah...' He looks down. 'Families. Not always easy.'

I laugh. 'How true.'

Celeste reappears with two towels.

'Now, would you like a hot bath or shower if you want to warm up?' I offer. 'Or I can light the fire in the sitting room? Or food first? Celeste and I were in the middle of supper.'

'Oh, I don't want to disturb you. May I sit somewhere while you finish eating?'

'Don't be ridiculous!' Celeste hands him the towels. 'We're not going to sit and eat supper while you're loitering in another room on your own. Have you eaten?'

'Well, I had a horrible sandwich hours ago in Bristol. I fear reports that British cooking has greatly improved may be ill-founded.'

'I'm Celeste, by the way, Natalie's sister. You're the secret brother, aren't you?'

'Ah. And have you been kept a secret too?' Stefan gives her that half-smile.

'I'm too stroppy and too noisy for anyone to keep me a secret. Not that Natalie could ever keep a secret for more than two minutes because she's incapable of lying, fortunately.'

'*Incapable*? Interesting. Tell me more. I like her already.'

Stefan dries his hair and face, removes his soaked jacket and comes through to the dining room. I fetch him a plate and Celeste serves him chicken casserole, potatoes, lemony cabbage and roasted carrots.

I pour him a glass of wine and he starts to eat.

'Oh, now I'm embarrassed with my crack about British cooking. This is *delicious*.'

'Thank you.'

'I see Carl's gone for an upgrade second time around. Antonia couldn't even cook toast.'

Celeste laughs but she also gives me a look. I'm not sure what to say. I mean, it's a joke, right? But a bit odd?

Stefan takes a gulp of his wine, then says, 'I'm sorry, that was a crass thing to say. I should not have compared you with Antonia. Please accept my apologies. I'm really nervous to be here.' The way he talks is interesting – it's quite formal. I wonder if he speaks several languages. People who do sometimes sound like that.

'Well... er...'

'It was inappropriate. I'm sure you are very different in many ways and no comparison is required. Or useful.'

'Well, actually, most of the time, I don't feel like an upgrade at all.' I pick up my wineglass and stare down into it. 'I feel like a bargain basement, crappy, cheap, knock-off wife who can't begin to compare to Wife Number One.'

'Oh, Nats. Don't say that – it's so not true.' Celeste leaps up from her seat and comes around the table and hugs me.

'Ach, it's the wine talking – take no notice.' I wipe my eyes with my napkin. 'Things have been... trickier than I thought for various reasons. Plus living a stone's throw from Mrs Bloody Perfect with her golden hair, immaculate kitchen and palatial house is not making it any easier. She's an *impossible* act to follow and I'm not even making a half-decent crack at it.'

A sudden snorting noise as Stefan bursts into laughter while drinking his wine. He dabs his face with his napkin.

He tries to say sorry but is laughing too much.

'Antonia, *perfect*?' He laughs again. 'Oh God! That's the stupidest thing I ever heard.'

'Thanks.'

'No. I'm so sorry. Really.' He wipes his face again and takes a gulp of his water. 'But you can't possibly think Antonia is perfect?'

'Oh, do tell,' says Celeste, leaning close in towards him. 'She's certainly well-groomed and glamorous, but...?'

'Oh, glamorous – who gives a shit about that?' It seems funny, hearing him swear. He looks so *proper*.

'Hey, thanks a bunch!' Celeste flicks her hair back in a self-mocking parody of a narcissistic woman.

'Don't be crazy.' Stefan raises his glass to her. 'Don't fish for compliments. You are clearly a very attractive woman. It demeans you. Never do it.' His voice is suddenly very serious.

Celeste, chastened, gives a tiny nod and raises her glass back.

'So, why is Antonia not as perfect as she appears then?' Celeste asks.

Stefan looks at her, then at me, then says, 'You know why Carl and Antonia split up?'

'No,' says Celeste.

'Um, well, I think it was a combination of things, wasn't it? And... well, yes, I do know about Antonia and... er... you.'

'What?' Celeste looks at me. 'You never told me that.'

'It's not my story to tell.'

Stefan nods. 'Can I ask, what did Carl tell you, exactly? Is it OK to ask?'

'Yes, it is. *But.*' I sigh. Is this wrong? Should I be talking like this when Carl's not here? And in front of Celeste? I look at the

antique ship's clock on the wall. Nearly quarter past nine. Carl
will be back soon.

'Celeste, I'm sorry. I don't think Carl would like it if I talked
about his private past in front of you.'

'Oh, come on, Nats. You can't make me miss out now.'

'Cely, I can't. It's not right.'

She sighs and gets up and starts clearing the plates.

'All right. I'll put the kettle on for coffee and go through to the
living room. But you've got three minutes, then I'm coming back.'

* * *

Stefan lowers his voice.

'So, you know Antonia and I slept together? Carl told you?'

'Yes, and then Antonia told me too.'

Stefan tips his head back and snorts. 'Christ – and what did
she tell you? That I seduced her when she was drunk? That I took
advantage of her, right?'

'Mm – more or less.'

'And did you believe her?'

I pause for a minute, thinking back.

'You know – I didn't completely. It didn't sound quite credible,
the way she said it.'

'And you have some experience of Antonia by now? Your
sister said you are incapable of lying, yes?'

'Well, I find it very difficult, that's true. Even when you should
lie, I mean, like when someone's had a new haircut and you're
supposed to say something nice about it. I find it really hard.'

'Well, Antonia is exactly the opposite of that. Sometimes she
lies when there is no reason to at all. Just because she can,
because she enjoys it, or whatever. It's a habit, like spending

money on things she doesn't need or having her hair done when it's already perfect. A very bad habit.'

'OK.' I nod. 'I can see that that might be true, but why should I believe what you say about your affair? You're not impartial either, are you?'

'I suppose that's true. But it wasn't an affair. We had sex one time. Literally once. It was *nothing*.'

'But, Stefan, come on.' I put my hand on his arm. 'You slept with your brother's wife. You can't pretend that's nothing. Look, I really don't give a toss about Antonia, but you hurt Carl. You really hurt him. He's your brother. That's not nothing.'

He looks down, then into my eyes.

'You are right.' He nods. 'It was wrong. I'm an adult and I shouldn't have let her—' He tuts at himself. 'No, I'm not a child! I believed their marriage was over – but no excuses. She had her reasons and none of them were anything to do with me. She used me because she was so angry with Carl. She could have used anyone, any man, but she wanted *me* – to hurt Carl. To hurt him as much as possible. And I was an idiot. And I was drunk.'

I look at him, brows raised.

'Yes, I see what you are thinking. No one poured vodka shots down my throat. You're telling me I have to take responsibility. For my part.'

'Yes. You do.'

He nods and says nothing.

Then he says, very quietly, 'I have missed him very much.'

'I don't doubt it. And I know he's missed you too. Listen, Carl won't talk about it. I didn't even know you existed until a few weeks ago. I tried – more than once – to ask him and he got furious with me, then clammed up. So I know it really matters to him. I love him, but it's so hard to get him to talk about anything difficult. When he's upset, he goes into himself and I can't get through to him and he acts as if I'm being an annoying nag.'

Stefan nods and takes a sip of his wine.

'He was the same way when he was a kid. If we had a fight, afterwards I would look for him to make it up, and he would be hiding – behind the shed at the bottom of the garden or under his bed, or in the pantry. And he wouldn't speak to me. Felix isn't like that. If Felix is cross, you go and tickle him or make a stupid face and he laughs, and all is forgiven. With Carl, the shutters slam shut and you can't get through. He changed later, in his twenties and thirties, and we became much closer, but I think maybe – I don't know, I'm not a psychologist or anything – but our parents were very... tough on Carl. More indulgent with Felix because he was the baby of the family. But hard on me as the eldest and I think even worse with Carl, on his case about work all the time. I am, you know, very sporty, very academic also...'

'And modest.'

He laughs.

'Ah, I miss English humour. This is the trouble with living abroad. In the Netherlands, it is great in many ways – more efficient than the UK, not so obsessed with class – but no one takes the piss as well as the English.'

'Maybe it should be our national motto.'

He nods, laughing.

'Our father was very strict, very old-fashioned. Not an understanding sort of dad, you know. Even now, being around him is... not easy. Carl goes to be with him because he is a dutiful son, but I can see it drains him.'

He's right. Carl looks shattered all the time now. It's not only the physical exhaustion from going to and from Bristol; it's being there, but when I try to draw him out, to tell me how it is with his dad, he shrugs and says it's OK.

Celeste comes back in, saying she's going to make coffee and tea.

'Are you finished yet? I don't see why I should have to miss out on all the interesting bits.'

'Don't be a vulture. We're talking about important family stuff.'

'So, can I sit or what? Or am I relegated to the living room again? It's boring in there on my own.'

'She can stay, yes?' Stefan gestures towards her seat. 'She is my family too now.'

'Well... but we're not like siblings or anything, are we?' She flushes suddenly and makes a show of fiddling with the cafetière, then returns to the kitchen and starts fussing over which cups to use. It's so unlike Celeste ever to be flustered about anything that I watch her roaming about the kitchen, apparently hunting for something.

I meet Stefan's eyes and he gives me a small smile and raises his eyebrows. Oh my goodness – they fancy each other. I know it.

'Nats, where's the sugar?'

'Not for me!' Stefan calls out. 'I don't take it.'

'Oh. Nor me.' Celeste pauses, then starts apparently looking for something in the larder. 'Chocolate?'

'In the fridge. It was really hot before the storm broke and it was going too soft.'

She comes back to the table, I see Stefan watching her, waiting for her to look at him.

Finally, she does, and he smiles at her. Not in a smug, I know you fancy me way, not in a creepy way, just acknowledging that he likes her too. And she smiles back. She doesn't start flirting ridiculously (as she has been known to do); she doesn't start laughing pointlessly or going all pouty. She simply pours Stefan his coffee and looks at him directly as she passes the cup to him.

Suddenly, I feel quite tearful because I sense I am witnessing the beginning of something – something important – and normally you don't get to see that. It makes me think back to when I first started seeing Carl and knowing for sure I wanted him in my life, that being around him made me feel soft and sane and *whole* in a way that was totally different from being with anyone else.

'By the way, I meant to ask you, how did you get here? Did you drive?'

Stefan says he came by train, then took a taxi from the station. The driver wouldn't come down the lane because he said the potholes are so bad for his suspension and that's why Stefan got soaked through.

'Well, I would certainly ask you to stay, but I should—'

'It's OK. I think there is a pub in the village, yes? I will call and see if they have a room. If not, there are hotels in Ashford. But I do want to talk to Carl. I *need* to talk to him. I can't stand the way it is in Bristol when we are there together.'

'Yes, I think you should.' I check the clock. It's after ten now. 'He should be back any minute.'

'Oh, but surely Stefan must stay here, Nats?' Celeste gives me a look over the rim of her coffee cup. Shameless.

I roll my eyes at her.

'It's not up to me. We have to wait for Carl.'

She sniffs and reaches for the chocolate.

'It's nice to see women actually eating,' Stefan says.

'Good.' Celeste shoves a piece of chocolate in her mouth and slides the bar over towards him.

'So many women seem to eat nothing at all. I go out for lunch with a colleague and she orders a salad then spends half an hour moving bits of it around the plate before pushing it away and saying she is stuffed. I don't understand it. Aren't they hungry?'

'I think maybe they eat in secret.' I reach for the chocolate.

'They think it's shameful or something. We've never been like that, have we?'

'Definitely not,' says Celeste through a mouthful of chocolate so the words come out like 'Hefennlee hnot', which makes us all laugh.

'Appetite is important,' Stefan says, smiling at Celeste.

She nods and smiles back.

'It certainly is.' I get the feeling she isn't talking about chocolate any more...

We move through to the big sitting room and I light the fire. Celeste draws the curtains while Stefan pushes the sofa a little nearer the fireplace. Outside, the rain is still thrashing down and the wind is howling.

There is a brief hesitation as we all wonder who should sit where. I bet Celeste is trying to decide if it would be good to be opposite Stefan, so they can look at each other, or next to him so she can be close to him.

'Here, please, take the sofa.' I gesture to both of them to sit there and I take the armchair.

We are talking and laughing, generally having a really good time, but as the weather is still raging, I don't hear Carl's car pull up and, as the sitting room door is shut tight, I don't hear the front door either.

The sitting room door opens suddenly and Carl says, 'Hi. God, I'm *absolutely drenched*.'

Then he spots Stefan.

'What the *fuck* is *he* doing here? Is this one of your silly schemes to try to get us to play Happy Families? Not cool, Natalie. Really. What on earth were you thinking?'

'Hey, hey!' Stefan stands up. 'It's not her fault, Carl. It was nothing to do with Natalie. I turned up on the doorstep.'

'*Why?* What do you want? There's nothing more to say.' Carl covers his face with his hands for a moment. 'Jesus wept. Natalie, why did you let him in? It's hard enough having to be around him at Dad's while dealing with Dad falling to pieces. I really don't *need* this. I've had a very long day and I'm shattered.'

I stand up and take Carl's hand.

'Come into the kitchen for a minute, please.'

We stand in the kitchen, face to face.

'Nat, really, what the fuck...? I know you like to see yourself as some amazing peacemaker and all that. Well, go and run the UN. I didn't ask you to interfere, did I? It's nothing to do with you. He's my bloody brother and if I don't fucking want to talk to him then I fucking well won't, OK? I didn't stick my nose in with you and your dad, did I? Keep out of it. I don't want to come back after a day with the kids, and them squabbling and whining and asking for ice cream every two minutes, to find the person I hate most in the world laughing and talking in my own living room.'

I wait for him to come to a halt.

'Finished?'

He nods.

'Right, now listen to me for a minute. Stefan turned up unexpectedly. I didn't invite him. He appeared because he's half off his head desperate to talk to you and you're being such a stupid, stubborn, child about it. And – because I'm a human being and don't work for the Stasi, and he was cold and wet and – oh, yes – he's family – I invited him in to get warm and to eat something. And we've been talking because that's what people *do*, Carl.

People talk to communicate, to try to understand things better. Otherwise, everything stays a mess for ever. If you know of a better way than talking, well, please enlighten me, but I don't. It *helps* – even if you can't explain it exactly the way you'd like to, even if it's less than perfect – it's always, *always* better than *not* talking.

'Yes, he slept with your wife so, yes, he did a terrible thing. But you know what? He didn't kill anyone, he didn't hurt your children. What he did was stupid and bad, but he's still your brother. And was that really what ended your marriage, if you're one hundred per cent honest with yourself?'

'Well, it didn't help!'

'I'm sure it didn't, and maybe it was the final straw, but wasn't the marriage already on its last legs by then?'

'I don't know.' He sighs. 'Yes, I guess so.'

'And – by the way, it is *not* OK for you to talk to me like that. You're not my boss, and if you were my boss and spoke to me like that, I'd be taking you to an industrial tribunal. Be angry if you want to be, but there's no excuse to talk to me as if I'm a bit of dogshit on your shoe. Do it again and I will be out the door in two seconds and heading for the M20 in my van – and you know I mean it. Do you *hear* me?'

He has the grace to look shamefaced.

'I'm sorry. I'm really sorry. I shouldn't have had a go at you. I'm just exhausted and cross.'

'I know you are, but you still can't go around talking to people like that. Especially not if you're married to them.'

Carl nods and looks at me properly then.

'I'm very sorry.'

'Good. So, will you go in there now and try to talk to Stefan, please? Or let him talk for a bit.'

'I don't want to.' Suddenly, he looks like a little boy, sulky and cross, and I bite my lip to stop myself laughing.

'I know you don't, but you can do it and I'd like you to at least try, OK?'

He nods.

'Is there any wine? I'd love a drink but I couldn't have anything as I was driving round all day.'

'I will bring you some wine, Husband.' I stretch up to on tiptoe to kiss him.

He goes in and greets Celeste properly and when I bring the wine, I beckon her to come out and I shut the door. She and I huddle in the kitchen, eat more chocolate and finish clearing up.

'So, what do you think of Stefan? As if I didn't know already.'

'God, he's gorgeous, isn't he? And funny and sharp. But don't tell me – he's married. No ring, though.'

'He's divorced but I don't know any more than that.'

'Would it be too weird? I mean, we are vaguely related. There's a definite spark, right? I'm not imagining it?'

'You're not imagining it – and it's fine. You've read *Emma*?'

'Oh, probably – years ago. But she ends up with the neighbour she's always been in love with without realising, doesn't she?'

'Yes, and he's also her brother-in-law. Sort of. Emma's sister is married to Mr Knightley's brother.'

'I'd completely forgotten that. Does that mean it's OK – because it's sanctioned by Jane Austen?'

'Yes, that means it's officially OK. But be warned, Carl might well throw him out on to the front path any minute now so you should probably take a moment to tuck your phone number into his jacket pocket or something.'

'Carl wouldn't really do that?'

'He might.' I shrug. 'Really, it could go either way...'

We stand there for a minute in silence, straining to hear for shouting or the throwing of heavy objects in the sitting room, but although I can hear the low murmur of voices, nothing scary so far.

Celeste and I creep closer to the door. Now it's weirdly silent.

'You don't think they've killed each other, do you?'

I knock lightly at the door and call out: 'Er... we're making more coffee. Anyone want anything?'

There's no response at first but then Carl suddenly opens the door. He looks different somehow, softer, less strained.

'OK?' I reach up to touch his cheek.

He nods and dips to kiss me, then draws me into the hallway to speak to me.

'I'm truly sorry about earlier. I don't know why you put up with me. I'm sorry I'm such a grumpy git half the time.'

'You're not. You're very stressed and very tired, and that makes anyone grouchy.'

He wraps his arms tightly around me.

'Love you, Wife. *So* much.'

'Love you, too, Husband.'

'So,' he says, raising his voice to normal volume. 'Can we find my bastard of a brother a bed for the night, do you think, or shall we make him sleep in the shed with the spiders?'

Behind him, Stefan laughs and makes an OK sign at me.

'Of course. Oh, except Celeste is here.'

Celeste raises one eyebrow and smirks and I know exactly what she's thinking.

'I can take the couch!' Stefan offers.

'We do have three bedrooms...' Carl and I have been sleeping in the second bedroom but the bigger mattress for the brass bed is leaning against the wall in the large room upstairs so we could certainly sleep on that. 'We're a bit short of bedding. But don't worry, we'll work it out.'

We give Stefan the third bedroom and Celeste the guest double, and I rustle up sheets and blankets. Carl and I shift our bedding from the guest room to the other room. Remind self to get another duvet and pillows as soon as I can.

'Well, good night, everyone – sleep tight. I'll do proper cooked breakfast in the morning – but no rush to get up. Whenever suits you is fine.'

'Would you like another pillow?' I hear Celeste offering as I start to shut our bedroom door.

* * *

The next morning, I get up first and leave Carl to lie in for a while. Celeste comes down after a few minutes, wearing a long, glamorous ivory satin robe like a film star and looking suspiciously gorgeous, with her hair all pretty and tousled and definitely a touch of mascara on. I peer at her closely.

'So?' I say.

'I *slept* very well, thank you for asking.' She looks at me. 'Honestly, Nats, I do have some self-control.'

'I know, I know, but all that offering him your pillow – you looked like you were about to pounce on him.'

'Give me some credit, will you? I gave him a pillow and he gave me a very brotherly good night kiss on the cheek. You said Jane Austen thinks it's OK, but he obviously doesn't.'

'Maybe he has something else going on in his life? Or maybe he wants to take things slowly. Just... don't rush it. Let things take their course.'

'Says the woman who got married after less than six months!'

'That was completely different. Don't be annoying.'

'I'll be nice if you make me breakfast.'

We are bustling about the kitchen, with Celeste getting out cutlery and slicing the bread, while I cook.

'So – good morning.' We both turn to see Stefan standing in the kitchen doorway, fully dressed.

'Good morning, Stefan. How did you sleep?'

'Very well, thank you. Is my brother up?'

'Don't think so. He was pretty tired. What do you fancy for breakfast?'

I cook bacon and eggs while Celeste makes toast. There is a large pot of tea and a cafetière of coffee, and our cottage feels like a proper *home* at last. All the time the house was being fixed up and decorated, I kept thinking: *once the last light switch is in, the last window frame has been painted, then it will feel like our home.* But that wasn't it at all. It's having people here that makes all the difference.

'So,' I say, topping up Stefan's coffee cup as we sit at the table, 'how did it go, talking to Carl last night? If I may ask?'

'Of course.' He nods his thanks for the coffee. 'I think you, Natalie, have achieved what no one else has ever been able to: you got my pig-headed kid brother to talk!'

'Who's pig-headed?' Carl is suddenly standing there, having entered the other way, via the little sitting room. Awkward.

'*You* are.'

'And you're a *bastard*,' Carl says.

Oh God, I thought they'd sorted things out last night...

Carl comes closer, then suddenly ruffles his brother's hair and bends to hug him.

'I still love you, though, shit-face.'

'And me you, pig-breath.'

Celeste and I look at each other.

'I guess it must be a brothers' thing.'

'Guess so.'

'Oh, I forgot to say happy birthday, Celeste!' Carl says. 'It was a couple of days ago, right?'

'Yes, Thursday.'

'Did you have a wild party?' Stefan asks. 'I didn't get my invite.'

She smiles at him. 'No wild party this year as I was feeling crappy about it. *Big* birthday. Don't feel you have to be polite and say I don't look forty.'

'Actually, I was going to say you look really good for fifty...' Stefan keeps a straight face and looks at her over the rim of his cup as he takes a sip of coffee.

'Is this supposed to be cheering me up? Because it's not working.'

Stefan raises his glass of orange juice towards her.

'I drink your health and wish you a belated happy birthday and a sweet, happy and healthy year ahead and, if you have no wild party plans next year, I promise to take you out for dinner anywhere you like. Paris, Amsterdam, New York. Anywhere.'

'Thank you, though that is quite a way off.'

She stands up and starts clearing the plates.

I pick up the teapot and take it across to the kettle. As I refill the kettle at the sink, Celeste leans towards me and whispers, 'Is he asking me on a *date* – but then why a whole year away? Does he like me or not?'

Suddenly, Stefan leans in behind us.

'Yes, he does like you but he has to go back to Amsterdam this evening. And also – he has excellent hearing!'

Celeste thwacks him playfully on his chest and he takes her hand.

'So, a year away is too long to wait?'

She shrugs.

'Don't play games, beautiful Celeste. Is it too long?'

'It is,' she says.

'Good. Next Friday, I have to come back to see my father. On Saturday, we can have dinner, yes? If you will be free?' He gets out his phone to take her number.

She nods.

'Where? Bristol? London? Kent?'

'I can come to Bristol,' she says, 'as you'll have come from Amsterdam. It's only fair.'

'Thank you.'

He picks up his bag and heads out the door for Carl to drive him to the station. Then a few moments later, as I'm clearing the rest of the table, I hear the door open again. I turn to see who it is. Stefan comes in, takes two strides towards Celeste. She moves towards him and he pulls her close and kisses her.

'Don't forget me before next Saturday!' he says.

* * *

I am lying in bed in the dark with my husband. Maybe it's the darkness, or maybe it's that at last he's managed to talk to Stefan, I don't know, but we are *talking*. Carl strokes my arm as he speaks.

'Nat, there's something else I didn't tell you ... about ... what happened with Stefan and Antonia.'

'Go on.'

'The marriage was over. *Over*. It was so over that it didn't even feel like a big deal when I slept with someone else while I was away on a trip. Back then, Stefan and I talked on the phone often. Things had been bad at home, really awful, with us arguing and shouting. Max was unhappy, retreating into himself, Saskia was playing up – because they were upset by what was going on with Antonia and me. Stefan used to call me every few days to check I was OK, and this time, I said, 'It's *over*. I can't do this any more. It's killing me. I'm exhausted and I'm so tense, it's affecting the children. I'm asking for a divorce as soon as I get back.'

'And then what happened?'

'I got home and before I could say anything, Antonia said she thought we should try again, maybe we could see a marital therapist or something, but we should at least try.'

I turn on my side towards him.

'What did you say?'

In the darkness, he strokes my hair away from my face and kisses me softly.

'I told her no, I didn't want to. Then I told her I'd slept with someone else. It seemed less hurtful than saying I hadn't loved her for such a long time.'

'She didn't take it well?'

He snorts.

'No, really not. But Stefan – all this time – I *blamed* him and told myself it was *his* fault, all his fault. My marriage had ended but it was nothing to do with me.' I hear his voice crack. 'It was Antonia and it was Stefan.'

I kiss him very, very tenderly, as if he's been badly injured.

'But it was *me*. The marriage was a disaster. And it was mostly my fault.'

'Darling, I'm sure it wasn't. Relationships are hard.' I think back. Look at how many arguments we've had – and that's without adultery or children to worry about.

'I know, but I was never *there*. I worked all the time, and left Antonia to do everything. She got angry and resentful. I was bringing in plenty of money but I was absent, and even when I *was* there, I might as well not have been: always glued to my phone or dashing off for another meeting, another party where I could network, always looking out for the next possible client.'

'Maybe it's not such a bad thing about your leaving the business?'

He kisses me and laughs.

'Thank you for phrasing it like that rather than saying I got my ass fired. You know, I think you might be right.'

'I am occasionally. Not often but every now and then, by chance. About what?'

'Maybe I should do something else. I don't know what yet, but I don't think I should go back to the way I was. I've been doing the same thing with you, haven't I, getting obsessed with work? I don't know if you've noticed.'

'Er... yes, yes I have.'

'Well, I want to explore other ideas. I'm going to give myself six months while I work out what I'd really like to do. We have enough money for that. And if I haven't come up with something by then, then I'll find a job down here – anything.'

'That's a good plan. And, Carl, my dad – he offered me some money. I said no but maybe... do you think I should accept it?'

There's a silence.

'Carl?'

'I think actually it's entirely up to you. I'm not saying it wouldn't be nice to have a bit extra, but he's your dad, and I know how you feel about him must be complicated.'

'I miss him. It's not that I'm not upset still. And angry, but...'

'Can you go and see him?'

'He's gone back to Portugal.'

'Well, it's not another planet, darling. We can go visit, if you like?'

'It's not the money.'

'I know. It never would be with you.'

'It's just – I – there is no other dad, you know. And he's not young. I think I want to spend a bit of time with him while I can.

Even if he was a criminal. I know he's a million miles from perfect but...'

'He's your dad.'

'Yes.'

He holds me in the darkness then. Until, at last, at last, we both slip into sleep.

40

RETURN OF THE MONSTER

The spider is *back*. Right there, on the stairs, where it was the very first time I came to the cottage, and Carl laughed at me. He thought it was funny that I was too scared to come downstairs and step over a silly little spider. But it's not little. It's HUGE.

This is ridiculous. I can't live in the countryside and not be able to cope with a lone spider. It's part of living in the country, understanding the wildlife – like knowing not to let your dog off the lead anywhere near sheep, or going around the top field of Mr Akerman's rather than through it because that's where he keeps the bull. Houses in the country have spiders. It's a fact.

That's the sensible bit of me. But the other bit of me (unfortunately, about ninety-eight per cent, in this instance) is going AAAAAARRRRRGGGHHHH – get me out of here. I don't feel in tune with the wildlife. I want Carl to come with his shoe or a heavy book and crush this particular piece of wildlife to oblivion. How can I kid myself I care about animals and the environment when all I can think now is DIE, DIE, DIE?!

But Carl has had to dash back to Bristol again. Who else can I call?

Right, I refuse to be a wuss about this, but I can't manage it from upstairs. For a start, there's nothing up here. The book I'm reading is normally by my side of the bed but I know I left it downstairs in the sitting room when I was reading last night. My phone is in the kitchen, to time the scones I'm baking, so I can't even reach it to call someone, anyone, for help. Would it be over the top to call the fire brigade?

Max says he removes a spider by placing a glass over it. Then he slides a piece of card underneath and lifts the whole thing and then releases it outside.

But to try to get the glass over it, I'd have to be on the step immediately above and lean right over – and we'd be nose to nose. OK, maybe a spider doesn't have a nose. But we'd be CLOSE. Too close.

If I could possibly get to the other side of it, then I'd be able to see better and also I could run out the front door if it suddenly moved. So long as I have an escape route, I'd feel braver, I'm sure I would.

It's only small, I tell myself, but then I look at it again and I can see that, objectively, it is very, very large. By spider standards, I mean.

'Yes, but it's so much smaller than you are,' I say out loud. 'You are now calmly going to walk downstairs, stepping over it, then you will fetch a glass and come back and deal with it the way Max told you.' I use my bossiest, no-nonsense voice.

'You *can* do this!' I know that's what self-help books are all about: positive affirmations, releasing your inner power.

Slowly, trying to step lightly, I descend one step. It – the Thing – is roughly halfway down.

I raise my hands in a gesture of peace.

'I mean you no harm,' I say out loud. 'But I do need to get downstairs, OK?'

The spider doesn't move. Perhaps it's dead?

I descend another step. It flexes one leg as if warming up for battle. Oh God, why isn't Carl here? What's the point of getting married and putting up with living on his ex-wife's doorstep if your bloody husband is never here to deal with spiders when you need him?

I like to think I can deal with anything. When I was growing up, there were thieves and drug dealers and all sorts hanging out at the flats – on the steps, on the litter-strewn green space outside, by the cars. How come I could manage that but can't deal with a single spider? My dad managed to survive a decade in prison. I must have some fearless genes in my DNA somewhere. Where the hell are they?

I go down another step.

I don't know where they are, but I *can't*. I don't care about bloody positive affirmations or The Giant Within. I don't have a giant within. I'm a small, hopeless woman on the outside and I'm also a small, hopeless woman within.

At this point, the timer starts bleeping on my phone, which is handily placed on the kitchen worktop, i.e. miles away from where I am, needing to call the emergency services to come and rescue me. I must take the scones out in the next couple of minutes too, or they'll burn.

Ah, I know – I grab the stair-rail to my right – if I can climb up on to it, then slowly lower myself to the hall that way, I won't need to tread on the Monster's step at all, or on the ones above or below it.

I get up close to the banister and bend over it so that my head is dangling over the side into the hall away from *IT* and I scrunch my legs up so that the Beast can't leap up on to them. It's awkward because I'm still wearing my apron, as I was baking. I slowly slide myself down the banister. Brilliant! I'm a genius. As I reach the newel post at the bottom, I attempt to dismount, but it's at this point that the skirt of my apron becomes wrapped around the ball of the newel post. I am upside down, suspended from the banisters like a pheasant hung up to tenderise. The timer is bleep-bleeping.

'Siri, shut up!' I bellow from the hall. Of course, it ignores me. Typical technology.

I start flailing around, trying to free myself, but my own weight is making it impossible, gravity tugging me down with the apron hooked round the post holding me fast.

This is ridiculous. How have I managed to get myself into this stupid position?

Suddenly the thought strikes me that it's not just 'this position', pinioned to the banisters. It's 'this position' in my life. It feels like a perfect fit. I suggested to Carl we move to be nearer his kids so he could see them more, be the kind of dad he wants to be, rather than the distant kind he had himself. So now here I am, living with his ex-wife monitoring my every move, popping in whenever she feels like it, telling me what to do and where to eat and what to wear. Hoist by my own petard.

And then I realise, yes, it *is* absolutely ridiculous – and I start to laugh because what else can I do other than despair and sink into a pit of self-blame, which will help no one? But I am bloody stuck whether I like it or not, and I cannot see how on earth to get myself free.

Suddenly there's a knock at the door. It's late morning. Thank goodness – it's probably Dave, the postman. He can help me. The door's not locked.

'*Dave!* Is that you? I'm stuck! Can you come in?'

There's a pause, then the door opens a little way.

'Natalie?

It's Antonia. Marvellous. Who is the one person on the planet I'd least like to see me stuck on a stair post upside down, looking like a stranded beetle?

'Oh... er, hello, Antonia. How are you?' I say politely, as if we've bumped into each other at the village fête.

'Are you all right?'

Yes, I'm absolutely fine. I often like to suspend myself upside-down from the banisters. It's a new form of yoga. Everyone's doing it, haven't you heard?

'Well, not as such, no.'

'Why are you...? Would you like a hand down?'

'Yes, please.'

And because she's tall and fit and I'm a miniature person, she physically lifts me up to release me, then sets me down on to the floor. I have never been so embarrassed in my life. I thank her and rush to rescue the scones, which are browner than usual but still look edible.

'Were you sliding down the banisters? It's awfully fun, isn't it? My brothers and I used to do it all the time. It drove our poor mother absolutely doolally. We were always careering off at the bottom and breaking things.'

I explain about the spider.

'Oh, Max is in the car. He deals with all the spiders in our house. I only popped in to ask you about the raffle.'

I point to the beast and Antonia shudders.

'That *is* huge! No wonder you didn't want to face it. Let me go and rustle up Max. You'll see, he's absolutely ace at this.'

* * *

'Hey, Natalie. Do you have a glass and a piece of card because I don't have my ones with me? That's what you need for a spider-catching set.'

'You're a star.' I go into the kitchen for a big plastic picnic glass and I take a card-backed envelope from the post pile on the hall table.

I am standing behind a small eleven-year-old boy. You're pathetic, I tell myself, while making sure I leave the front door open so I can make a run for it if I have to.

'That's a whopper! I hope the glass is big enough. I don't want to trap its legs or anything.'

Max kneels on the second step and carefully lowers the glass over the spider. It moves suddenly and I jump backwards, banging into Antonia.

'Ow!'

'I'm so sorry – it's... it... moved, you see.'

'Ha, you're even worse than I am! Well, nice to see you're not perfect, at least.'

What's that supposed to mean? How could Antonia ever have thought I was perfect?

I'm about to respond but then Max says: 'Here, have a look.' He's holding it up towards me.

'Er, it's OK thanks.'

I lean back away from it.

'And, Maxie, take it far, far away, OK?' Antonia points to the field beyond the pond. 'Miles away so it can't find its way back again.'

'Thank you.' I look down, then back at her and offer her a tea or coffee. 'I know it's pathetic, but I really can't help it.'

'It's fine. No one's good at everything, are they?'

'Well, you seem to be. You're so glamorous and gorgeous and

your house is perfect, and you host parties and do stuff for charity
and—'

'Oh, Natalie, don't be absurd. I make a massive effort with my
appearance and my hair and so on, but only because I look so
bloody awful if I don't. You should see me first thing in the
morning before I've done my make-up. I won't even do the school
run without at least doing my face.'

'Really?'

'Absolutely. And look at you – are you even wearing any
make-up at all? I'd love to have that kind of proper natural beauty
where you don't even have to try. So unfair!'

I put the kettle on and fetch our nicest cups from the dresser.

'Now, I did want to ask you about raffle prizes. I've been
landed with sorting out the prizes for the village harvest festival;
we always do a raffle to raise funds at the same time. And did you
have a word with Carl about playing Santa at Christmas, because
if he can't, then I'll need to find someone else?'

'Yes – and he said yes. Sorry, I meant to text you but I forgot. I
must admit I was really surprised.'

'Well done, you, then.'

'Actually, it wasn't down to me at all. He wants to do it because
he thought Max and Saskia would find it funny to see him in
costume with a big white beard.'

She smiles and nods. 'Yes, they'll get a kick out of that, I'm
sure.'

We chat about that for a bit, then she bites her lip and looks
out of the window to the garden.

'Natalie, I know I told you a bit about... well, how my
marriage to Carl ended.'

'Mm.' I fetch a couple of plates and the butter dish and a pot
of jam. 'Scone?'

'It's just... I can see that I made it sound as if it was all his fault: he slept with someone, so I did, and that's what ended the marriage, but that wasn't quite it.'

Max suddenly comes rushing back in.

'Ooh, can I have a scone?'

'Sure. Help yourself. There's butter and jam there.'

'I love scones. Did you make them?'

'Yes.'

'Mum, why don't you ever do baking, like Natalie?' He breaks one open and slathers it in butter and jam, then takes a huge bite. 'It's *so* good,' he says, his mouth full.

Antonia rolls her eyes.

'Max, can you run off and play for a bit? Go on. Careful round the pond, please. Not too close.

'But also,' she suddenly cups her hands over her mouth as if she can't quite bring herself to speak, 'to be honest, the marriage was over by the time Carl slept with someone else. I think he was desperately lonely, you know? And I was, too. We were living separate lives practically. He was obsessed with work, hardly ever at home, and I was focusing on the kids. He spends much more time with the kids now than he did when we were together.'

'It's a pity he has to be in Bristol so much, but I know it won't always be that way.'

'Of course. How do you find Carl's parents – if you don't mind my asking?'

'Well...'

I don't want to be disloyal to Carl but on the other hand Antonia is the only other person I know who knows what they're like, and who's been in exactly the same position as me.

'I really don't know them at all well. We had one dinner with each of them before we got married, then they were at the wedding, but that's about it. They seem quite... er... reserved.' I can't think how else to say they were both incredibly unfriendly.

'But they're a horror show, right?'

I laugh. It's so unexpected. I had assumed that they must adore her.

I push the scones towards her. Maybe she is human, after all?

'Oh, bollocks to the endless fucking diet,' she says, taking one.

'Well, they are a bit of a horror show – you're right.'

'His mother! What a judgemental cow! The way she looks at you, as if she can't believe she's having to be in the same room as you.'

'I thought she was just like that with me, because I'm not posh.'

'Not a bit of it. She'd be like that if the Queen came to tea. *No one* is good enough. No wonder Carl's got such a preposterous complex about trying to be the best all the time – trying to show her he's not a failure. And his father's a horrible, horrible man. I bet seeing him so much in Bristol is putting Carl in an absolutely foul mood, am I right? I'm sure trying to prove himself to his parents is why Carl's always worked so hard – constant competition, constant striving to show he's the best.'

'I hadn't thought of it that way, but I can see it makes sense. He's always been so intense about pitching for clients.'

'Look, I know it's not for me to say, but don't let him be the way he was with me. Don't let him get away with making work the be-all and end-all of everything. You know one of the things that first made me fall in love with Dom?'

'No – what?' That's nice. Carl implied that Antonia only went for Dominic because he's rich, so I'm glad to know that he's wrong.

'He'd offered to cook dinner for me. He's a great cook, which is just as well, as I can barely boil an egg. So I showed up – this was at the house he lived in before we got married and moved to this one – and he said, "Hang on a tick, must shut down for the day." He went into his studio and switched off the computers and everything, and closed the door. Then we talked while he cooked. That whole evening, he didn't check his phone once. It even rang a couple of times but he said his kids – they're grown-up now – had different ringtones so he knew it wasn't anyone important, and he ignored it. I felt like the most special woman on earth. Dom makes me feel I'm the most important person in his life, that I really *matter*. With Carl, I always felt there were at least five or six projects above me – not only the kids, which is natural, but pitching for this, or drafting copy for that. And always, always on his bloody phone.'

I grab another couple of scones from the cooling rack as we seem to have eaten the first ones.

'That's all any of us want maybe – to feel like we *matter*,' I say.

She nods through a mouthful of scone.

'And to eat whatever we want without worrying about getting fat.'

We go outside then and stand by the pond, and when Max comes running up, I say, 'Max, I want to thank you very, very much for dealing with the Beast of Rose Cottage. I couldn't tackle it myself. I think you're incredibly courageous. I try to be brave but I'm really not.'

'No one is brave about everything. That's what Mrs Hicks said when I didn't want to do the zip-wire at Outward Bound.'

'She's right.'

'Natalie, can I tell you how spiders get bigger?'

'Sure. Shoot.'

'They moult. They shed their outer layer – like when I come back from school and get rid of my coat in the hall.'

'Really? I didn't know that. I've never thought about it before.'

'When they're ready to get bigger, the outside bit of them goes kind of hard like a shell and then the spider inside creeps out and it's all soft and new, only it's bigger. Spiders are amazing!'

I'm not sure I'll ever come around to thinking spiders are amazing, but the moulting thing is kind of extraordinary. Maybe that's what I need to do. I know I'm not going to get taller at this point, but maybe there's a new, more grown-up me that's been hiding inside and is now ready to come out?

41

POWER CUT

There's another thunderstorm but I'm all warm and snug in the kitchen. I'm cooking myself some supper – pan-fried sole bought from the fish shack right on the beach, with boiled potatoes and samphire and a salad – when the power suddenly cuts out. It gives me a bit of a shock, but I'm not completely plunged into darkness because I have two pans on the go, on the gas hob. I use the light on my phone to go and grab the big torch, then I check the fuse board but all the switches are up so I assume the power failure must be because of the storm? I light the candles in our two lanterns and immediately the room feels not only brighter but cosy and welcoming.

I text Carl to tell him about the power and reassure him that I'm fine. He's in Bristol so there's not much he could do even if I weren't. He texts back almost at once:

Thank you for making me talk to Stefan. It's so much better now and makes it bearable being here. You always want to do the right thing. No wonder I love you so much. x

Carl's not normally one for expressing himself much in texts. His usual communications are more along the lines of: On way. C U 30 mins. x

He's always so certain about everything, but since so much has happened over the last few months – his dad becoming ill, Stefan coming back to England so often, being let go by his work partners – Carl seems more hesitant, more fragile, as if he's lost the outer armour that made him undefeatable. He seems more vulnerable now. More... human, too.

I'm about to send a soppy text back when my phone rings. I guess it'll be Carl but then I see it's Antonia. She probably wants to check I'm using the must-have most stylish lanterns and not just any old thing. I'm tempted to ignore it but maybe she needs something. Knowing her, all her candles are super-posh, over-priced scented ones that she wouldn't waste by actually lighting them during a storm.

'Antonia. Hi.' I've become a bit more business-like in my dealings with her now. I'm friendly but I no longer fawn at her feet like an unworthy underling seeking approval.

'Oh, Natalie – thank goodness. I'm so glad you picked up.' She sounds genuinely distressed, not just hamming it up in her usual way – oh no, my beautician can't come at two thirty!

'What is it? Are you all right?'

'No. Yes. I don't know.' She sounds on the verge of tears.

'Hey, hey – it's OK. Sit down and take a breath. Tell me, what can I do to help?'

'You're always so nice!'

Now I feel mean for being so unkind about her. She was genuinely kind when I got stuck on the banisters. She could so easily have taken the piss out of me but she didn't, and she got Max to deal with the spider.

'I'm really not – but is your power out? Is that it?'

'Yes, how did you know?'

'Well, because ours is too.'

'Oh, of course. Dom's away on his trip so we're all alone here.'

'You mean the three of you?' So, not alone then.

'Yes, we're *completely* alone,' she repeats.

I am *actually* all alone here as Carl's away, and the cottage is much more isolated, but I can tell I'm a lot less bothered about the power being out than Antonia is.

'It's so *dark*, Natalie. Even the LED display on the oven is out.'

For some reason, this small detail makes me feel softer towards her. It's the kind of thing a child would notice.

'How are the kids doing?'

'Well...' Her voice drops to barely above a whisper so I can hardly hear her. 'Hang on – I'm going into the utility room.' I hear the sound of a door closing. 'Max *hates* the dark, he really hates it. He keeps crying and I don't know how to cheer him up.'

Oh, that's right, he did tell me he's scared of the dark. I should have rung them as soon as the power went.

'Is Carl back? Could he perhaps come over?'

I explain that he's still in Bristol and wonder if I should offer to go over myself – but maybe she only wants a big strong man for protection?

'Oh – could – would *you* come, Natalie? Is it awful of me to ask?'

'It's fine. Of course I'll come.'

'Would you really? You know I'm not much use at this sort of thing – a crisis, I mean.'

It's hardly a crisis, just a power cut, but she has had such an easy life that it probably feels like one to her. I check if there's anything she needs me to bring, then tell her I'll be there in ten minutes and to get a fire going in the wood-burning stove as that'll be cheerful and give out some light.

'Oh, I've no idea how to light it. Dom always does it.'

She's lived there for two years. How can she not know how to light a fire?

'I'll do it when I get there.'

I grab my big torch, plus a spare to leave there in case she doesn't have one, as well as some candles, a couple of lanterns, and the lemon cake I made earlier.

When I step outside, I look up. The sky is absolutely beautiful – ink dark and I can see thousands and thousands of stars.

I get in the van and head to Antonia's.

* * *

I knock on the front door and call out, 'Antonia – it's me, Natalie.'

'Thank God.' She opens the door and gives me a huge hug, not her usual *mwah-mwah* artful kiss-kiss but a proper, relieved hug.

'It's all right, don't worry – it's just dark.'

'I know.' She's sniffling. She lowers her voice. 'You'll think I'm so ridiculous, and I'm so useless, Natalie! Max is so scared of the dark and I tried to comfort him but – but – I...' I give her another squeeze. I can feel her trembling. 'I know it's silly but actually I'm awfully scared of the dark, too. We always leave the landing light on at night. Even when I'm trying to be strong for Max, what I'm really thinking is: I hate it, I hate it.'

I turn on my big torch and head for the kitchen. I'm really surprised to see that the only light there is coming from three tealights on a plate in the middle of the table. Max and Saskia are sitting close together at the end of the table, leaning over a tablet, watching cartoons.

'It's the only thing that was charged.' Antonia nods towards the tablet.

'Well, hello, guys,' I say, thinking I must stop trying to sound matey. But for once Saskia doesn't make a face at my attempts to be friendly, or if she does, luckily, it's too dark to see. 'I've brought candles and lanterns and, most important of all – cake!'

Max brightens up at once.

'Is it the banana one you made before?'

'Nope – this one is lemon but I think it needs to be tested.'

I light the two lanterns and put them on the table and immediately the room looks a whole lot brighter and I sense all three of them relaxing a little.

'Now, why don't I light the fire in the sitting room so we can keep warm and cosy in there?' I pick up one of the lanterns.

They all trail after me and I suddenly feel like a mother duck with my little ducklings following me around. I wonder if Carl and I will have children. I had hoped so, but it's hard to have sex when he's two hundred miles away...

I ask Antonia if there are any more logs as there are only a couple by the stove.

'I don't know – or... yes, sorry – of course there are. But someone else usually brings them in. They're in the log store behind the garage.'

'Right, I'll go and get some.'

'Don't leave us!' Antonia says.

'Tell you what, I'll start with kindling and these logs, then get more once it's going, OK?'

Antonia perches on the edge of the sofa while the kids sit on the rug really close to me. I think they need a distraction.

'So, who's going to help light this fire then?'

'I will!' Max, of course.

I show them how to make newspaper firelighters, using elaborate concertinaed strips. Max and Saskia kneel by the coffee table, carefully folding the strips. You can make twists of paper instead, of course, but they need something to occupy them and these do last longer than twists.

'Antonia, shall we have some tea or something to go with the cake?'

'Oh, yes, of course.' Honestly, does she ever do anything herself?

'Where's Katja?'

'Um, she – she – decided to go back to Slovenia.'

'Oh, right.'

I bet Katja had just had enough. Carl says Antonia's helpers rarely last long.

'Um, but how do I make tea if there's no power for the kettle?'

'Isn't your hob gas?'

'Oh, yes – yes, it is.'

Do I really need to explain how to boil water?

'Have you got matches because, of course, the ignition won't work. You'll have to light the hob.'

'Will I?'

'Yes.'

In some ways, Antonia is really like a child. Maybe that's how I should treat her?

'I'm not one hundred per cent sure where I put the matches...'

I've assembled the paper and kindling so I pass the matches to Saskia and point where she should light the fire.

She strikes the match with great concentration as if she's never done it before.

The fire lights up immediately because of the paper and Saskia's face is lit up too. She looks entranced.

'I need to keep an eye on the fire, otherwise it might go out – if you can manage the tea. I'd probably boil some water in a saucepan on the hob. With a lid – you know, to speed it up.' I pass the matches to Antonia.

'Oh, yes,' she says. 'With a lid. Of course.'

'Here, take my torch. Max, why don't you go and help your mum with the tea?'

'OK.'

'The fire's really pretty,' Saskia says.

'Isn't it? When I was your age, and younger, I always used to dream about living in the country and having a real fire. So I could stare into it. And make toast.'

'Couldn't you have one where you lived?'

I laugh. 'No – well, no one did where we lived. It was a modern block of flats: no fireplaces, no gardens, not much space. I shared a room with my sister until I left for university.'

'You didn't have your own bedroom?' She sounds really shocked.

'No. Lots of people don't, you know.'

'But didn't you mind? I'd hate to share with Max. He's so annoying!'

'Well, I'm afraid *I'm* the annoying little sister. Celeste is my big sister, like you are to Max. We did argue but we didn't know any different. We'd always shared so that's just how it was. And if it's normal for you, then, well, it's normal. There were good things, too – lying in the dark, talking. Sometimes it's easier to talk in the dark, don't you think?'

I feel her shuffle a little closer.

'Max is really scared of the dark,' she says.

'Lots of people are. I suppose it's a throwback to prehistoric times, when staying in the cave by the fire meant you were safe. The fire would keep away any wild animals.'

'But there aren't any really dangerous ones in Kent, are there?'

'No, course not, but people are quite primitive underneath. We still have fears about not being safe.'

'I don't like the dark all that much either.' Her voice is almost a whisper.

I fiddle with the fire, adjusting the up-draught to keep it going.

'We really need to get more logs or this won't last long. Care to show me the log store?'

'But it's so dark outside!'

'We can take a torch.'

We go through to the kitchen where Antonia is standing by the stove, boiling the water.

'I need to get more logs.'

'Oh – do you need the lantern?'

In the dim light, I can see she looks worried.

'No, it's fine – I'll take the second torch. Who wants to come?'

Max looks at his mum, then at me.

'We could all go.' Antonia says. 'I'll just make the tea.' She pours the water into the teapot.

It feels slightly mad – four people going to fetch a few logs – but I realise they feel happier if we're all together.

We put the door on the latch and step outside, Max entrusted with the lantern and Saskia with the torch.

'It's so dark,' Saskia says.

'And also so beautiful,' I point out.

We go and put some logs from the store in a bucket. Then I ask them to hang on a tick.

'Here – look up.' I suggest Saskia points the torch downwards and Max sets down the lantern.

'Gosh,' says Antonia. 'I hadn't realised there were so many stars.'

'It's one of the things I love about being down here rather than in London. In the city, you can only see a handful of stars because there's too much light from the houses and the street-lamps, but here...'

And it really *is* exquisite. You can't *not* see it. Next to me, Max curls his hand into mine and I give it a squeeze. Antonia puts her arm around Saskia.

'That's the Plough there. See?' I point.

'*Where?*' they all say at once, and we laugh. I take it in turns to line them up, with my pointing finger. 'There, the constellation like a saucepan? In America, they call it the Big Dipper. And sometimes the Great Bear. But I do think it's more like a saucepan than anything else.'

'Do you know any others?'

'Not many, but let's see...' I point out the handful that I know.

Then we go in and I build up the fire and we all sit on the rug close together, having tea and lemon cake, and play an increasingly silly game of 'My aunt went to Morocco and brought back...' until we're all in fits of giggles. I take a picture of the kids on my phone, their faces lit up by the lantern, and send it to Carl and he calls to say hello to us all.

Then Dom rings. Antonia goes through to the kitchen to talk to him, and Max follows along too.

'Are you scared down at the other house?' Saskia asks. 'When Daddy's not there?'

'Not really. I mean, I miss him a lot, but I'm used to being on my own.'

'But what do you *do*?'

'Well, soon I hope to have my shop set up in Canterbury, so then I'll be there most days, but for now I read, I cook, I do the garden, things for the house – like making curtains – go for walks, swim in the pond.'

'In the pond! You don't! Yuck.'

'It's not yucky at all. The water's very clear.'

'But aren't there bugs and stuff?'

'Some, yes, but nothing horrible.'

'You can swim in our pool, if you like.'

'Thank you, but sometimes it's, you know... er... easier to be in your own place.'

'Oh. Max likes it when you go in with him and play games. Mum doesn't really do that. And Dom just swims up and down. He's so boring.'

'I mostly swim up and down too usually – for exercise – but I like to mess about in the water too. And it's good for kids; it helps with water confidence.'

'What's that?'

'Having confidence while you're in the water – trusting it.'

'I don't get it.'

'Well, relaxing in the water is partly about feeling at ease that it will hold you up. As long as you have air in your lungs, you're like a ball. When you swim, you learn to manage your breathing so that you don't run out of puff, as that can make you panic. But getting your breathing right is tricky – it takes practice. And of course, lots of people find swimming scary.'

'Do they?'

'Absolutely. My mum for one. She can swim a little but she doesn't enjoy it. She had a bad experience with school swimming when she was a kid and she just couldn't face it. My dad always took me when I was small, instead, and I loved it.'

'Is your dad still alive? My mum's dad died.'

'Yes, he's alive.' It feels funny saying that out loud. 'He lives abroad, though.'

'Like Uncle Stefan.'

'Exactly.'

'Maybe the next time you come to use the pool...?' Saskia says.

'It would be nice if you'd come in at the same time.'

'Maybe. I'm not... you know. Very good. I can't really do much.'

'It's OK. Did Max tell you he had to rescue me from a huge spider?'

'Yes, he did. He was really proud of himself.'

'He should be – it was practically the size of a building.'

She laughs.

'And Max told me something his teacher said that I thought was really helpful, because I'm so hopeless when I see a spider. He said: no one is brave about everything. That's true for everyone.'

42

LEARNING TO FLOAT

Antonia has asked me over for a swim and supper. She sounded tentative on the phone, as if she were inviting me on a date.

When I get there, Max is already in his swimming trunks and waiting for me.

'Mum said I had to wait until you got here before I can go in the pool. I've been waiting for *ages*.'

'But I'm not late at all!' I check my watch.

'But I've still been *waiting*! I've been *waiting* since seven o'clock this morning because I *knew* you were coming and, now, we can play underwater games. Mum won't swim underwater because she says it makes her hair all yucky but I said you're brilliant because you don't care about your hair or what you look like or anything.'

'Er, thanks. I guess that's sort of true.'

I quickly change. I have a new swimsuit. Another Speedo but this one is bright red. I must admit it is nicer than my plain black and navy ones, but I worry it's too ostentatious.

Max declares it is much less boring than my others as we get in the pool.

'Can you teach me proper backstroke, Natalie? When I try to do it, I end up crashing into the side!'

'You're probably stronger on one side – most people are. Here, let me show you...'

We practise for a bit. Saskia, as usual, is reclining on a sun lounger a little way away from the pool. Astonishingly, though, she is reading a book rather than fiddling with her phone.

'I guess it's nearly Back to School time, isn't it, Max? How are you feeling about moving up to big school?'

'Mm.'

Carl told me that Max said he's not going to go, that he's going to stay on at his junior school, which, obviously, isn't actually possible. Carl thought Antonia was fretting too much about it and that it would magically sort itself out, that Max was going through a phase. I suppose it stems from his own parents being so distant about everything, but maybe it would be good to try to get to the bottom of why he doesn't want to move up.

I ask Max if other boys from his class will be going to the same school and he says 'uh' and nothing else.

Saskia is at a girls' secondary school, so Max won't have her looking out for him.

'Does your new school have a swimming pool?'

'Yes, but it was closed when we went to visit on the open day, so I didn't get to see it.'

'That's a shame. Perhaps you could find a picture of it online? On the school website?'

His face lights up for a moment.

'I might not be going anyway.' He suddenly plunges underwater to go and sit on the bottom. I put on my goggles and swim round him underwater, and make silly faces, and we both surface again.

'Oh, yeah? Why's that, then?'

'I think I'll stay at my other school.'

'I see. Don't you have to move up at your age?'

'I'm going to ask Mum if I can stay a bit longer.'

I lean back and float on my back with my arms outstretched and Max joins me, the two of us happily floating. Maybe it'll be easier if we're not face to face.

'Shall I tell you about my secondary school?'

'Yes. What was it like?'

'Well, like most things, it was a mixture – lots of good bits plus a few less good bits, like having to play hockey in winter when it was so cold and we got all muddy and frozen. Or school macaroni cheese.'

'I love macaroni cheese!'

'Me too, but this one was disgusting – like all the pasta had been glued together. It made me gag.'

'But did you like the rest of it?'

'In the end, you know, I absolutely *loved* it. Even though I was shy, I made some great friends and I liked most of the teachers, too. The main problem I had was with this group of really mean girls. One of them, called Elisa, was the sort of ringleader whom the others all followed, and she said I was a witch.'

'Why?'

'Oh, it was stupid – only because I have dark hair and it was so frizzy and tangly, not all smooth and shiny like hers. She didn't like me. Sometimes a person decides not to like you for no good reason, but because of what *they're* like inside.'

'We have boys like that in our school.'

'So maybe moving up to big school will be better?'

'I don't think so.'

'Are any of those boys going to the big school, too?'

The tiniest of nods, then he ducks underwater again. I wait for him to surface.

'Max? Those boys – they don't hurt you or do anything really bad, do they?'

'Uh-huh. They say mean things to everyone. Not just me. But at your school – what did *you* say when they said you were a witch?'

'The first time it happened, I got very upset and then Elisa started calling me "Nitch the Witch" every time she saw me, and getting her gaggle of friends to join in. Once, they all stood in a circle round me, chanting "Nitch the Witch" and it was horrible. After that, I could feel myself flinching, tightening up inside and feeling sick as I got closer to school.

'Then one day she leaned in really close – with her face right up to mine – and she said, "You're a weird witchy witch and I hate you." Now, as a grown-up, I know that it's stupid and pathetic, but when I was a kid, things got to me sometimes – because I felt powerless and I didn't know how to make it stop.'

'What did you say?'

'You know, the strangest thing happened. It suddenly somehow *clicked* that it was nothing to do with me or what I was like. It was only that *she* liked to feel she had power over people. So I did something she didn't expect.'

'What?'

'I *smiled*. I gave a very slow smile, like I had a special secret, and I said: "I'm wondering which spell I'm going to put on you." And she jerked back as if she'd been stung.'

'Did you really know a spell?'

'No, course not. I don't believe in magic or spells. But maybe *she* did? I only had to make her believe that maybe I could make something bad happen to her. I nodded my head very slowly and said, "I do think it's going to be something nasty..."

'And she said, "You wouldn't? No – please don't!"

'After that, all I had to do was look at her in a certain way and she'd run off so she couldn't see me.'

'But you let her think you were a witch!'

'So what? I didn't care. It was enough to get her off my back. It worked. Still, I wish I'd done judo or kick-boxing or something. Those things can give you more confidence, especially for people who aren't tall, like me.'

'Or me.'

'And if you're more confident, you walk differently, you seem strong, and you don't get bothered by bullies. Kick-boxing is supposed to be a lot of fun.'

'Could you ask Dad for me if I can do it? Or Mum?'

'Course I will. And if anyone ever gives you trouble at school and you're not sure how to sort it out, you let me know and I'll come in and put a spell on them.'

He giggles then and we go back to swimming, and I show him how to make his backstroke straighter and how to keep track so you don't bump your head at the end.

I sense, rather than see, Saskia watching us.

Eventually she comes and perches on the Roman steps with her feet in the water.

Antonia comes out and calls Max to go in for his bath before supper and to come and warm up as he's been in for ages.

'Why do you like swimming so much?' Saskia says, apparently addressing the steps rather than me.

'I suppose because my dad used to take me when I was little, while my sister had a tap dance class, so it was just me and him.'

She nods but says nothing.

'It's great that you have a pool here so you can swim when you want to.' I push off on my back and float in the shallow end. 'If you want to.'

'But what if you drown?'

'Well, you have to respect the water – it's true – but the better a swimmer you are, the less likely you are to get into problems. I would never swim in rough seas or where there are dangerous currents or anything like that. I love it but I'm still cautious.'

'Max loves it. He'd live in the pool if he could.'

I'd like to help her, but I'm worried if I offer, she'll flounce off.

'You could get your suit on if you fancy a splash,' I say, keeping my voice light. I don't look at her directly, but push off on to my back, relaxed and effortless. 'It's lovely and warm.'

'Do you have to go soon? I could change maybe?'

'Your mum asked me for supper so I'm here for a while.'

'Will you wait? I mean, could you...?'

'I'll be here.' I move my hands and make myself wheel round in a circle. 'No rush.'

Five minutes later, Saskia emerges in a very stylish turquoise bikini, her hair pulled back in a tight ponytail.

'Is Max in the bath?'

'Yes. Probably got his goggles on.'

I laugh.

'Did you get a new swimsuit?' She nods towards my suit.

'Mm. Not sure if red is my colour exactly, but it's definitely more cheerful than my others.'

'It looks good. But you could get a bikini. I mean – you're not fat. You could totally wear one.'

'Thanks, but I really prefer a one-piece for swimming as they don't move around so much.'

'But you can – I mean, people can swim in a bikini?' Sometimes, she suddenly sounds incredibly young and unsure of herself. I admit that I actually prefer it when she's like this.

'Yes, absolutely, especially one as pretty as that.'

She smiles but still hasn't entered the pool.

I swim towards the steps and tell her there is an easy way to practise floating on your back.

'Some people feel nervous about floating in the middle of the pool at first.' I sit on one of the lower steps and stretch my legs out. 'But with steps like these, you can gently lower your head and float while still being at the edge to feel more secure.' I tip my head back. 'See? You have to be careful not to move suddenly or you could bang your head but it's fine if you can relax and let yourself *be* in the water.'

Finally, she descends the steps, though the look on her face suggests she's far from relaxed.

I talk her through it, almost as if I'm reminding myself rather than instructing her. I can see how tense she is.

The sky is still very bright, the sun still strong. A few little clouds skit across the expanse of blue in the light breeze.

Saskia slowly lowers her head into the water.

'Now, can you ease your legs out?'

'I – I'm scared.'

'I promise you'll be OK. The steps are right beneath you. And I'm next to you. Focus on your feet – can you point them like a dancer?'

She smiles unexpectedly. Ah, yes, she used to do ballet when she was younger.

'Now really stretch your legs out as if your pointed toes are trying to reach the other end.'

'I'm sinking in the middle!'

'Here, may I give you a little boost?'

She nods and I lightly slip my hand under her lower back.

'Try to keep your head tipped back. It might feel odd at first, but as your head's so heavy, if it's in the water, it helps your hips stay up – head up, hips go down. Like a see-saw.'

She's floating, though I still have my hand beneath her.

'Shall I move my hand away?'

'Not yet!' She clutches for my hand.

'I won't until you say it's OK. Take your time, nice slow breaths, look at the clouds, let the water hold you.'

'Can you float next to me? You can move your hand now.'

I remove it from her back and she wobbles for a second but then steadies, and the two of us float there, side by side, for a whole minute.

'I'm floating!' she says.

'You certainly are! Well done.'

'I must show Dad when he comes.'

'He'll be very proud of you.'

Afterwards, we climb out and she runs back into the house to shower and I go into the changing pavilion. I actually had a nice time with Saskia – only for a few minutes but still, for once, I didn't make it worse and she didn't storm off or say something bitchy. Maybe she's growing up a bit?

Or maybe I am?

* * *

We have a delicious chicken pie Antonia bought at the deli and, after supper, the kids go off to watch TV while I help Antonia clear up.

Suddenly, she turns round from the dishwasher and says, 'Natalie, if I tell you something, will you promise not to hate me?'

Oh, no – is she going to confess that she still has feelings for Carl? Just because he doesn't love her any more doesn't mean she doesn't love him.

'Well, I suppose it depends on what it is.'

I turn to face her.

'It's a kind of confession.'

I knew it. I put down my mug. I feel slightly sick. I'm not sure I want to know. I take a deep breath.

'OK.'

Now she looks away, putting the dishes carefully into the dish-washer as if it requires all her concentration, as if she can't bring herself to look at me.

'God, this stupid cutlery thing is so fiddly – it takes half an hour to get the bloody forks in!'

'Antonia?'

'Sorry... I'm sorry. I'm so embarrassed, but I think I do need to come clean if we're to... to... be friends.'

'Can you please tell me?'

'Well, actually it's two things.'

Great. This gets better and better.

'Right...?'

'You remember that very first time you and Carl came over to the house so you and I could meet, only I was coming back with the kids and we were so late that you had to leave?'

'Yes, of course. You got held up.'

'Yup. Only – well, actually, we weren't held up. I picked Saskia up from riding and Max from his friend's house and we were heading home, but then I offered to take them both for ice cream sundaes on the way. Of course, they both jumped at it, so that's what we did and I let them dawdle for ages until I knew it would be too late. I'm really sorry.'

'But *why*?'

At the time, I did wonder if she'd made herself run late on purpose but I dismissed the thought as mad. What possible reason could she have? The only lingering niggle was I thought perhaps she was trying to put me in my place somehow, send me a message that she didn't consider meeting me important enough to bother with. But when I tried to say that to Carl, he said I was being paranoid and that Antonia honestly wasn't that malicious; she was simply disorganised and constantly tearing around from one thing to another because she never left enough time to get from A to B.

'I realise this must sound awfully silly.' She looks at me, then away again. 'It's just I was *so* nervous about meeting you. I wanted to put if off as long as I possibly could. I felt like I was the has-been, the old ex-wife, and you would be this new, younger version. I was so daunted by the prospect of finally meeting you that I wanted to avoid it, even though it was stupid because of course I couldn't do that forever.

'And then, when I realised I absolutely couldn't put it off any longer, I invited you to that pool party, because I couldn't face it unless I had the supportive shield of my friends around me. Team Antonia.' She laughs then carries on. 'I even asked them all to dress up and do proper make-up so we'd look our best, and we all posed at the end of the pool as if we were models – it was bonkers.'

'Then I showed up in my Speedo and felt like a schoolkid who'd wandered on to the set of a Bond film. And then you said I had fantastic tits and I was totally flummoxed.'

'Oh Good Lord – I *did* say that!' Antonia covers her face with her hands. 'I'm *so* sorry. What on earth must you have thought? I was so nervous, I ended up babbling and saying anything that came into my head. I must have sounded completely crazy.'

'But I'm just *me*! Why were you nervous once you'd seen me? I'm not at all daunting. Am I?'

'Well, actually, you know you *are* in some ways. Not in the ways I expected, to be honest. I mean, I thought maybe you'd be impossibly glamorous and – and...'

I laugh because, really, what else could I do?

'OK, so you're not all that glamorous, but still...'

'How am I daunting? There's absolutely nothing daunting about me!'

'Now that's not true!' She turns to look at me. 'That was the second thing. You *are* daunting. I feel like you're an impossible act to live up to. You've always worked, run a business. You're clever and capable. You can cook and bake and sew curtains and light a fire and apparently master absolutely anything you turn your hand to. You're completely unafraid.'

'I'm *not*—'

'Except for spiders. But you're not a *scared person*, Natalie. You're tough and you're strong. And, most of all, you're completely straight. There's no, I don't know, hidden agenda. You say what you mean. And you have substance. I feel like such a – a – lightweight next to you. I don't work, I can't *do* anything. I have no skills at all other than making my home look nice. It's not exactly one for the CV, is it? Dom's pretty easy-going, but even he was saying the other day that perhaps I should consider going back to work. Only I haven't worked for years. Who on earth would hire me?'

'I'm sure you could find something if you really wanted to. And you're so popular! You could be a party planner. You're like the Queen of the Village. Everyone looks up to you.'

'Oh, Natalie, now you're being naïve. They really don't. My friends gather round me partly because we have a gorgeous swimming pool, and I'm always ready to have their kids over if they want a couple of hours off, and the booze flows pretty freely at our house.'

'But surely they like you as a friend? They must do.'

'A couple of them do probably, yes. But sometimes it's hard to think that anyone comes over because they really want to see me, rather than they like the house and the pool.'

I cover my face with my hands for a moment.

'Oh, Antonia.'

'What? What is it?'

'I really am a fool. That first time – when we were supposed to meet – I was absolutely petrified about meeting you. Then I saw how incredible your house was, and I built you up in my head as this rival. And then it got worse and worse. When I met you at last – at that pool party, I can't tell you how awful I felt. There you were, this golden *goddess* sashaying forwards to meet me, and I felt like a poor schoolgirl in my boring swimsuit and tatty old bathrobe.'

'But then you got in the water – and it was like watching a beautiful mermaid or something, the way you moved was so natural, so fluid. I felt like a clunky robot – I couldn't wait to get out of the water so I could stop feeling so stiff and awkward.'

I laugh.

'Antonia, this really is ridiculous. You and me. How we've built each other up in our heads to be something other than what we are.'

She smiles.

'So, are we OK then?'

'More than OK.'

'Now I'm honestly so glad I told Carl about the cottage and took him to see it. It's been fantastic for the kids to see him so easily and pop to the beach or the café with him – though I must admit when we were at the auction and Carl actually got the house, my first thought was: Oh God, what on earth have I done!'

'*You* took him to see it?'

'Yes, of course – only round the outside. Then he must have got the agent to show him the inside the next day, I think. He told me that you'd suggested moving down here so he could see the children more often. That's right?'

'Yes, that's right...' I don't understand about the timing. I suddenly feel chilled to the bone. 'Sorry – *when* did you show him the house?'

'Let me see – when was it? The auction was a Friday, I think. So, I suppose it must have been the previous weekend when he came to take the children out. I can't remember now if it was the Saturday or the Sunday, but I think that's when it was.'

43

A QUESTION OF TIMING

Carl is back from Bristol, his dad has improved a little, and we are having supper at the cottage when I brave the subject.

'Carl, do you remember when you very first saw the house? *This* house?'

'Hmm, I don't know, Nat. It's ages ago now, I can't remember exactly. Right before the auction, I suppose.'

'Not a few days beforehand?'

He reaches for his wine and takes a deep swallow.

'Because if you saw it, say, the previous weekend, it seems odd that you didn't mention it as soon as you saw it, that you didn't say: "Hey, I've seen this great house! Come down and see it."'

'Maybe I thought you wouldn't want to be so near my ex-wife. But remember it was *your* idea. *You* were the one who suggested moving nearer the children.'

'That's true. I did. But I'm not claiming I don't remember. I *know* I suggested it. But I don't believe that you don't remember when you first saw this house. If you loved it the moment you saw it, the way you say you did, then you must remember.'

'OK, OK, I suppose I must have seen it... well... perhaps it was a little before the auction. I can't recall exactly...'

'It's not an impeachment hearing, Carl. "I can't recall exactly..." isn't going to cut it.'

'Oh, come on, darling – what does it matter now anyway?'

'And it was Antonia who told you about it? And showed it to you?'

'Erm... I suppose it might have been. Does it matter?'

'That's fine, Carl. There's nothing wrong with her wanting you to be nearby for the kids.'

'Probably so she could have more child-free time than anything else. But really, darling, let's leave it, eh? It's a lovely house. You love it, I know you do.'

'Yes, I do.'

'Well, then – what else matters?'

'It *matters* to me, Carl, because this was the biggest decision we had to make together – the first major decision of our married life – and you took it without me.'

'I didn't. I called you from the auction, remember?'

'Oh, come on. You manipulated me into it, you know you did. You made it impossible for me to say no.'

'But I knew you'd love it! Why does it matter when you've ended up with your dream house? I found you a place with a duck pond, for God's sake!'

'That's not the point, Carl, and you know it's not the point. *When* did you see the house? The auction was a Friday.'

'At some point that morning, I suppose.'

'Really? The auction was first thing. That seems tight.'

'Well, possibly it was the night before... I don't know.'

He looks down into his glass.

'Or maybe the weekend before? In fact, you could have called me as soon as you'd seen it and I would have come straight down?'

He shrugs.

'I suppose so.'

'So why didn't you?'

He shrugs again but he looks cross and sulky like a child who's broken one of the best teacups and now the pieces have been discovered beneath the sofa.

'Carl? Why didn't you ask me to come to see it? If you were so sure I'd love it, what were you afraid of?'

'I suppose I didn't think of it.'

'Well, obviously that's not credible even for a second. You have to be able to come up with a better lie than that, surely?'

'Look, Natalie, I don't want to lie to you.'

'Good, I don't want you to lie to me either. So why didn't you call me straight away?'

'Now promise you won't get cross?'

'I'm already cross. I'm not going to throw a saucepan at you, if that's what you're worried about. Believe me, I'm already cross. I don't see how you finally telling me the truth could possibly make me any angrier.'

'It's a perfectly good reason when you look at it dispassionately. Without getting all het up about it.'

'Fine. Tell me then.'

'OK.' He clunks his coffee mug down on the table and faces me. Sighs.

'Look, I was honestly going to tell you. As soon as I saw it – the house and the land and the pond and the ducks – I knew you'd *love* it. I *knew* it. I couldn't wait to tell you, to show it to you. I was so excited. I'd looked round and I was thinking, it'll look so much better once we rip out those sad brown carpets and strip off the woodchip wallpaper. I hope Natalie will see past all that, and all this awful old furniture. And then I thought about that time you were supposed to book a villa for us to go on holiday to France and – you remember?'

I nod. Of course I do.

'You couldn't *decide*. You promised you'd sort out the holiday, but then you weren't able to make up your mind. And while you were faffing about for days and days, trying to decide which villa you liked best...'

'They all got booked up. And we ended up having to stay in that horrible poky place where everything was slightly damp and the beach stank of rotting seaweed, like sewage, and the village didn't have a restaurant, just a depressing bar with a slot machine and stale sandwiches.'

'Well, yes. I didn't tell you I'd seen the house because – well, because – now don't take this the wrong way, darling – but you are quite... well, *very*... indecisive and I thought – I *knew* – that if I involved you, you'd only start fretting about every tiny flaw and fail to see the bigger picture, and we would lose our only chance to get a house so close to Saskia and Max. Or you'd be really disturbed about what happened with the previous owner and get hung up on that. And I thought you'd get flustered by buying a house at auction because you have to be really decisive and go for it if you want it and—'

'*What!*' my voice is louder than I meant. I was planning to be all calm and reasonable but that comment about the auction has flipped me over the edge. I can't believe what I'm hearing.

'So – let me get this right – the person who actually goes to auctions at least once a month and who earns a living partly by successfully choosing what to bid on and for how much, and has done so for over ten years, has to be kept out of the way like mad

Mrs Rochester hidden away in the attic? And the person who's never bought anything at auction goes and gets carried away and allows himself to be pushed too high because he can't resist trying to get one up on his supposed rival? And the person who will have to oversee the building and decorating work, the person who will have to make decisions about every paint colour, every curtain, every light switch, can't be trusted to be involved? But the person who had to hire an interior decorator to choose his blinds, his taps, even the sofa he should sit on – that person is the one who should be trusted to make the decision on his own? Hilarious.'

'Well, when you put it that way, I can see it doesn't sound so great.'

I say nothing.

'Natalie, I'm really sorry.' He reaches out to pat my arm but I pull away from him. 'Come on, darling, forgive me. I can see it was a bit of a daft thing to do but can't you see—'

'No, Carl. "A bit of a daft thing" is going to the supermarket to get food for supper and coming back with a bunch of flowers and a bottle of wine. This is not that. I *can't* see. All I can see is that you don't think of me as your equal, you don't see me as someone who matters, a grown-up who can make decisions on how to run her own life, and our life. You think that because I can't make up my mind over what to order in a restaurant, that it means I can't be trusted with anything important.'

'No, I don't, I really don't—'

'You're wrong, Carl – so wrong. I decided to marry you, didn't I? When it comes to something that really matters, I'm *more* decisive, not less. I didn't hesitate. We'd only known each other a few months but it was enough for me to know that I loved you and that I'd go on loving you, no matter what.'

He smiles.

'So, you do forgive me then, darling. My love.' He comes towards me, starts to put his arms around me but I shove him away.

'Don't – just don't call me that. I love you but I don't want to live with you – not now, not ever – if that's how you see me. I can't. Not if you see me as some fluffy little hamster you're really fond of, but not as your equal.'

'I don't see you like that.'

'The evidence says you do.'

'Hey, calm down, darling, calm down. You're getting all het up.' He reaches for me again. 'There's no need to get so emotional about it.'

'No! Don't tell me to calm down. You can't run a marriage as if it's a campaign where you call all the shots. And you can't say emotions are irrelevant. You've orchestrated things and decided for me as if I were a baby – enough!' I stab the air with my finger in front of him. 'Enough!'

Carl looks shell-shocked. For once, he doesn't have a ready answer.

'I love you so much, but I can't be with you if you think I'm just a child who can't make up her own mind.' I grab my bag and my jacket and head for the door. 'I'm sorry.'

I'm quite hoarse from shouting and I feel strange, fired up and angry but also oddly excited. My skin is tingling and it seems as though my blood is sprinting round my body. I run to the van and, as I start to drive up the track, I hear Carl shouting behind me. I watch him running after the van in my mirror as I speed away, then he slows and stands there, getting smaller and smaller.

He phones, of course. He phones again and again in the next few hours, but I don't answer it. I feel shaky and anxious but also hopeful. I can do this. I don't have to have Carl telling me what to do, what to think, when to wipe my nose. I'm thirty-six, for God's sake. If I'm not going to have a go at being a grown-up now and running my own life, then I'll never be one. I'll acquire more wrinkles without more wisdom and be some dumb little girl stuck in an ageing body. Thanks, but no thanks.

44

SAYING GOODBYE

I know it's probably the wrong thing to do. No doubt it will make me feel even more awful. But I don't care – I'm doing it. To be honest, I don't see how I could possibly feel any worse than I do already. My whirlwind romance turned out to be a tornado in the end, and I'm a fragment of the wreckage. Carl has called so many times over the last couple of weeks. He sent flowers with a note saying: 'I'm so sorry, my love. Please forgive me. Carl xxx'. It should have said, 'Sorry I treated you like a little kid who has to have her decisions made for her. Sorry I forgot that you are my equal.'

But then yesterday he sent a text:

Natalie, I think you're being unfair. I did what I thought was best at the time. I accept now that it was wrong, but – as you said – we all make mistakes. I'm in Bristol. I'll leave you in peace. x

Well, it sounds as if he managed to get over the 'terrible pain' he claimed to be in quite quickly, in one of the many messages he left on my voicemail. I wish I could shrug it off so easily. *I'll leave you in peace.*

So that's that then.

Does Carl really think I'm being unfair? He lied to me about the cottage because he thought if he let me see it, I'd um and ah and dither and he'd lose the only house in the world that is within easy walking distance from his kids.

Am I being unfair? Could he be *right*? Not about pretending he hadn't seen the cottage, no. Not about making the decision jointly with him. I don't mean that because I still think what he did was plain wrong. But am I overreacting? Still, I feel if I said, oh well, never mind, it's done now, then there would be other things further down the line – important decisions where he'd somehow contrive to exclude me to speed things up or 'forget' to tell me something vital because I'd only complicate matters by wanting to *talk* about everything. I could imagine that, before I knew it, I'd find our child shipped off to boarding school because Carl would have already paid the first term's fees, having 'forgotten' to ask me how I feel about sending my child away.

For a moment, an image flits into my head of a little boy, with thick, dark hair and blue-grey eyes like Carl, running across the grass at the cottage to talk to the ducks. I slump into the sofa. A sick feeling of loss and grief for something I haven't even had yet churns my stomach. Our *child*.

I'm nearly thirty-seven. Even if I met another man tomorrow – not all that likely given that, a) I'm not exactly in the mood to get out there and start trying to chat men up, and b) I'm still desperately (pathetically) in love with my infuriating husband – I'd have to crack on and try to get pregnant and, as far as I know, it's not ideal on a first date to be saying: 'I think I'll have a caffe latte and by the way – children – one or two? What do you think?'

Oh, Carl. How did we get ourselves into such a mess?

I know, I know. I said 'we'. I've blamed him, but I know it's not all his fault. Am I doing what he did with Stefan and Antonia, blaming someone else because it's so, so much easier than looking in the mirror to examine my own innumerable flaws? He was an idiot but I didn't exactly help matters, did I? I go on and on about how important it is to communicate: *oh, Carl, you need to open up more! You need to talk to me when you're not happy!* I lectured him and made pronouncements as if I was some kind of expert on marriage and happiness when the truth is that I know absolutely nothing.

When I thought Carl was still in love with Antonia, I should have asked him – but I didn't. I bailed. I ran away from the party like a teenager storming out from a row with her parents. And that's what I've done with every relationship I've ever had. As soon as there was a problem, I jumped ship or sabotaged it somehow – before the other person did. So I wouldn't be the one left behind, the one who wasn't wanted.

Why did I let myself get into such a state about Antonia anyway? In my head, I built her up and built her up to be this superwoman – so glamorous, her hair so perfect and bouncy, her clothes so stylish, her house devoid of mess and cobwebs and builder's dust (OK, so she didn't knock down her own ceiling when in a strop – probably wise). But she's only a *person*. Flawed – sometimes selfish, sometimes kind, sometimes bitchy, sometimes generous. Human, then. Just like the rest of us. Maybe not so very different from me after all. A slightly different set of insecurities wrapped up in a carapace of confidence, muddling through, pretending we're proper grown-ups when half the time we have no idea what we're doing and we only act as if we do so as not to freak out the children.

I'm going to the cottage. I need to say goodbye to it, which no doubt sounds daft and sentimental but I don't care. I won't say I need closure because even the word 'closure' makes me want to vomit. That's not it. It's only that – I – I've come to love Rose Cottage. Really love it. Somehow, the fact that it took so long and needed so much work has made me love it more than I ever could have done if it had been all ready to move in to. Every curtain I've sewn myself, every tile I've chosen, every paint chart I've pored over to try to find the right colour, every picture I've hung – every room in that house has a little bit of me in it, and I can't deal with losing it as well as losing Carl. It's too much. I don't know how to say goodbye to Carl. Well, I suppose I already did when I told him I couldn't be with him any more. That should have done the trick. His text looks like he can manage without me just fine. But I want to see the cottage one last time. Look at the rooms, walk along the stream to the field, maybe swim in the pond if it's not too cold.

Carl's text yesterday said he was back in Bristol. There's zero danger of running into him, so at least I don't need to worry about that.

* * *

At the gate, I unlock the big padlock for what I suppose is the last time. I drive down the track. I love this – the way the trees on the banks either side arch over the lane. Stop it. I must stop dwelling on 'this is the last time I'll do the padlock... this is the last time I'll drive down the track...' It's not helping me feel better. Right. Shoulders back. This isn't a maudlin wander down memory lane. I'll grab my clothes from the wardrobe, take a look round the house to say goodbye to it, then leave without a backwards glance. OK, maybe a small glance, but no lingering.

I park and take my swimming kitbag from the van. As I reach the cottage, the clouds part and the sun shines right down on the front path. Yes, I will have a swim once I've had a look round. It's still pretty mild today, though you can sense the first whiff of autumn in the air.

I let myself in. The air smells a bit stale. Maybe Carl hasn't been here for a while. I wonder where he's been staying. Perhaps he's had to rent another flat in London.

I stand by the worktop in the kitchen and put the kettle on. I do love those pretty blue shelves on this side, the old dresser over there, the big wooden table in the dining area up the steps, with its eclectic collection of mismatched chairs. It seats ten. I thought we'd have lots of relaxing meals with friends and family gathered around that table, talking and eating and laughing, but we hadn't got around to that yet. I had Celeste and Mum there, and Stefan came. Mostly it was Carl and me, or just me. I liked the way he always used to touch me when he went past. I don't know if he even noticed he was doing it, but if he passed me in the kitchen to fetch something or put the kettle on or go to the fridge, for a moment, he'd lay his hand on my back or my waist or touch my arm. I miss that. I know: such a small thing. It's not the only thing, of course.

I make myself a cup of tea but the only milk in the fridge is on the turn. There's a lemon, though, so I have the tea with that instead. I take a chocolate biscuit from the tin. Go through into the big sitting room.

This room is beautiful now. It's finally come together – the red walls are amazing, though they look even better at night when we switch on the lamps and the fire's going. There's the big, old, nicely weathered leather armchair I got at auction, plus the large grey velvet sofa, long enough for even Carl to stretch out on. I'd love to lie on it now, let myself drift off, maybe slip into a dream where everything is all right again. But I don't allow myself that indulgence. Instead, I perch on the edge of it, sipping my tea, as if I'm a guest who isn't sure I'm welcome. Next door, the little sitting room looks light and bright and pretty, with its pale green walls and sprigged curtains and small white sofa.

At the foot of the stairs, I pause for a few moments, wanting to go up and wanting to stay downstairs. Stop being a pathetic coward! They're only rooms. This is your one chance. Don't make a big deal of it – go up, retrieve your clothes, shove them in the van. It won't take a minute.

It's so bizarre, seeing the house like this. I feel like a stranger, looking round it for the first time as if I'm considering whether to make an offer.

In one way, I do wish that it had looked so lovely the first time I saw it. Maybe then I'd have had more confidence that I was doing the right thing, marrying Carl and moving so close to his ex-wife. As it was, I remember feeling so awful, being weighed down by the sense of having made a terrible, terrible mistake.

I did enjoy doing the house up, though I hated the fact that Carl was never here and that whenever I asked him about anything to do with the house – whether he was in Bristol to see his father or up in London for work – he always said: 'I don't know' or, 'I don't mind' or, 'You choose' – as if he didn't care about any of it. Maybe he didn't? To me, it felt as if he wasn't bothered about me either, about our marriage or spending time with me, as if, somehow, I had become part of the house, a problem that would get sorted out in due course, but not worth too much attention.

Now, of course, I know Carl wasn't only worrying about his dad. He did have a serious problem with work, only he didn't tell me. He said he didn't want to worry me, but what's the point of being married if you never talk about anything that really matters?

I wonder if Carl will at least try to live here on his own. I hope for his sake, and for Saskia and Max's, that he does. He could probably still afford a small flat in London if he needs to be up in town for work. Perhaps he'll try to get another job rather than start his own business? Or maybe he will change careers completely? He's an incredible man – he could do anything he set his mind to, I know. I wish I could help.

I can't think about this. I brace myself and go up to the bedroom.

The ceiling really did turn out well in the end. It looks stunning, with the beams soaring right up to the ridge. The bed is beautiful in here, now that the parts have been bolted together at last. It looks as if it belongs to the room. Or almost as if the room belongs to it. I can't believe we never got to sleep in the bed together.

On 'my' side of the bed, unexpectedly, there's a jug of slightly wilted flowers. Not shop-bought, but wild ones of the sort you see around the pond and down in the meadow, and along the hedgerows and verges when you walk into the village: red valerian, field scabious, purple vetch and frothy meadowsweet, I think. Did Carl pick these? For me? I can't imagine him picking flowers. He must have been so sure I'd come back.

On his side of the bed, there's a small photograph – not framed, but lying on top of his book on the bedside cabinet. I sit down on the edge of the bed. It's a picture of me looking into the pond. I don't remember his taking this. I'm lying on my front and it's a close-up of my face peeping through the long waving grasses at the edge, transfixed by the reflections on the water and all the life I can see. I don't usually like looking at photos of myself; all I can see is frizzy hair and freckles and a scowly expression unless I've been instructed to smile, and then you can see I look tense, trying to smile properly and failing. But in this photograph, I look completely relaxed because I'm looking at the water rather than into the camera.

I want to curl up in the bed beneath the covers and undo it all. Well, not absolutely all of it. But if I could go back, what would I do differently? How would I magically make everything all right?

The truth is, wouldn't I make the same mistakes all over again? Or maybe different ones? I'd still be me, turning Antonia into some impossible rival. Carl would still be Carl, too wrapped up in work to pay enough attention to the rest of his life. How do I... moult... become the better, stronger me I now believe I could be? How does anyone manage to change? I don't suppose there's an easy answer I will happen across one day. Maybe the important thing is to keep trying, no matter how hard it feels.

I ought to pack my clothes and the few bits of jewellery I have here, but I can't face it yet. I'll have a dip in the pond first, restore myself. Then I can scoop the clothes into black bin bags and dump them in the back of the van and sort them out at the flat.

I change in the downstairs shower room and pad out, down past the trees, to the pond in my flip-flops.

I can't believe this. Carl must have got Steve to build a deck here. It's absolutely perfect. Months ago, I did a scrappy sketch on a paper napkin when I was telling Carl about swimming in the pond and trying to explain how great it would be to make a small, simple wooden platform at the edge with a ladder going down into the water and a vertical post to hold when getting in and out. Carl must have kept the sketch and asked Steve to build this as a surprise for me.

The wind is blowing the reeds slightly, but it's still warm. The last of the late summer sun sparkles on the water. All I can hear are the ducks occasionally giving the odd quack, birds singing as if for the joy of being alive, the drowsy hum of bees.

There's no one else around. One of the things I love most about this cottage – loved – is that it isn't overlooked at all.

I glance around once more. I remember that day, months ago now, when Carl and I swam naked in the pond together. I strip off my swimsuit and climb down the ladder into the water. The deck and ladder are wonderful – so much better than trying to launch myself awkwardly from the slippery bank.

It is colder than last time, inevitably. Early September now. Oh, I think it's Max's first day at big school tomorrow. I should at least have sent a card. I hope he'll be all right. I will miss him. Saskia too, now. And Antonia. If only I'd had more time... I felt at last we were getting somewhere.

* * *

I swim lazily, languidly, relishing the water and the late dragon-flies swooping and soaring. Humphrey the duck suddenly appears by my side, as ever totally unperturbed that I am sharing his domain. He honestly looks pleased to see me. Well, that's what I'm telling myself. The only relationship I haven't messed up.

Then I turn on to my back and let myself float. I could do this all day. When I'm here, looking up at the sky, feeling the water hold me, nothing else seems to matter so much. I know, I know – eventually, I will have to get out of the water and face up to everything that's happened. I'll have to look at all the things that I got wrong because it wasn't just Carl, and I know that now. If I'd been more of a grown-up at the start of our marriage, someone he could respect, it would never have occurred to him to buy a house without letting me see it first.

It's so peaceful. You can't hear anything – well, obviously not, as my ears are under water so even the birdsong is drowned out now. I know everything is awful but, for now, there is no ruined marriage, no failure, no Carl being angry or disappointed. There is just the water and the air and the late sun and that is enough for now. I hadn't realised how tense I've become. At last, at long last, I can feel myself starting to relax. Floating here, looking up at the sky and the birds wheeling overhead, I feel for once that it's not so terrible to be me.

The thought crosses my mind that I'm about to have years and years of making decisions all on my own. I might meet someone else eventually... but he wouldn't be Carl. I think of Carl's face – the way he bites his lip on one side when he's worried about something, the way he pushes his hair back from his forehead on the left-hand side when he's tired and can't think any more, the way he looks at me sometimes as if he can't believe he's lucky enough to have found me. The same way I feel about him. Felt, I mean.

Is that a noise? Funny, I thought I heard something. Probably the ducks having an altercation.

No, it's a shout. But who on earth—

Suddenly, there's a huge splash, sending a wave of water over me. I breathe in at the wrong moment and inhale water through my nose. Flail at the water, choking and coughing. What's happening? I can't see with so much water in my eyes. Then I'm grabbed round my waist. I scream my head off as loudly as I can and thrash out wildly at my attacker.

'Nat, Natalie – my love, my love – oh God, are you OK?' Carl shakes me vigorously.

'What the hell are you—'

'Natalie – I – arrgggh – no! No!'

The two of us are floundering and flailing about, but now Carl looks really panicked.

'It's OK, I'm OK,' I tell him. 'What is it?'

'I thought you were drowning – but now I'm stuck. Nat, *help* me.'

'How are you stuck?' I bring myself upright and tread water but the pond looks like a murky puddle. He must have churned his feet into the bottom and I can't see a thing.

'I put my feet down to the bottom when I grabbed you, but I'm stuck. Nat, help me. I'm sinking in the mud. I can't free my feet.'

And he is: the water's just over his shoulders.

'Have you got shoes on?'

'Yes. I jumped in. I was trying to – to – save you. I thought... Nat – what do I do?'

'OK – try to keep calm. Tilt your head back slowly so it's resting on the water and move your arms like you're treading water to keep your upper half up and reduce your weight. I'll have to release you from your shoes. And don't panic – I won't be able to see at all so I'm going to have to hold on to your body, OK?'

'OK.'

I take a big breath and clamp my eyes shut, then flip upside down, using Carl's legs to haul myself down. At his feet, I feel for his laces. Business shoes. Bugger. The laces are thin and harder to grab than the fat ones on trainers. And he's made a double bow. I release one bow then have to come up for air.

'Have you done it? My feet are still stuck.' The water is now right up to his chin.

'Going again. Stay calm. Trust me.'

He nods.

Down again. I manage to undo the first lace and I grab his leg by his sock and tug as hard as I can. Again. Finally, it comes free.

Up to the surface for air.

'Nat. I do love you, you know.'

'I love you, too. When you feel me tug, try to pull your leg up if you can.'

A huge breath. Down again.

The second shoe. The lace, tugging. Nothing.

Up I come. The water is lapping around Carl's face.

Another breath and down to the depths.

I pull at the sock, but his foot seems to be wedged in the shoe. Then I loosen the laces as best I can, tugging at them, pulling them, trying to stay calm. Finally, I can tug up the tongue of the shoe and I grab his sock and yank as hard as I can and I can feel Carl pulling too, and up I come, gasping for air.

Carl is treading water but far from calm. I help him on to his back and I tow him to the deck and the steps. He climbs up in his sodden clothes, shaking. Together then, we sprawl on the grass by the pond, exhausted, scared, relieved.

'Why did you jump in with all your clothes on, you daft pillock?' I punch his arm. 'You scared the hell out of me.'

'*You* scared *me*! I thought you were drowning. I thought maybe you'd... you know, had enough of everything and...'

'I was *floating*, you twit.'

'Natalie.'

'Yes?'

He pulls me towards him on the grass.

'I don't think I can actually live without you.'

'Course you can. Easy. You lived without me before, didn't you? You'll manage.'

'No. I can *survive*, but that's all it would be. When you're not there, I can't do *anything*. I can't *think*, I can't *concentrate*, I can't *eat*. You are part of me, Nat. I love you but I also *need* you. When you're not there, it's like I'm not properly *me* any more. I know that must sound stupid when I managed before I met you, but that's exactly it – I was *managing*. I was getting by. No more than that. When you said you couldn't be with me, I felt as if I were shattering into a thousand pieces, that I couldn't hold myself together as a person. I need you. And I love you. What can I do to make you love me again? I can't bear it if you don't love me. Just tell me what to do.'

'Oh, Carl, I never stopped loving you. Don't you know that? I couldn't stop loving you. It would be like ceasing to breathe. Even when I'm furious with you, I still love you. But...' I let out a deep breath as if I've been holding it in for months.

'Yes...? Tell me.'

'I do want you to treat me as your equal. Don't bypass me when it comes to decisions. Don't assume you know best. If there's a problem – like your colleagues getting pissed off with you, or what happened with Stefan, or you feeling crap about your dad, don't hide it. Share it. Even if I can't help or I can't solve it, I can at least listen. Don't exclude me.'

He nods. 'I am, honestly, deeply sorry I was such an idiot and that I underestimated you so badly.'

'Nobody's perfect.'

He puts his arms around me and draws me on top of him. Kisses me.

'You really are quite extraordinarily muddy, you know,' he says.

'Look who's talking.' But I kiss him anyway.

'Does this mean you'll come home?'

'Hmm. Well, for today, at least. But I'll tell you one thing, I'm not going down again to get your bloody posh shoes.'

'Fuck the shoes – the frogs can play in them. Nat?'

'Do you promise to appreciate me from this day forward until death do us part?'

'I do,' he says.

'Do you vow to include me in all important decision-making, including, but not confined to, issues relating to property, work, ex-wives and future children?'

'I *do*,' he says, smiling.

'And do you promise to love me even when I overreact, get the wrong end of the stick, or otherwise make things a lot, lot worse?'

'I really do,' he says.

'And you?' Carl says, kissing me. 'Do you vow to put up with me even when I make one stupid mistake after another, so long as I keep on trying?'

'I *do*,' I say, looking at my imperfect, perfect husband, because in the end, that's all any of us can do – keep on trying. 'I really *do*.'

ACKNOWLEDGMENTS

Writing a book is a peculiar thing to do; you make up characters, then unleash them on to the page to tell their story. At times, it feels as if your head has too many people in it, all competing for attention. At other times, it is a lonely business. Luckily, I had help and support from the following people:

Sarah Ritherdon, my wonderful editor at Boldwood Books, whose pertinent questions and comments prompted me to push myself further on certain aspects of the story.

The rest of the lovely team at Boldwood, including Amanda, Nia, Ellie, and Megan. Also, Yvonne Holland, who copy-edited the book, with a beady eye for detail and any continuity glitches, and proofreader Trish Bellamy, who sniffed out any remaining problems like a bloodhound. Alice Moore for the brilliant, eye-catching cover, and Chuwy for the great image.

Charlotte Robertson, my agent at Robertson Murray, who is fantastically supportive and encouraging, and always the voice of sanity and reason.

Shazia Ahmed, who patiently answered my queries about sentencing, parole and early release for criminal offenders.

My son, Leo, who acted as unofficial hall monitor during lockdown, pouncing on me when I dared to leave my study: 'Didn't you have a tea ten minutes ago?'

Larry, whose opinion still matters more than anyone else's.

My favourite sister, Stephanie, who has always been my chief cheerleader.

AUTHOR'S NOTE ON THE SETTING AND LOCATION:

One of the enjoyable aspects of writing a novel is weaving in multiple elements from real life and synthesising them into something new from your imagination.

Little Wyford is very loosely based on the Kentish village of Wye (though Little Wyford has more shops and cafés), which nestles at the foot of the downs between Ashford and Canterbury. Wye does have a beautiful flint and stone church at one end of the High Street, but the village green is not at the other end; it is tucked round one corner off the main street. None of the shops or shopkeepers in the book is remotely based on anyone in Wye.

When I was seven, my dad bought an ex-farmhouse in Kent, which was the inspiration for Rose Cottage. It had a large barn but the house itself was the size of a cottage, with only three bedrooms. It was down a private, extremely potholed track outside the tiny village of Mersham, which is about five miles from Wye. The house was made of Kentish ragstone with a catslide roof covered in handmade tiles, which were indeed stolen – more than once. The house did have a lovely, natural pond (but too small and too muddy for swimming) and three ducks when we first bought it, named Hansel, Gretel and Colonel Blimp.

The pond in the book was inspired by one I saw at a wedding, which was held at a house in rural Wiltshire. This pond was a really good size, with a small wooden deck (where the wedding ceremony took place) and a ladder for easy access for swimming as the hosts swam there often. When I walked round the pond after the wedding, I noticed just how much wildlife was whizzing about on and above the surface, especially the phenomenal number of dragonflies. It was enchanting.

MORE FROM CLAIRE CALMAN

We hope you enjoyed reading *A Second-Hand Husband*. If you did, please leave a review.

If you'd like to gift a copy, this book is also available as an ebook, digital audio download and audiobook CD.

Sign up to Claire Calman's mailing list for news, competitions and updates on future books.

http://bit.ly/ClaireCalmanNewsletter

Growing Up for Beginners another uplifting read from Claire Calman is available now.

ABOUT THE AUTHOR

Claire Calman is a writer and broadcaster known for her novels that combine wit and pathos, including the bestseller *Love is a Four-Letter Word*. She has appeared on BBC Radio 4's Woman's Hour and Loose Ends.

 twitter.com/clairecalman

 bookbub.com/authors/claire-calman

ABOUT BOLDWOOD BOOKS

Boldwood Books is a fiction publishing company seeking out the best stories from around the world.

Find out more at www.boldwoodbooks.com

Sign up to the Book and Tonic newsletter for news, offers and competitions from Boldwood Books!

http://www.bit.ly/bookandtonic

We'd love to hear from you, follow us on social media:

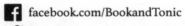 facebook.com/BookandTonic

twitter.com/BoldwoodBooks

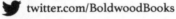 instagram.com/BookandTonic

Lightning Source UK Ltd.
Milton Keynes UK
UKHW040657100621
385172UK00003BA/163